CLASS
ACT

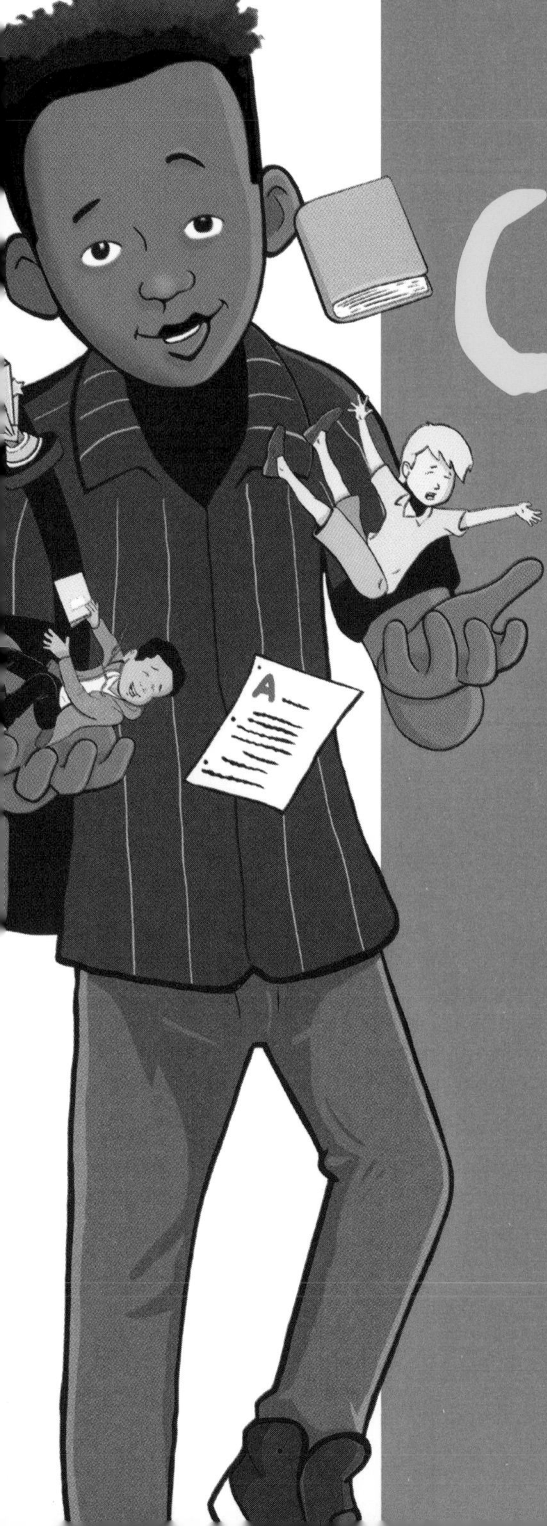

JERRY CRAFT

CLASS ACT

Quill Tree Books
Imprints of HarperCollinsPublishers
HARPER alley

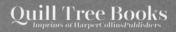

Quill Tree Books and HarperAlley are imprints
of HarperCollins Publishers.
Class Act
Copyright © 2020 by Jerry Craft
All rights reserved. Printed in the United States of America.
No part of this book may be used or reproduced in any manner
whatsoever without written permission except in the case of
brief quotations embodied in critical articles and reviews.
For information address HarperCollins Children's Books,
a division of HarperCollins Publishers,
195 Broadway, New York, NY 10007.
www.harperalley.com

Library of Congress Control Number: 2020937195
ISBN 978-0-06-288550-0 (paperback) - ISBN 978-0-06-288551-7
(hardcover)

21 22 23 24   PC/LSCC   10 9 8
❖
First Edition

Be kind.
Be fair.
Be you.

SKETCH DIARY of a Shrimpy Kid

CHAPTER 1

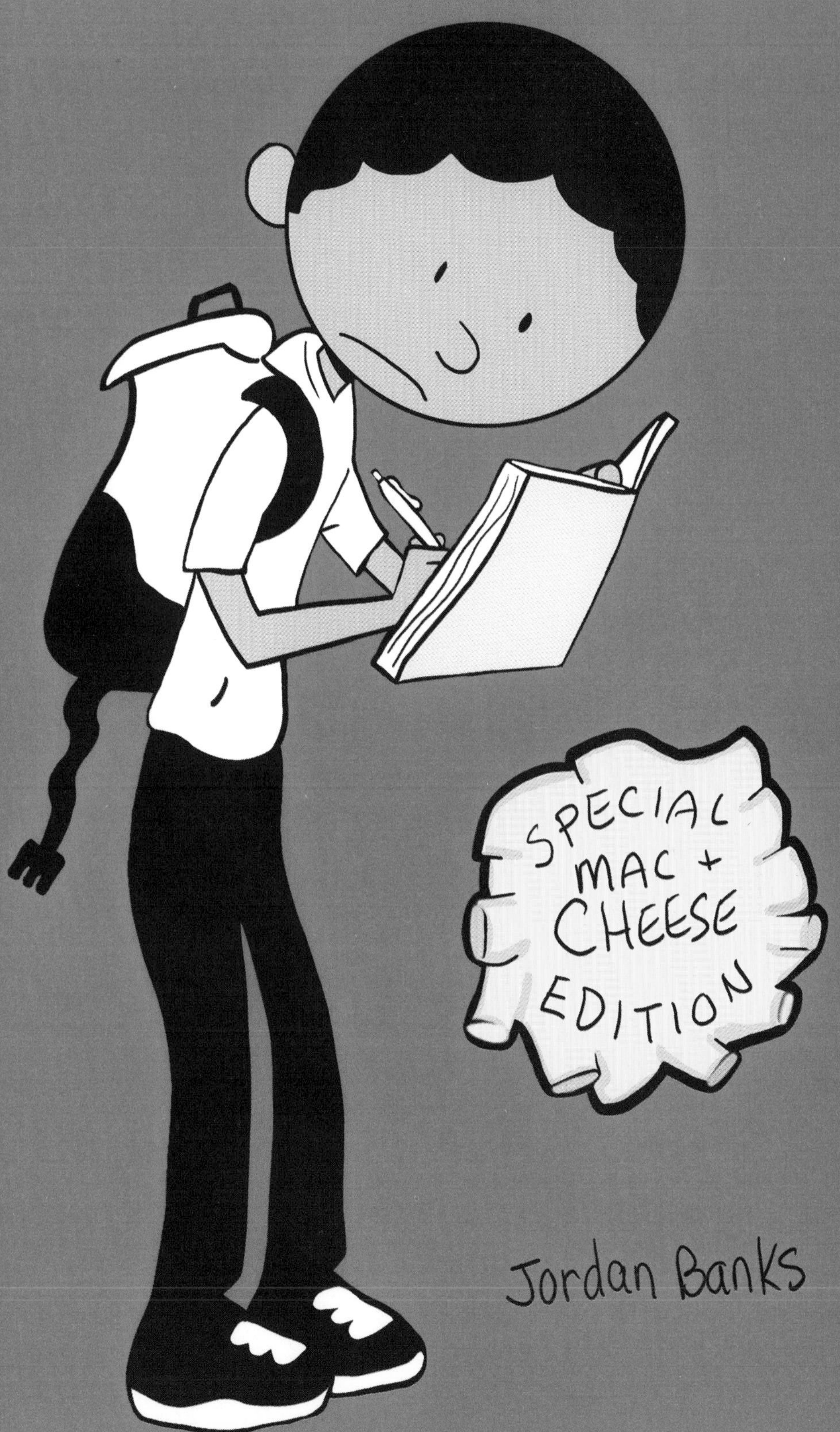
SPECIAL MAC + CHEESE EDITION
Jordan Banks

My Life Till Now!

by Jordan Banks

My name is Jordan Banks. All my life, I have wanted to be an artist.

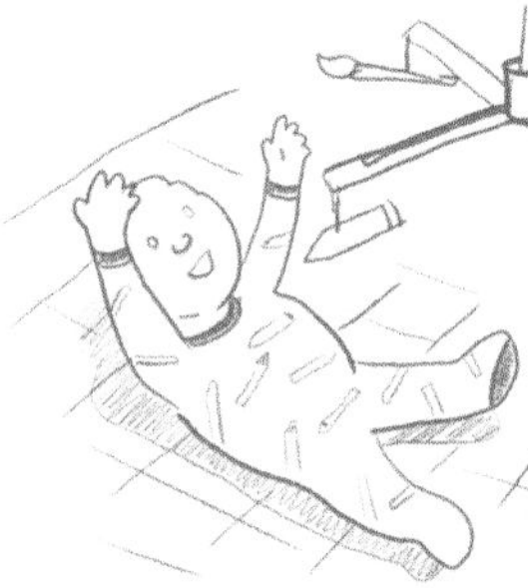

MY plan was to stay at St. Harwell's, my old school, until the eighth grade.

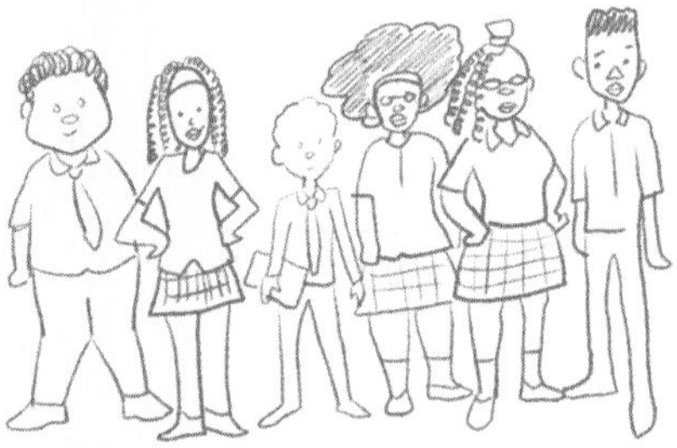

Then I wanted to go to the High School of Music, Art, and Mime . . .

That was my dream.

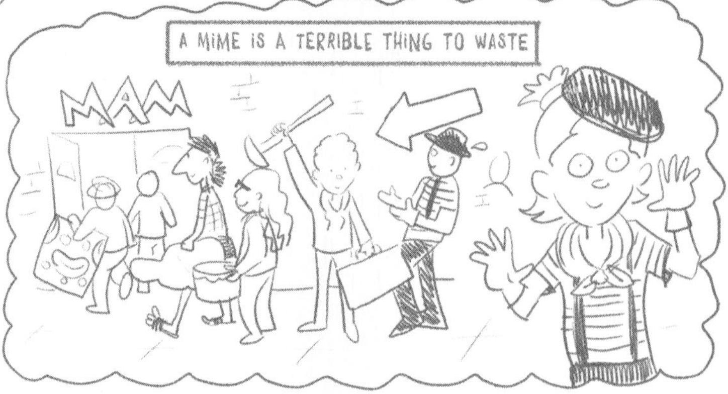
A MIME IS A TERRIBLE THING TO WASTE
MAM

Unfortunately, my dream met my mom!

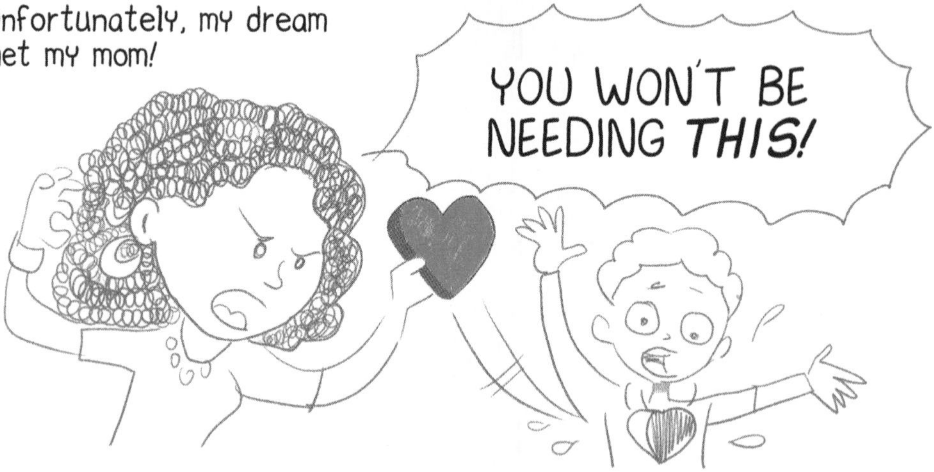
YOU WON'T BE NEEDING *THIS!*

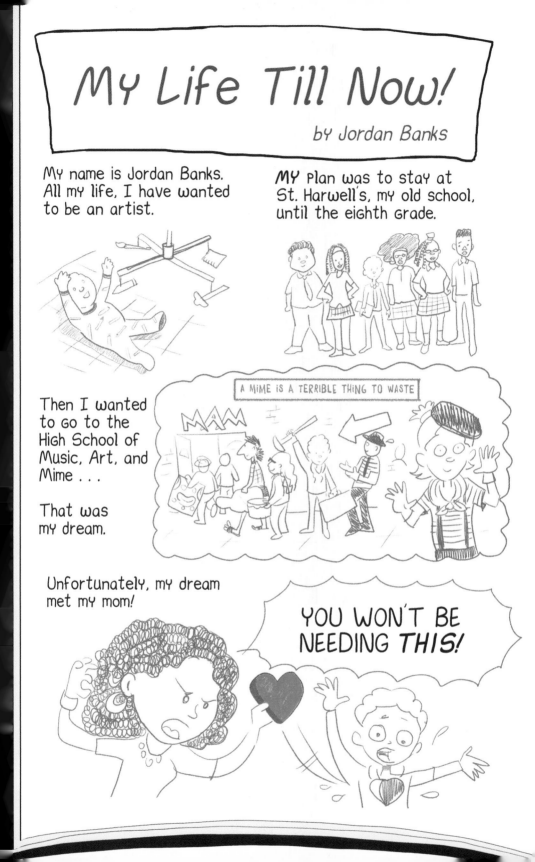

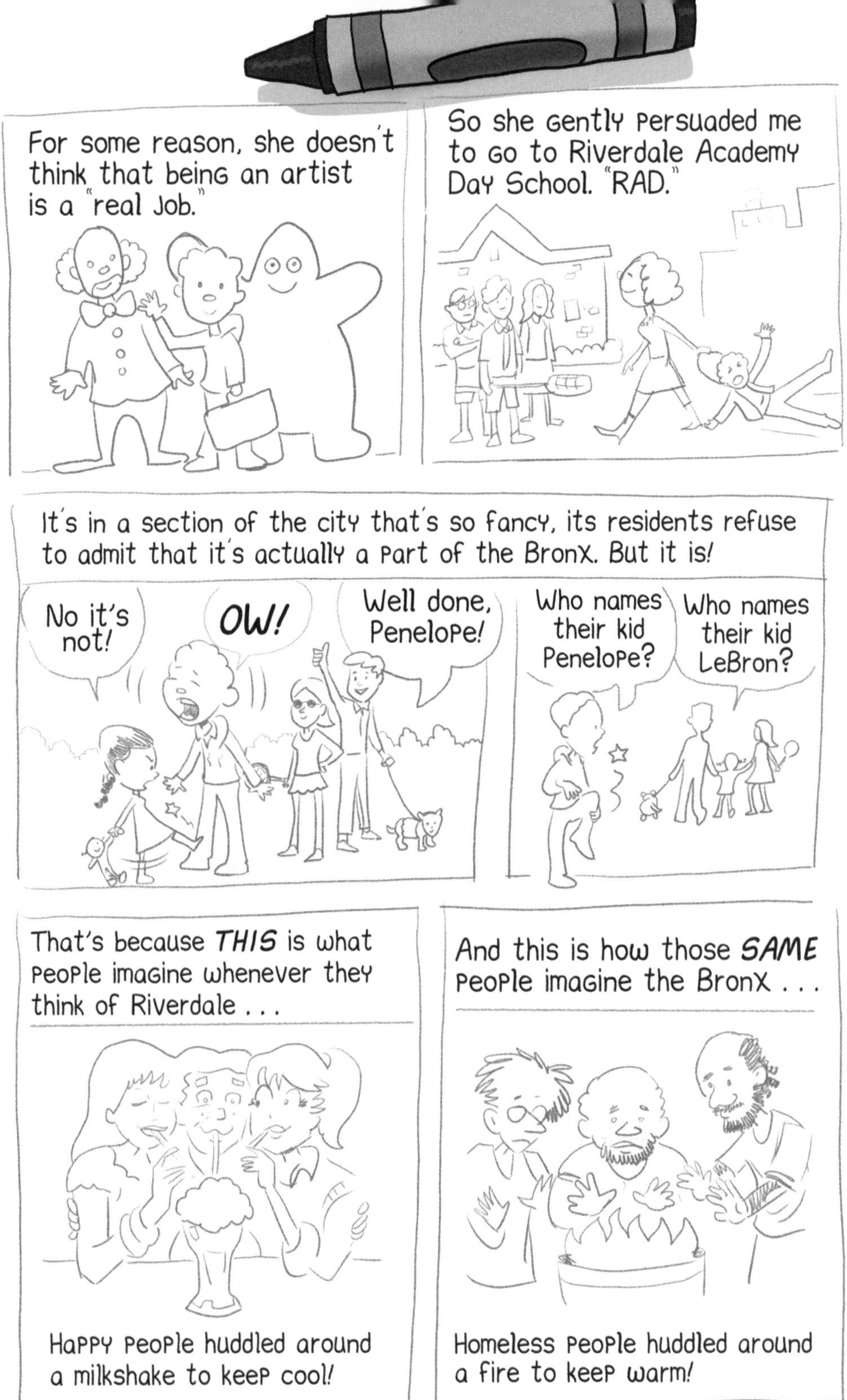
For some reason, she doesn't think that being an artist is a "real job."
So she gently persuaded me to go to Riverdale Academy Day School. "RAD."
It's in a section of the city that's so fancy, its residents refuse to admit that it's actually a part of the Bronx. But it is!
No it's not!
OW!
Well done, Penelope!
Who names their kid Penelope?
Who names their kid LeBron?
That's because THIS is what people imagine whenever they think of Riverdale . . .
Happy people huddled around a milkshake to keep cool!
And this is how those SAME people imagine the Bronx . . .
Homeless people huddled around a fire to keep warm!

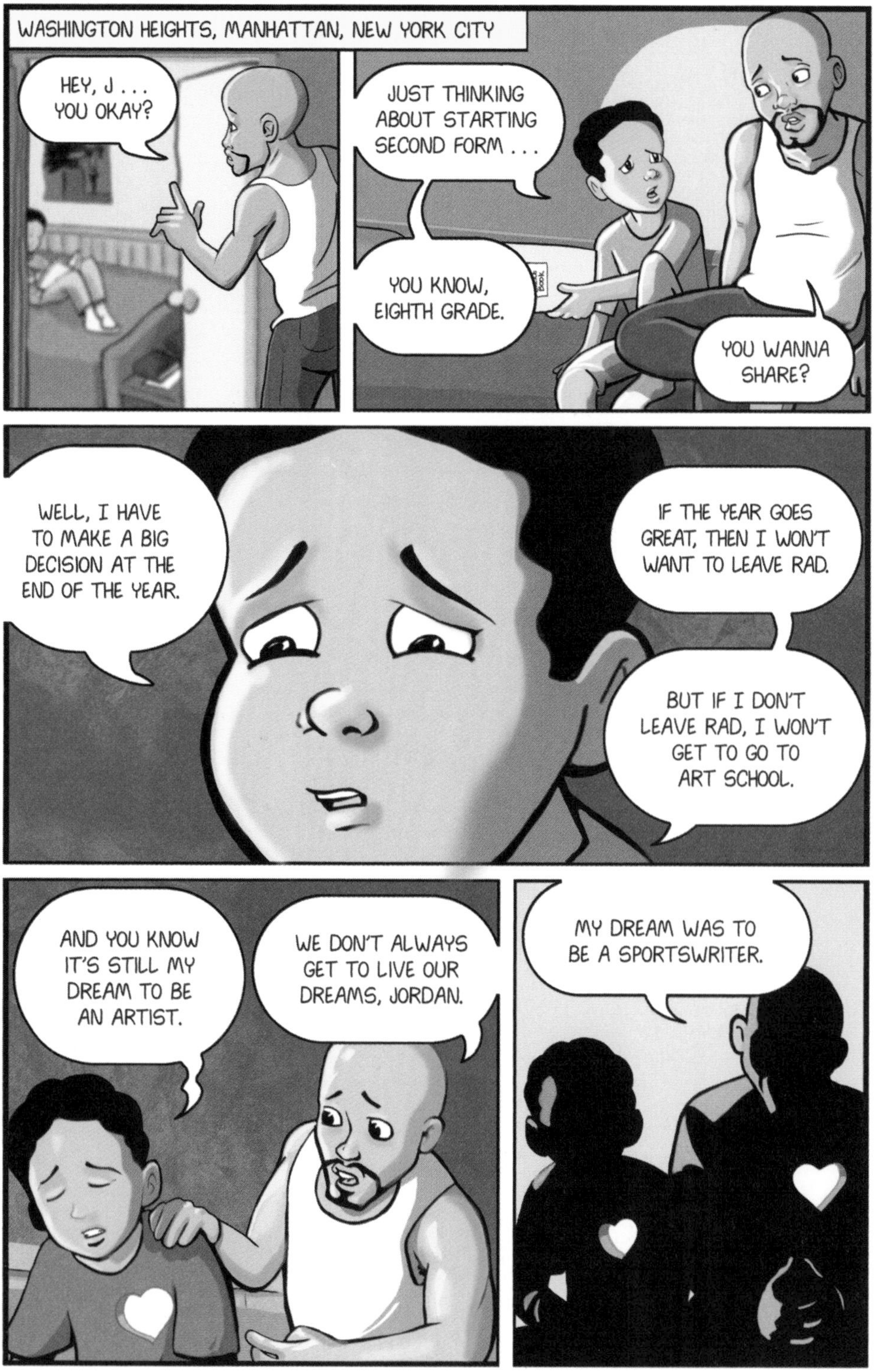
WASHINGTON HEIGHTS, MANHATTAN, NEW YORK CITY
HEY, J . . . YOU OKAY?
JUST THINKING ABOUT STARTING SECOND FORM . . .
YOU KNOW, EIGHTH GRADE.
YOU WANNA SHARE?
WELL, I HAVE TO MAKE A BIG DECISION AT THE END OF THE YEAR.
IF THE YEAR GOES GREAT, THEN I WON'T WANT TO LEAVE RAD.
BUT IF I DON'T LEAVE RAD, I WON'T GET TO GO TO ART SCHOOL.
AND YOU KNOW IT'S STILL MY DREAM TO BE AN ARTIST.
WE DON'T ALWAYS GET TO LIVE OUR DREAMS, JORDAN.
MY DREAM WAS TO BE A SPORTSWRITER.

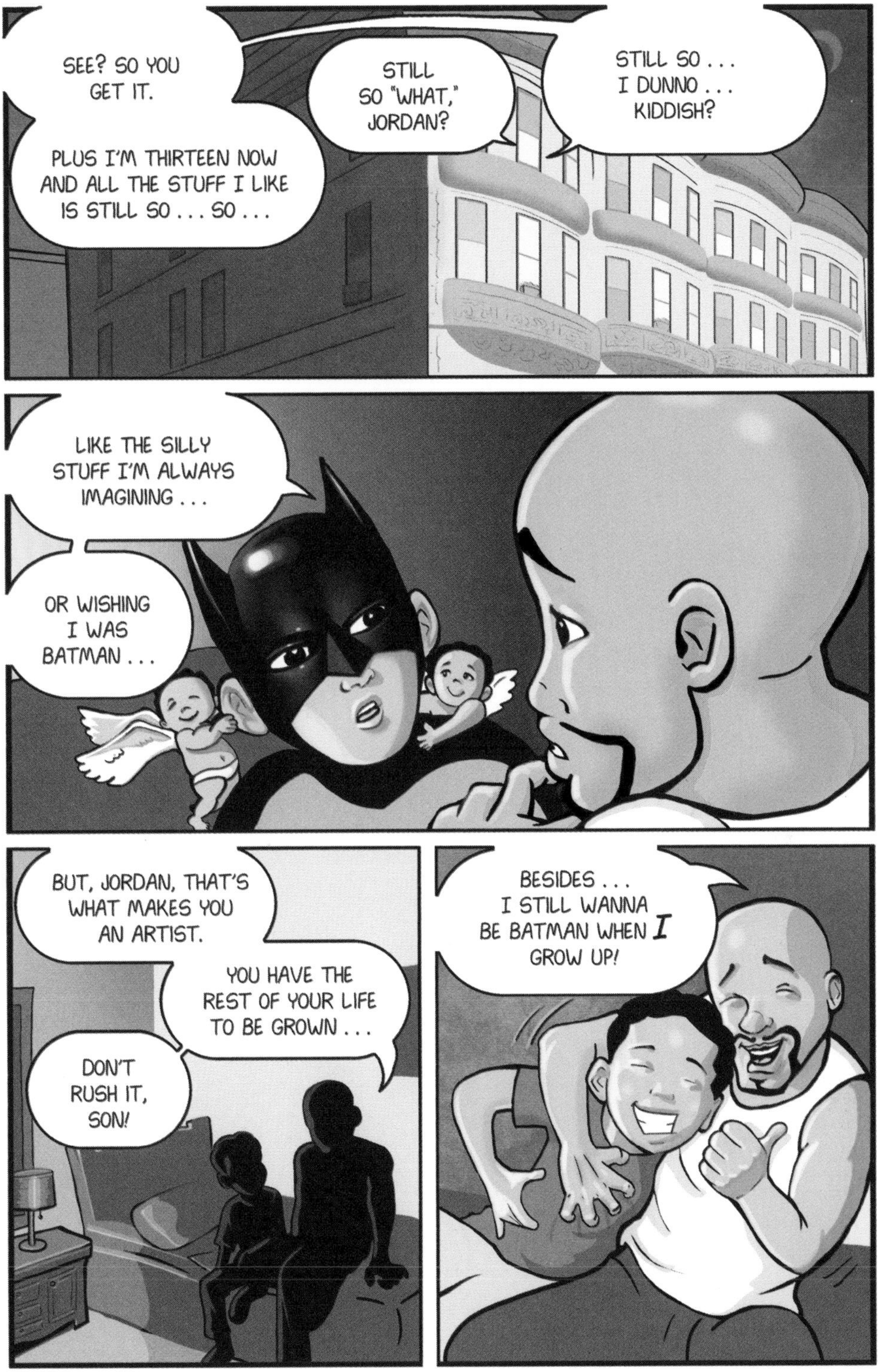
SEE? SO YOU GET IT.
PLUS I'M THIRTEEN NOW AND ALL THE STUFF I LIKE IS STILL SO . . . SO . . .
STILL SO "WHAT," JORDAN?
STILL SO . . . I DUNNO . . . KIDDISH?
LIKE THE SILLY STUFF I'M ALWAYS IMAGINING . . .
OR WISHING I WAS BATMAN . . .
BUT, JORDAN, THAT'S WHAT MAKES YOU AN ARTIST.
YOU HAVE THE REST OF YOUR LIFE TO BE GROWN . . .
DON'T RUSH IT, SON!
BESIDES . . . I STILL WANNA BE BATMAN WHEN I GROW UP!

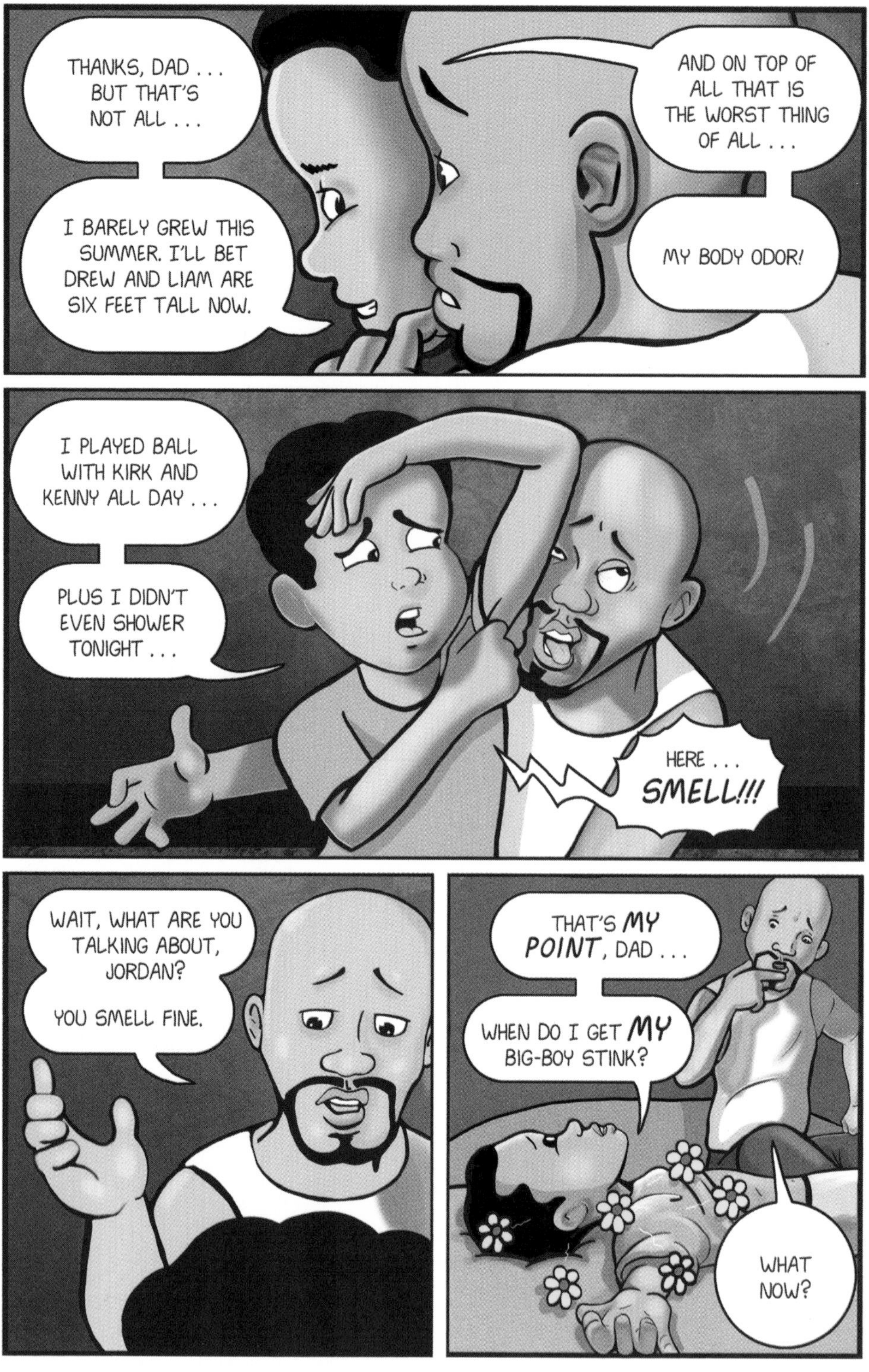
THANKS, DAD . . . BUT THAT'S NOT ALL . . .
I BARELY GREW THIS SUMMER. I'LL BET DREW AND LIAM ARE SIX FEET TALL NOW.
AND ON TOP OF ALL THAT IS THE WORST THING OF ALL . . .
MY BODY ODOR!
I PLAYED BALL WITH KIRK AND KENNY ALL DAY . . .
PLUS I DIDN'T EVEN SHOWER TONIGHT . . .
HERE . . . SMELL!!!
WAIT, WHAT ARE YOU TALKING ABOUT, JORDAN?
YOU SMELL FINE.
THAT'S MY POINT, DAD . . .
WHEN DO I GET MY BIG-BOY STINK?
WHAT NOW?

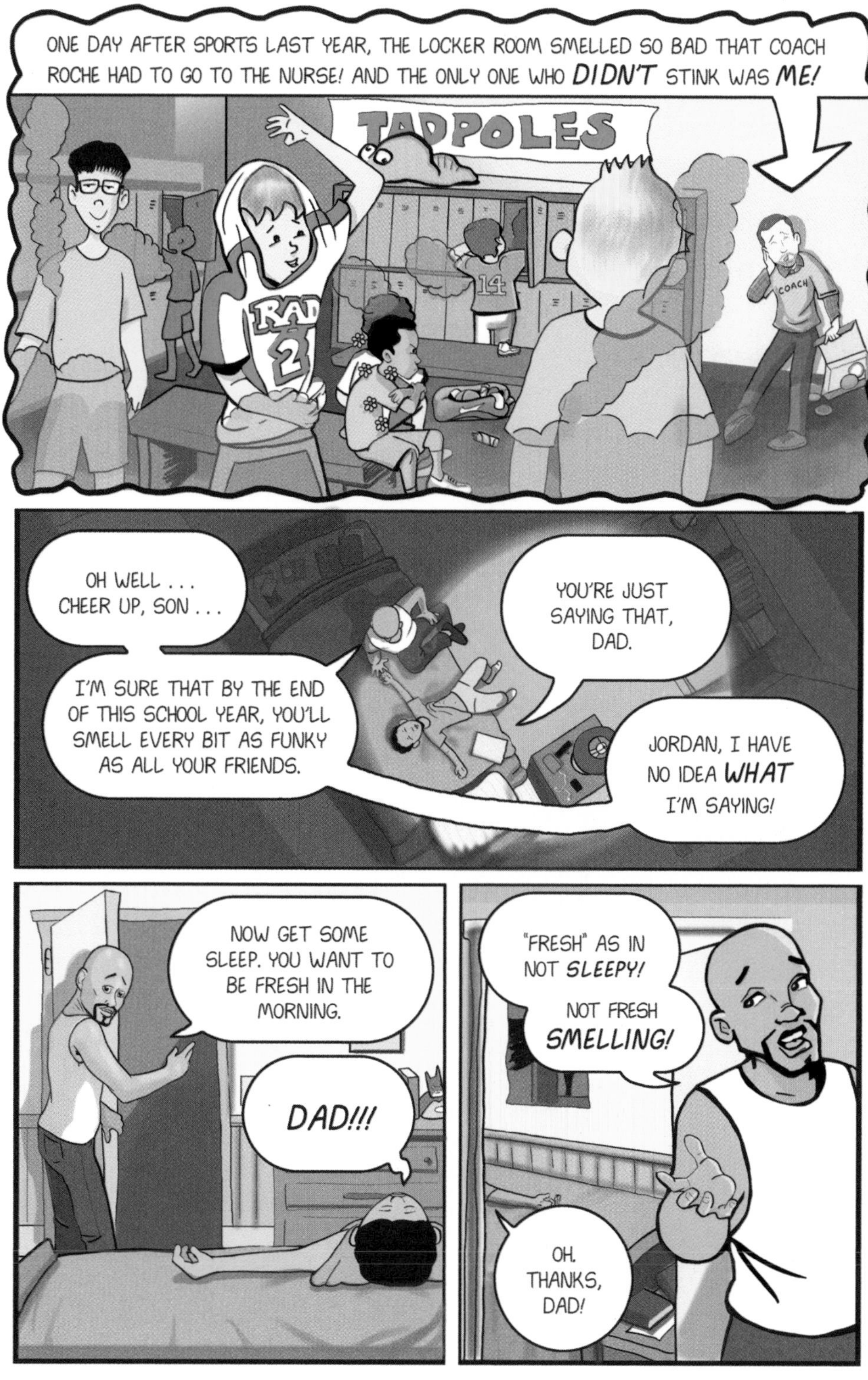
ONE DAY AFTER SPORTS LAST YEAR, THE LOCKER ROOM SMELLED SO BAD THAT COACH ROCHE HAD TO GO TO THE NURSE! AND THE ONLY ONE WHO DIDN'T STINK WAS ME!
TADPOLES
14
COACH
OH WELL . . . CHEER UP, SON . . .
I'M SURE THAT BY THE END OF THIS SCHOOL YEAR, YOU'LL SMELL EVERY BIT AS FUNKY AS ALL YOUR FRIENDS.
YOU'RE JUST SAYING THAT, DAD.
JORDAN, I HAVE NO IDEA WHAT I'M SAYING!
NOW GET SOME SLEEP. YOU WANT TO BE FRESH IN THE MORNING.
DAD!!!
"FRESH" AS IN NOT SLEEPY!
NOT FRESH SMELLING!
OH. THANKS, DAD!

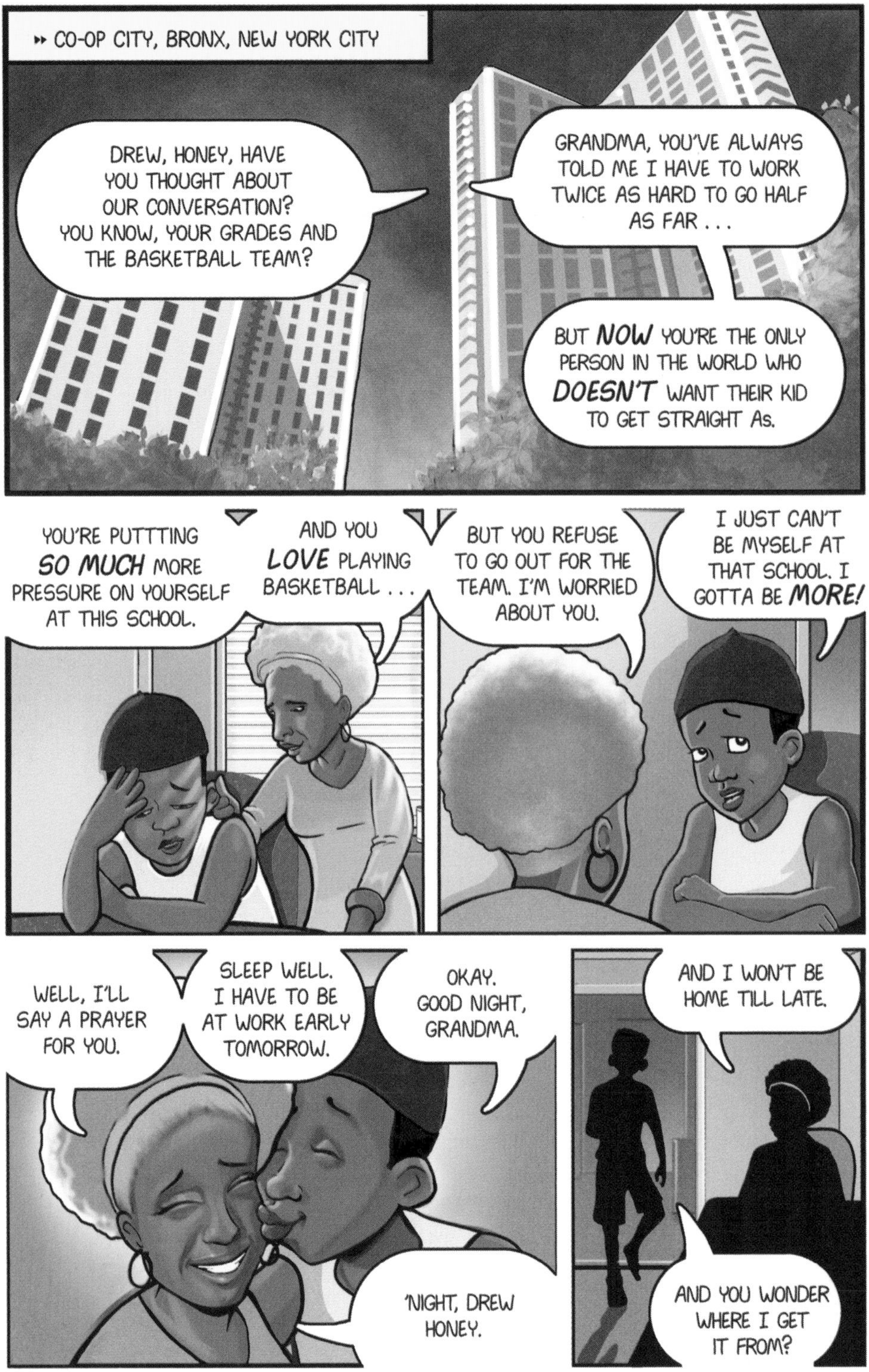
CO-OP CITY, BRONX, NEW YORK CITY
DREW, HONEY, HAVE YOU THOUGHT ABOUT OUR CONVERSATION? YOU KNOW, YOUR GRADES AND THE BASKETBALL TEAM?
GRANDMA, YOU'VE ALWAYS TOLD ME I HAVE TO WORK TWICE AS HARD TO GO HALF AS FAR . . .
BUT NOW YOU'RE THE ONLY PERSON IN THE WORLD WHO DOESN'T WANT THEIR KID TO GET STRAIGHT As.
YOU'RE PUTTTING SO MUCH MORE PRESSURE ON YOURSELF AT THIS SCHOOL.
AND YOU LOVE PLAYING BASKETBALL . . .
BUT YOU REFUSE TO GO OUT FOR THE TEAM. I'M WORRIED ABOUT YOU.
I JUST CAN'T BE MYSELF AT THAT SCHOOL. I GOTTA BE MORE!
WELL, I'LL SAY A PRAYER FOR YOU.
SLEEP WELL. I HAVE TO BE AT WORK EARLY TOMORROW.
OKAY. GOOD NIGHT, GRANDMA.
'NIGHT, DREW HONEY.
AND I WON'T BE HOME TILL LATE.
AND YOU WONDER WHERE I GET IT FROM?

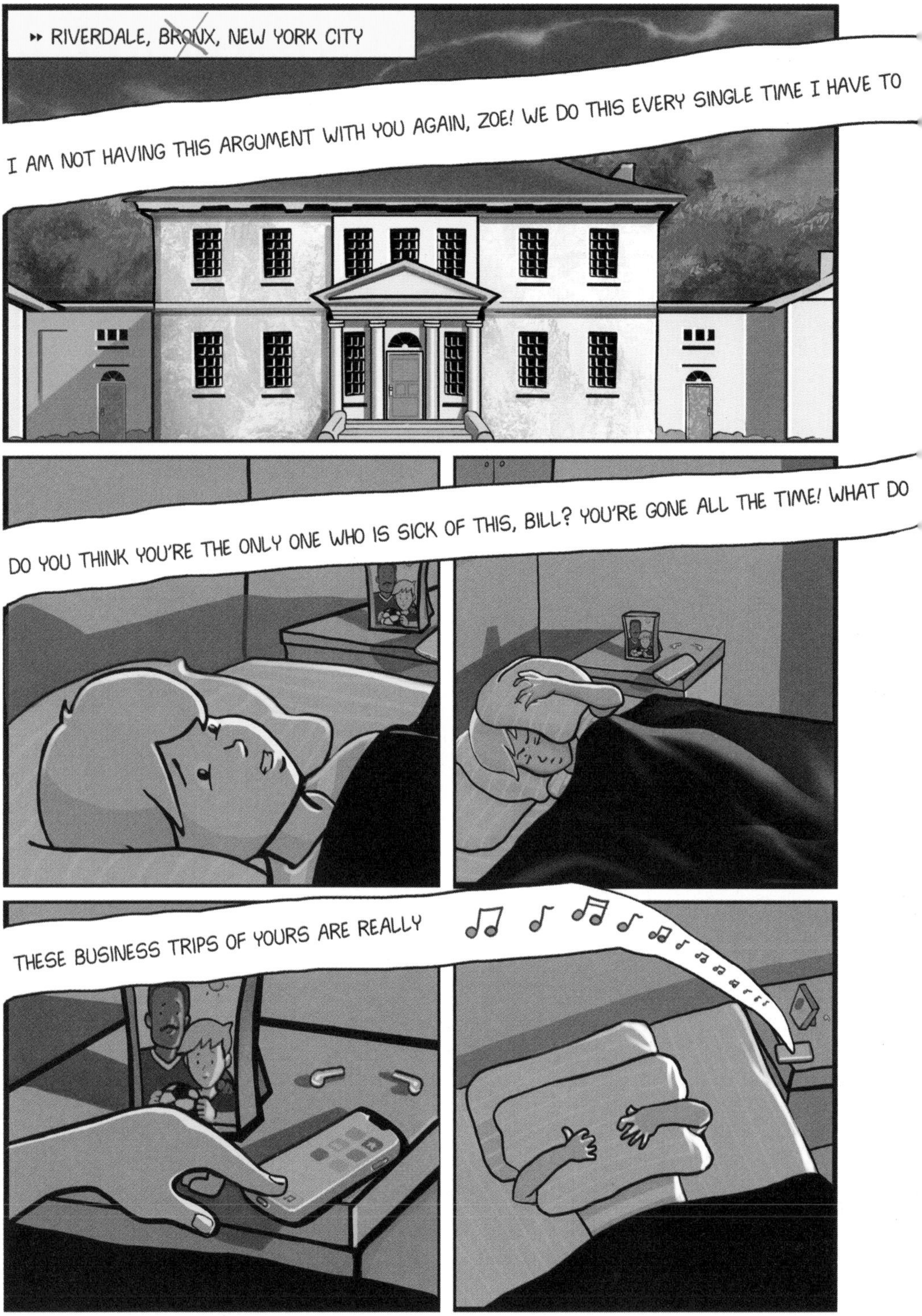
RIVERDALE, BRONX, NEW YORK CITY
I AM NOT HAVING THIS ARGUMENT WITH YOU AGAIN, ZOE! WE DO THIS EVERY SINGLE TIME I HAVE TO
DO YOU THINK YOU'RE THE ONLY ONE WHO IS SICK OF THIS, BILL? YOU'RE GONE ALL THE TIME! WHAT DO
THESE BUSINESS TRIPS OF YOURS ARE REALLY

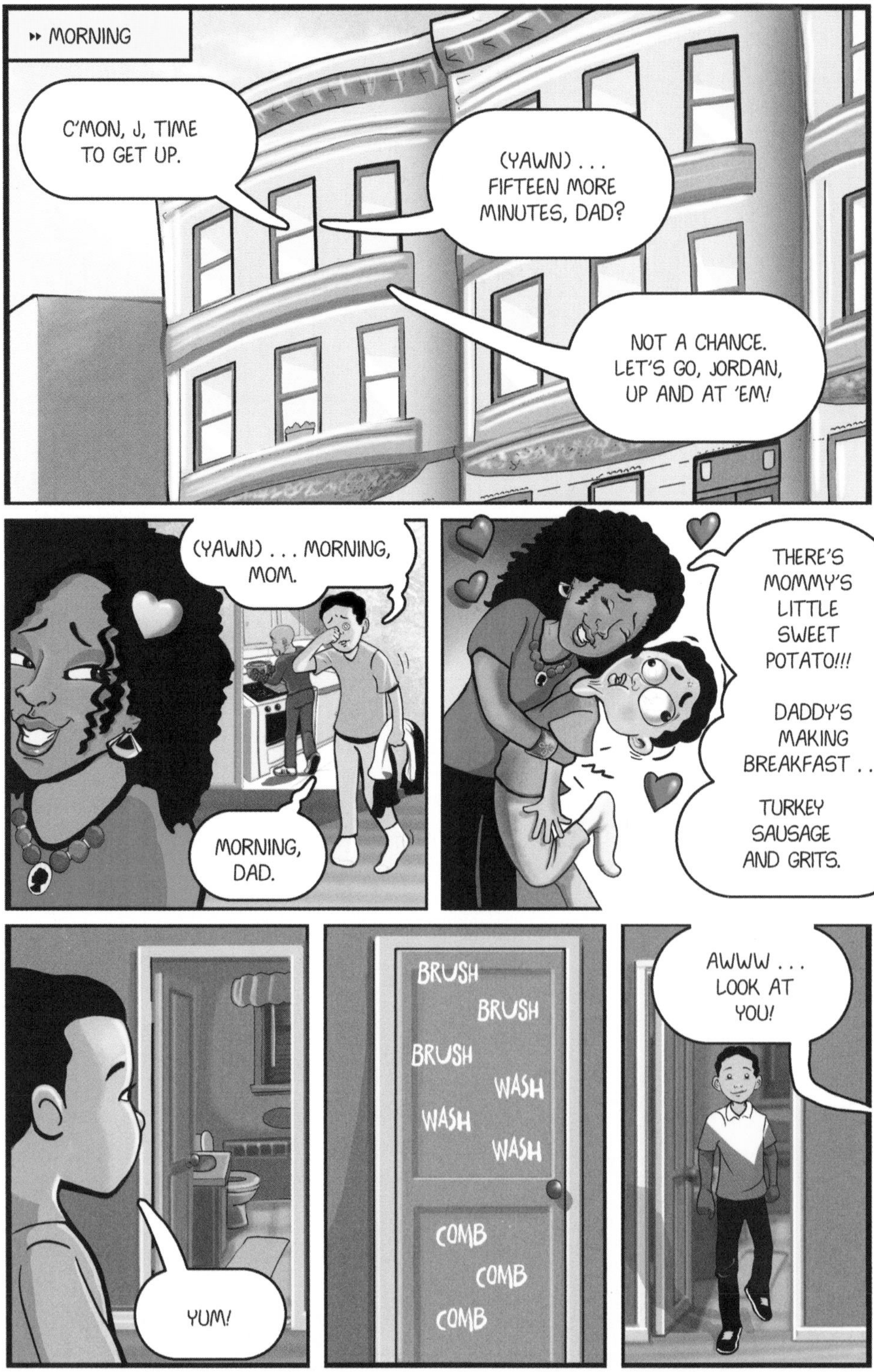

MORNING
C'MON, J, TIME TO GET UP.
(YAWN) . . . FIFTEEN MORE MINUTES, DAD?
NOT A CHANCE. LET'S GO, JORDAN, UP AND AT 'EM!
(YAWN) . . . MORNING, MOM.
MORNING, DAD.
THERE'S MOMMY'S LITTLE SWEET POTATO!!!
DADDY'S MAKING BREAKFAST . . .
TURKEY SAUSAGE AND GRITS.
YUM!
BRUSH
BRUSH
BRUSH
WASH
WASH
WASH
COMB
COMB
COMB
AWWW . . . LOOK AT YOU!

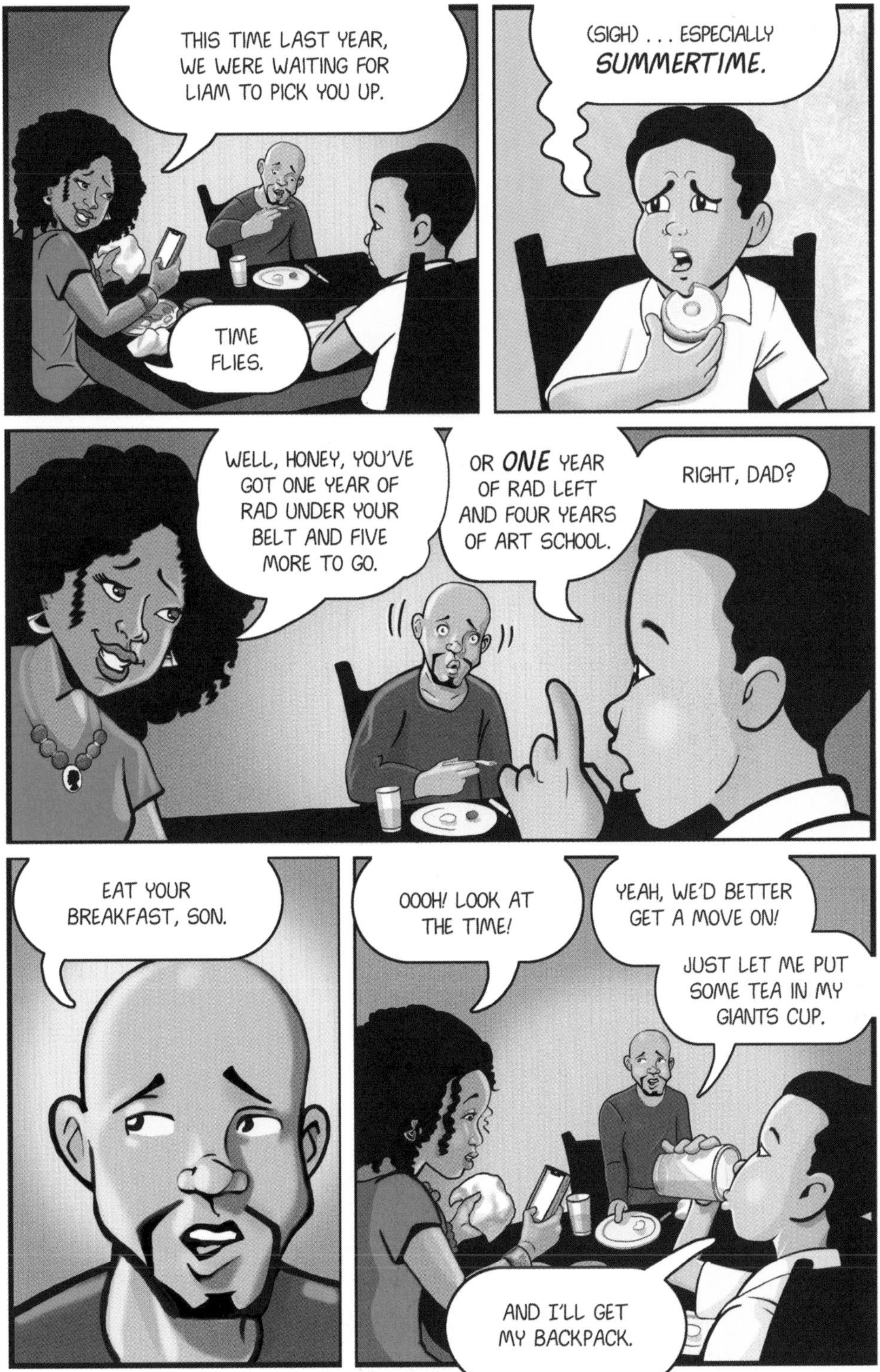
THIS TIME LAST YEAR, WE WERE WAITING FOR LIAM TO PICK YOU UP.
TIME FLIES.
(SIGH) . . . ESPECIALLY *SUMMERTIME.*
WELL, HONEY, YOU'VE GOT ONE YEAR OF RAD UNDER YOUR BELT AND FIVE MORE TO GO.
OR *ONE* YEAR OF RAD LEFT AND FOUR YEARS OF ART SCHOOL.
RIGHT, DAD?
EAT YOUR BREAKFAST, SON.
OOOH! LOOK AT THE TIME!
YEAH, WE'D BETTER GET A MOVE ON!
JUST LET ME PUT SOME TEA IN MY GIANTS CUP.
AND I'LL GET MY BACKPACK.

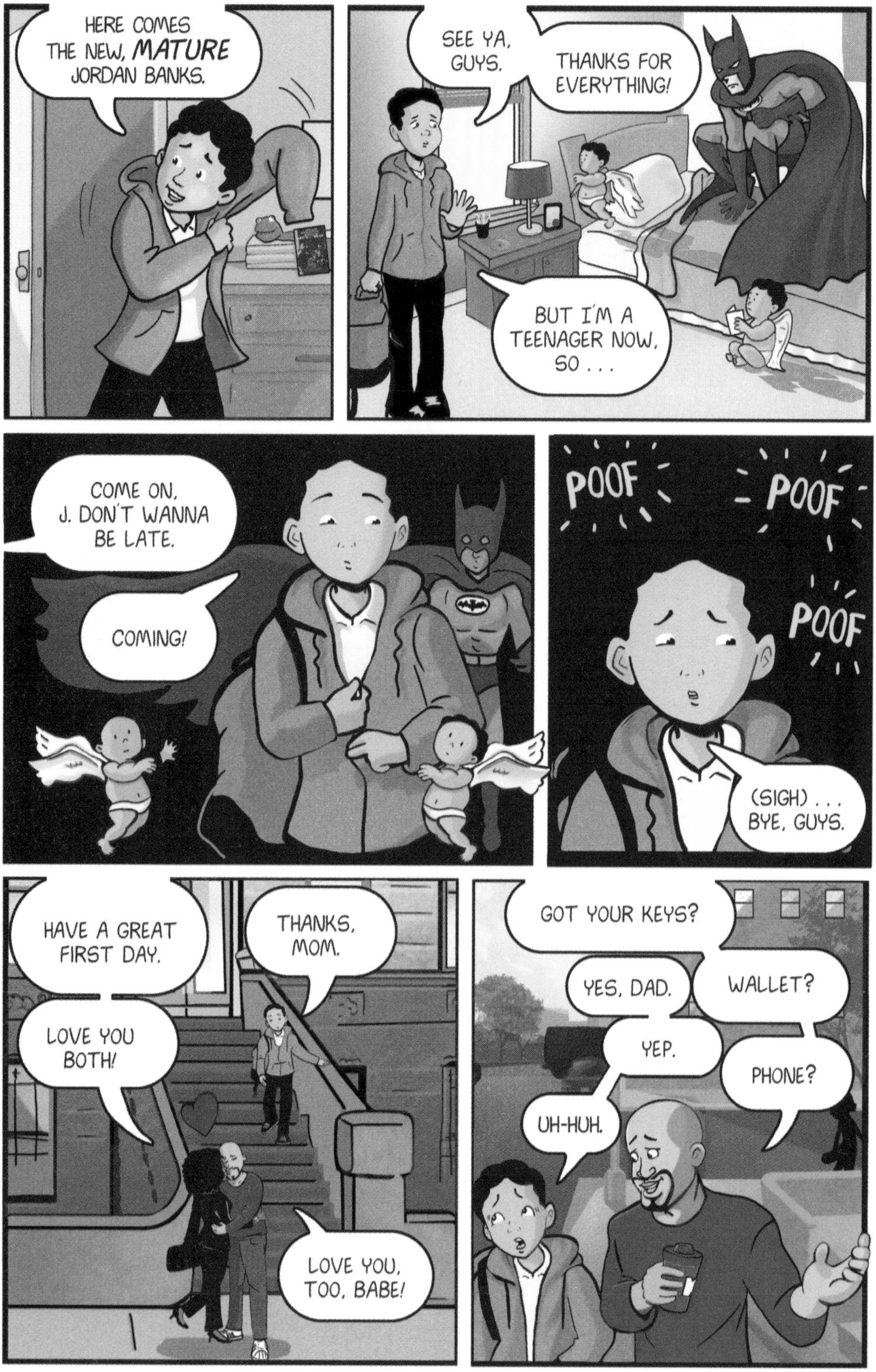
HERE COMES THE NEW, MATURE JORDAN BANKS.
SEE YA, GUYS.
THANKS FOR EVERYTHING!
BUT I'M A TEENAGER NOW, SO . . .
COME ON, J. DON'T WANNA BE LATE.
COMING!
POOF
POOF
POOF
(SIGH) . . . BYE, GUYS.
HAVE A GREAT FIRST DAY.
THANKS, MOM.
LOVE YOU BOTH!
LOVE YOU, TOO, BABE!
GOT YOUR KEYS?
YES, DAD.
WALLET?
YEP.
PHONE?
UH-HUH.

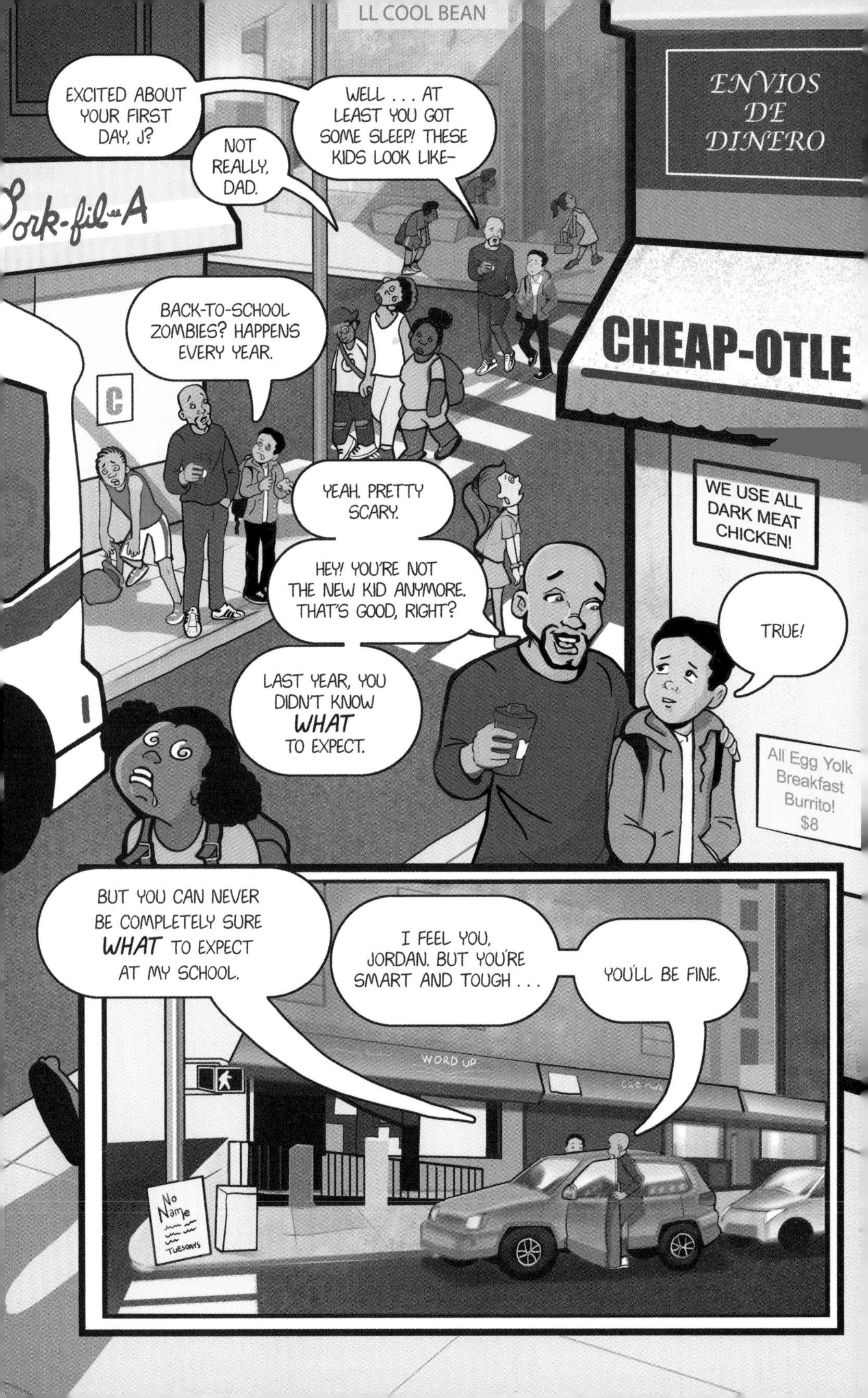
LL COOL BEAN
ENVIOS DE DINERO
EXCITED ABOUT YOUR FIRST DAY, J?
NOT REALLY, DAD.
WELL . . . AT LEAST YOU GOT SOME SLEEP! THESE KIDS LOOK LIKE–
Pork-fil-A
BACK-TO-SCHOOL ZOMBIES? HAPPENS EVERY YEAR.
C
CHEAP-OTLE
YEAH. PRETTY SCARY.
WE USE ALL DARK MEAT CHICKEN!
HEY! YOU'RE NOT THE NEW KID ANYMORE. THAT'S GOOD, RIGHT?
TRUE!
LAST YEAR, YOU DIDN'T KNOW ***WHAT*** TO EXPECT.
All Egg Yolk Breakfast Burrito! $8
BUT YOU CAN NEVER BE COMPLETELY SURE ***WHAT*** TO EXPECT AT MY SCHOOL.
I FEEL YOU, JORDAN. BUT YOU'RE SMART AND TOUGH . . .
YOU'LL BE FINE.
WORD UP
No Name
TUESDAYS

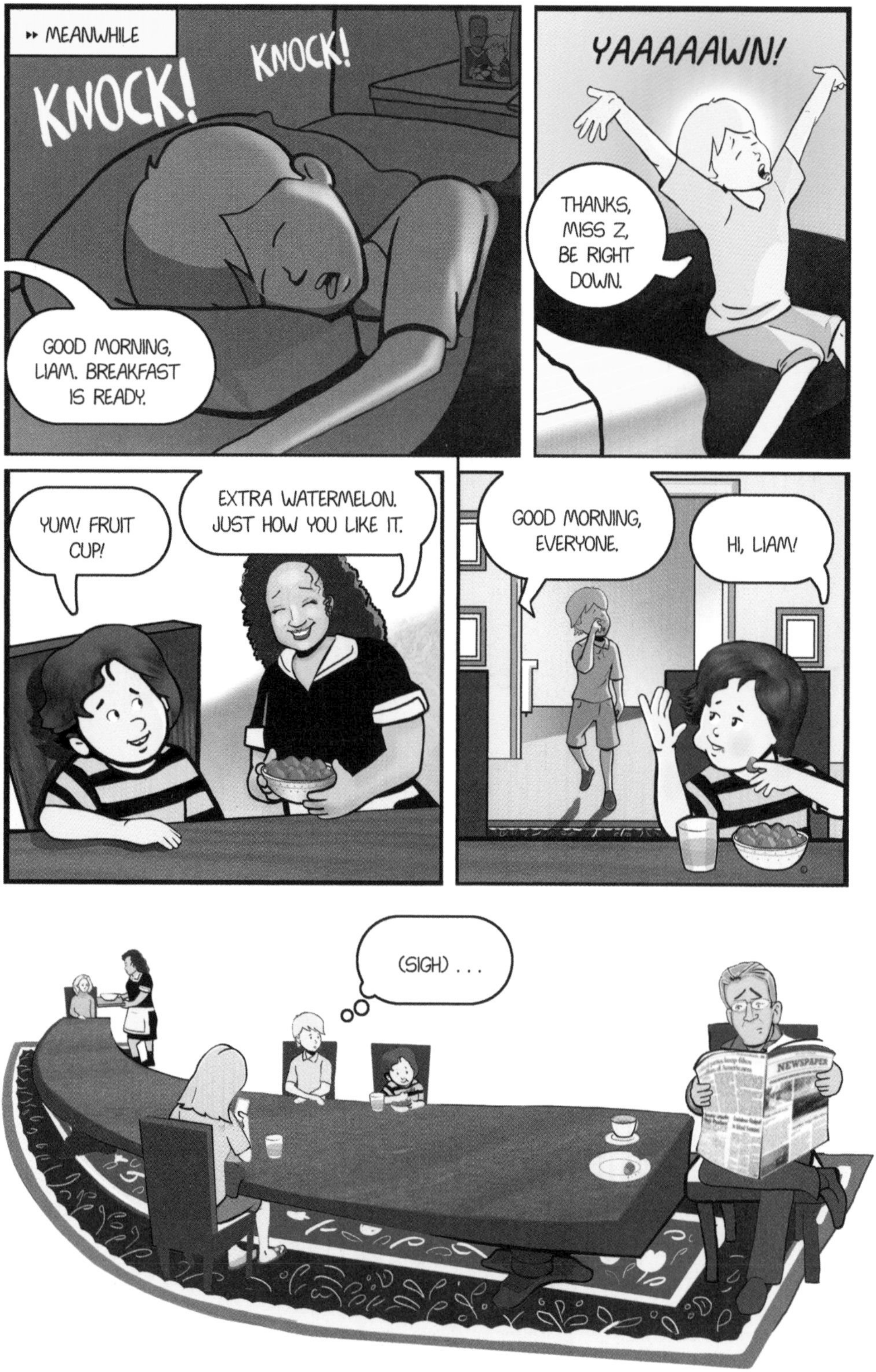
MEANWHILE
KNOCK!
KNOCK!
GOOD MORNING, LIAM. BREAKFAST IS READY.
YAAAAAWN!
THANKS, MISS Z, BE RIGHT DOWN.
YUM! FRUIT CUP!
EXTRA WATERMELON. JUST HOW YOU LIKE IT.
GOOD MORNING, EVERYONE.
HI, LIAM!
(SIGH) . . .
NEWSPAPER

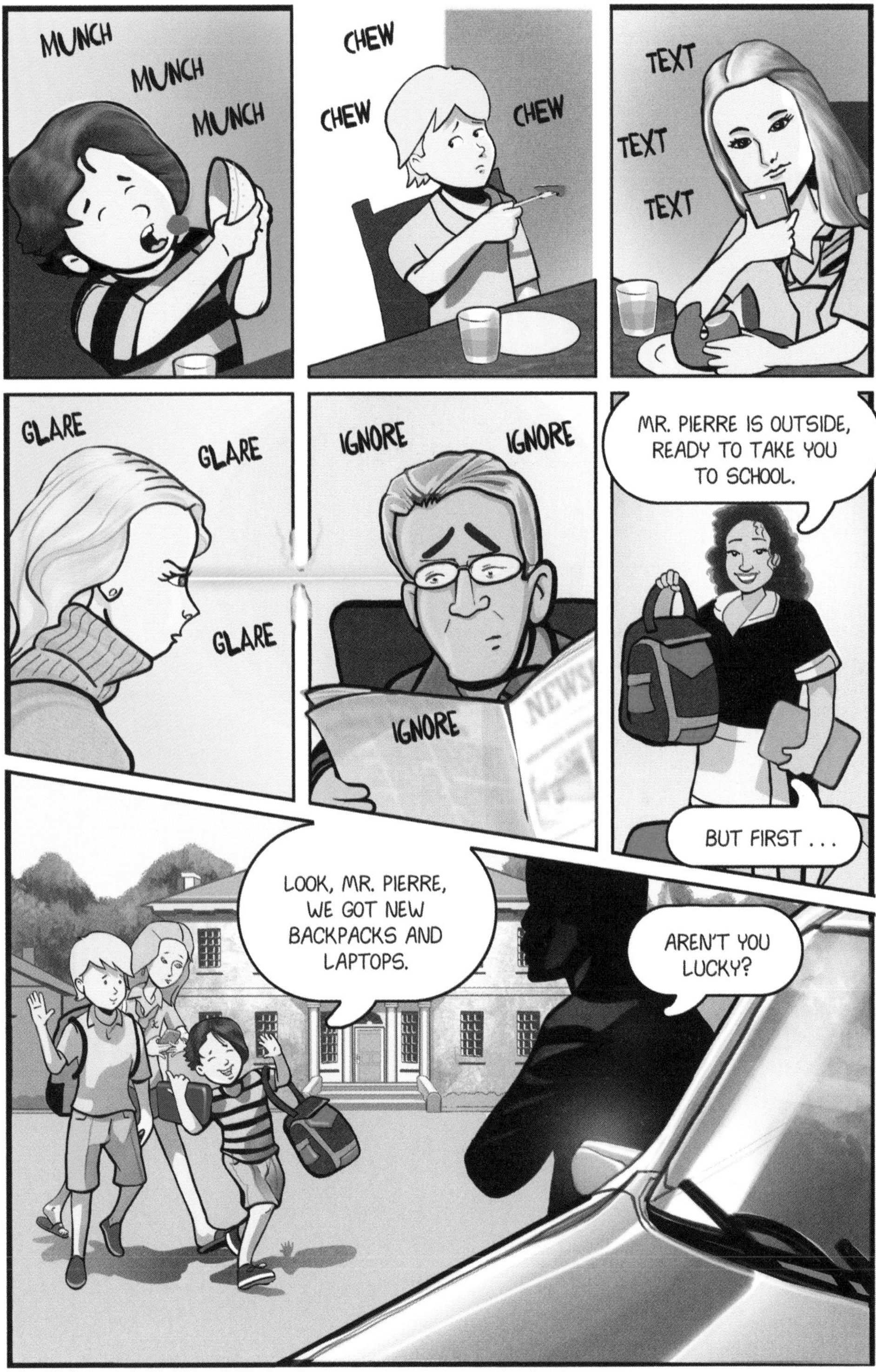
MUNCH
MUNCH
MUNCH
CHEW
CHEW
CHEW
TEXT
TEXT
TEXT
GLARE
GLARE
GLARE
IGNORE
IGNORE
IGNORE
MR. PIERRE IS OUTSIDE, READY TO TAKE YOU TO SCHOOL.
BUT FIRST . . .
LOOK, MR. PIERRE, WE GOT NEW BACKPACKS AND LAPTOPS.
AREN'T YOU LUCKY?

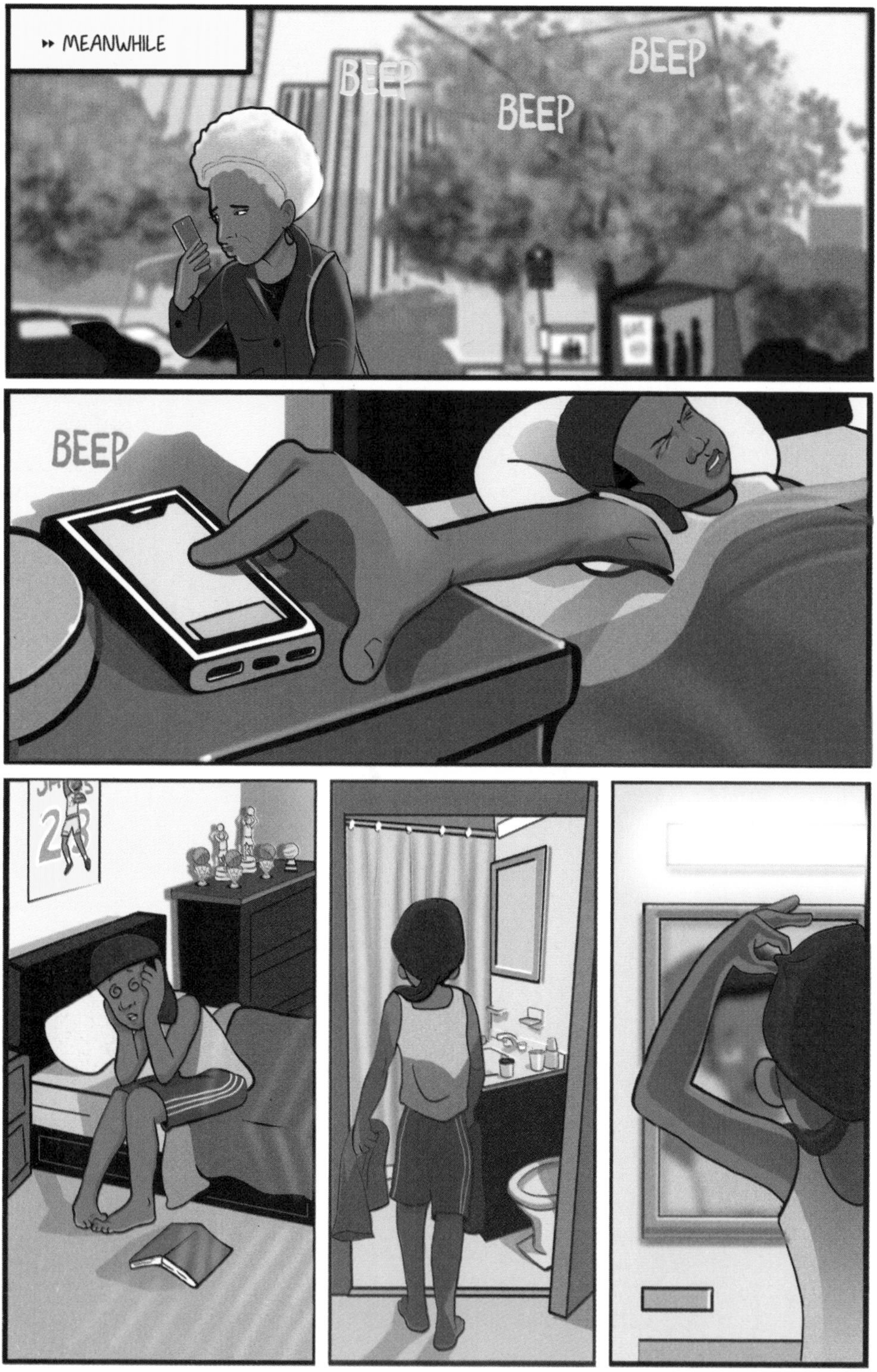
MEANWHILE
BEEP
BEEP
BEEP
BEEP

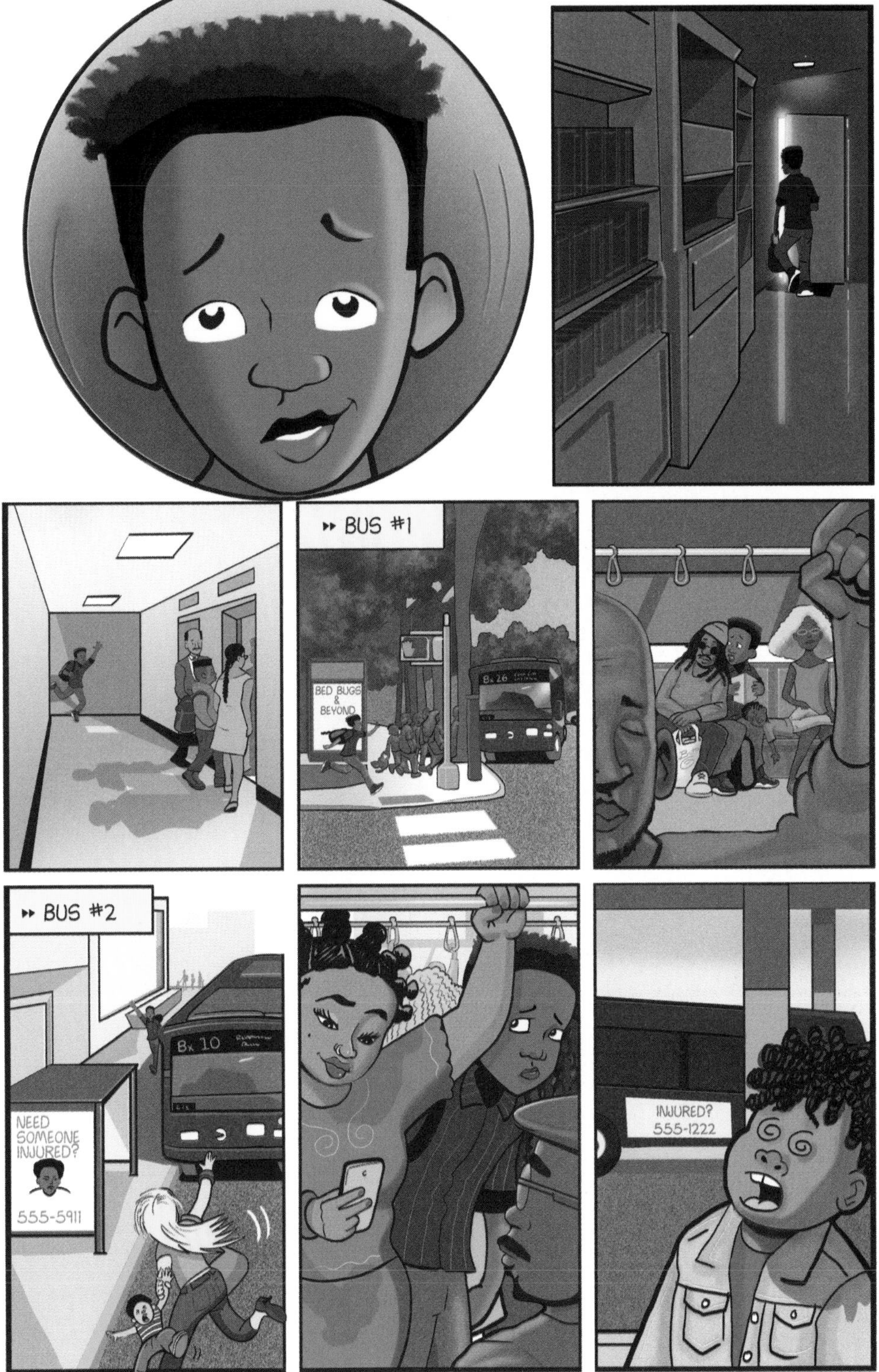
▸▸ BUS #1
BED BUGS & BEYOND
Bx 26
▸▸ BUS #2
Bx 10
NEED SOMEONE INJURED?
555-5911
INJURED?
555-1222

CHAPTER 2

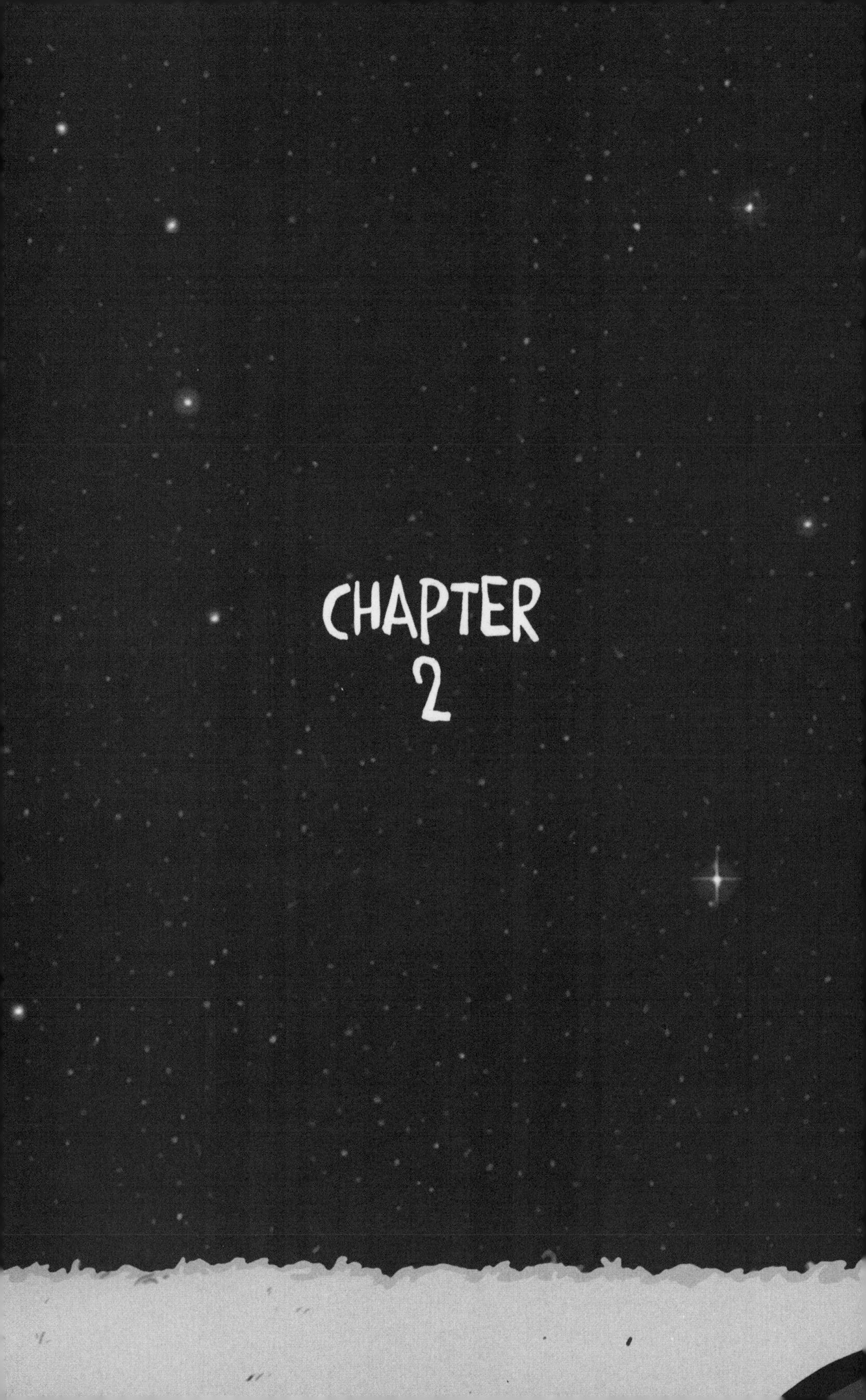

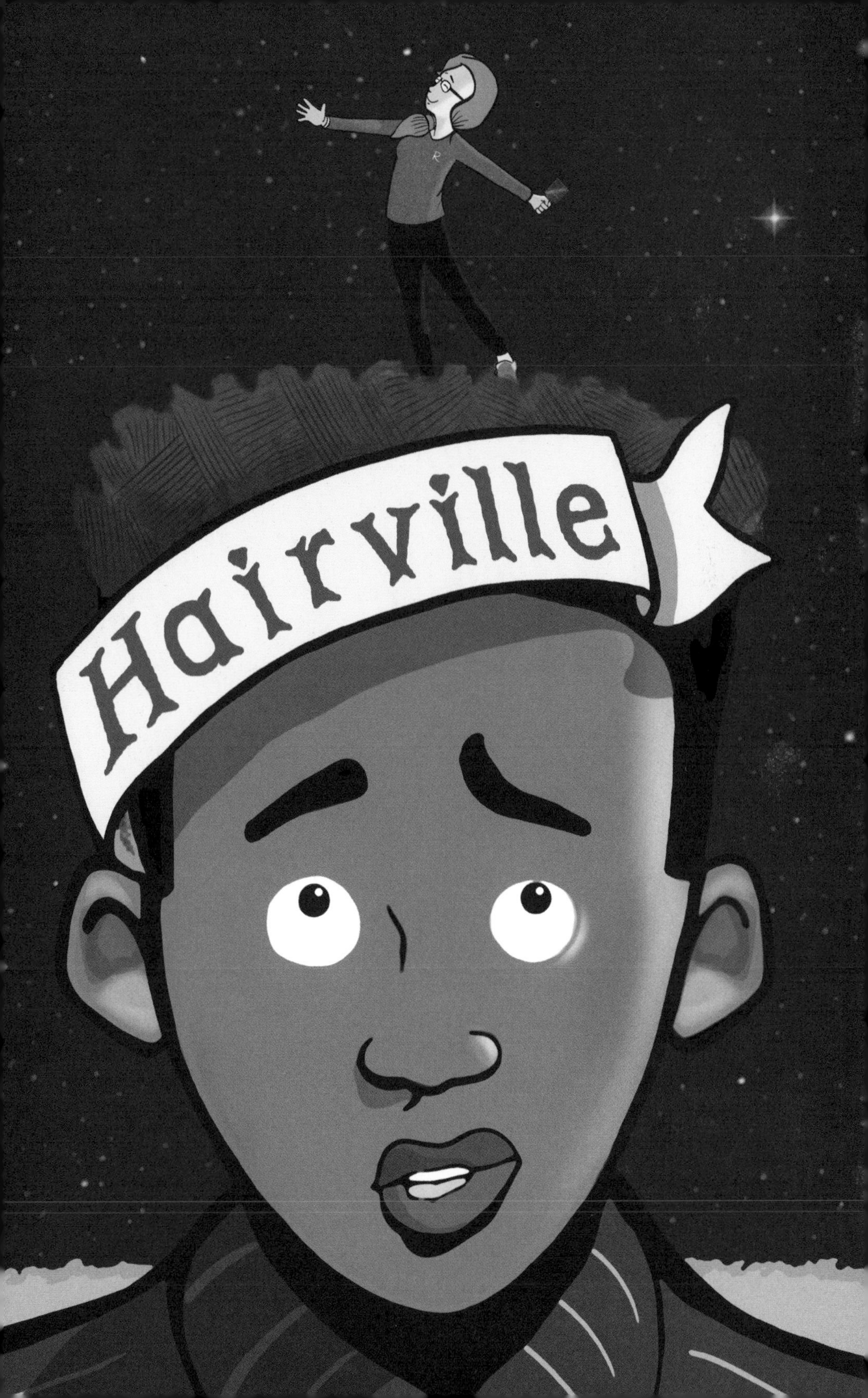
Hairville

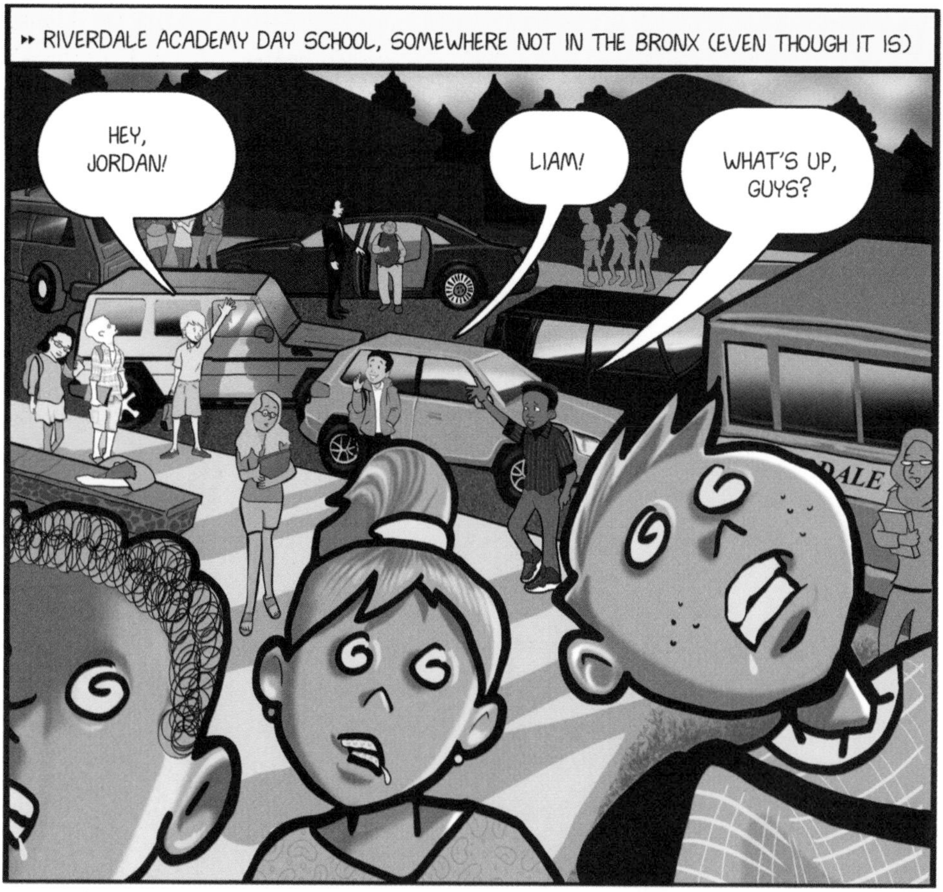

▸▸ RIVERDALE ACADEMY DAY SCHOOL, SOMEWHERE NOT IN THE BRONX (EVEN THOUGH IT IS)
HEY, JORDAN!
LIAM!
WHAT'S UP, GUYS?
DALE

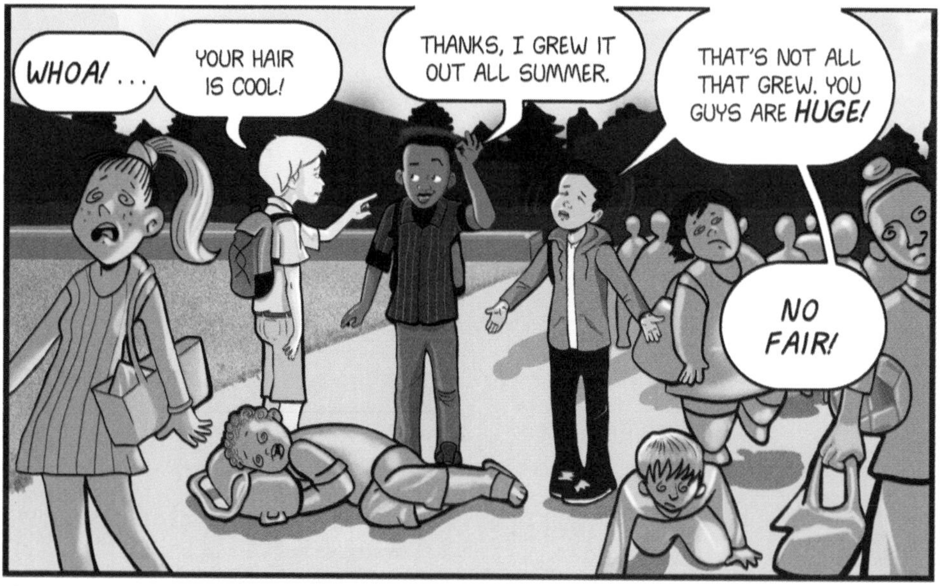

WHOA! . . .
YOUR HAIR IS COOL!
THANKS, I GREW IT OUT ALL SUMMER.
THAT'S NOT ALL THAT GREW. YOU GUYS ARE **HUGE!**
NO FAIR!

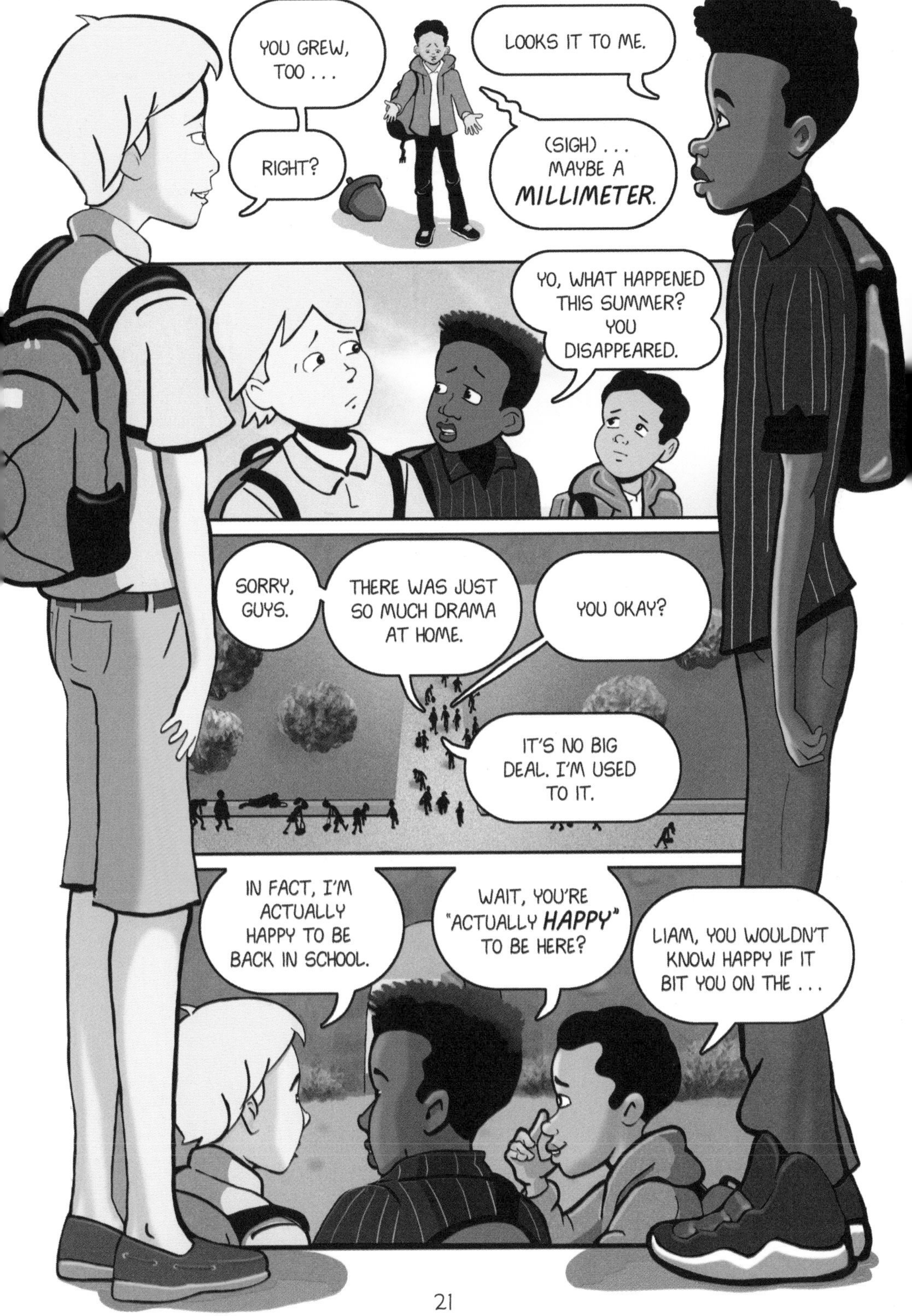
YOU GREW, TOO . . .
RIGHT?
LOOKS IT TO ME.
(SIGH) . . . MAYBE A MILLIMETER.
YO, WHAT HAPPENED THIS SUMMER? YOU DISAPPEARED.
SORRY, GUYS.
THERE WAS JUST SO MUCH DRAMA AT HOME.
YOU OKAY?
IT'S NO BIG DEAL. I'M USED TO IT.
IN FACT, I'M ACTUALLY HAPPY TO BE BACK IN SCHOOL.
WAIT, YOU'RE "ACTUALLY ***HAPPY***" TO BE HERE?
LIAM, YOU WOULDN'T KNOW HAPPY IF IT BIT YOU ON THE . . .

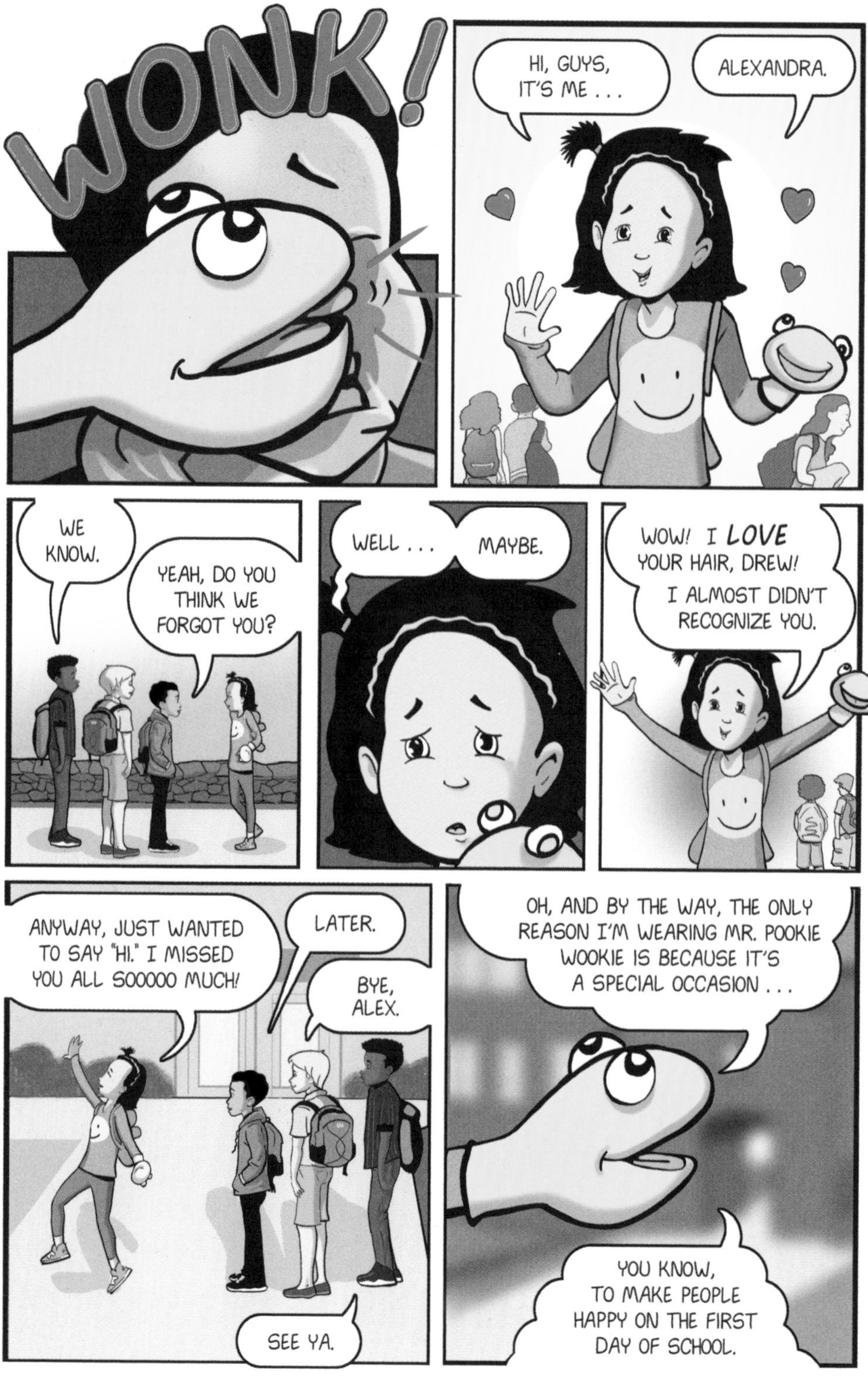
WONK!
HI, GUYS, IT'S ME . . .
ALEXANDRA.
WE KNOW.
YEAH, DO YOU THINK WE FORGOT YOU?
WELL . . .
MAYBE.
WOW! I **LOVE** YOUR HAIR, DREW!
I ALMOST DIDN'T RECOGNIZE YOU.
ANYWAY, JUST WANTED TO SAY "HI." I MISSED YOU ALL SOOOOO MUCH!
LATER.
BYE, ALEX.
SEE YA.
OH, AND BY THE WAY, THE ONLY REASON I'M WEARING MR. POOKIE WOOKIE IS BECAUSE IT'S A SPECIAL OCCASION . . .
YOU KNOW, TO MAKE PEOPLE HAPPY ON THE FIRST DAY OF SCHOOL.

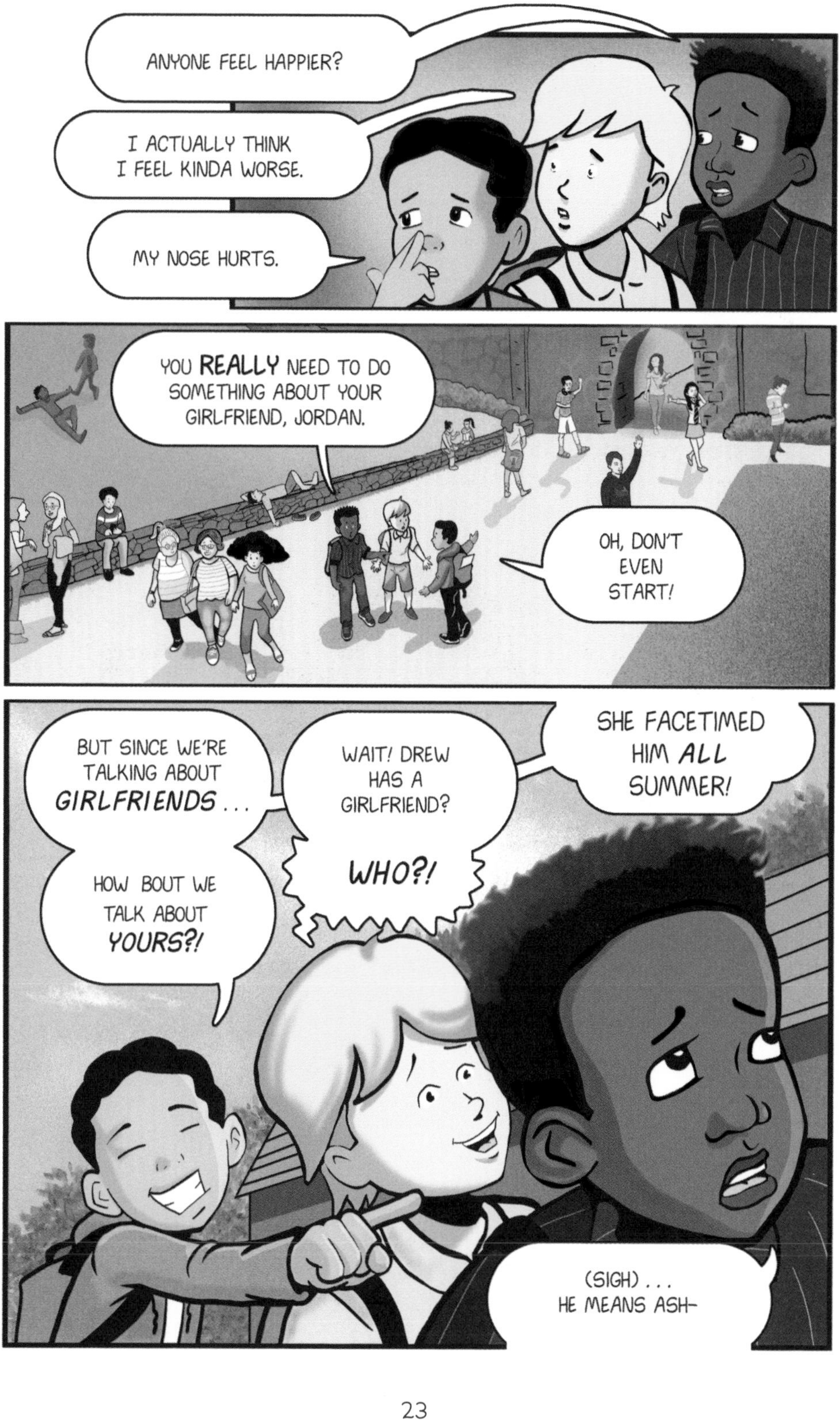
ANYONE FEEL HAPPIER?
I ACTUALLY THINK I FEEL KINDA WORSE.
MY NOSE HURTS.
YOU **REALLY** NEED TO DO SOMETHING ABOUT YOUR GIRLFRIEND, JORDAN.
OH, DON'T EVEN START!
BUT SINCE WE'RE TALKING ABOUT ***GIRLFRIENDS*** . . .
HOW BOUT WE TALK ABOUT ***YOURS?!***
WAIT! DREW HAS A GIRLFRIEND?
WHO?!
SHE FACETIMED HIM ***ALL*** SUMMER!
(SIGH) . . . HE MEANS ASH–

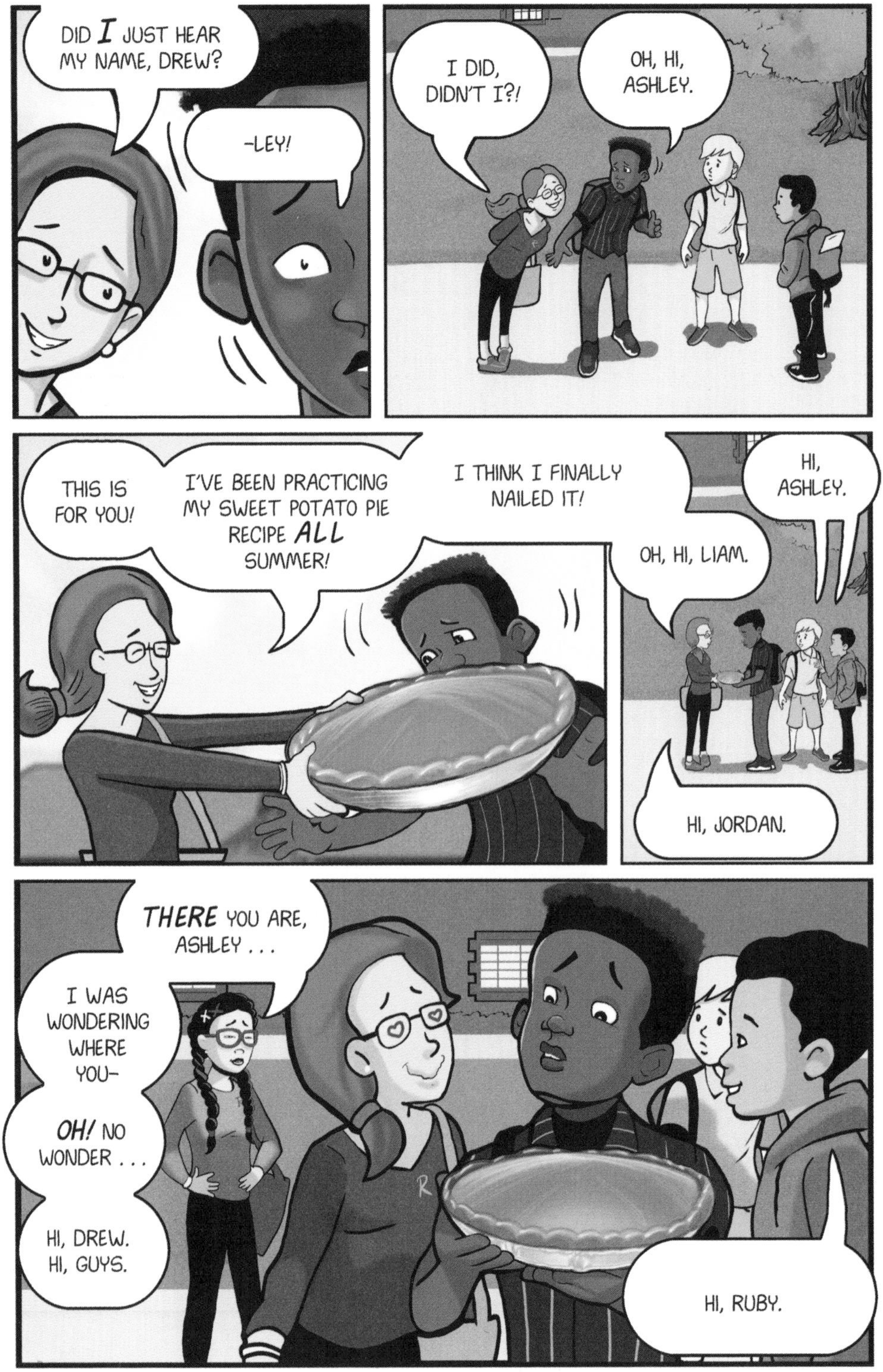
DID I JUST HEAR MY NAME, DREW?
-LEY!
I DID, DIDN'T I?!
OH, HI, ASHLEY.
THIS IS FOR YOU!
I'VE BEEN PRACTICING MY SWEET POTATO PIE RECIPE ALL SUMMER!
I THINK I FINALLY NAILED IT!
HI, ASHLEY.
OH, HI, LIAM.
HI, JORDAN.
THERE YOU ARE, ASHLEY . . .
I WAS WONDERING WHERE YOU-
OH! NO WONDER . . .
HI, DREW. HI, GUYS.
HI, RUBY.

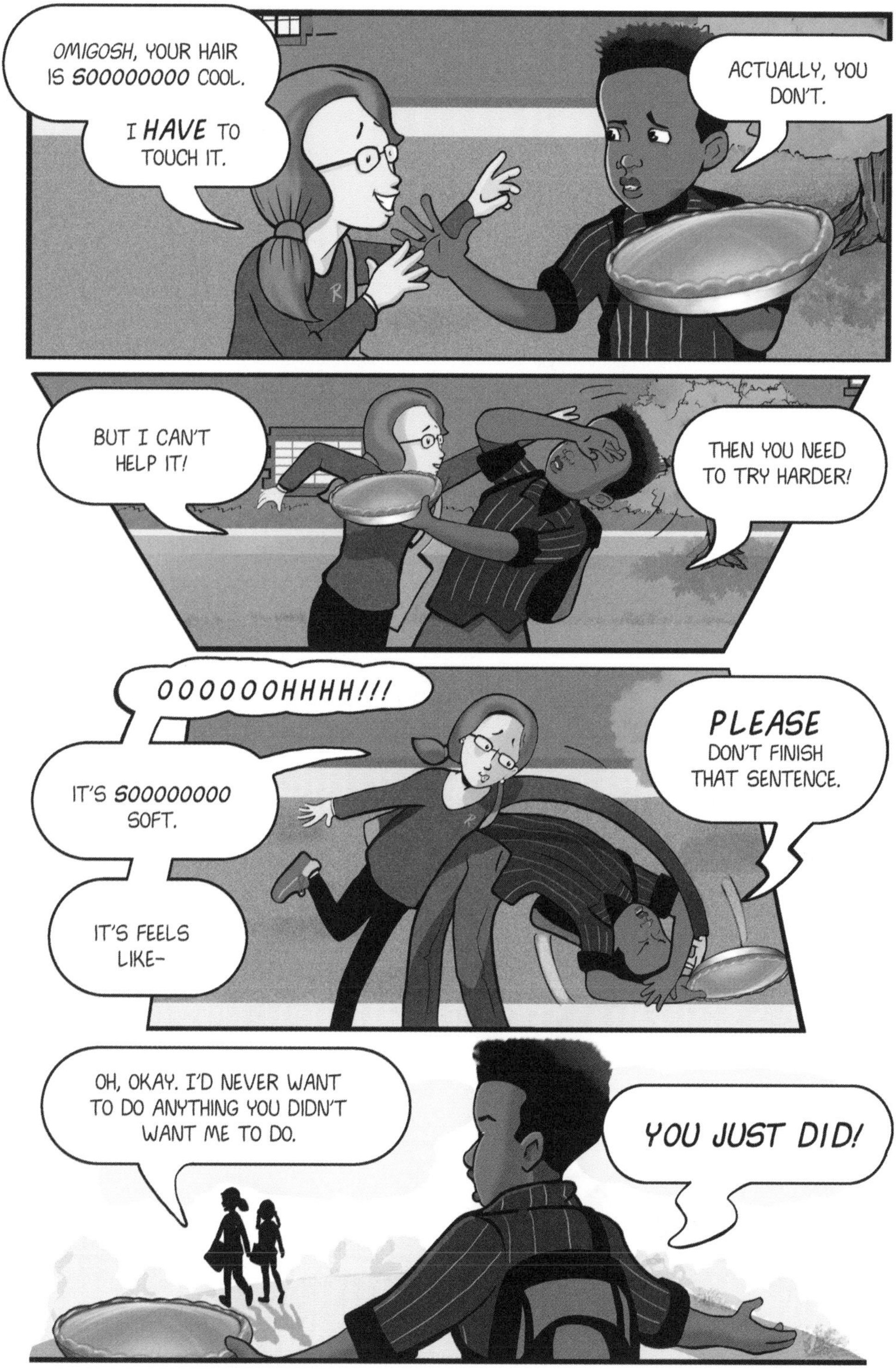
OMIGOSH, YOUR HAIR IS SOOOOOOOO COOL.
I HAVE TO TOUCH IT.
ACTUALLY, YOU DON'T.
BUT I CAN'T HELP IT!
THEN YOU NEED TO TRY HARDER!
OOOOOOHHHH!!!
IT'S SOOOOOOOO SOFT.
IT'S FEELS LIKE-
PLEASE DON'T FINISH THAT SENTENCE.
OH, OKAY. I'D NEVER WANT TO DO ANYTHING YOU DIDN'T WANT ME TO DO.
YOU JUST DID!

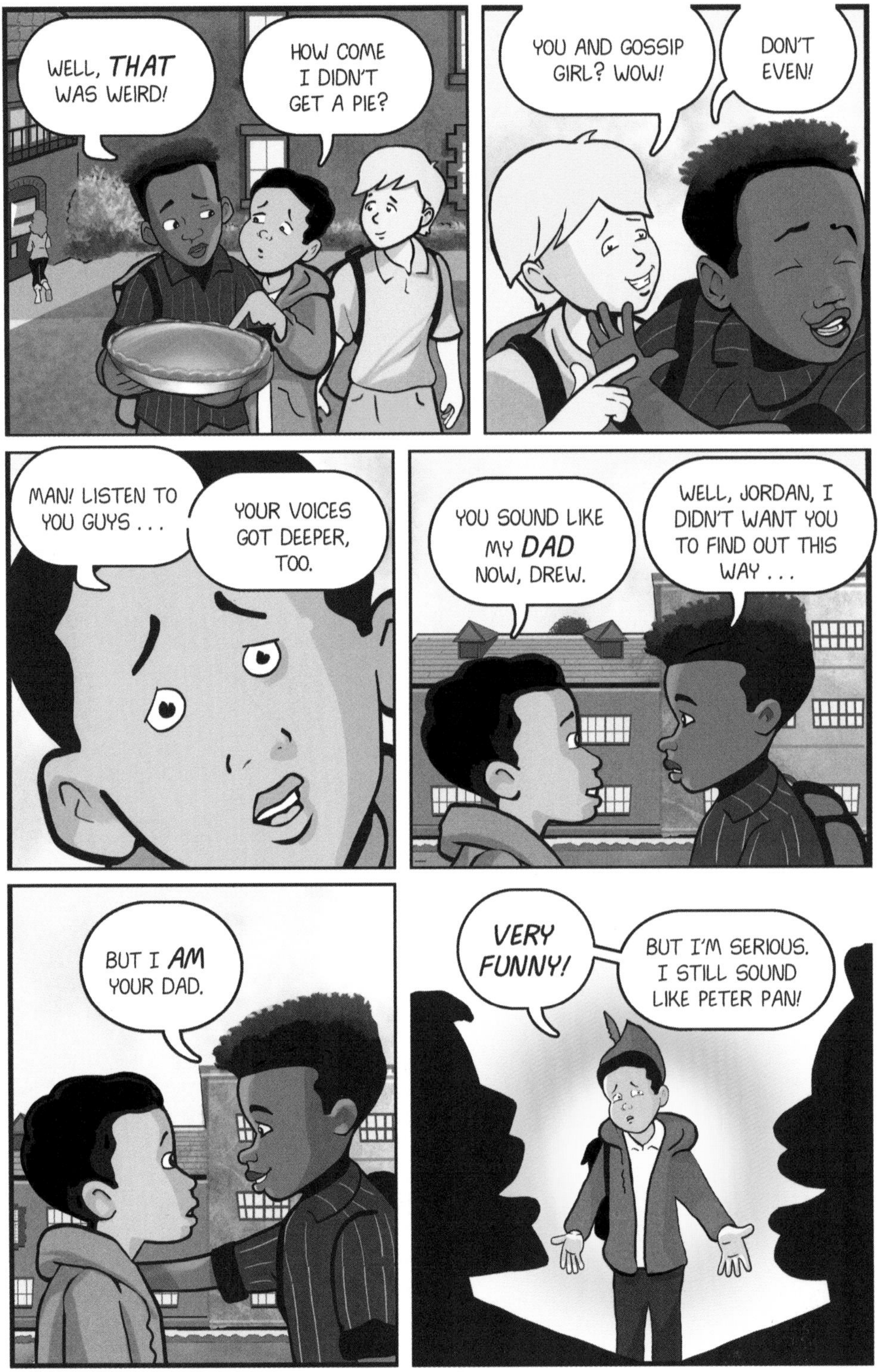
WELL, THAT WAS WEIRD!
HOW COME I DIDN'T GET A PIE?
YOU AND GOSSIP GIRL? WOW!
DON'T EVEN!
MAN! LISTEN TO YOU GUYS . . .
YOUR VOICES GOT DEEPER, TOO.
YOU SOUND LIKE MY DAD NOW, DREW.
WELL, JORDAN, I DIDN'T WANT YOU TO FIND OUT THIS WAY . . .
BUT I AM YOUR DAD.
VERY FUNNY!
BUT I'M SERIOUS. I STILL SOUND LIKE PETER PAN!

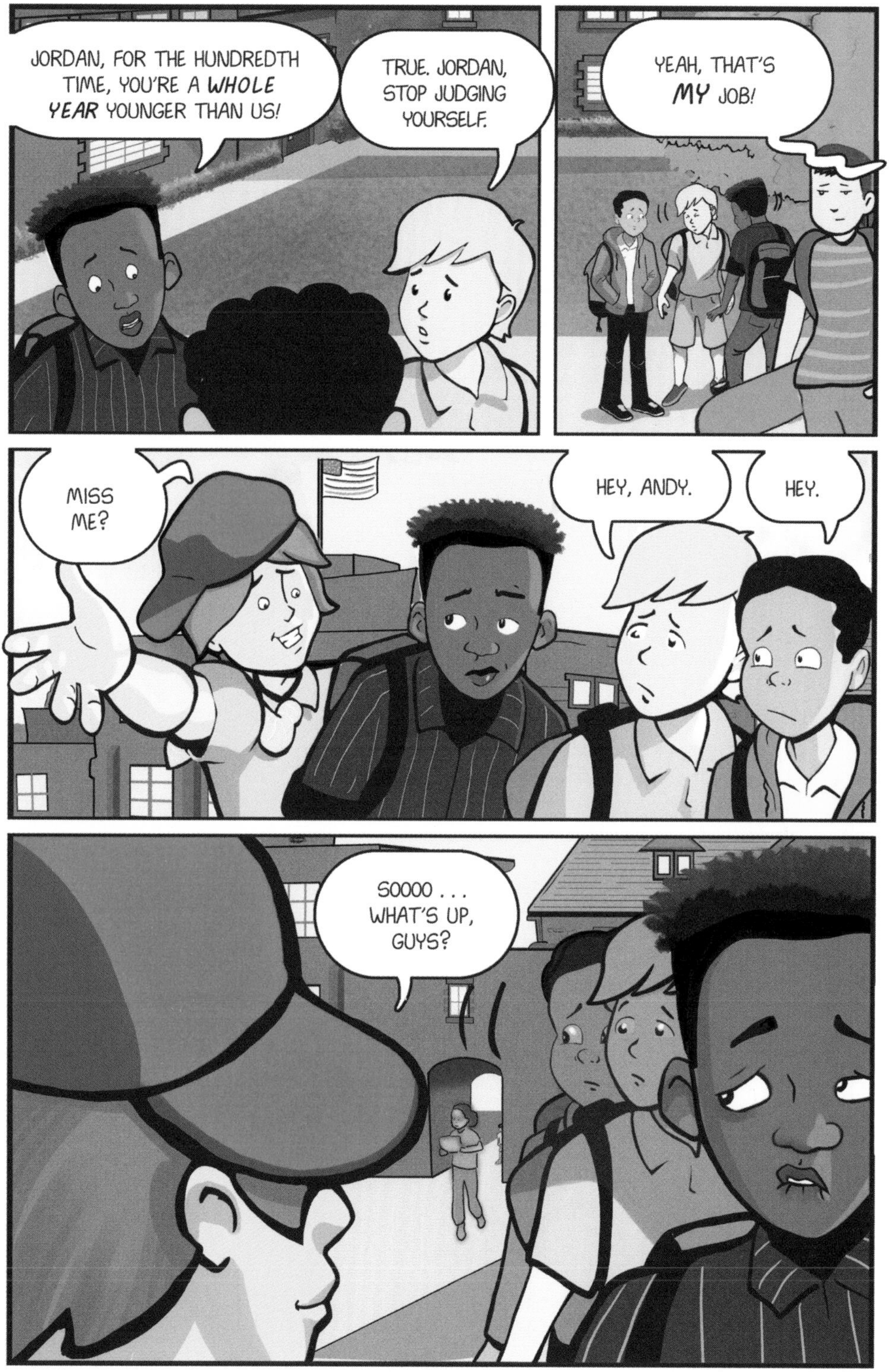
JORDAN, FOR THE HUNDREDTH TIME, YOU'RE A WHOLE YEAR YOUNGER THAN US!
TRUE. JORDAN, STOP JUDGING YOURSELF.
YEAH, THAT'S MY JOB!
MISS ME?
HEY, ANDY.
HEY.
SOOOO . . . WHAT'S UP, GUYS?

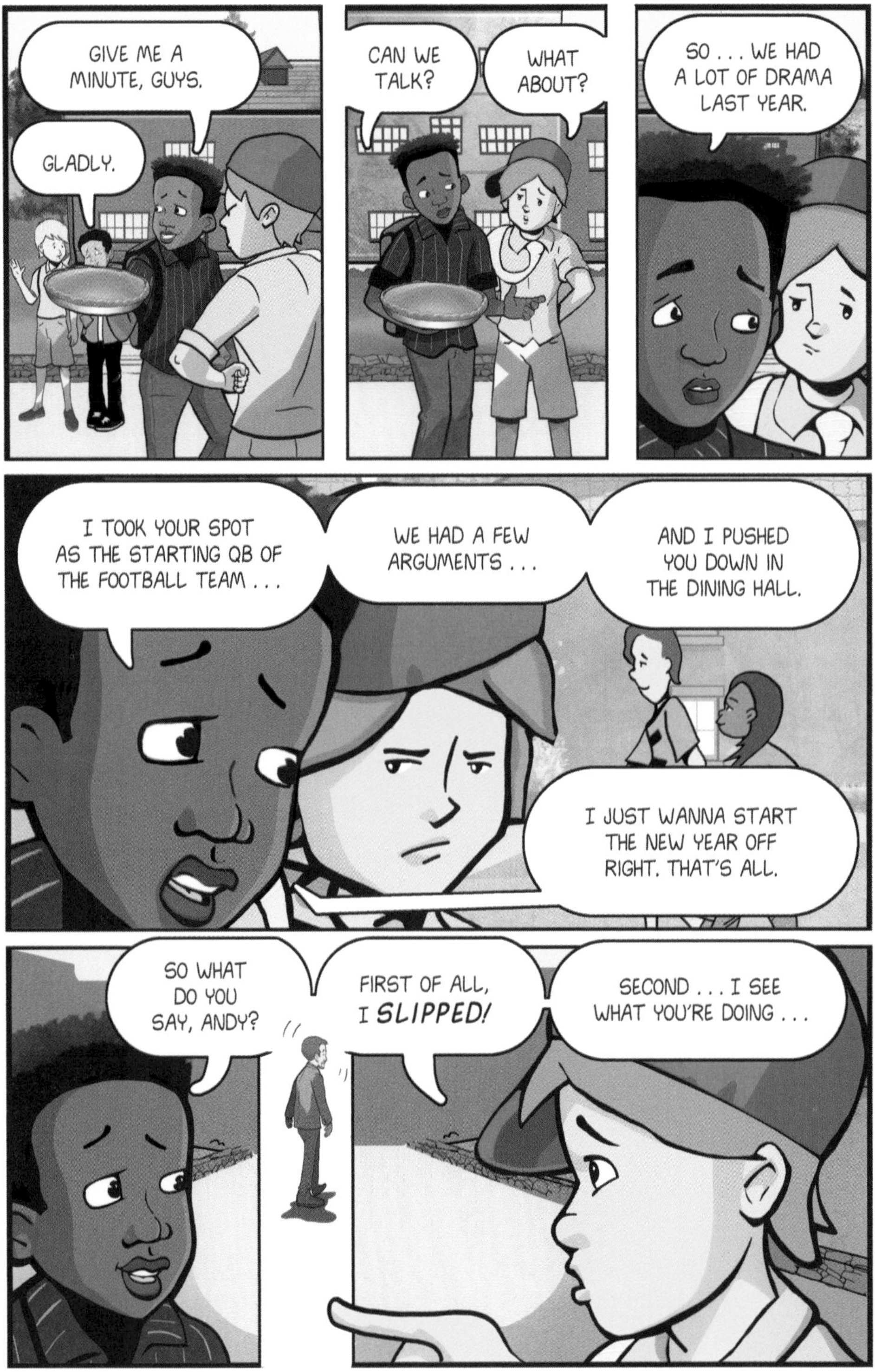
GIVE ME A MINUTE, GUYS.
GLADLY.
CAN WE TALK?
WHAT ABOUT?
SO . . . WE HAD A LOT OF DRAMA LAST YEAR.
I TOOK YOUR SPOT AS THE STARTING QB OF THE FOOTBALL TEAM . . .
WE HAD A FEW ARGUMENTS . . .
AND I PUSHED YOU DOWN IN THE DINING HALL.
I JUST WANNA START THE NEW YEAR OFF RIGHT. THAT'S ALL.
SO WHAT DO YOU SAY, ANDY?
FIRST OF ALL, I *SLIPPED!*
SECOND . . . I SEE WHAT YOU'RE DOING . . .

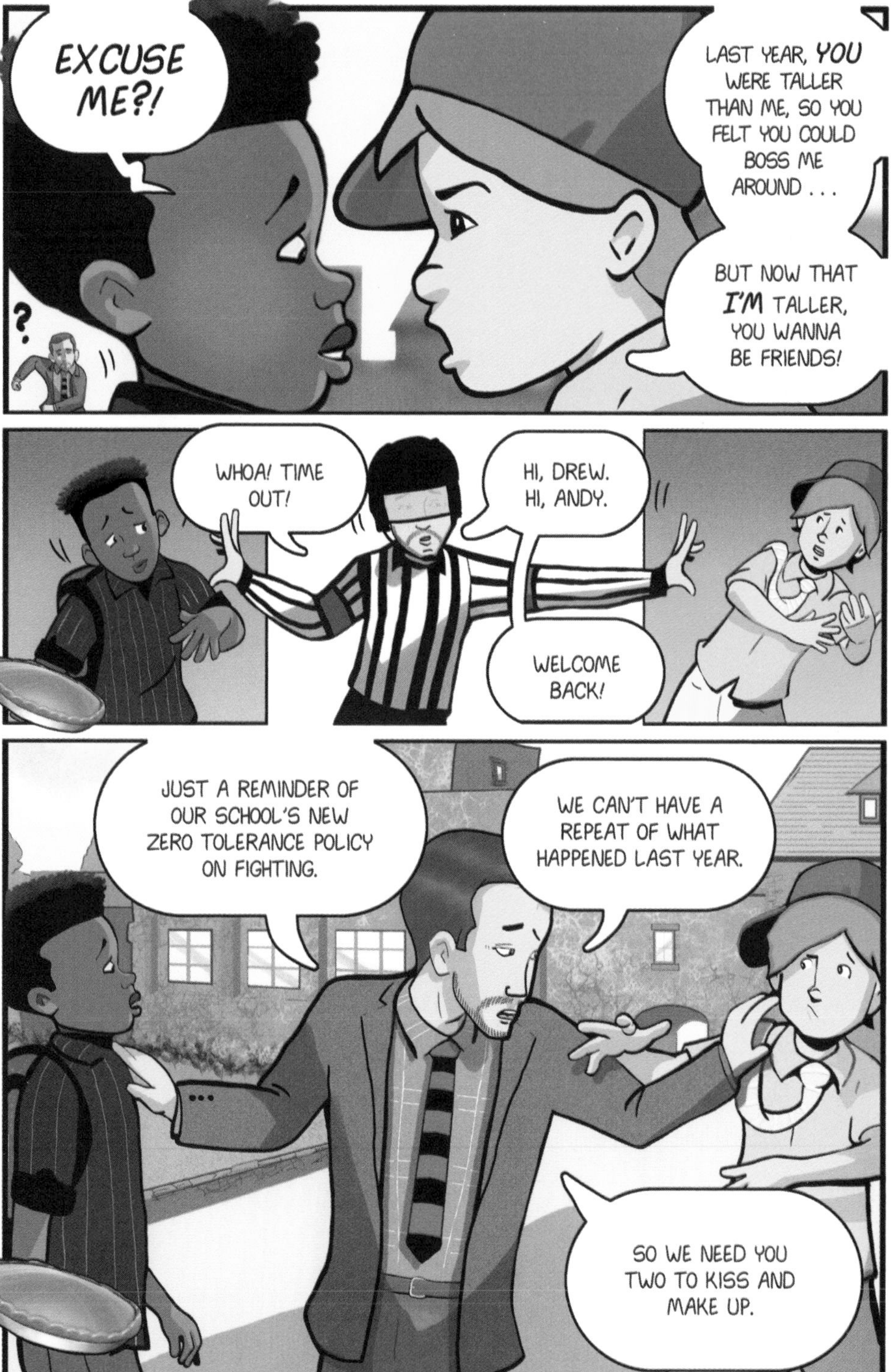
EXCUSE ME?!
LAST YEAR, YOU WERE TALLER THAN ME, SO YOU FELT YOU COULD BOSS ME AROUND . . .
BUT NOW THAT I'M TALLER, YOU WANNA BE FRIENDS!
?
WHOA! TIME OUT!
HI, DREW. HI, ANDY.
WELCOME BACK!
JUST A REMINDER OF OUR SCHOOL'S NEW ZERO TOLERANCE POLICY ON FIGHTING.
WE CAN'T HAVE A REPEAT OF WHAT HAPPENED LAST YEAR.
SO WE NEED YOU TWO TO KISS AND MAKE UP.

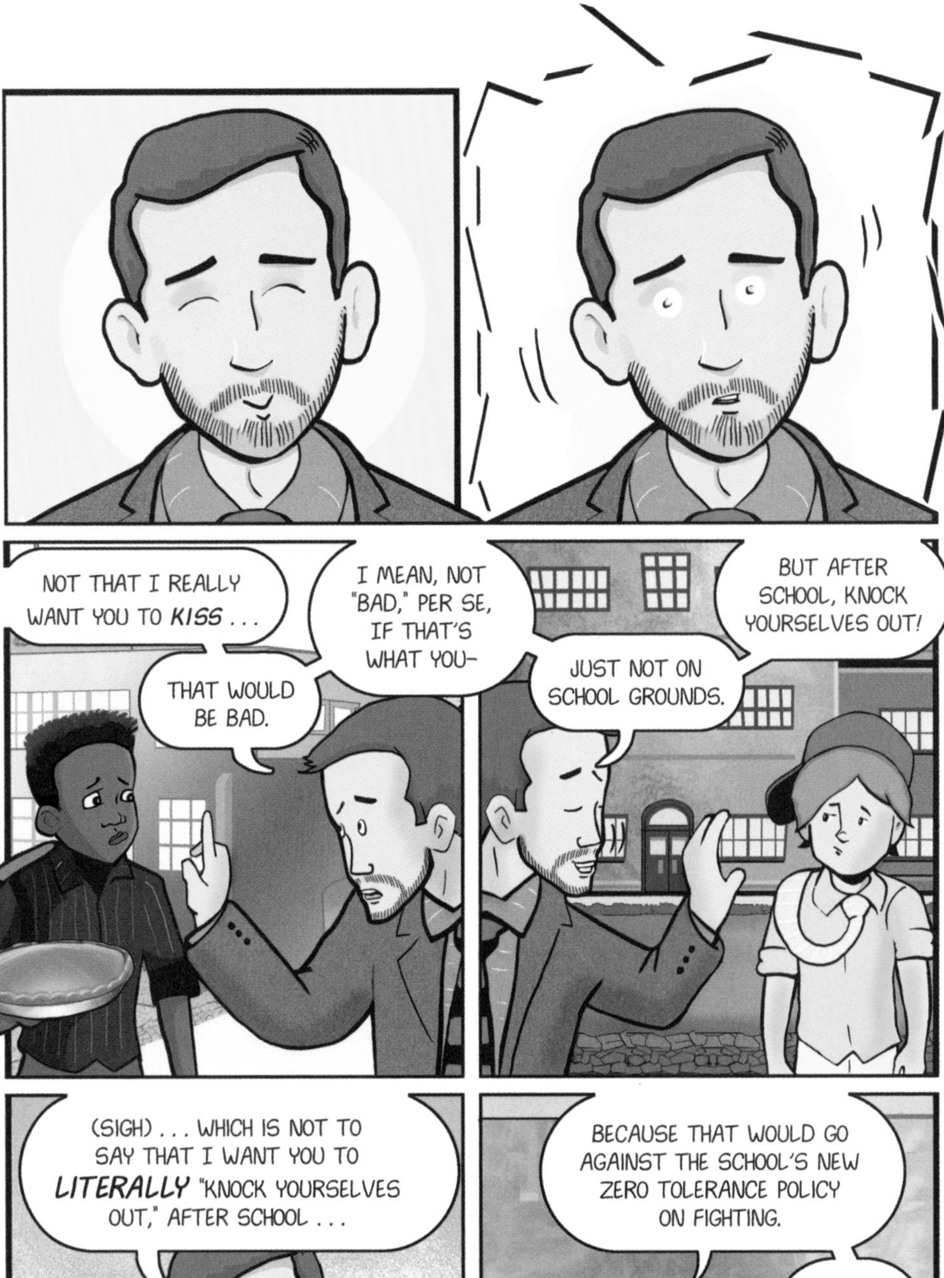
NOT THAT I REALLY WANT YOU TO **KISS** . . .
THAT WOULD BE BAD.
I MEAN, NOT "BAD," PER SE, IF THAT'S WHAT YOU–
JUST NOT ON SCHOOL GROUNDS.
BUT AFTER SCHOOL, KNOCK YOURSELVES OUT!
(SIGH) . . . WHICH IS NOT TO SAY THAT I WANT YOU TO **LITERALLY** "KNOCK YOURSELVES OUT," AFTER SCHOOL . . .
BECAUSE THAT WOULD GO AGAINST THE SCHOOL'S NEW ZERO TOLERANCE POLICY ON FIGHTING.
(SIGH) . . . I THINK I HEARD THE BELL. GOTTA GO!

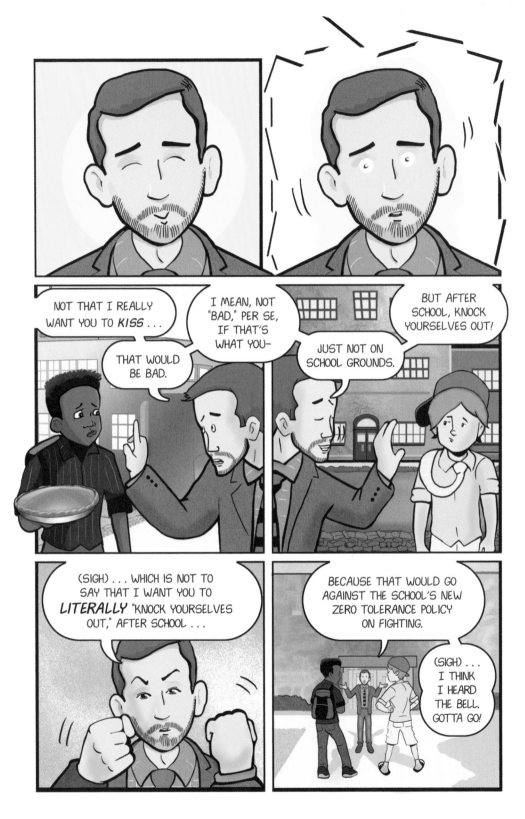

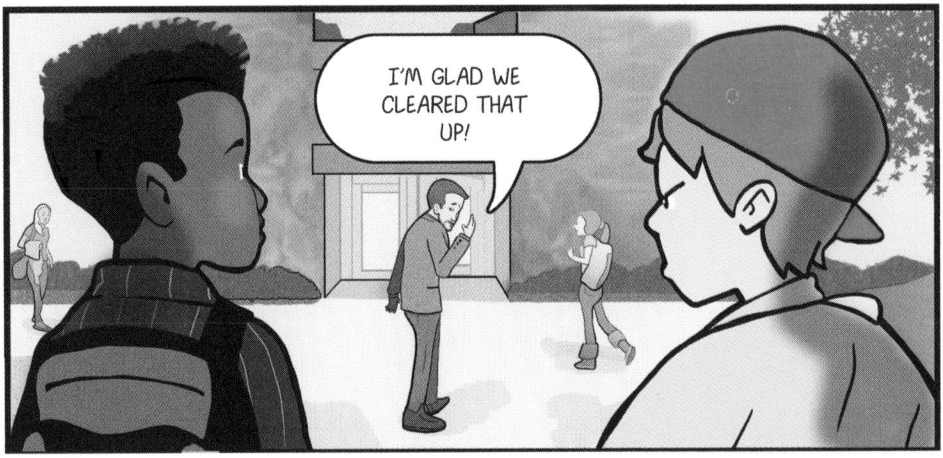
I'M GLAD WE CLEARED THAT UP!

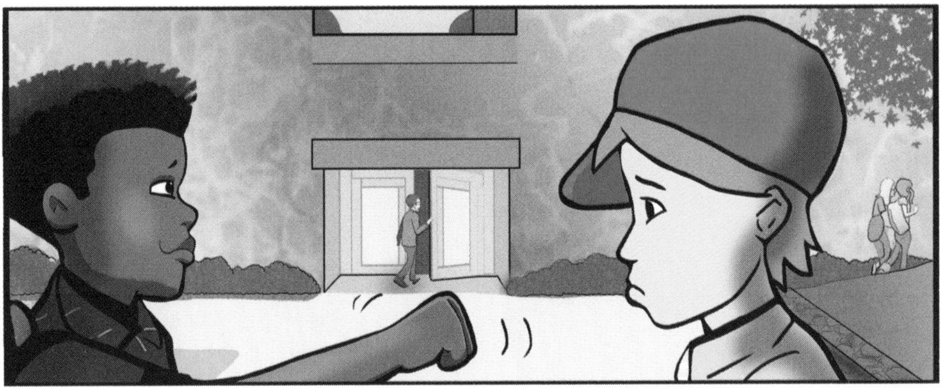

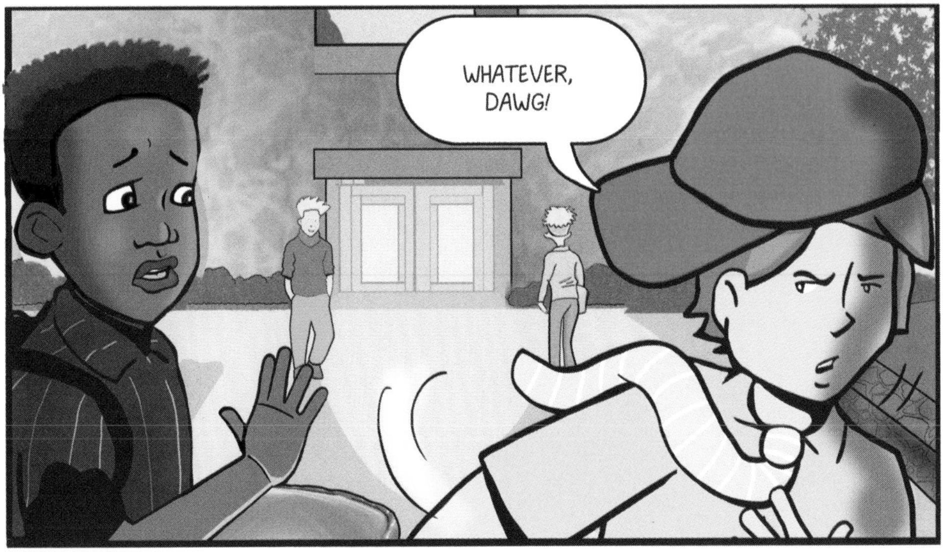
WHATEVER, DAWG!

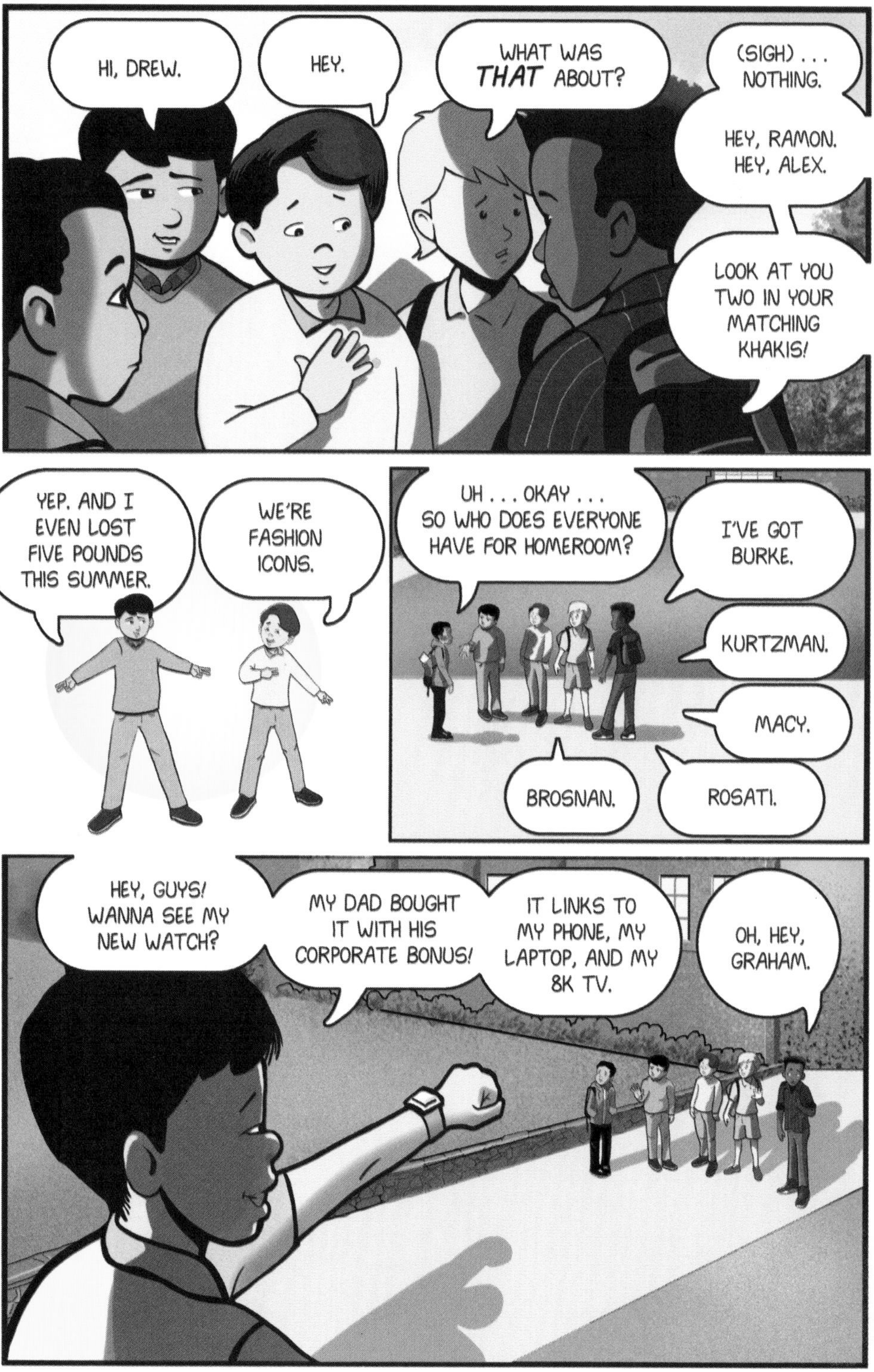
HI, DREW.
HEY.
WHAT WAS *THAT* ABOUT?
(SIGH) . . . NOTHING.
HEY, RAMON. HEY, ALEX.
LOOK AT YOU TWO IN YOUR MATCHING KHAKIS!
YEP. AND I EVEN LOST FIVE POUNDS THIS SUMMER.
WE'RE FASHION ICONS.
UH . . . OKAY . . . SO WHO DOES EVERYONE HAVE FOR HOMEROOM?
I'VE GOT BURKE.
KURTZMAN.
MACY.
ROSATI.
BROSNAN.
HEY, GUYS! WANNA SEE MY NEW WATCH?
MY DAD BOUGHT IT WITH HIS CORPORATE BONUS!
IT LINKS TO MY PHONE, MY LAPTOP, AND MY 8K TV.
OH, HEY, GRAHAM.

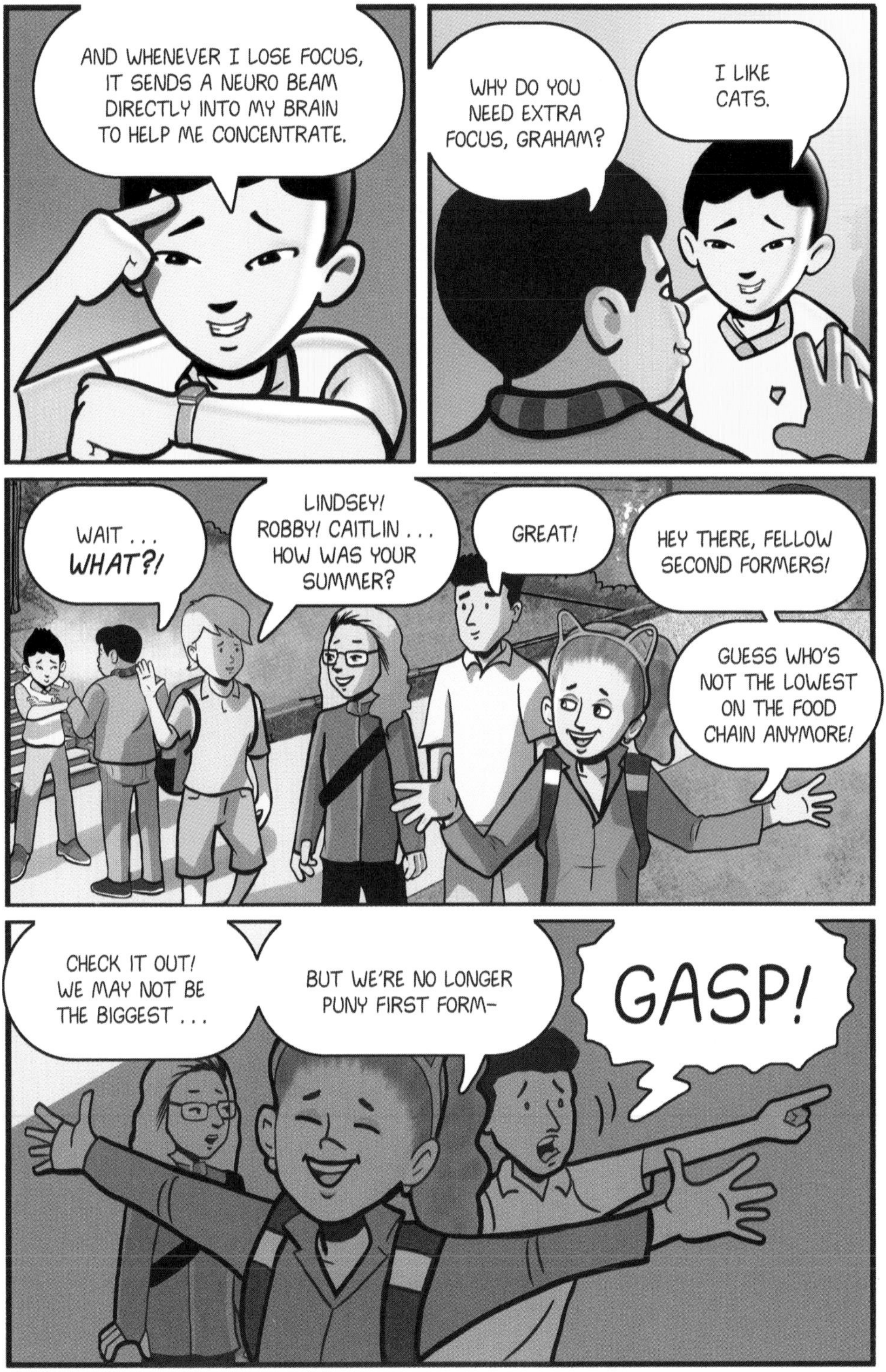
AND WHENEVER I LOSE FOCUS, IT SENDS A NEURO BEAM DIRECTLY INTO MY BRAIN TO HELP ME CONCENTRATE.
WHY DO YOU NEED EXTRA FOCUS, GRAHAM?
I LIKE CATS.
WAIT . . . WHAT?!
LINDSEY! ROBBY! CAITLIN . . . HOW WAS YOUR SUMMER?
GREAT!
HEY THERE, FELLOW SECOND FORMERS!
GUESS WHO'S NOT THE LOWEST ON THE FOOD CHAIN ANYMORE!
CHECK IT OUT! WE MAY NOT BE THE BIGGEST . . .
BUT WE'RE NO LONGER PUNY FIRST FORM–
GASP!

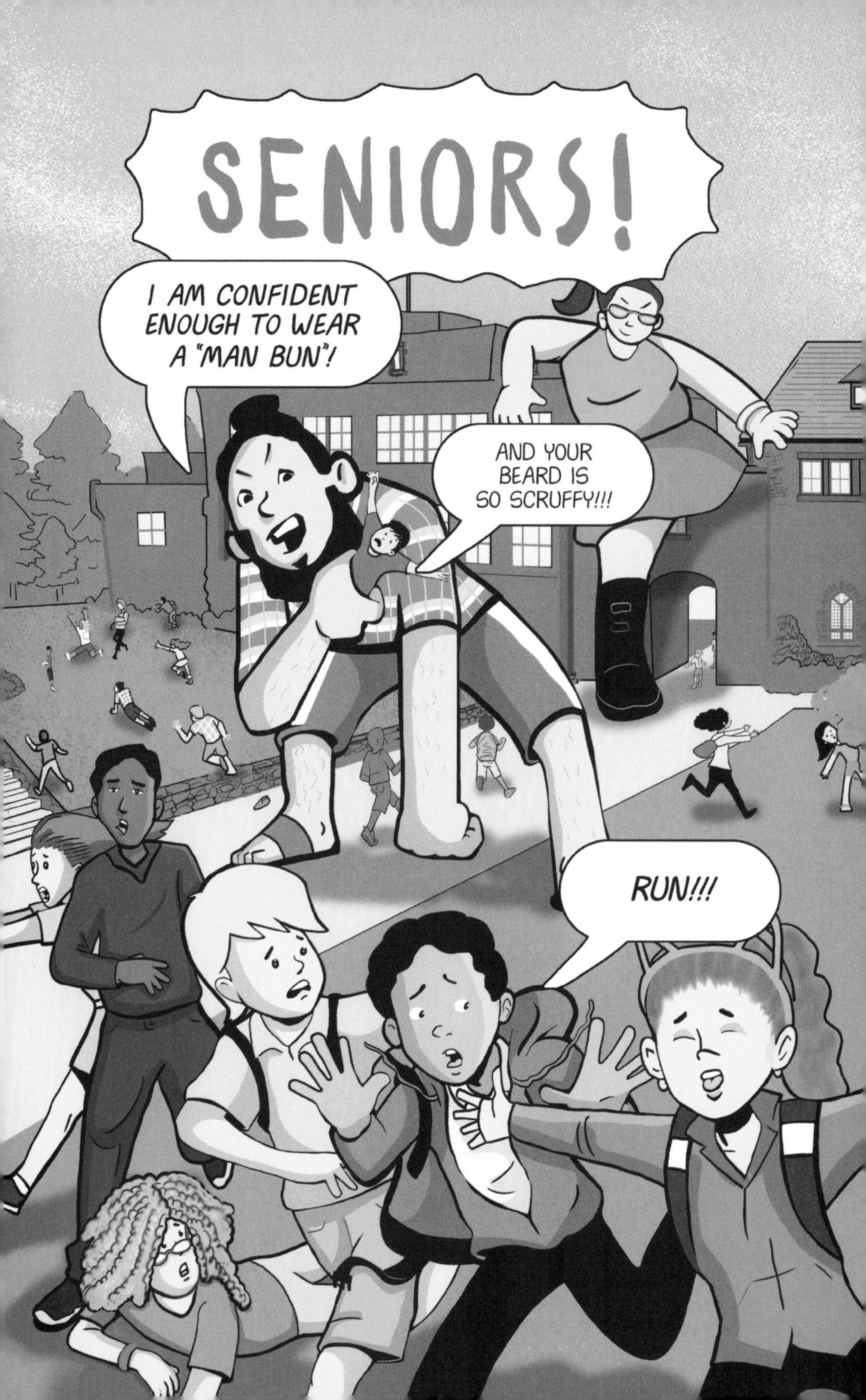
SENIORS!
I AM CONFIDENT ENOUGH TO WEAR A "MAN BUN"!
AND YOUR BEARD IS SO SCRUFFY!!!
RUN!!!

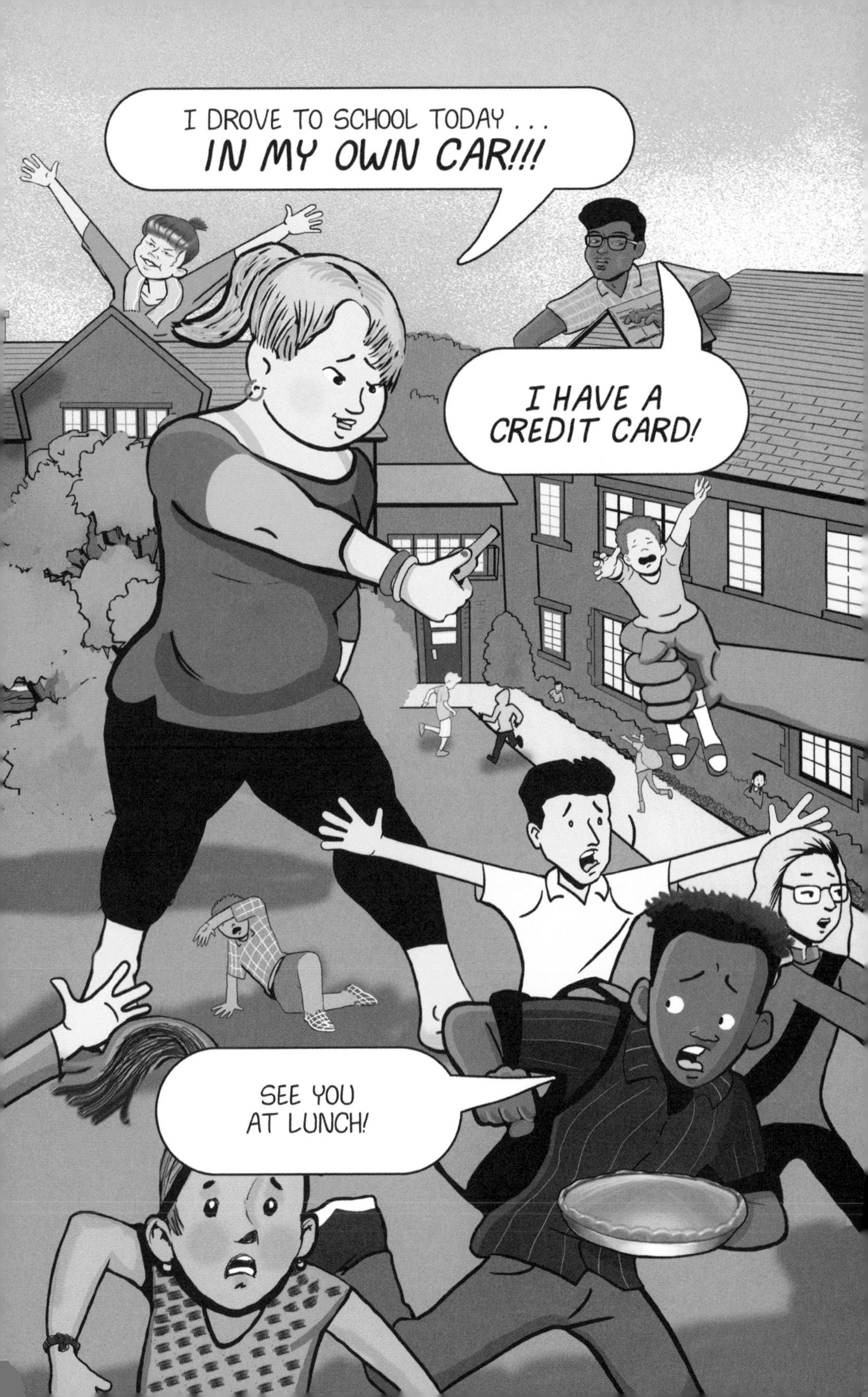
I DROVE TO SCHOOL TODAY . . .
IN MY OWN CAR!!!
I HAVE A CREDIT CARD!
SEE YOU AT LUNCH!

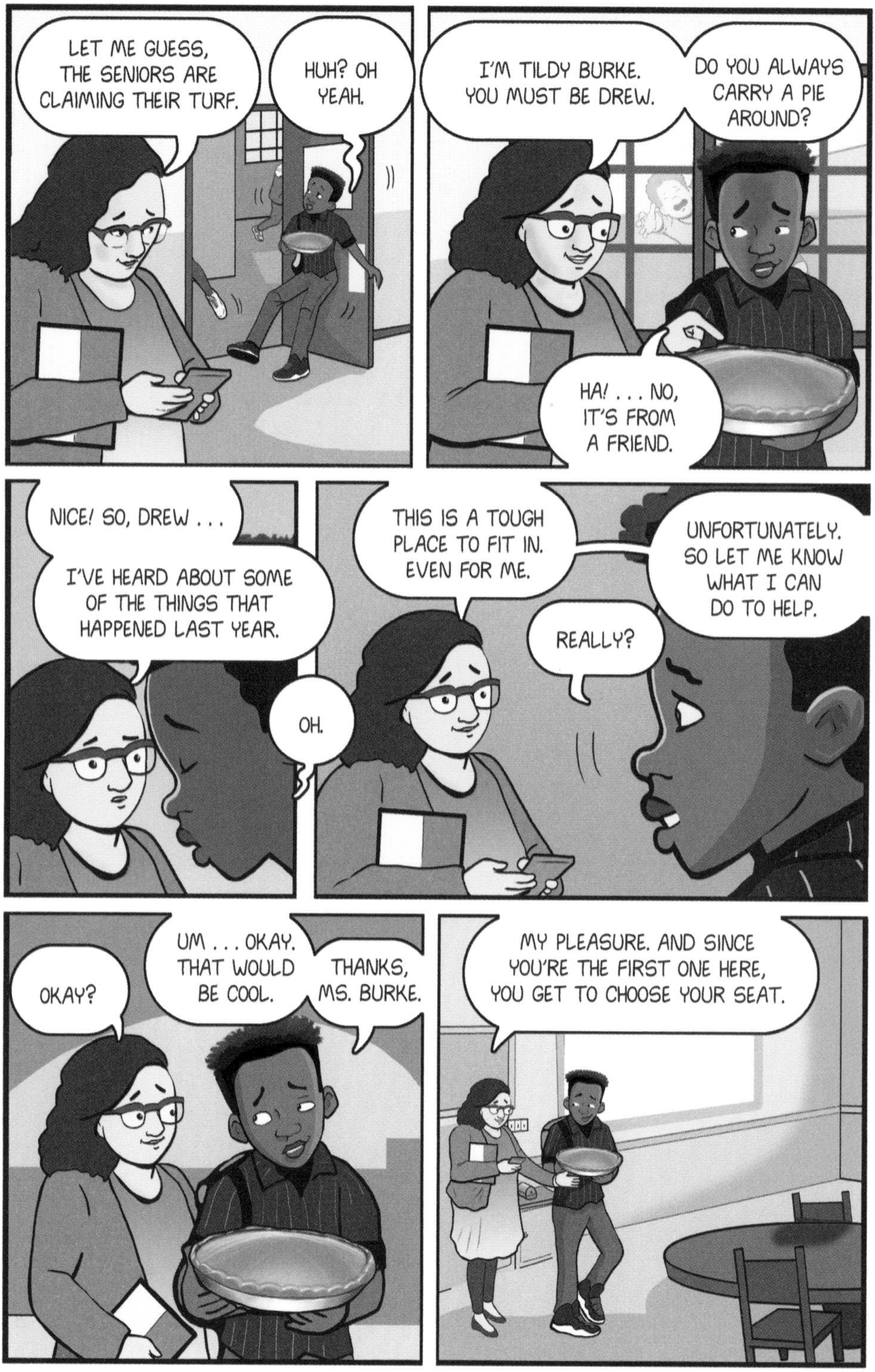
LET ME GUESS, THE SENIORS ARE CLAIMING THEIR TURF.
HUH? OH YEAH.
I'M TILDY BURKE. YOU MUST BE DREW.
DO YOU ALWAYS CARRY A PIE AROUND?
HA! . . . NO, IT'S FROM A FRIEND.
NICE! SO, DREW . . .
I'VE HEARD ABOUT SOME OF THE THINGS THAT HAPPENED LAST YEAR.
OH.
THIS IS A TOUGH PLACE TO FIT IN. EVEN FOR ME.
UNFORTUNATELY. SO LET ME KNOW WHAT I CAN DO TO HELP.
REALLY?
OKAY?
UM . . . OKAY. THAT WOULD BE COOL.
THANKS, MS. BURKE.
MY PLEASURE. AND SINCE YOU'RE THE FIRST ONE HERE, YOU GET TO CHOOSE YOUR SEAT.

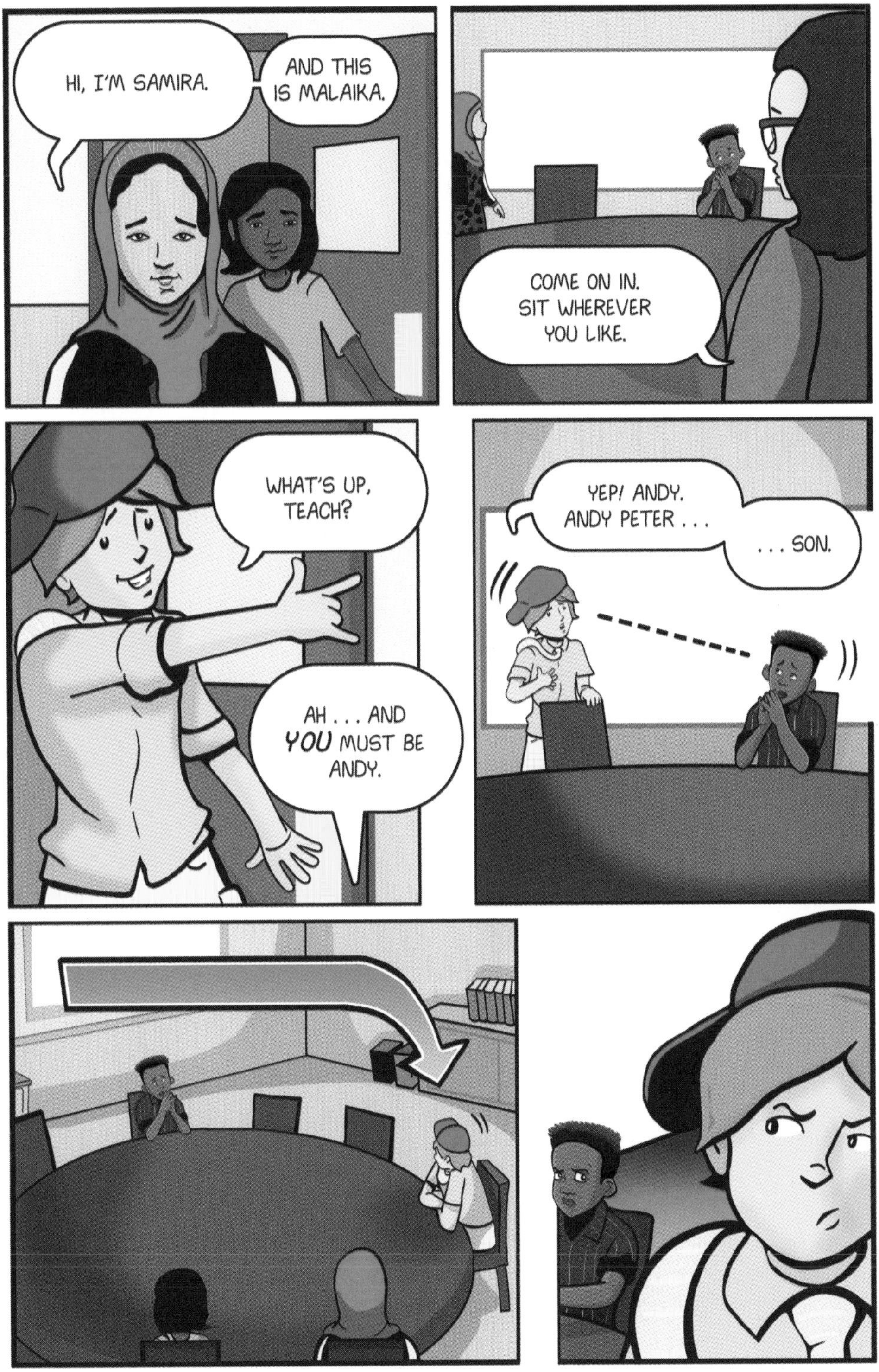
HI, I'M SAMIRA.
AND THIS IS MALAIKA.
COME ON IN. SIT WHEREVER YOU LIKE.
WHAT'S UP, TEACH?
AH . . . AND *YOU* MUST BE ANDY.
YEP! ANDY. ANDY PETER . . .
. . . SON.

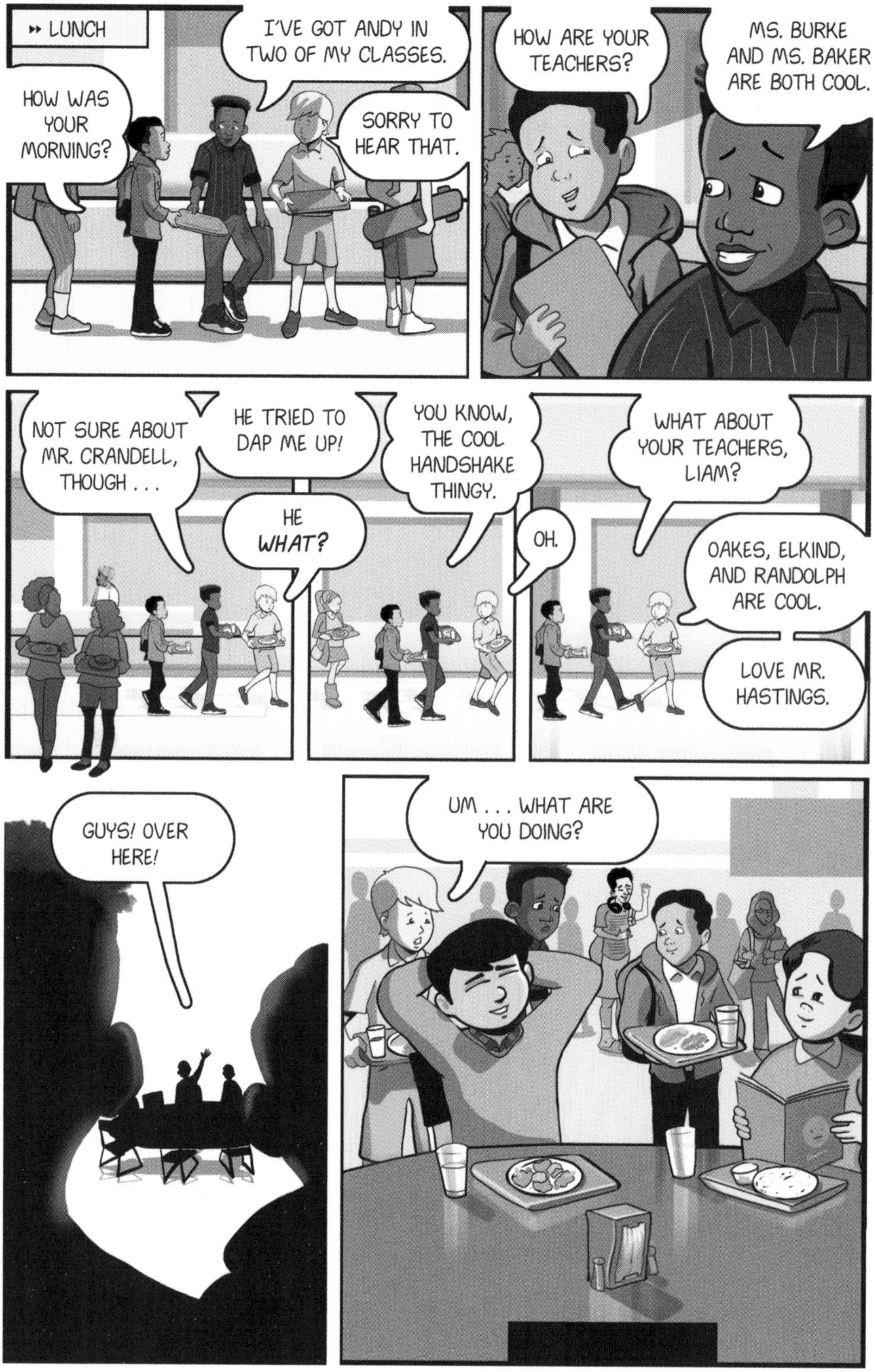
▸▸ LUNCH
HOW WAS YOUR MORNING?
I'VE GOT ANDY IN TWO OF MY CLASSES.
SORRY TO HEAR THAT.
HOW ARE YOUR TEACHERS?
MS. BURKE AND MS. BAKER ARE BOTH COOL.
NOT SURE ABOUT MR. CRANDELL, THOUGH . . .
HE TRIED TO DAP ME UP!
HE *WHAT?*
YOU KNOW, THE COOL HANDSHAKE THINGY.
OH.
WHAT ABOUT YOUR TEACHERS, LIAM?
OAKES, ELKIND, AND RANDOLPH ARE COOL.
LOVE MR. HASTINGS.
GUYS! OVER HERE!
UM . . . WHAT ARE YOU DOING?

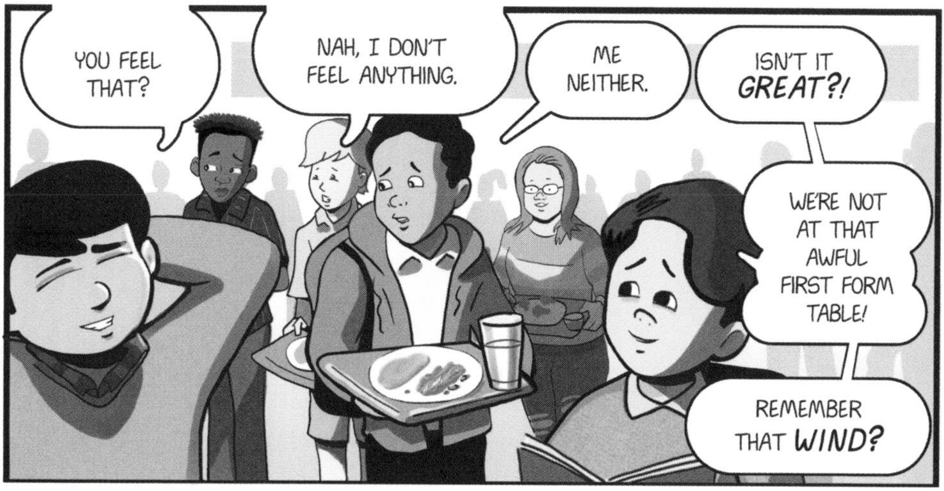
YOU FEEL THAT?
NAH, I DON'T FEEL ANYTHING.
ME NEITHER.
ISN'T IT **GREAT?!**
WE'RE NOT AT THAT AWFUL FIRST FORM TABLE!
REMEMBER THAT **WIND?**

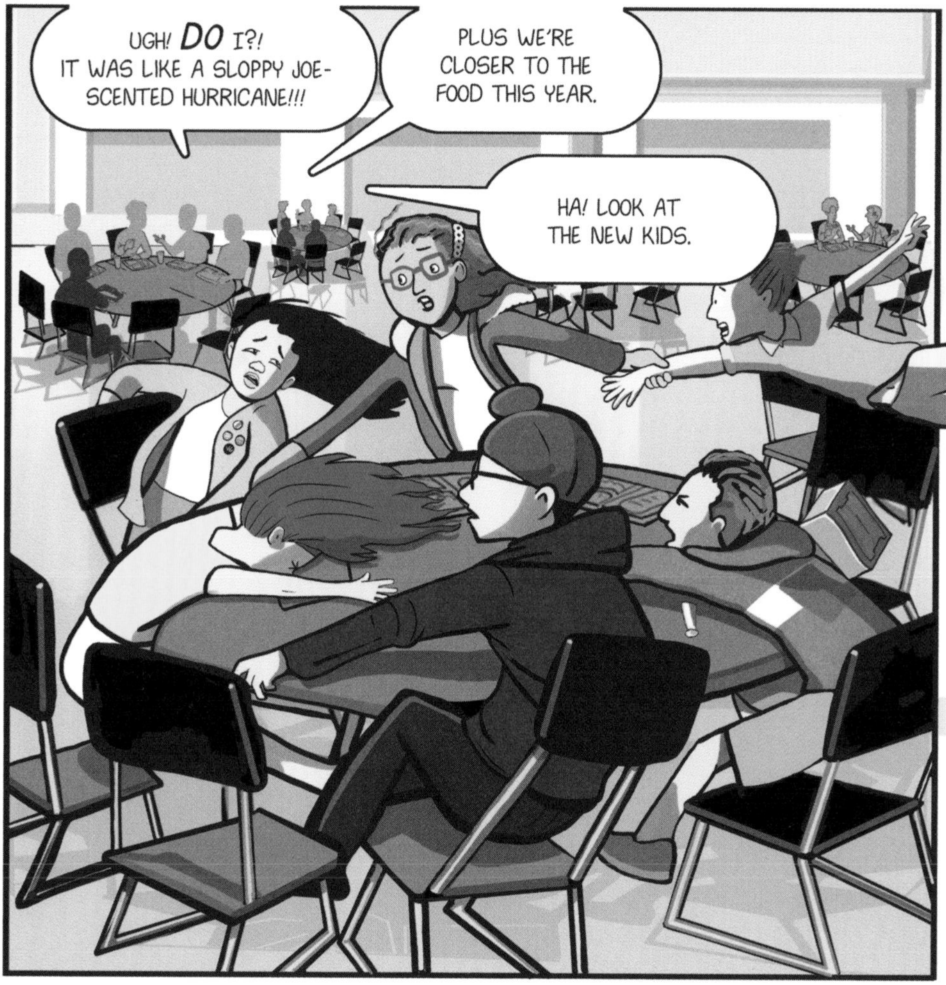
UGH! **DO** I?! IT WAS LIKE A SLOPPY JOE-SCENTED HURRICANE!!!
PLUS WE'RE CLOSER TO THE FOOD THIS YEAR.
HA! LOOK AT THE NEW KIDS.

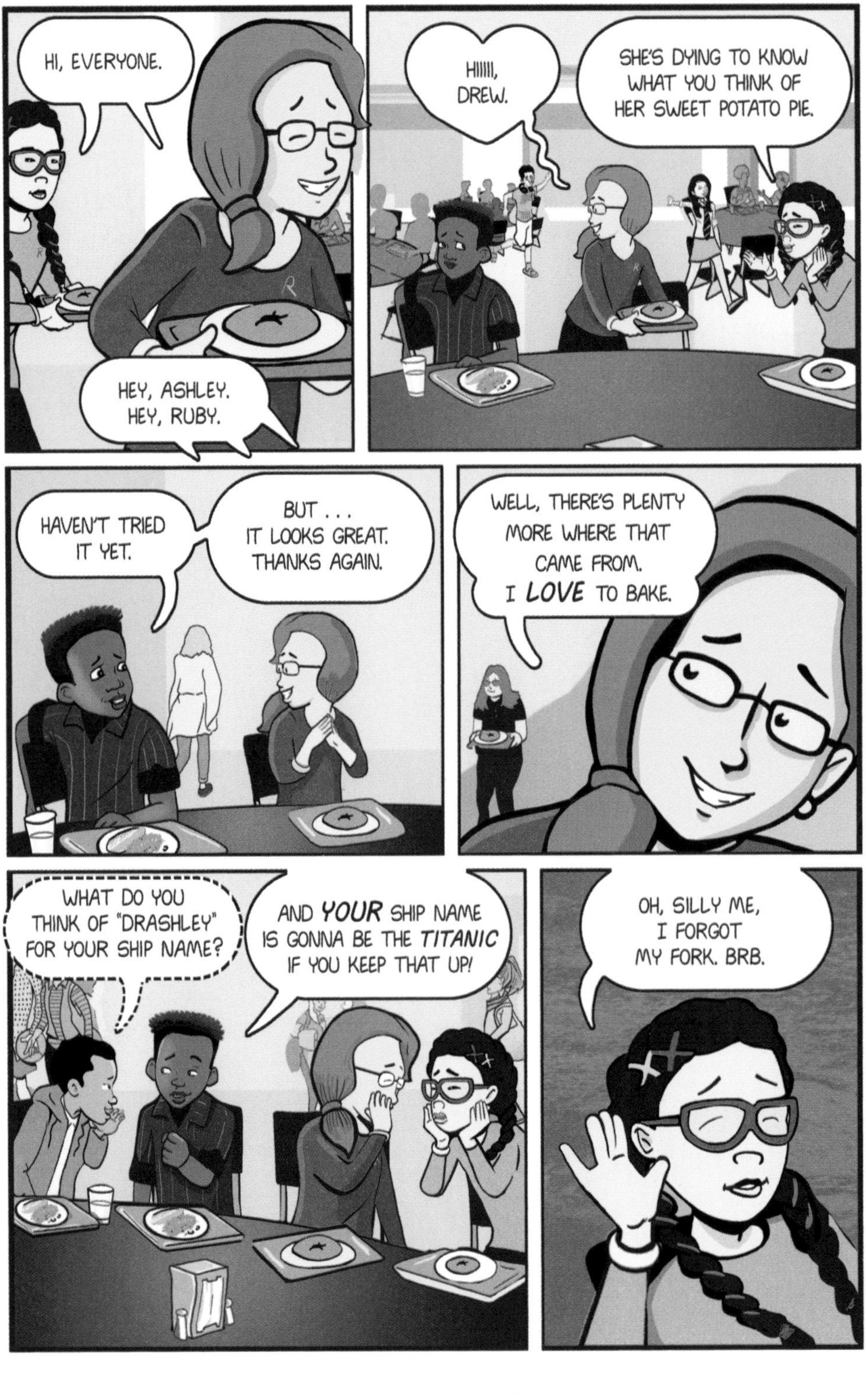
HI, EVERYONE.
HEY, ASHLEY. HEY, RUBY.
HIIIII, DREW.
SHE'S DYING TO KNOW WHAT YOU THINK OF HER SWEET POTATO PIE.
HAVEN'T TRIED IT YET.
BUT . . . IT LOOKS GREAT. THANKS AGAIN.
WELL, THERE'S PLENTY MORE WHERE THAT CAME FROM. I **LOVE** TO BAKE.
WHAT DO YOU THINK OF "DRASHLEY" FOR YOUR SHIP NAME?
AND ***YOUR*** SHIP NAME IS GONNA BE THE ***TITANIC*** IF YOU KEEP THAT UP!
OH, SILLY ME, I FORGOT MY FORK. BRB.

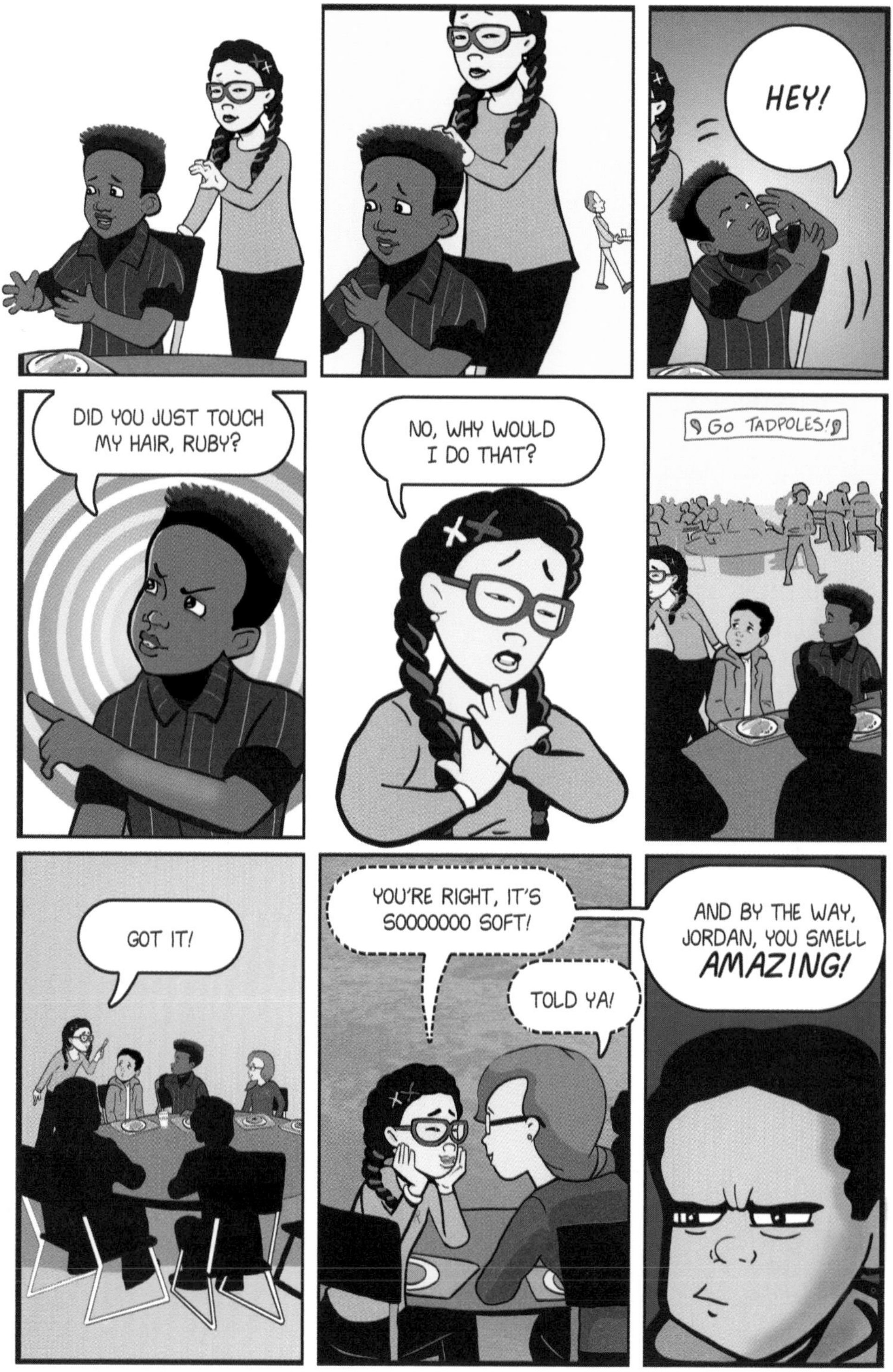
HEY!
DID YOU JUST TOUCH MY HAIR, RUBY?
NO, WHY WOULD I DO THAT?
GO TADPOLES!
GOT IT!
YOU'RE RIGHT, IT'S SOOOOOOO SOFT!
AND BY THE WAY, JORDAN, YOU SMELL AMAZING!
TOLD YA!

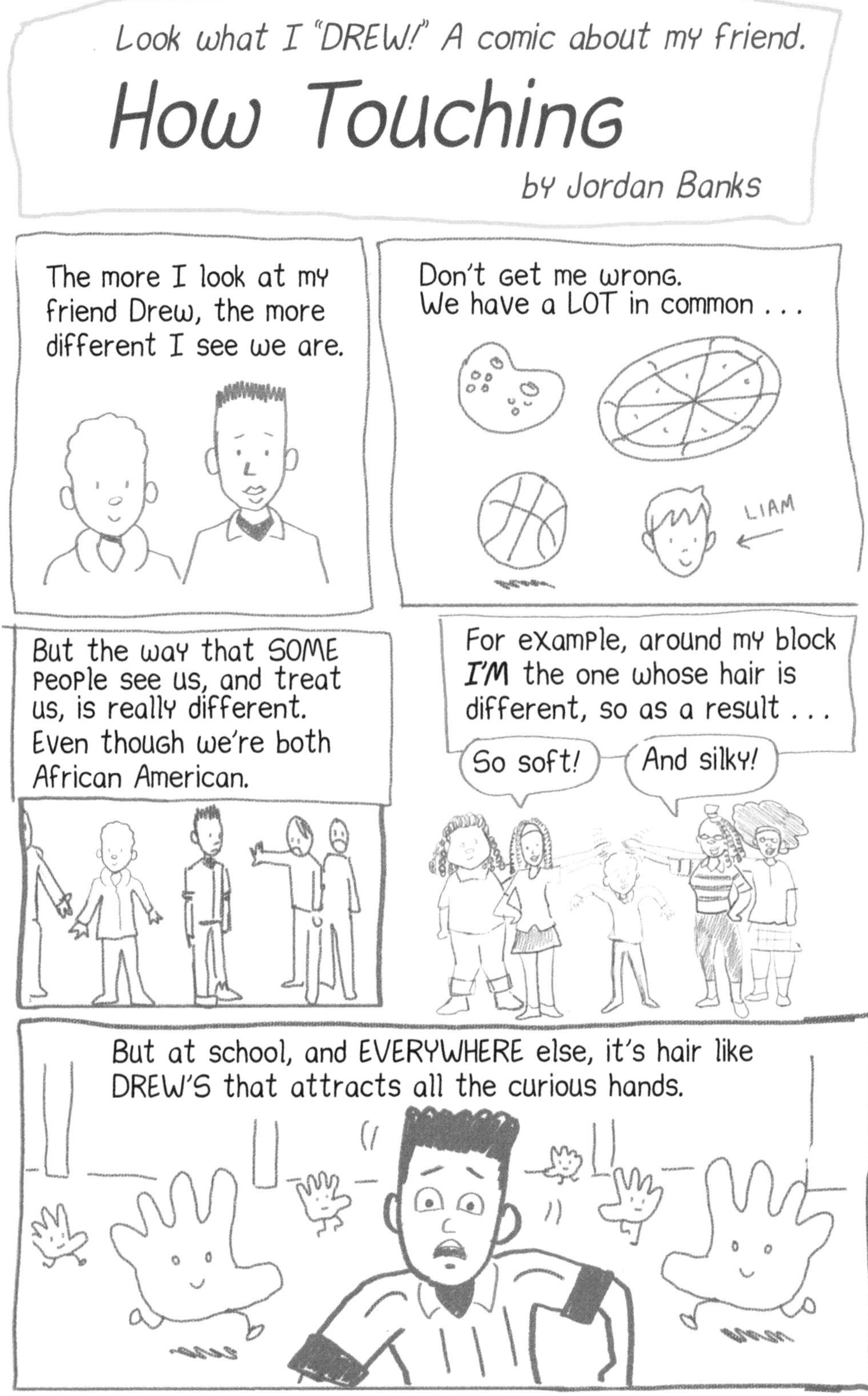
Look what I "DREW!" A comic about my friend.
How Touching
by Jordan Banks
The more I look at my friend Drew, the more different I see we are.
Don't get me wrong. We have a LOT in common . . .
LIAM
But the way that SOME people see us, and treat us, is really different. Even though we're both African American.
For example, around my block I'M the one whose hair is different, so as a result . . .
So soft!
And silky!
But at school, and EVERYWHERE else, it's hair like DREW'S that attracts all the curious hands.

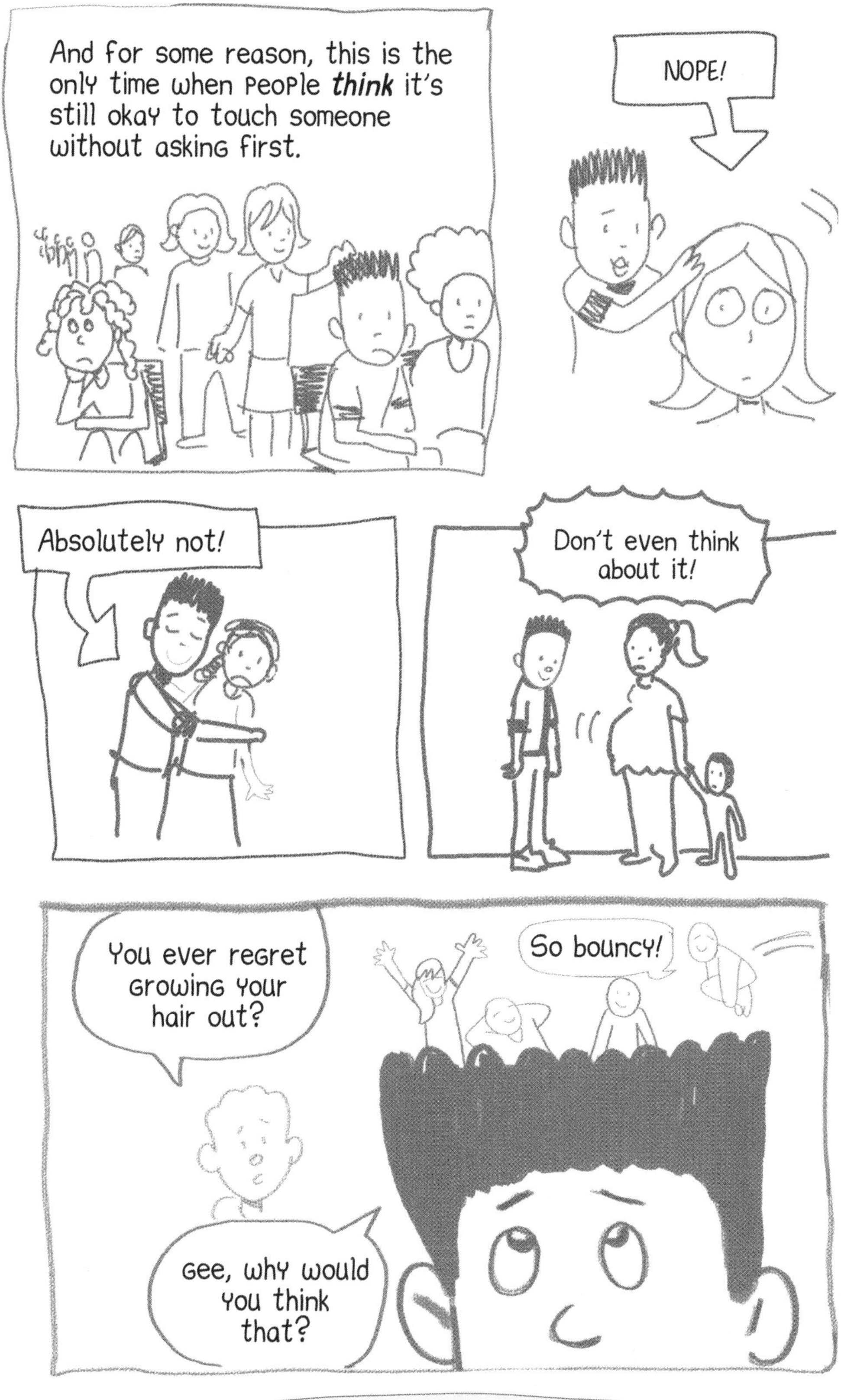
And for some reason, this is the only time when people *think* it's still okay to touch someone without asking first.
NOPE!
Absolutely not!
Don't even think about it!
You ever regret growing your hair out?
So bouncy!
Gee, why would you think that?

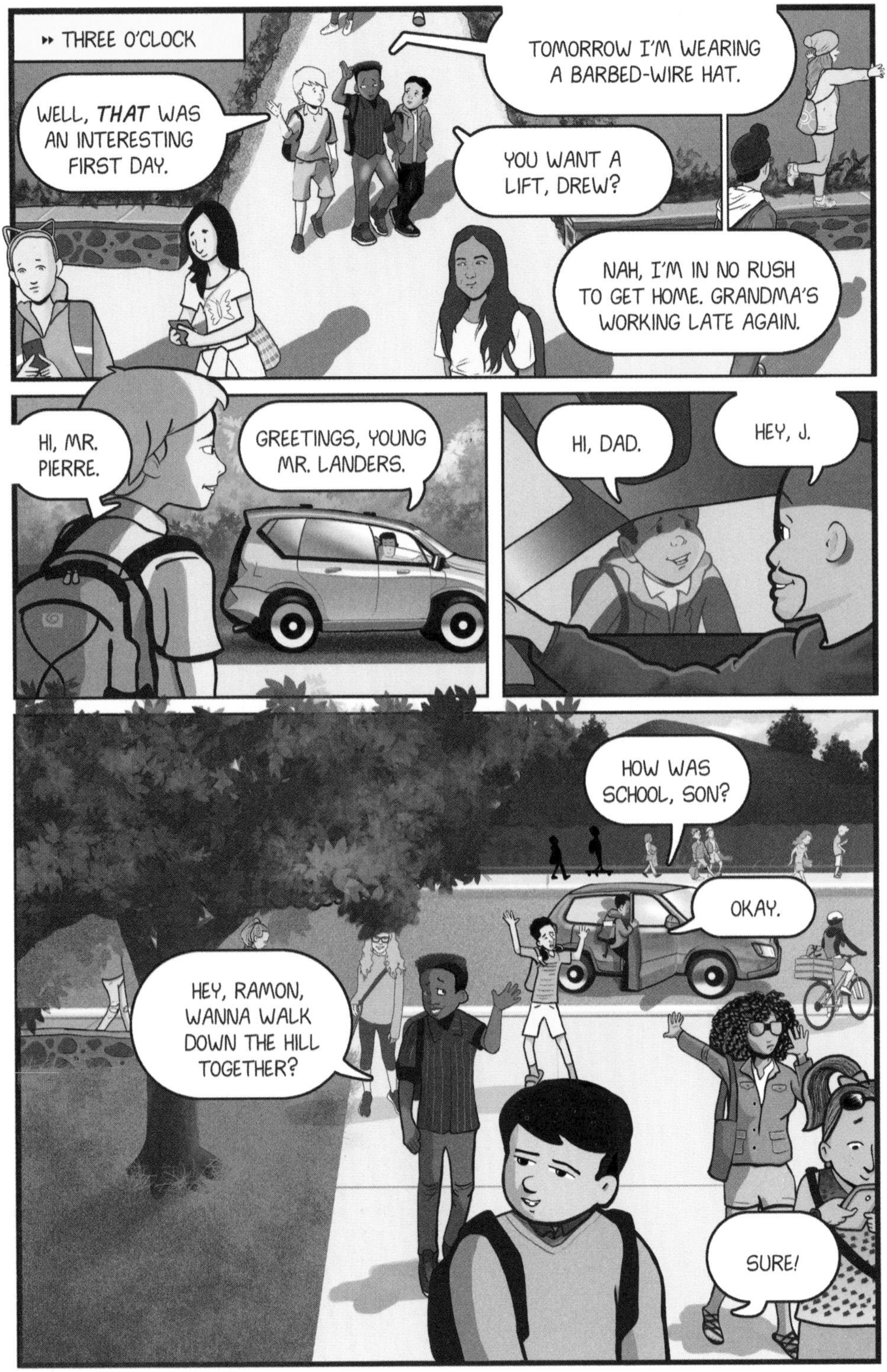
THREE O'CLOCK
WELL, *THAT* WAS AN INTERESTING FIRST DAY.
TOMORROW I'M WEARING A BARBED-WIRE HAT.
YOU WANT A LIFT, DREW?
NAH, I'M IN NO RUSH TO GET HOME. GRANDMA'S WORKING LATE AGAIN.
HI, MR. PIERRE.
GREETINGS, YOUNG MR. LANDERS.
HI, DAD.
HEY, J.
HOW WAS SCHOOL, SON?
OKAY.
HEY, RAMON, WANNA WALK DOWN THE HILL TOGETHER?
SURE!

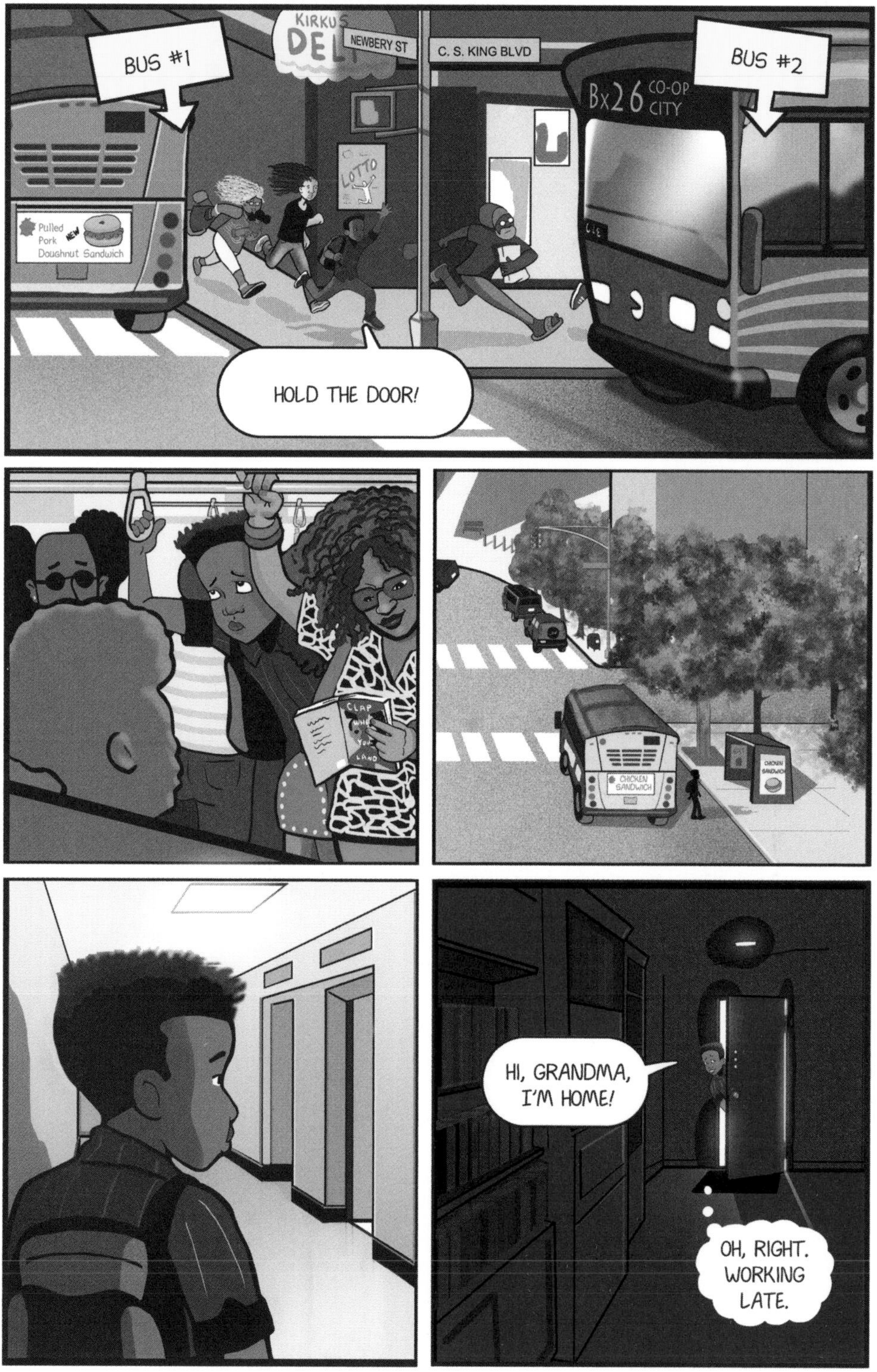
BUS #1
KIRKUS DELI
NEWBERY ST
C. S. KING BLVD
BUS #2
Bx26 CO-OP CITY
LOTTO
Pulled Pork NEW Doughnut Sandwich
HOLD THE DOOR!
CLAP WHEN YOU LAND
CHICKEN SANDWICH
HI, GRANDMA, I'M HOME!
OH, RIGHT. WORKING LATE.

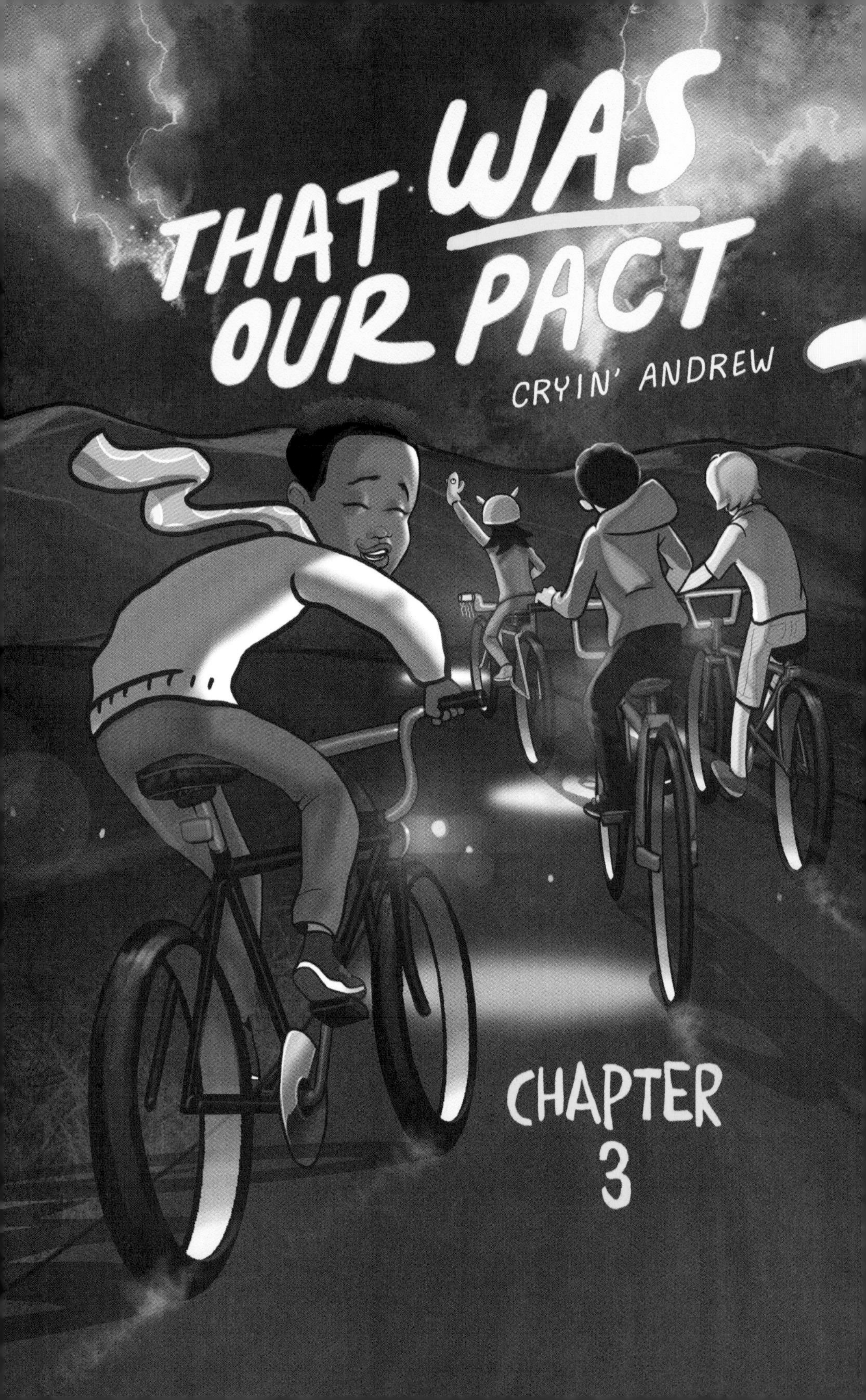
THAT WAS OUR PACT
CRYIN' ANDREW
CHAPTER
3

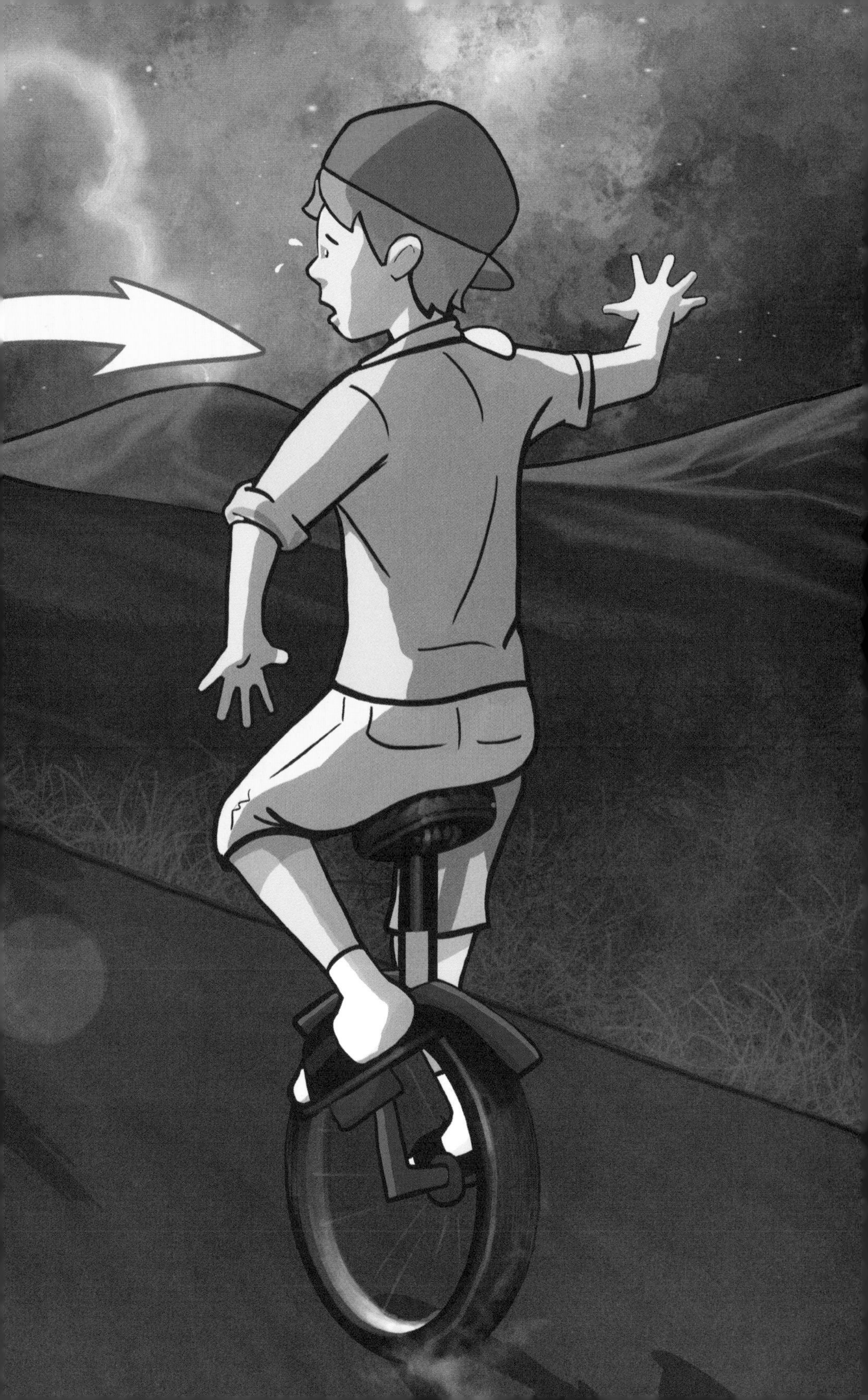

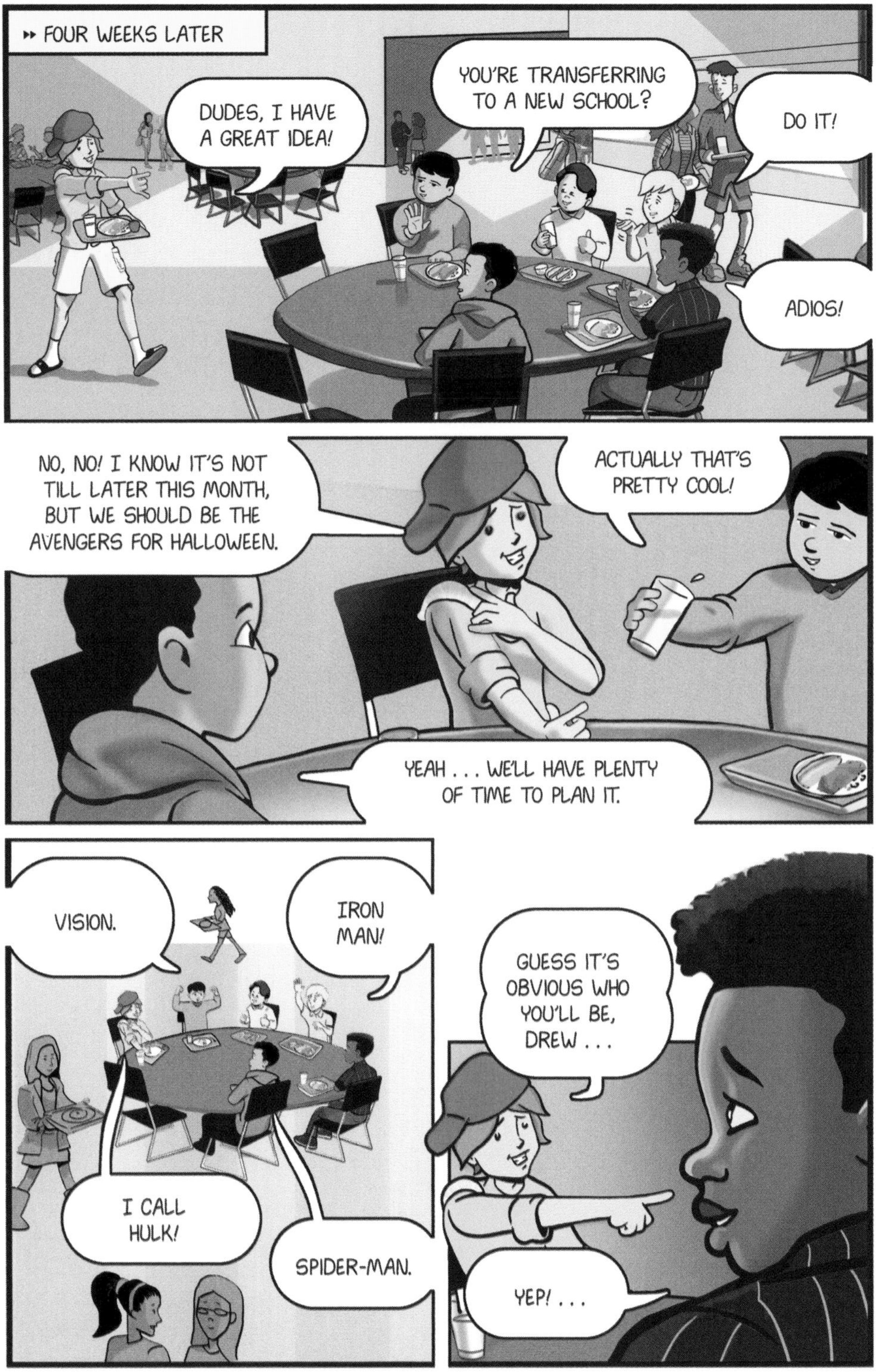
FOUR WEEKS LATER
DUDES, I HAVE A GREAT IDEA!
YOU'RE TRANSFERRING TO A NEW SCHOOL?
DO IT!
ADIOS!
NO, NO! I KNOW IT'S NOT TILL LATER THIS MONTH, BUT WE SHOULD BE THE AVENGERS FOR HALLOWEEN.
ACTUALLY THAT'S PRETTY COOL!
YEAH . . . WE'LL HAVE PLENTY OF TIME TO PLAN IT.
VISION.
IRON MAN!
I CALL HULK!
SPIDER-MAN.
GUESS IT'S OBVIOUS WHO YOU'LL BE, DREW . . .
YEP! . . .

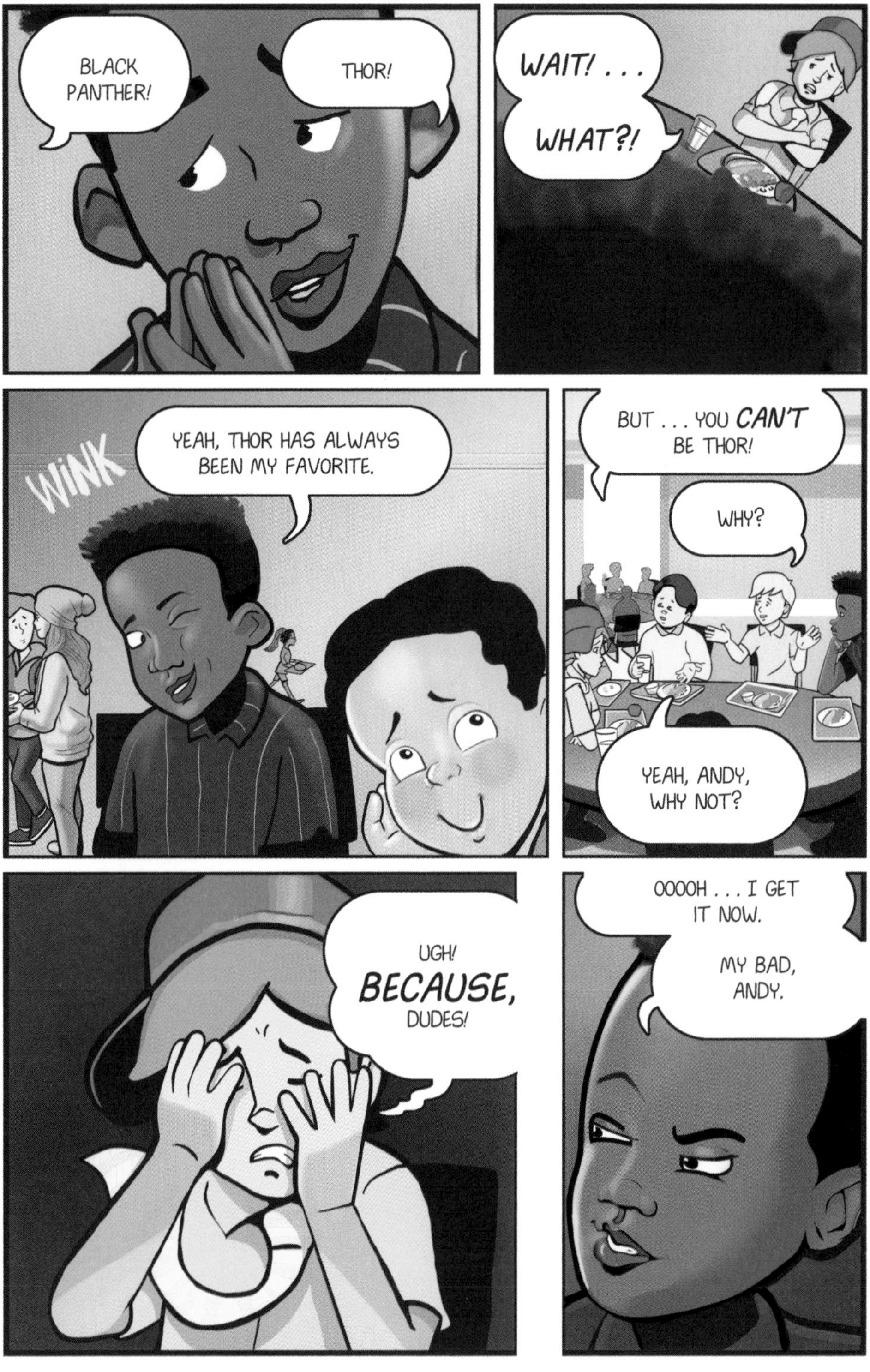
BLACK PANTHER!
THOR!
WAIT! . . .
WHAT?!
WINK
YEAH, THOR HAS ALWAYS BEEN MY FAVORITE.
BUT . . . YOU CAN'T BE THOR!
WHY?
YEAH, ANDY, WHY NOT?
UGH! BECAUSE, DUDES!
OOOOH . . . I GET IT NOW.
MY BAD, ANDY.

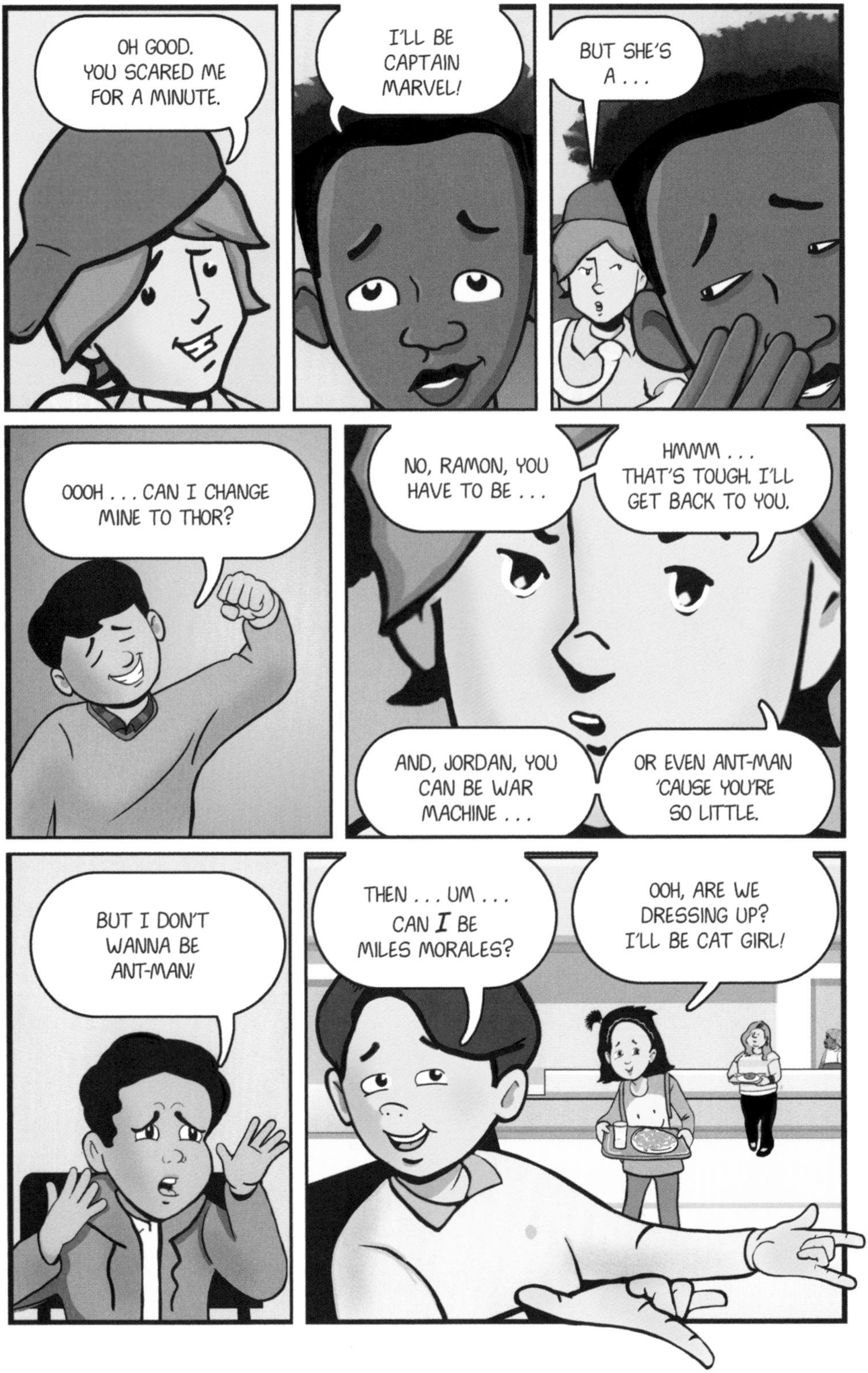
OH GOOD. YOU SCARED ME FOR A MINUTE.
I'LL BE CAPTAIN MARVEL!
BUT SHE'S A . . .
OOOH . . . CAN I CHANGE MINE TO THOR?
NO, RAMON, YOU HAVE TO BE . . .
HMMM . . . THAT'S TOUGH. I'LL GET BACK TO YOU.
AND, JORDAN, YOU CAN BE WAR MACHINE . . .
OR EVEN ANT-MAN 'CAUSE YOU'RE SO LITTLE.
BUT I DON'T WANNA BE ANT-MAN!
THEN . . . UM . . . CAN *I* BE MILES MORALES?
OOH, ARE WE DRESSING UP? I'LL BE CAT GIRL!

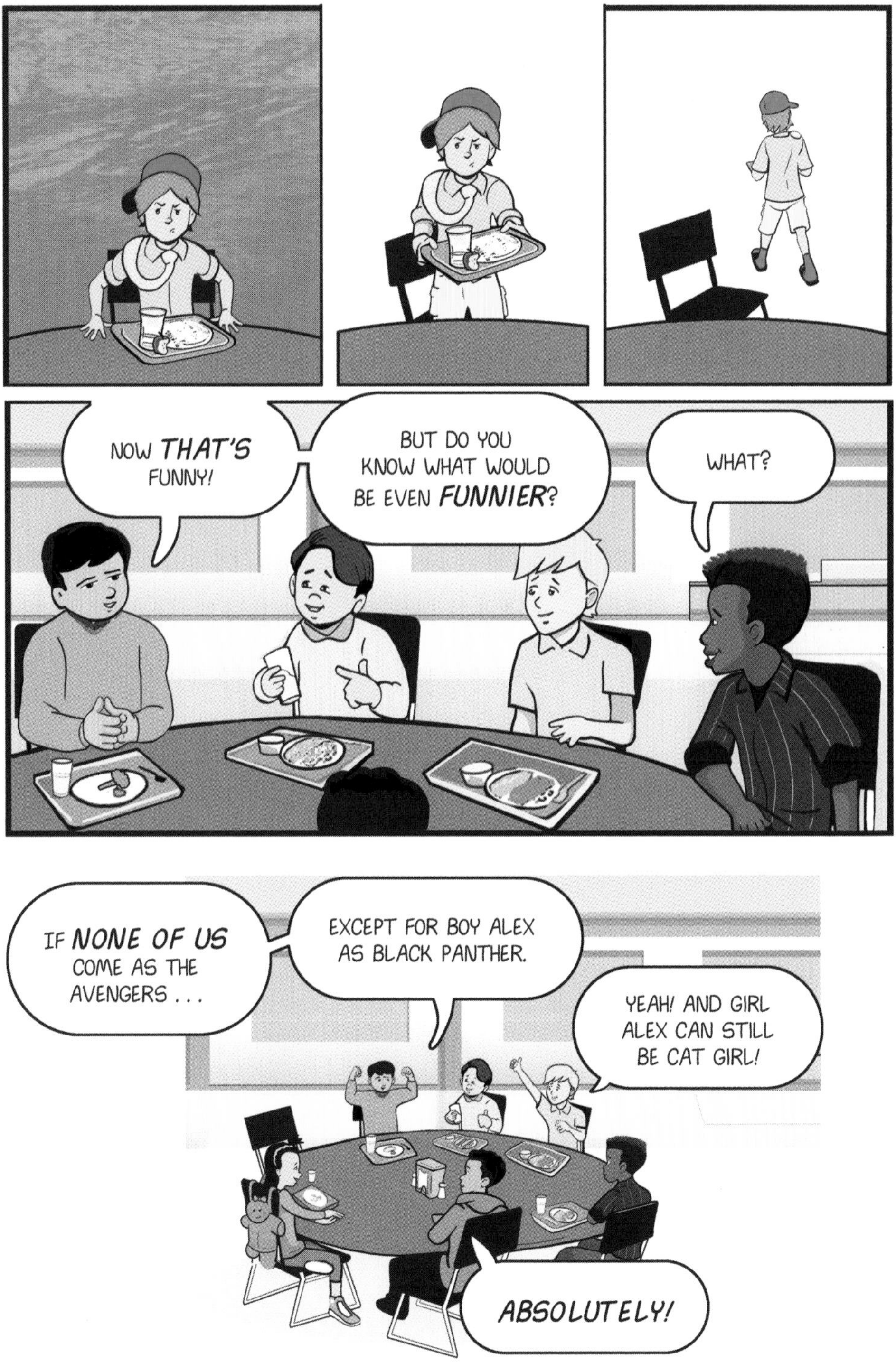
NOW THAT'S FUNNY!
BUT DO YOU KNOW WHAT WOULD BE EVEN FUNNIER?
WHAT?
IF NONE OF US COME AS THE AVENGERS . . .
EXCEPT FOR BOY ALEX AS BLACK PANTHER.
YEAH! AND GIRL ALEX CAN STILL BE CAT GIRL!
ABSOLUTELY!

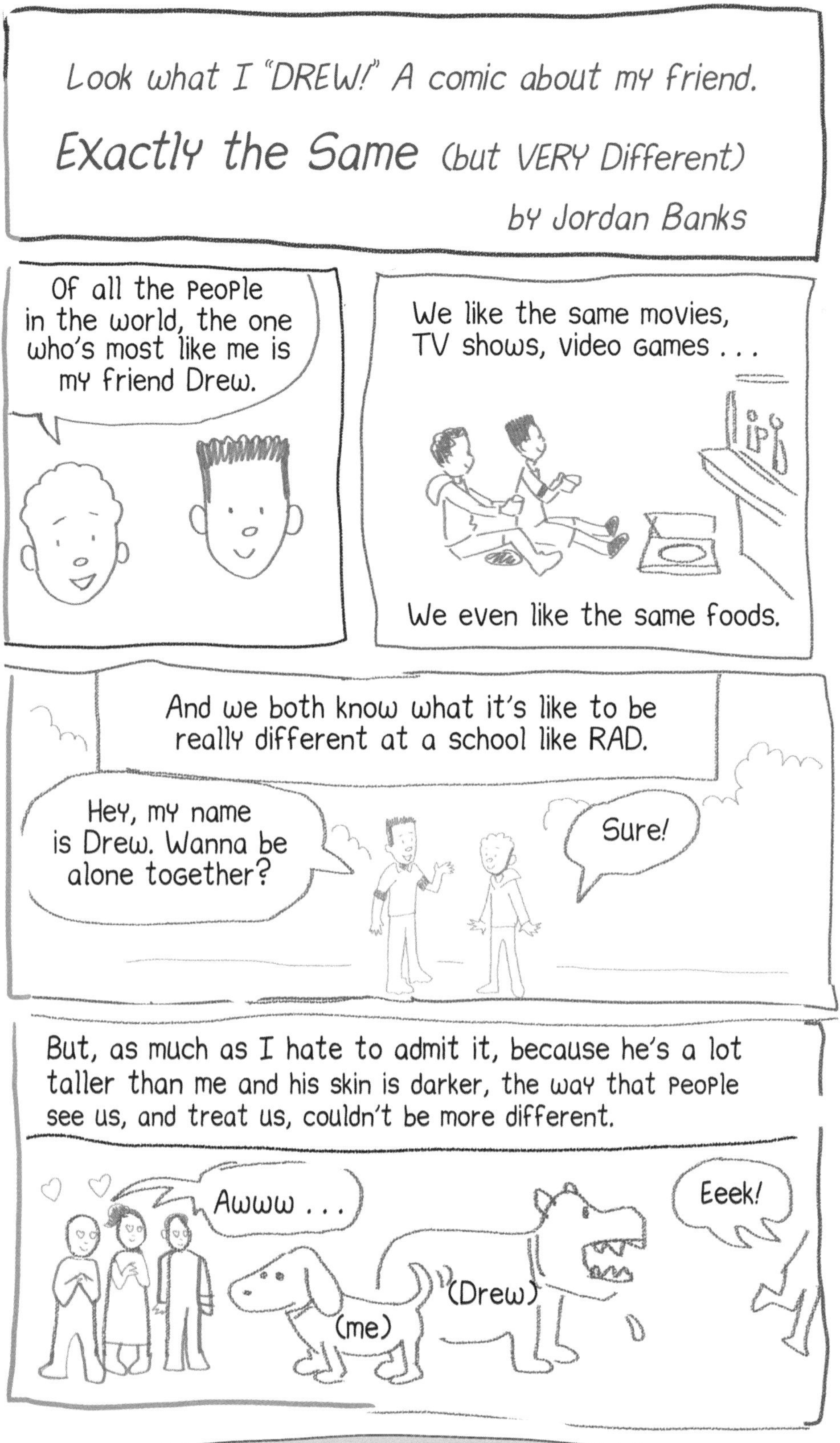
Look what I "DREW!" A comic about my friend.
Exactly the Same (but VERY Different)
by Jordan Banks
Of all the people in the world, the one who's most like me is my friend Drew.
We like the same movies, TV shows, video games . . .
We even like the same foods.
And we both know what it's like to be really different at a school like RAD.
Hey, my name is Drew. Wanna be alone together?
Sure!
But, as much as I hate to admit it, because he's a lot taller than me and his skin is darker, the way that people see us, and treat us, couldn't be more different.
Awww . . .
(me)
(Drew)
Eeek!

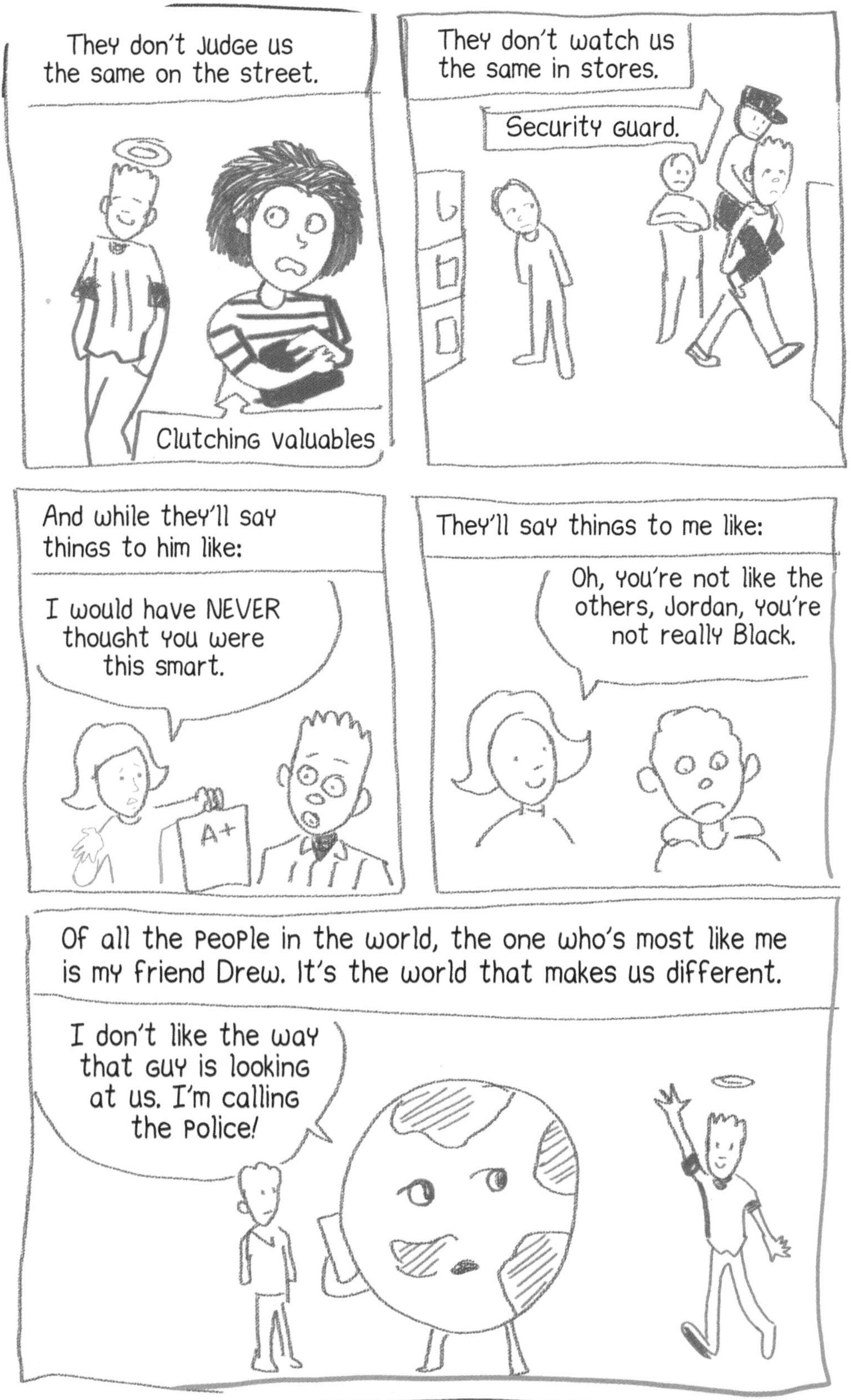
They don't judge us the same on the street.
Clutching valuables
They don't watch us the same in stores.
Security guard.
And while they'll say things to him like:
I would have NEVER thought you were this smart.
A+
They'll say things to me like:
Oh, you're not like the others, Jordan, you're not really Black.
Of all the people in the world, the one who's most like me is my friend Drew. It's the world that makes us different.
I don't like the way that guy is looking at us. I'm calling the police!

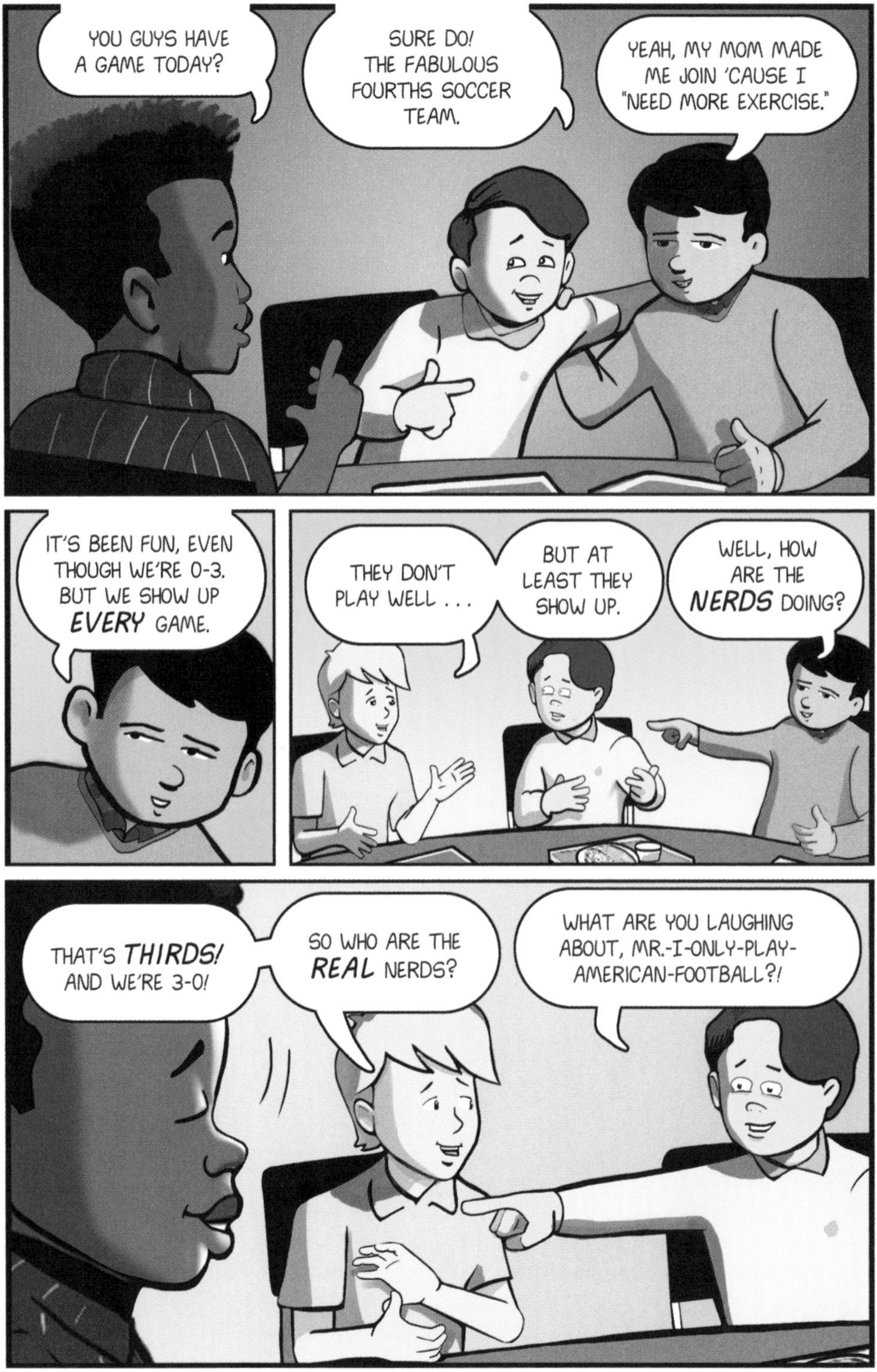
YOU GUYS HAVE A GAME TODAY?
SURE DO! THE FABULOUS FOURTHS SOCCER TEAM.
YEAH, MY MOM MADE ME JOIN 'CAUSE I "NEED MORE EXERCISE."
IT'S BEEN FUN, EVEN THOUGH WE'RE 0-3. BUT WE SHOW UP EVERY GAME.
THEY DON'T PLAY WELL . . .
BUT AT LEAST THEY SHOW UP.
WELL, HOW ARE THE NERDS DOING?
THAT'S THIRDS! AND WE'RE 3-0!
SO WHO ARE THE REAL NERDS?
WHAT ARE YOU LAUGHING ABOUT, MR.-I-ONLY-PLAY-AMERICAN-FOOTBALL?!

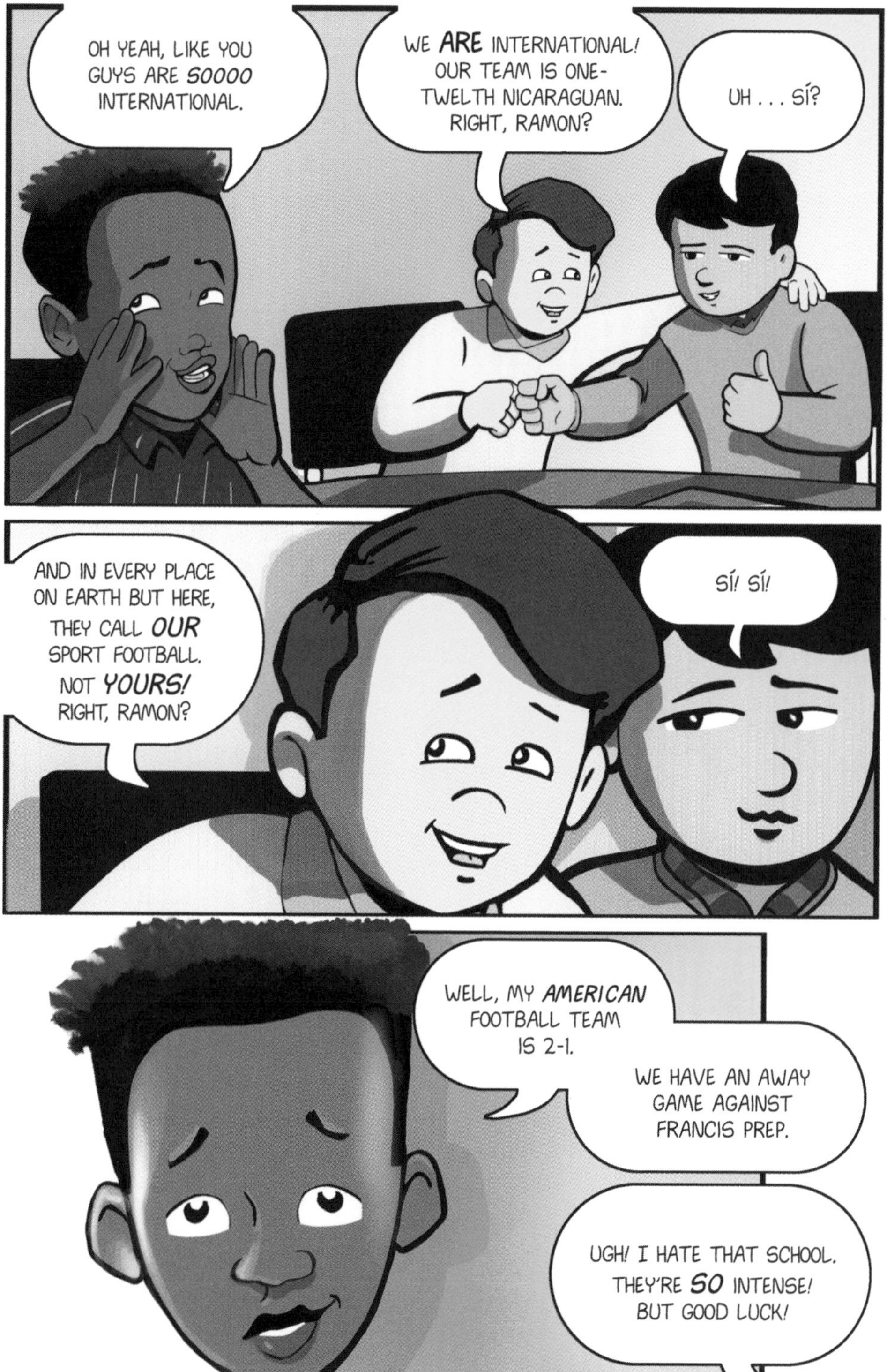
OH YEAH, LIKE YOU GUYS ARE SOOOO INTERNATIONAL.
WE ARE INTERNATIONAL! OUR TEAM IS ONE-TWELTH NICARAGUAN. RIGHT, RAMON?
UH . . . SÍ?
AND IN EVERY PLACE ON EARTH BUT HERE, THEY CALL OUR SPORT FOOTBALL. NOT YOURS! RIGHT, RAMON?
SÍ! SÍ!
WELL, MY AMERICAN FOOTBALL TEAM IS 2-1.
WE HAVE AN AWAY GAME AGAINST FRANCIS PREP.
UGH! I HATE THAT SCHOOL. THEY'RE SO INTENSE! BUT GOOD LUCK!

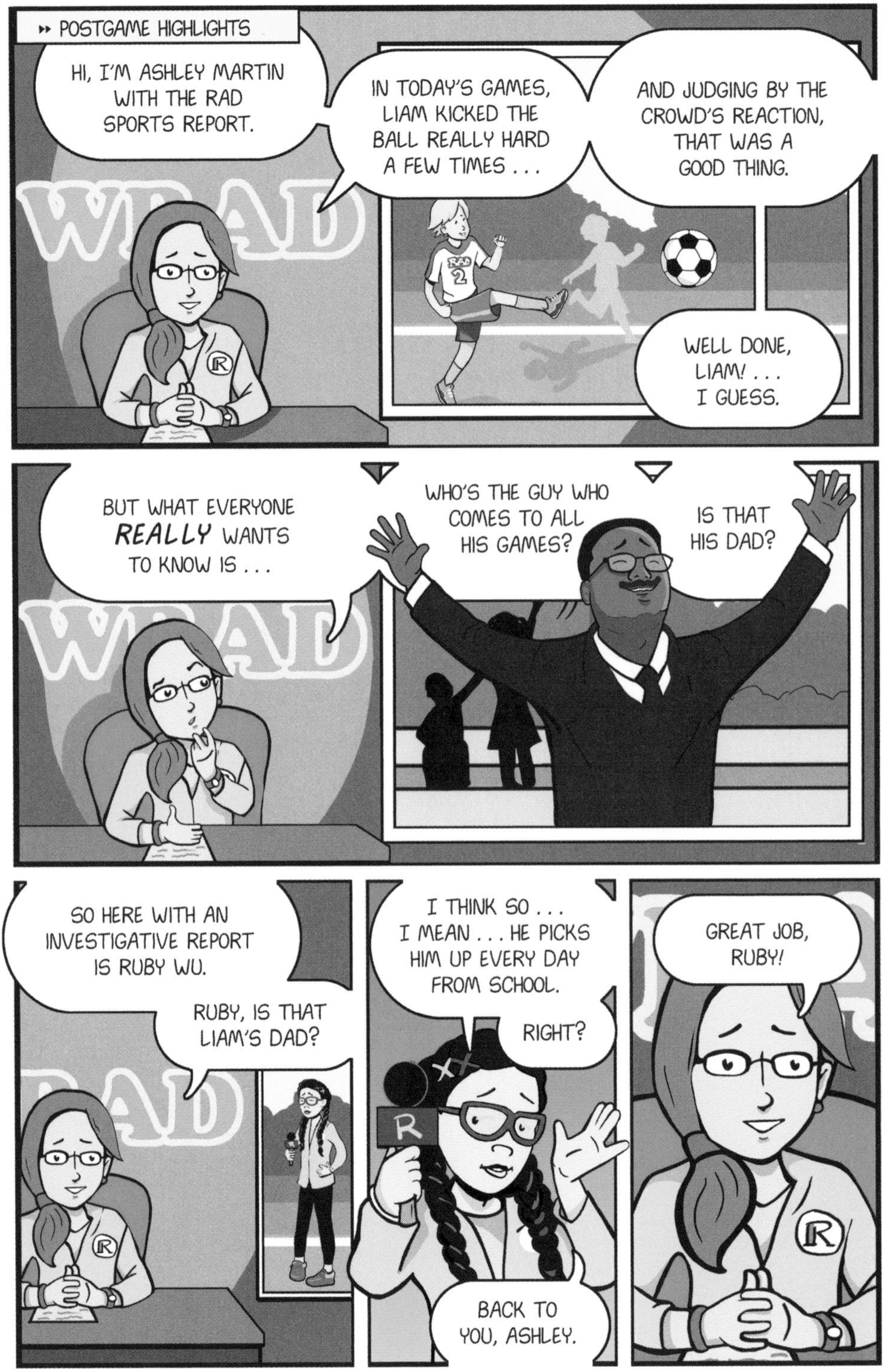
POSTGAME HIGHLIGHTS
HI, I'M ASHLEY MARTIN WITH THE RAD SPORTS REPORT.
IN TODAY'S GAMES, LIAM KICKED THE BALL REALLY HARD A FEW TIMES . . .
AND JUDGING BY THE CROWD'S REACTION, THAT WAS A GOOD THING.
WELL DONE, LIAM! . . . I GUESS.
BUT WHAT EVERYONE *REALLY* WANTS TO KNOW IS . . .
WHO'S THE GUY WHO COMES TO ALL HIS GAMES?
IS THAT HIS DAD?
SO HERE WITH AN INVESTIGATIVE REPORT IS RUBY WU.
RUBY, IS THAT LIAM'S DAD?
I THINK SO . . . I MEAN . . . HE PICKS HIM UP EVERY DAY FROM SCHOOL.
RIGHT?
BACK TO YOU, ASHLEY.
GREAT JOB, RUBY!

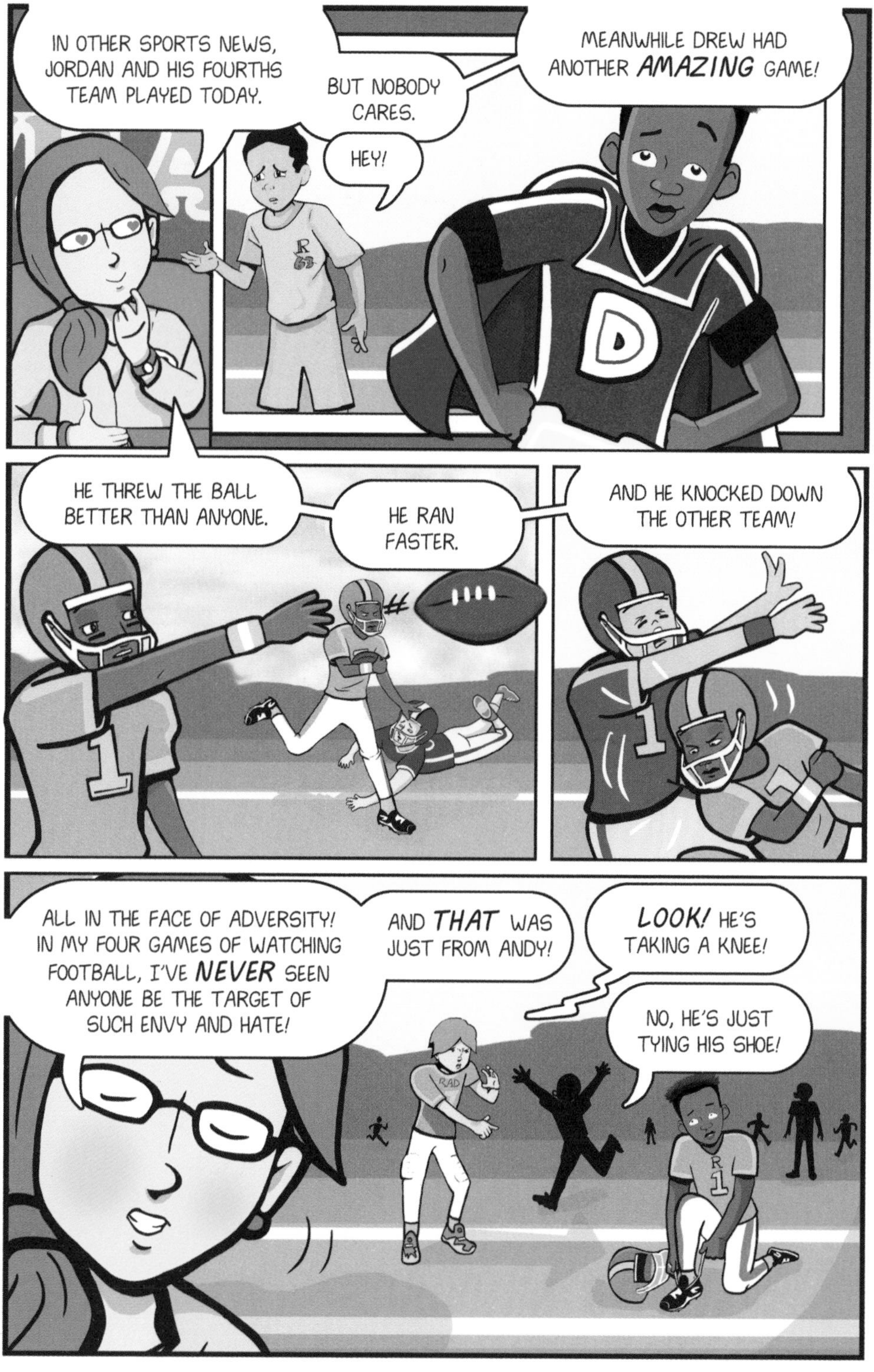
IN OTHER SPORTS NEWS, JORDAN AND HIS FOURTHS TEAM PLAYED TODAY.
BUT NOBODY CARES.
HEY!
MEANWHILE DREW HAD ANOTHER AMAZING GAME!
D
HE THREW THE BALL BETTER THAN ANYONE.
HE RAN FASTER.
AND HE KNOCKED DOWN THE OTHER TEAM!
ALL IN THE FACE OF ADVERSITY! IN MY FOUR GAMES OF WATCHING FOOTBALL, I'VE NEVER SEEN ANYONE BE THE TARGET OF SUCH ENVY AND HATE!
AND THAT WAS JUST FROM ANDY!
LOOK! HE'S TAKING A KNEE!
NO, HE'S JUST TYING HIS SHOE!

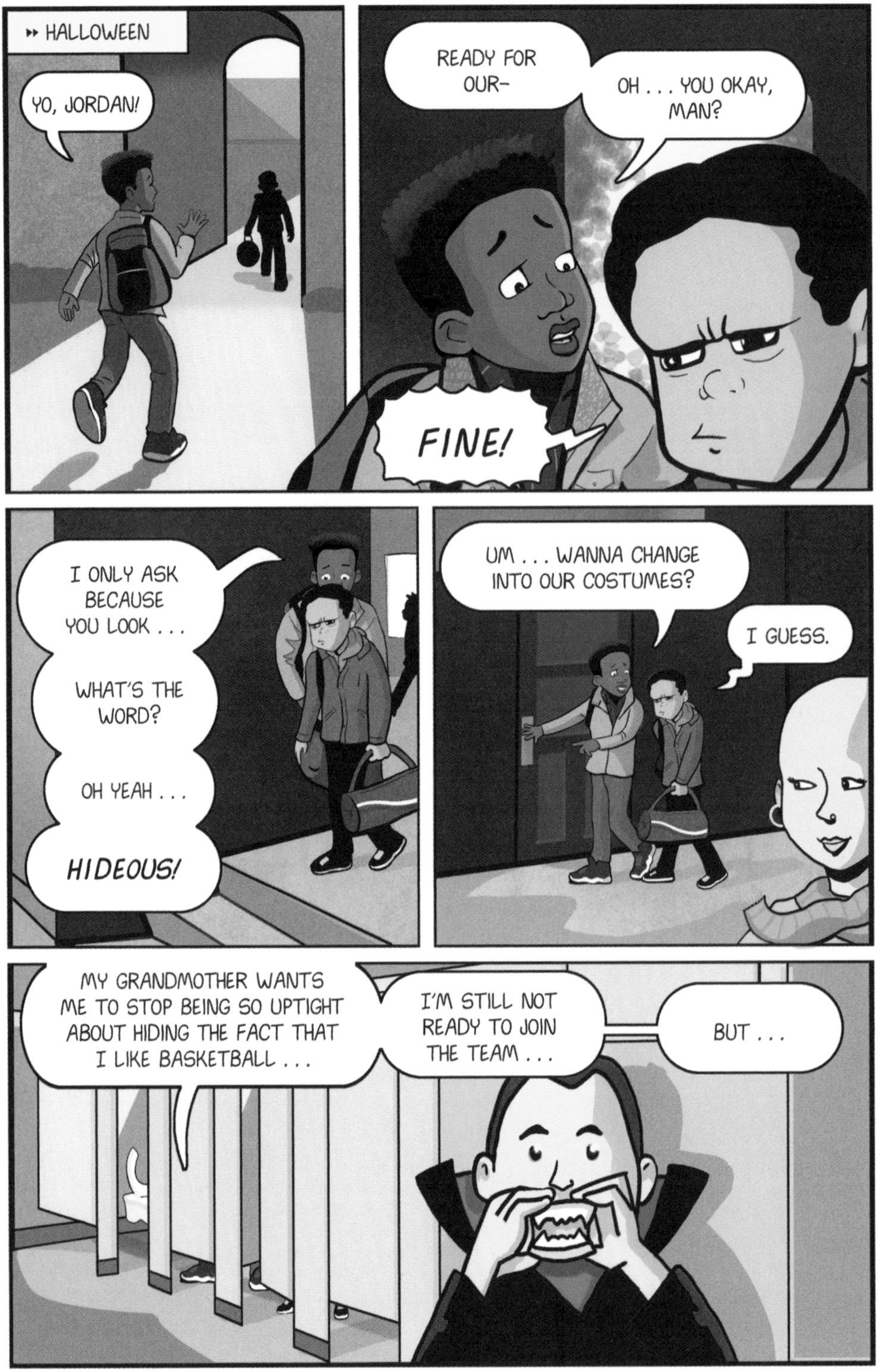
HALLOWEEN
YO, JORDAN!
READY FOR OUR–
OH . . . YOU OKAY, MAN?
FINE!
I ONLY ASK BECAUSE YOU LOOK . . .
WHAT'S THE WORD?
OH YEAH . . .
HIDEOUS!
UM . . . WANNA CHANGE INTO OUR COSTUMES?
I GUESS.
MY GRANDMOTHER WANTS ME TO STOP BEING SO UPTIGHT ABOUT HIDING THE FACT THAT I LIKE BASKETBALL . . .
I'M STILL NOT READY TO JOIN THE TEAM . . .
BUT . . .

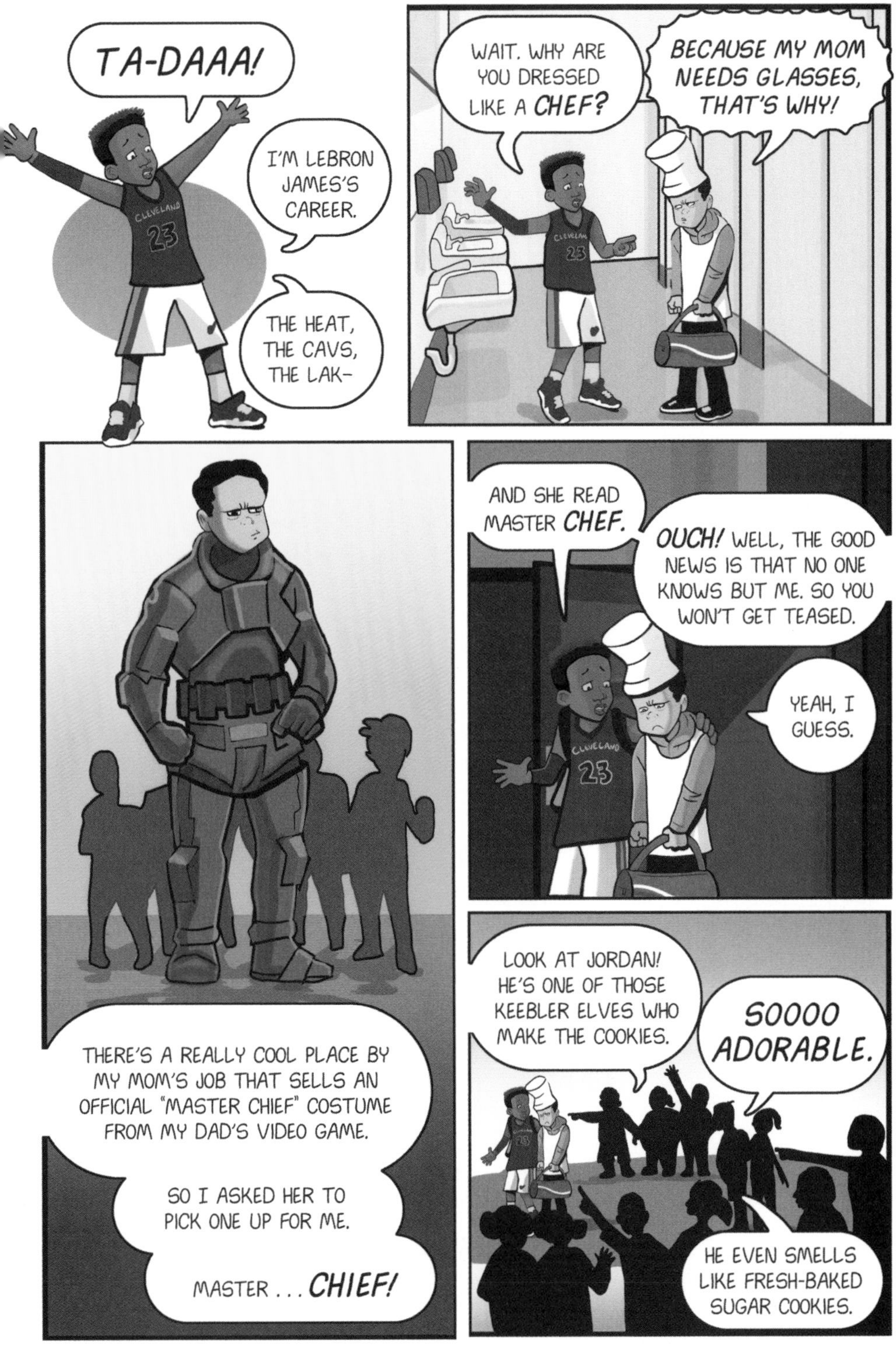
TA-DAAA!
I'M LEBRON JAMES'S CAREER.
THE HEAT, THE CAVS, THE LAK–
WAIT. WHY ARE YOU DRESSED LIKE A CHEF?
BECAUSE MY MOM NEEDS GLASSES, THAT'S WHY!
CLEVELAND 23
THERE'S A REALLY COOL PLACE BY MY MOM'S JOB THAT SELLS AN OFFICIAL "MASTER CHIEF" COSTUME FROM MY DAD'S VIDEO GAME.
SO I ASKED HER TO PICK ONE UP FOR ME.
MASTER . . . CHIEF!
AND SHE READ MASTER CHEF.
OUCH! WELL, THE GOOD NEWS IS THAT NO ONE KNOWS BUT ME. SO YOU WON'T GET TEASED.
YEAH, I GUESS.
LOOK AT JORDAN! HE'S ONE OF THOSE KEEBLER ELVES WHO MAKE THE COOKIES.
SOOOO ADORABLE.
HE EVEN SMELLS LIKE FRESH-BAKED SUGAR COOKIES.

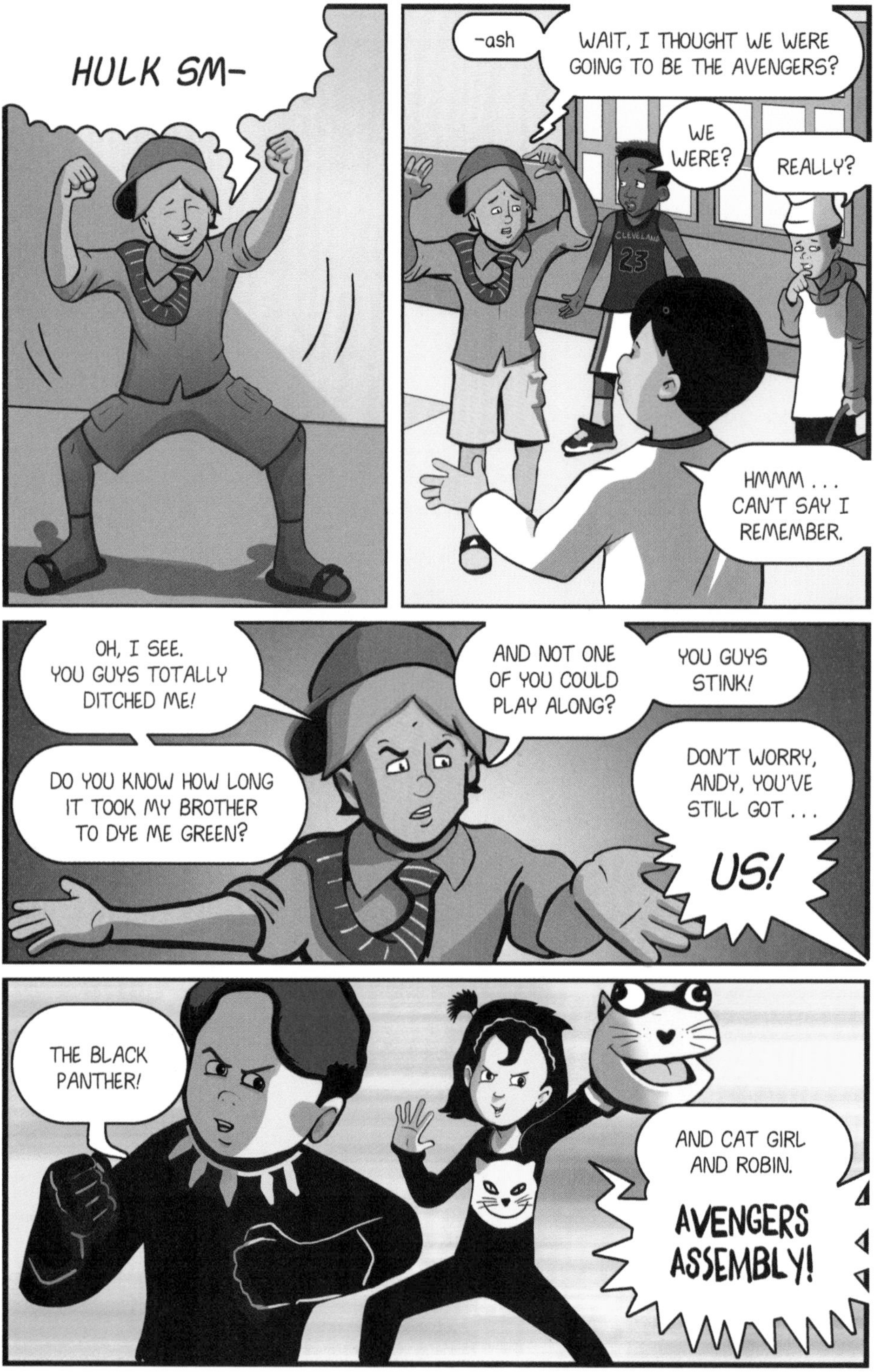
HULK SM–
-ash
WAIT, I THOUGHT WE WERE GOING TO BE THE AVENGERS?
WE WERE?
REALLY?
HMMM . . . CAN'T SAY I REMEMBER.
OH, I SEE. YOU GUYS TOTALLY DITCHED ME!
DO YOU KNOW HOW LONG IT TOOK MY BROTHER TO DYE ME GREEN?
AND NOT ONE OF YOU COULD PLAY ALONG?
YOU GUYS STINK!
DON'T WORRY, ANDY, YOU'VE STILL GOT . . .
US!
THE BLACK PANTHER!
AND CAT GIRL AND ROBIN.
AVENGERS ASSEMBLY!

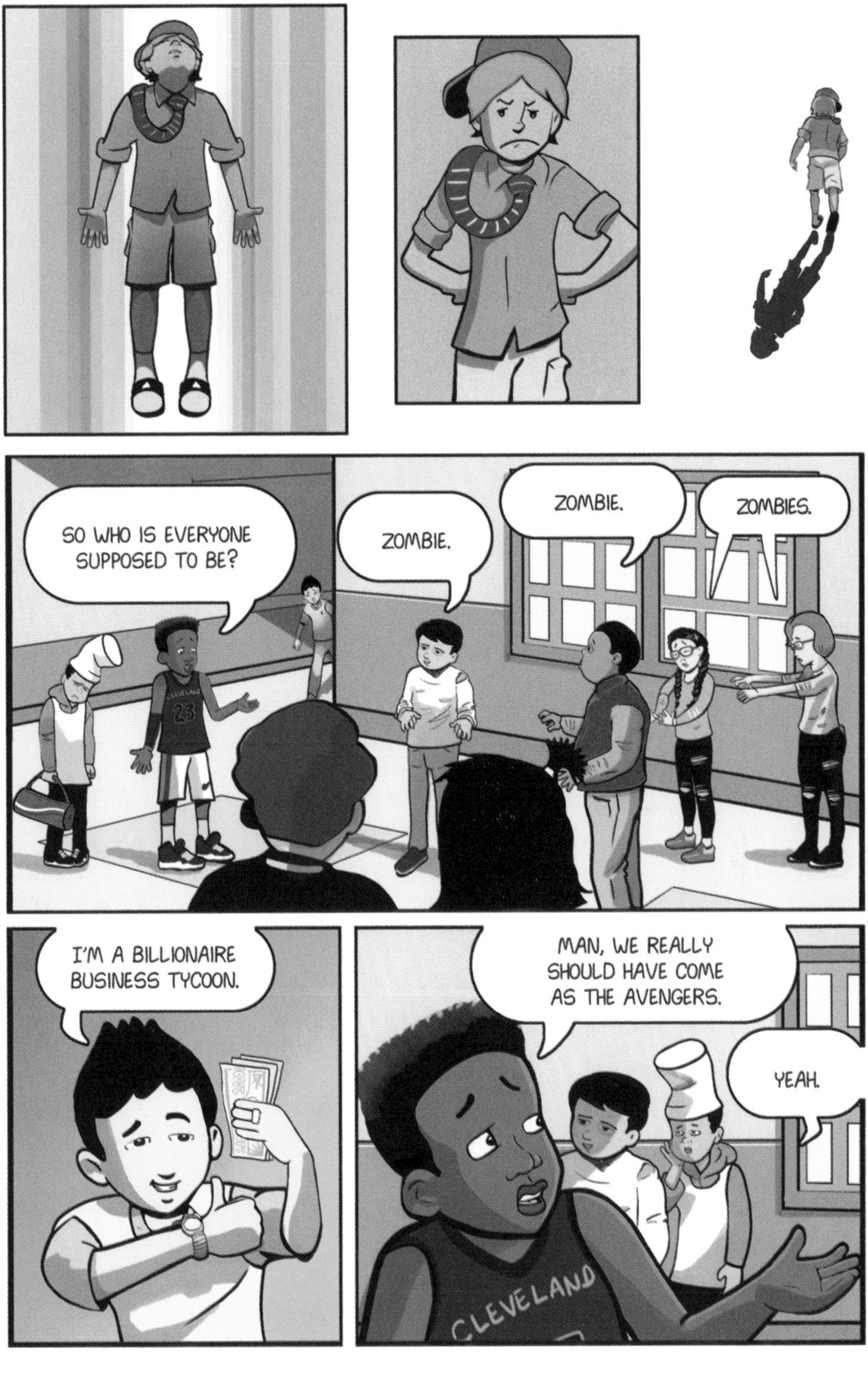
SO WHO IS EVERYONE SUPPOSED TO BE?
ZOMBIE.
ZOMBIE.
ZOMBIES.
I'M A BILLIONAIRE BUSINESS TYCOON.
MAN, WE REALLY SHOULD HAVE COME AS THE AVENGERS.
YEAH.

TEAL FRIENDS

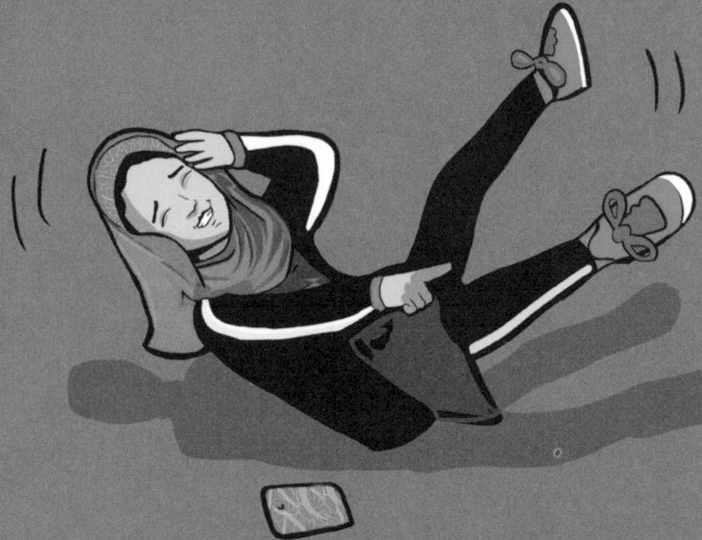

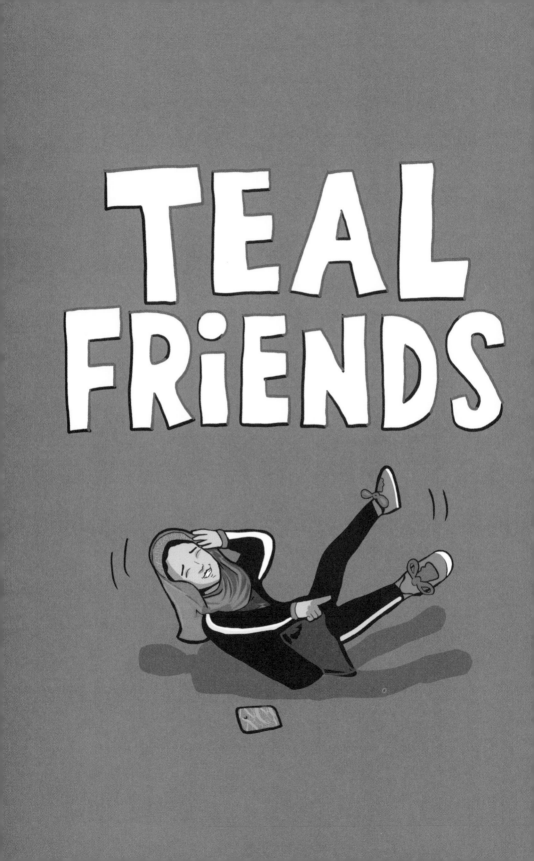

CHAPTER 4

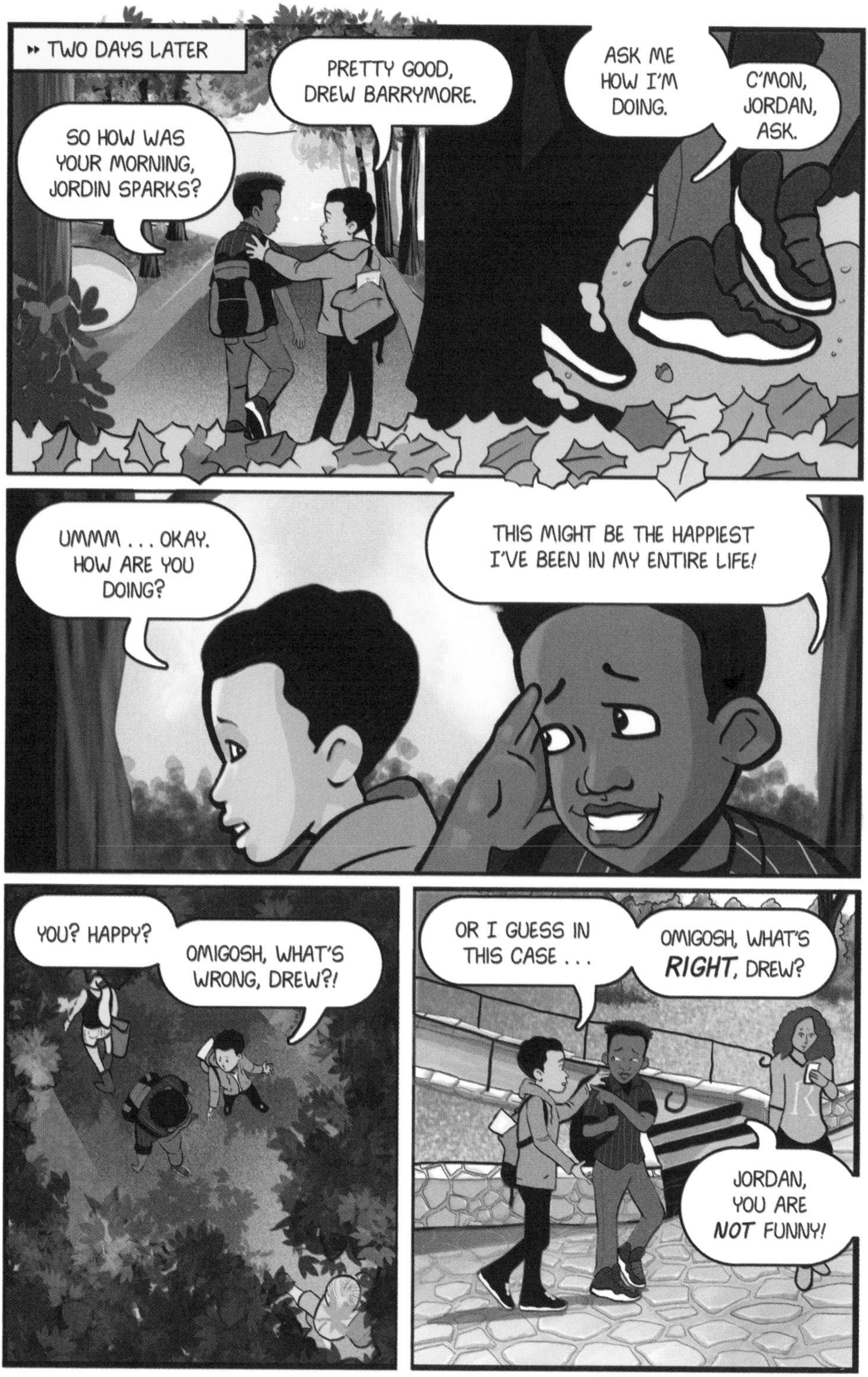
TWO DAYS LATER
SO HOW WAS YOUR MORNING, JORDIN SPARKS?
PRETTY GOOD, DREW BARRYMORE.
ASK ME HOW I'M DOING.
C'MON, JORDAN, ASK.
UMMM . . . OKAY. HOW ARE YOU DOING?
THIS MIGHT BE THE HAPPIEST I'VE BEEN IN MY ENTIRE LIFE!
YOU? HAPPY?
OMIGOSH, WHAT'S WRONG, DREW?!
OR I GUESS IN THIS CASE . . .
OMIGOSH, WHAT'S ***RIGHT***, DREW?
JORDAN, YOU ARE ***NOT*** FUNNY!

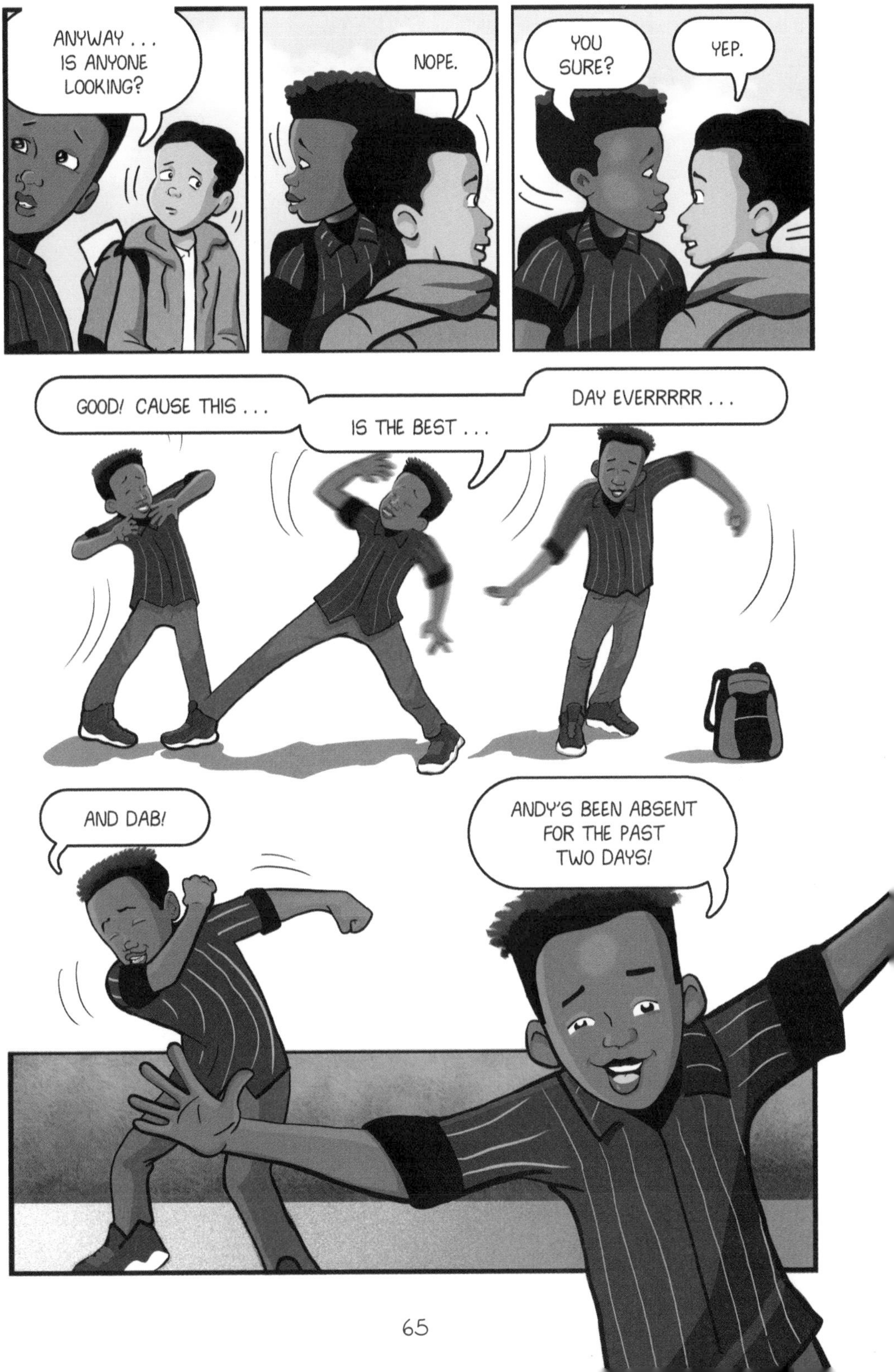
ANYWAY . . . IS ANYONE LOOKING?
NOPE.
YOU SURE?
YEP.
GOOD! CAUSE THIS . . .
IS THE BEST . . .
DAY EVERRRRR . . .
AND DAB!
ANDY'S BEEN ABSENT FOR THE PAST TWO DAYS!

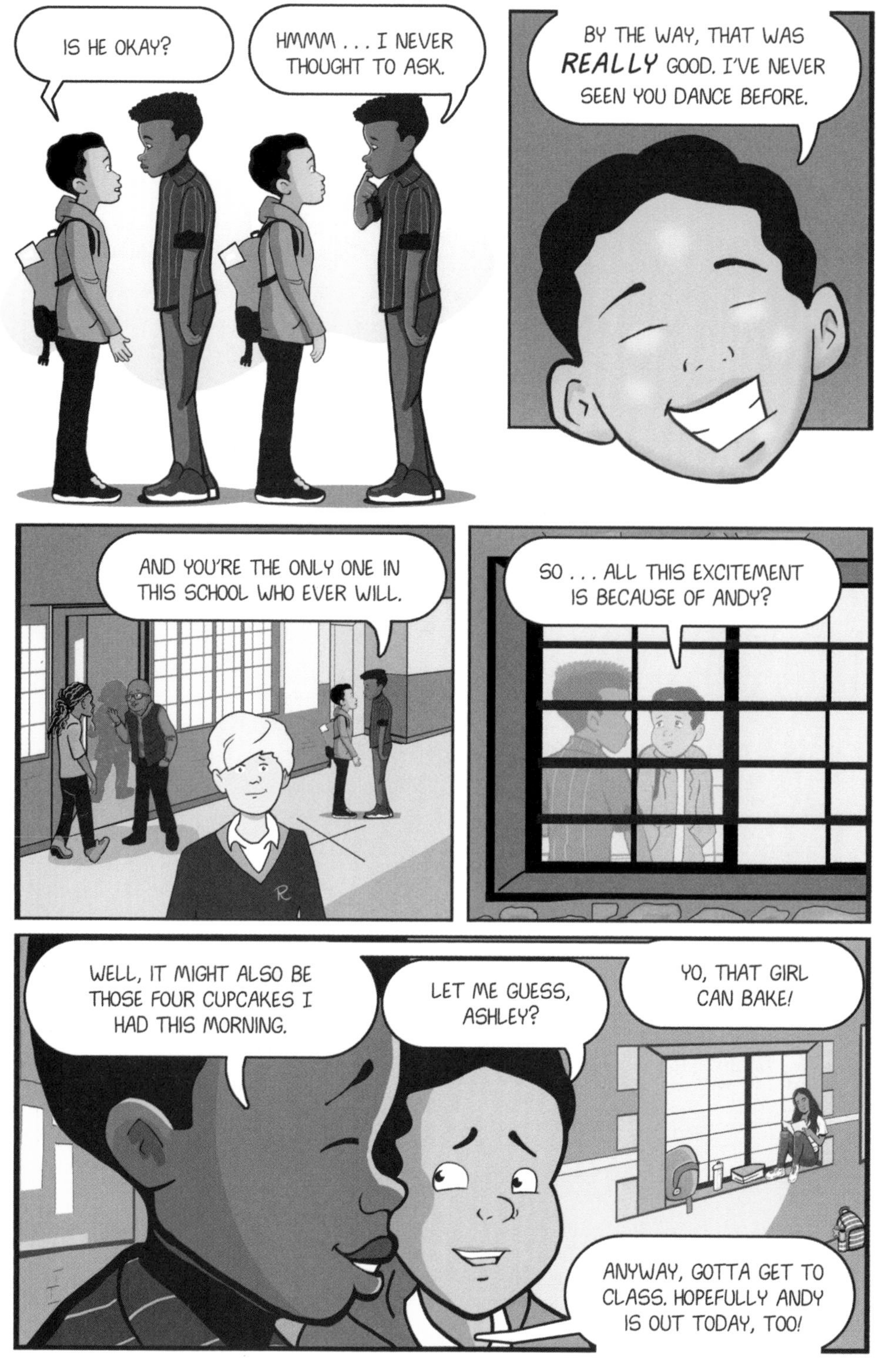
IS HE OKAY?
HMMM . . . I NEVER THOUGHT TO ASK.
BY THE WAY, THAT WAS REALLY GOOD. I'VE NEVER SEEN YOU DANCE BEFORE.
AND YOU'RE THE ONLY ONE IN THIS SCHOOL WHO EVER WILL.
SO . . . ALL THIS EXCITEMENT IS BECAUSE OF ANDY?
WELL, IT MIGHT ALSO BE THOSE FOUR CUPCAKES I HAD THIS MORNING.
LET ME GUESS, ASHLEY?
YO, THAT GIRL CAN BAKE!
ANYWAY, GOTTA GET TO CLASS. HOPEFULLY ANDY IS OUT TODAY, TOO!

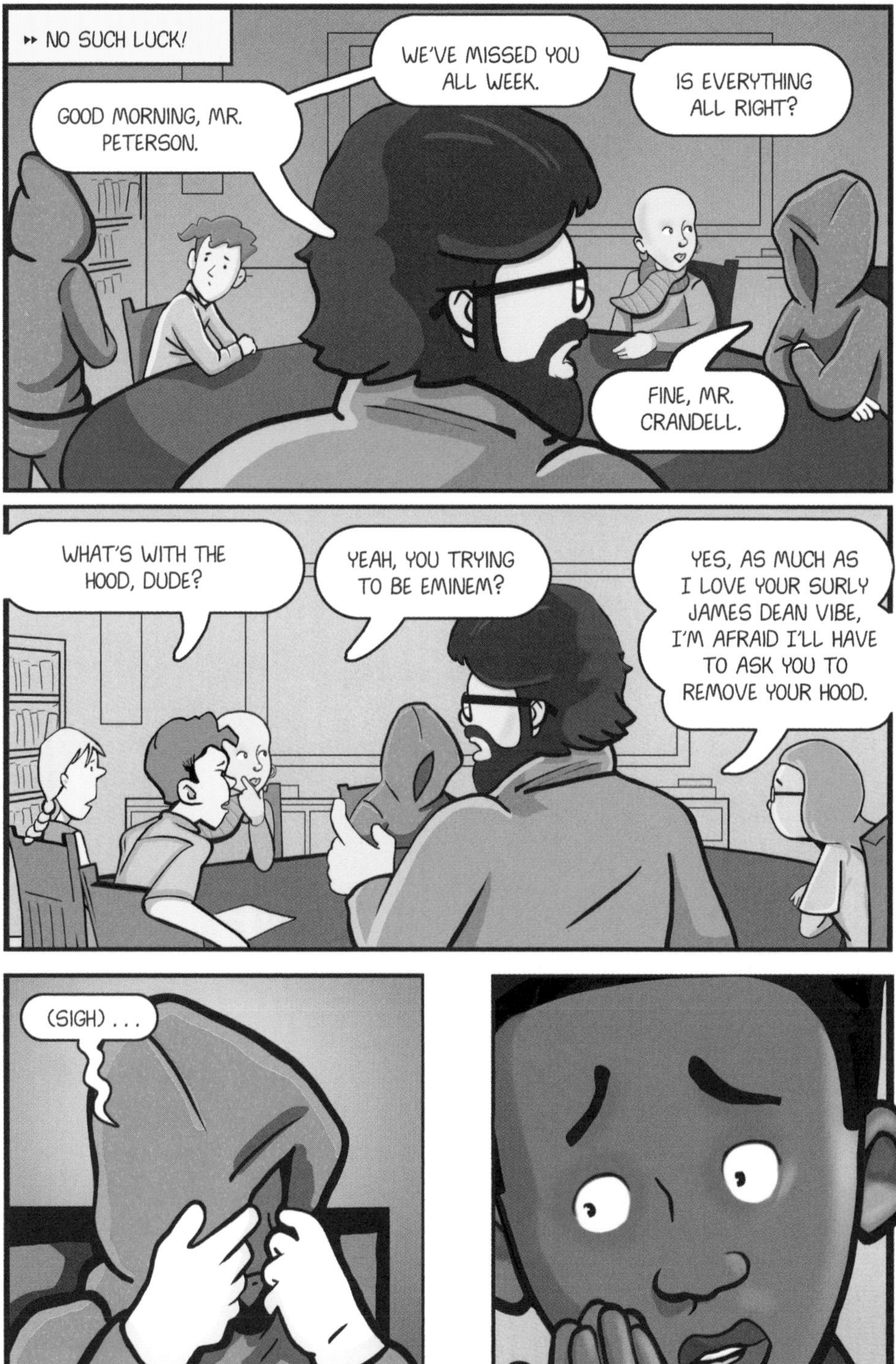

▸▸ NO SUCH LUCK!
GOOD MORNING, MR. PETERSON.
WE'VE MISSED YOU ALL WEEK.
IS EVERYTHING ALL RIGHT?
FINE, MR. CRANDELL.
WHAT'S WITH THE HOOD, DUDE?
YEAH, YOU TRYING TO BE EMINEM?
YES, AS MUCH AS I LOVE YOUR SURLY JAMES DEAN VIBE, I'M AFRAID I'LL HAVE TO ASK YOU TO REMOVE YOUR HOOD.
(SIGH) . . .

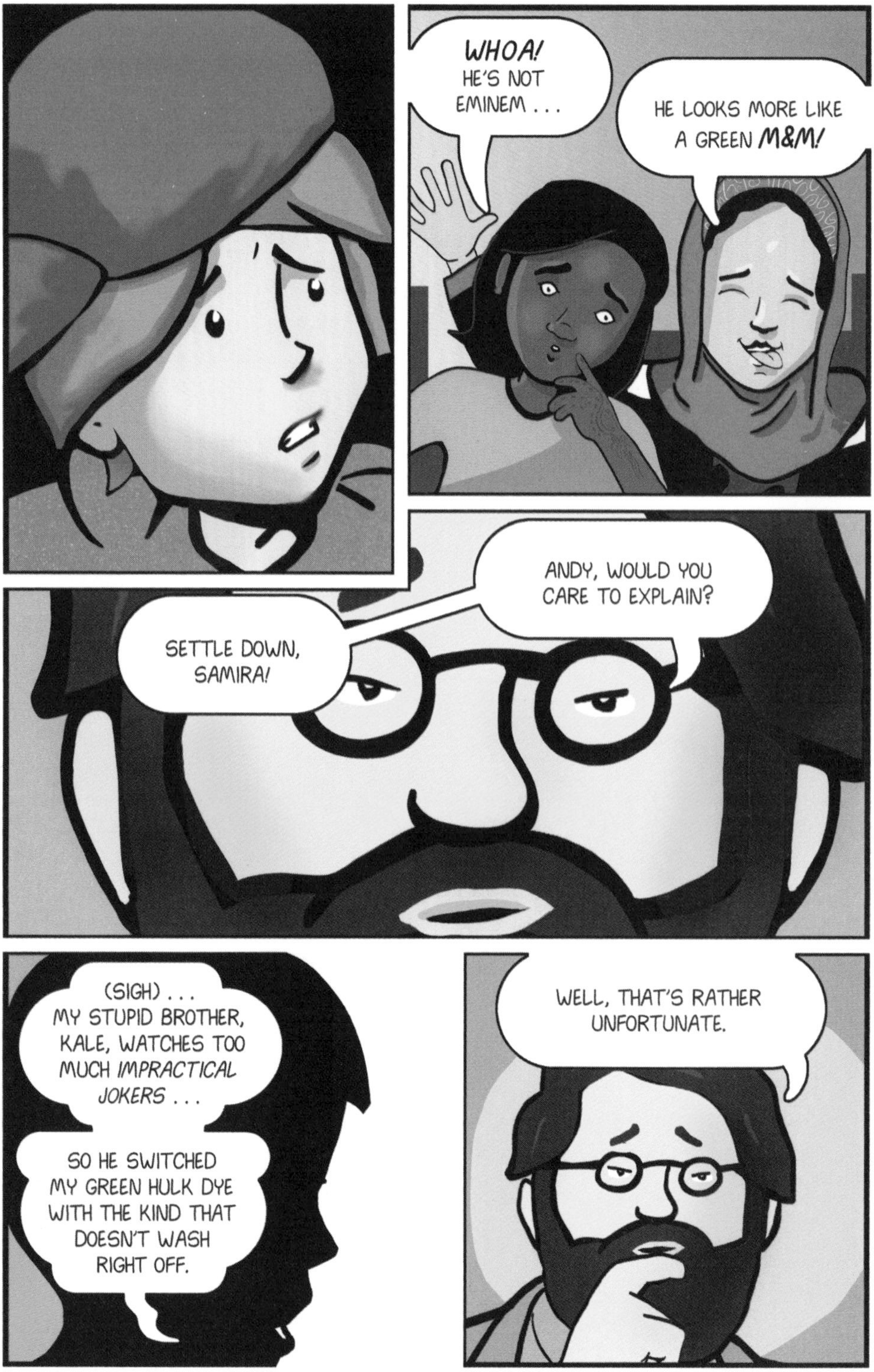
WHOA! HE'S NOT EMINEM . . .
HE LOOKS MORE LIKE A GREEN M&M!
ANDY, WOULD YOU CARE TO EXPLAIN?
SETTLE DOWN, SAMIRA!
(SIGH) . . . MY STUPID BROTHER, KALE, WATCHES TOO MUCH *IMPRACTICAL JOKERS* . . .
SO HE SWITCHED MY GREEN HULK DYE WITH THE KIND THAT DOESN'T WASH RIGHT OFF.
WELL, THAT'S RATHER UNFORTUNATE.

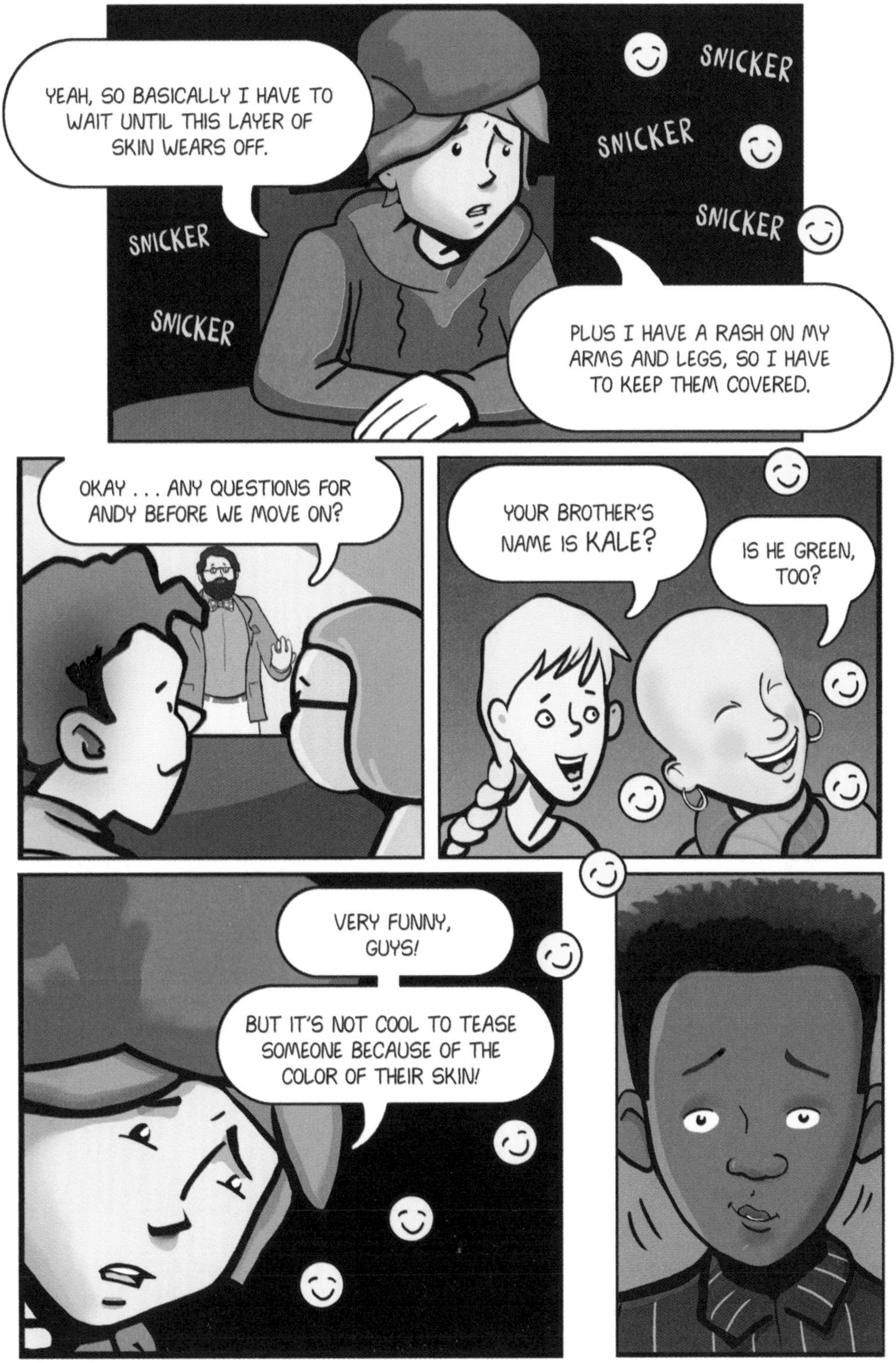
YEAH, SO BASICALLY I HAVE TO WAIT UNTIL THIS LAYER OF SKIN WEARS OFF.
SNICKER
SNICKER
SNICKER
SNICKER
SNICKER
PLUS I HAVE A RASH ON MY ARMS AND LEGS, SO I HAVE TO KEEP THEM COVERED.
OKAY . . . ANY QUESTIONS FOR ANDY BEFORE WE MOVE ON?
YOUR BROTHER'S NAME IS KALE?
IS HE GREEN, TOO?
VERY FUNNY, GUYS!
BUT IT'S NOT COOL TO TEASE SOMEONE BECAUSE OF THE COLOR OF THEIR SKIN!

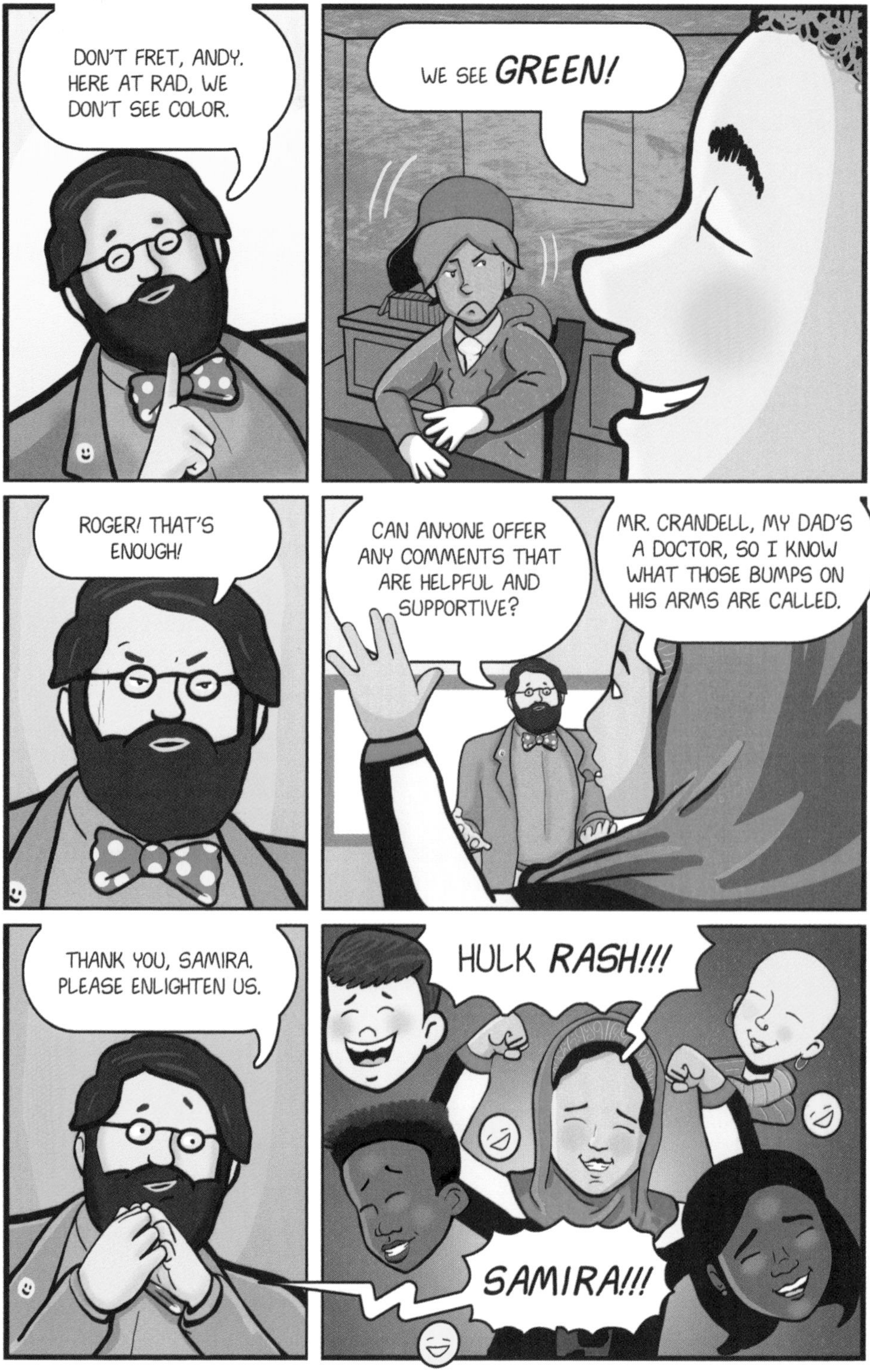
DON'T FRET, ANDY. HERE AT RAD, WE DON'T SEE COLOR.
WE SEE GREEN!
ROGER! THAT'S ENOUGH!
CAN ANYONE OFFER ANY COMMENTS THAT ARE HELPFUL AND SUPPORTIVE?
MR. CRANDELL, MY DAD'S A DOCTOR, SO I KNOW WHAT THOSE BUMPS ON HIS ARMS ARE CALLED.
THANK YOU, SAMIRA. PLEASE ENLIGHTEN US.
HULK RASH!!!
SAMIRA!!!

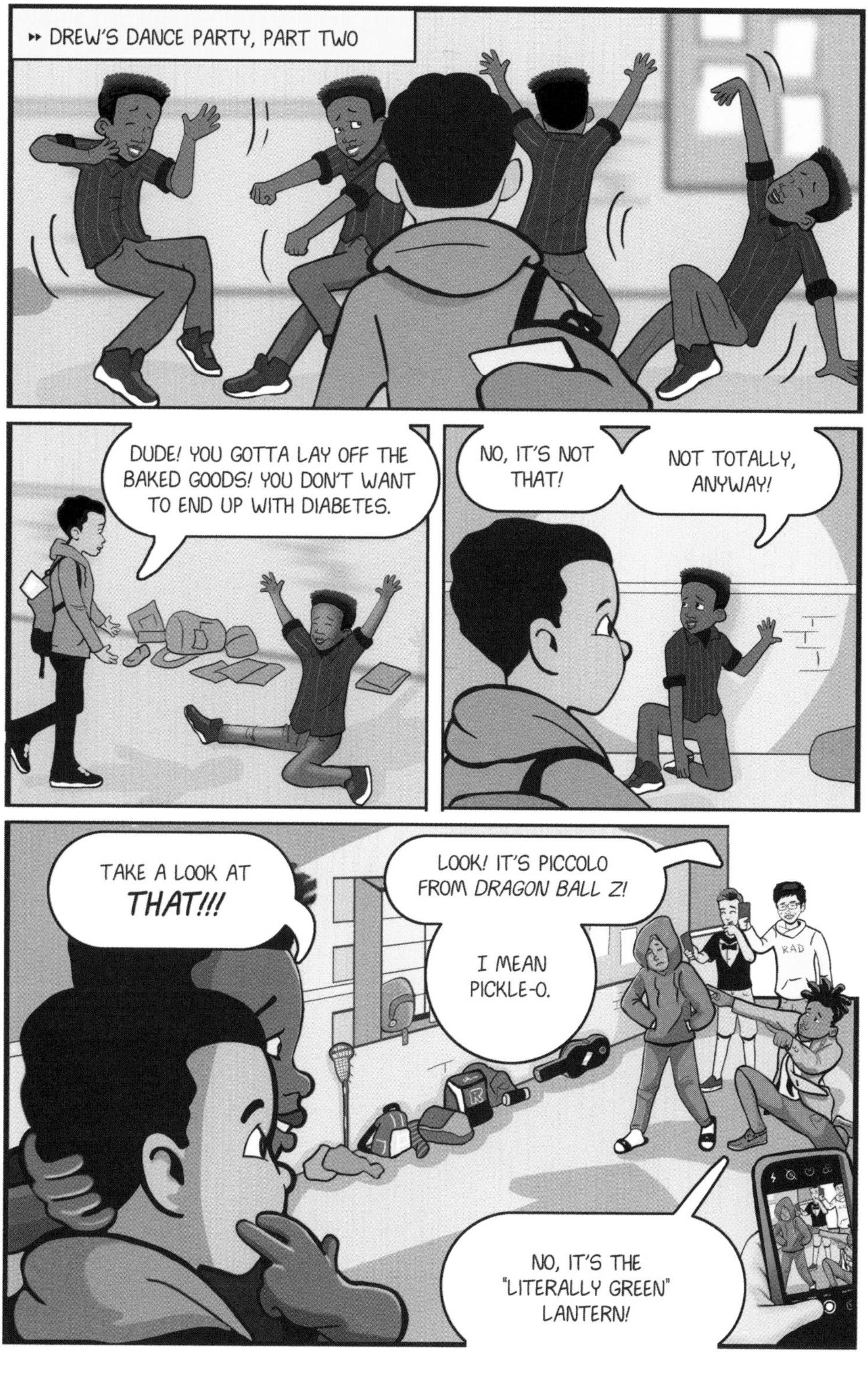

▸▸ DREW'S DANCE PARTY, PART TWO
DUDE! YOU GOTTA LAY OFF THE BAKED GOODS! YOU DON'T WANT TO END UP WITH DIABETES.
NO, IT'S NOT THAT!
NOT TOTALLY, ANYWAY!
TAKE A LOOK AT THAT!!!
LOOK! IT'S PICCOLO FROM DRAGON BALL Z!
I MEAN PICKLE-O.
NO, IT'S THE "LITERALLY GREEN" LANTERN!
RAD

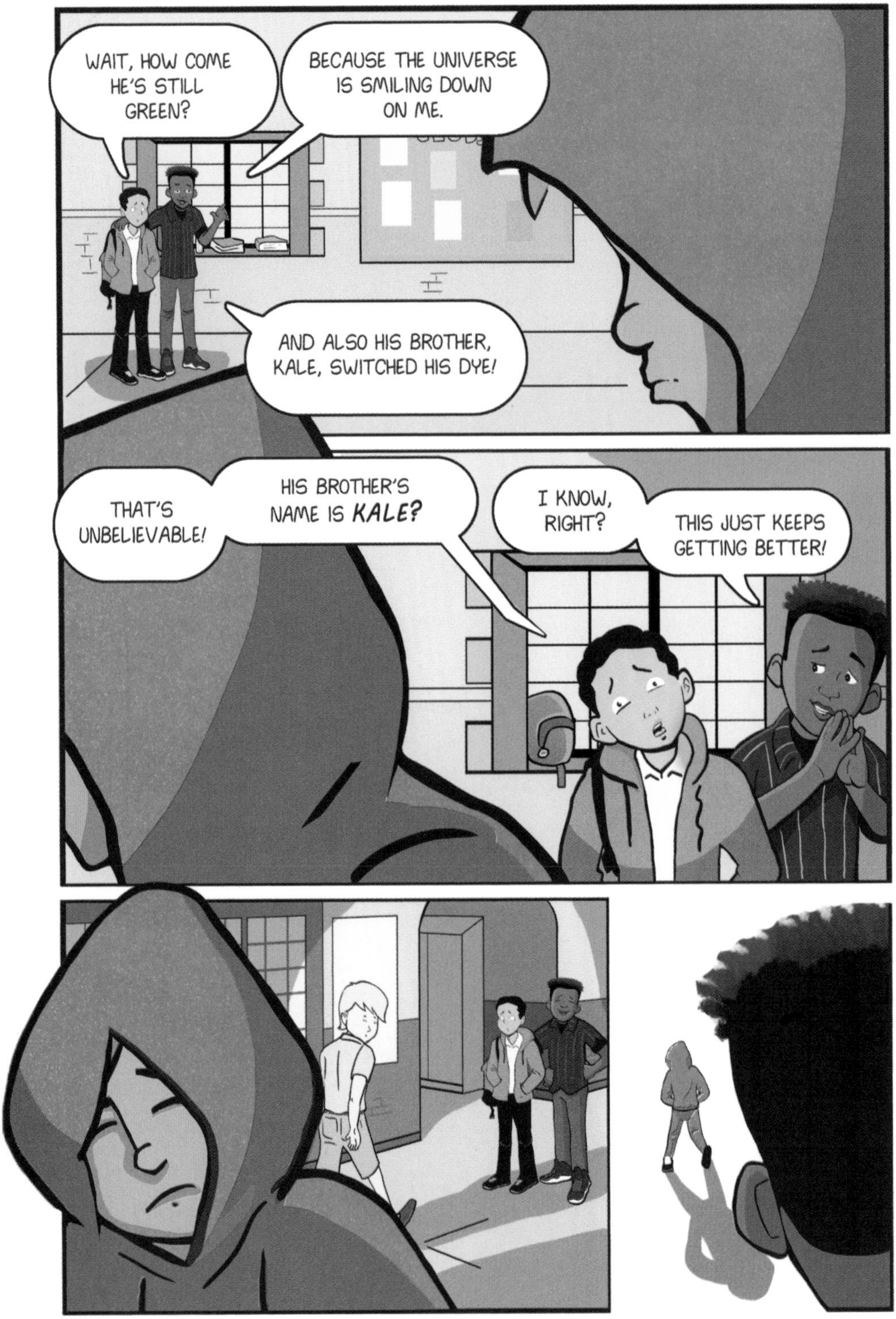
WAIT, HOW COME HE'S STILL GREEN?
BECAUSE THE UNIVERSE IS SMILING DOWN ON ME.
AND ALSO HIS BROTHER, KALE, SWITCHED HIS DYE!
THAT'S UNBELIEVABLE!
HIS BROTHER'S NAME IS **KALE?**
I KNOW, RIGHT?
THIS JUST KEEPS GETTING BETTER!

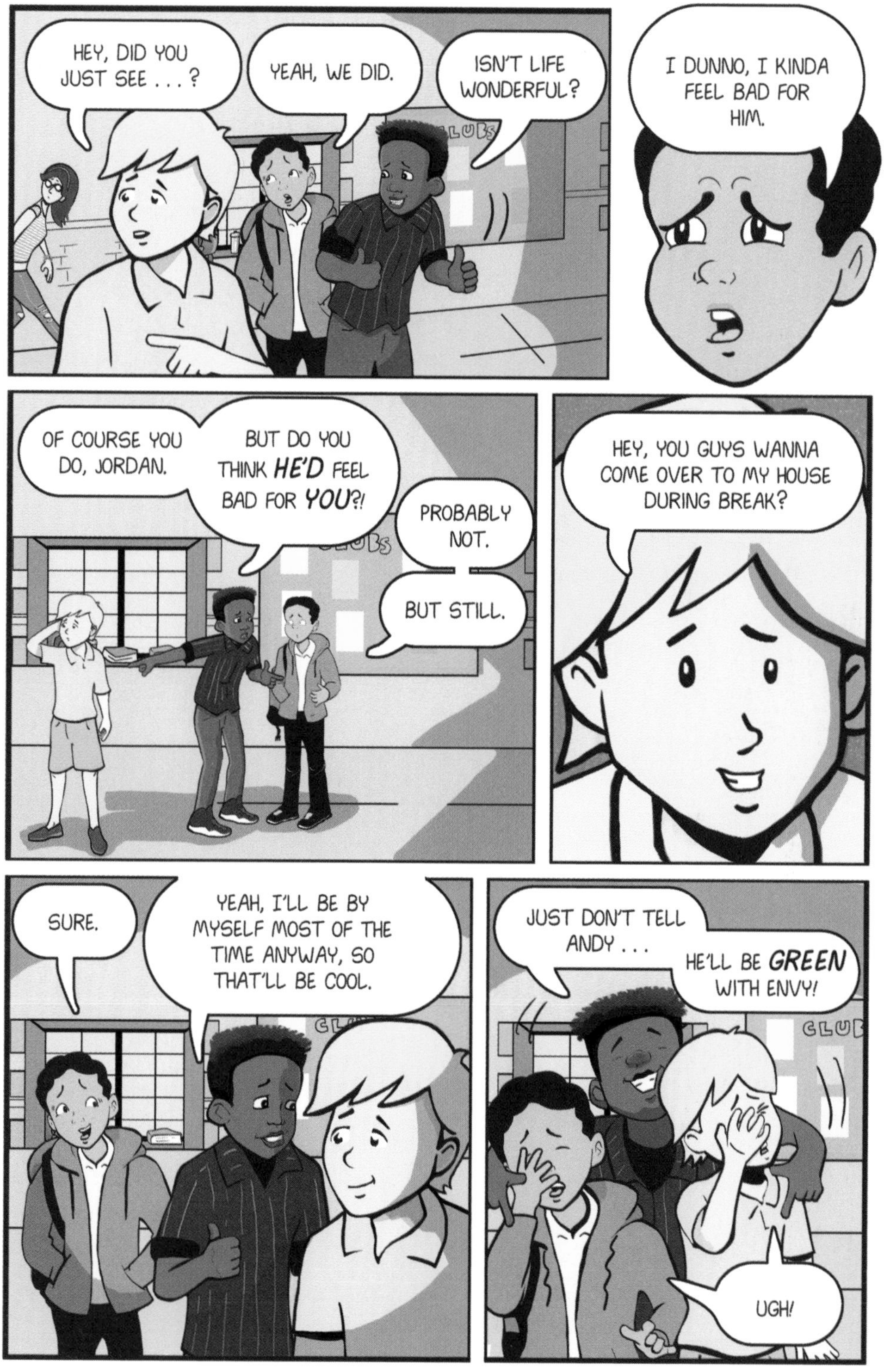
HEY, DID YOU JUST SEE . . . ?
YEAH, WE DID.
ISN'T LIFE WONDERFUL?
I DUNNO, I KINDA FEEL BAD FOR HIM.
CLUBS
OF COURSE YOU DO, JORDAN.
BUT DO YOU THINK HE'D FEEL BAD FOR YOU?!
PROBABLY NOT.
BUT STILL.
HEY, YOU GUYS WANNA COME OVER TO MY HOUSE DURING BREAK?
SURE.
YEAH, I'LL BE BY MYSELF MOST OF THE TIME ANYWAY, SO THAT'LL BE COOL.
JUST DON'T TELL ANDY . . .
HE'LL BE GREEN WITH ENVY!
UGH!

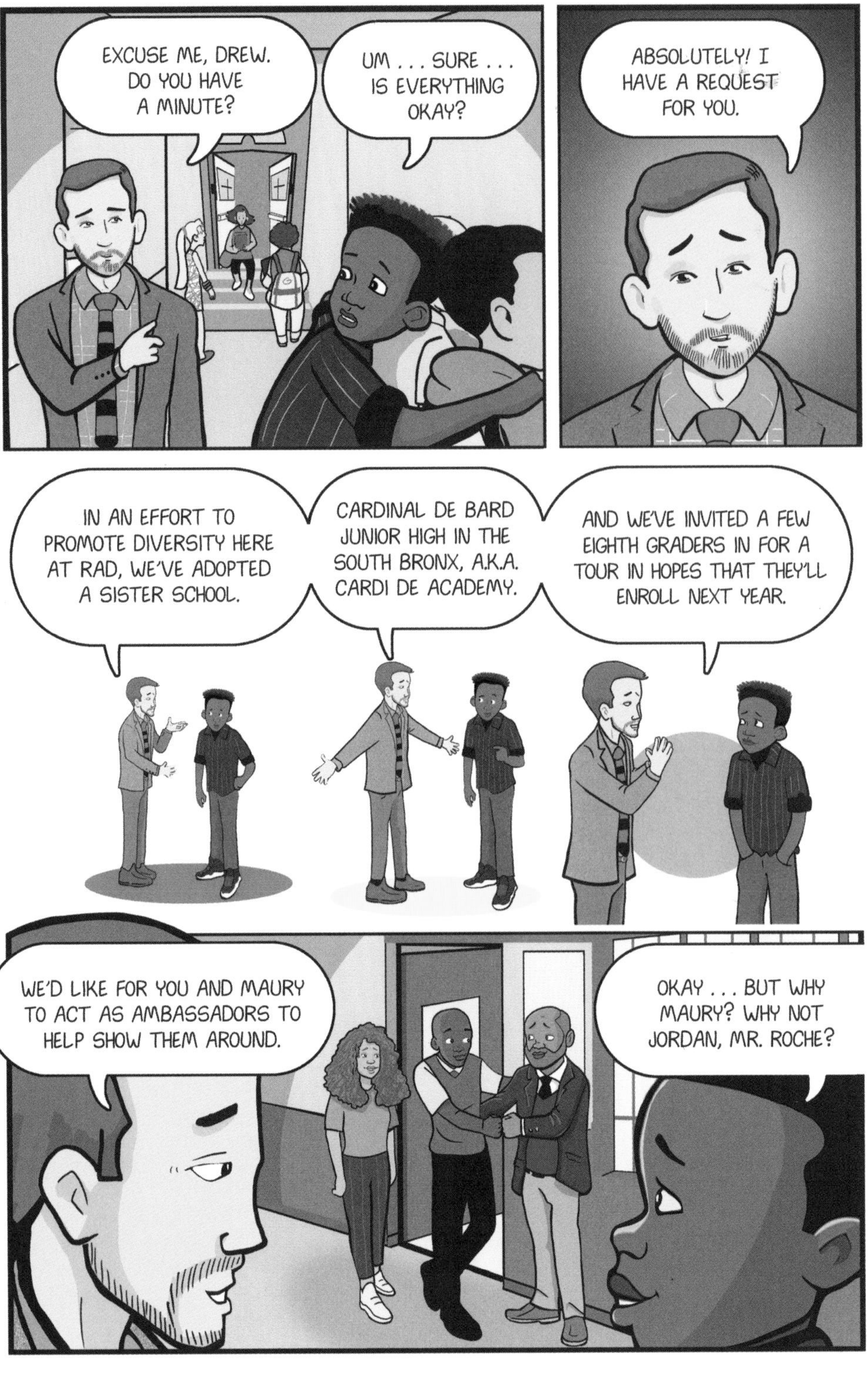
EXCUSE ME, DREW. DO YOU HAVE A MINUTE?
UM . . . SURE . . . IS EVERYTHING OKAY?
ABSOLUTELY! I HAVE A REQUEST FOR YOU.
IN AN EFFORT TO PROMOTE DIVERSITY HERE AT RAD, WE'VE ADOPTED A SISTER SCHOOL.
CARDINAL DE BARD JUNIOR HIGH IN THE SOUTH BRONX, A.K.A. CARDI DE ACADEMY.
AND WE'VE INVITED A FEW EIGHTH GRADERS IN FOR A TOUR IN HOPES THAT THEY'LL ENROLL NEXT YEAR.
WE'D LIKE FOR YOU AND MAURY TO ACT AS AMBASSADORS TO HELP SHOW THEM AROUND.
OKAY . . . BUT WHY MAURY? WHY NOT JORDAN, MR. ROCHE?

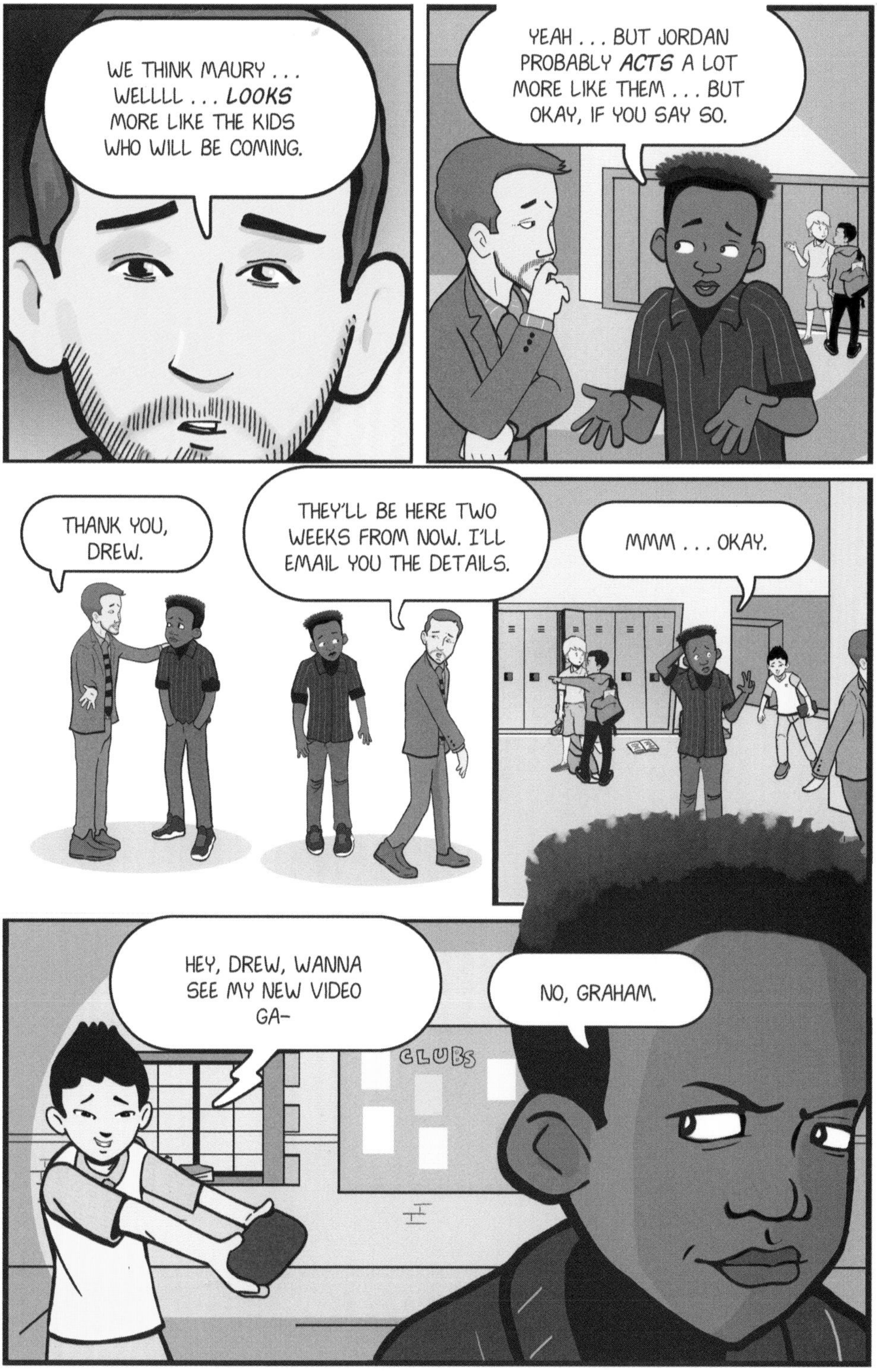
WE THINK MAURY . . . WELLLL . . . LOOKS MORE LIKE THE KIDS WHO WILL BE COMING.
YEAH . . . BUT JORDAN PROBABLY ACTS A LOT MORE LIKE THEM . . . BUT OKAY, IF YOU SAY SO.
THANK YOU, DREW.
THEY'LL BE HERE TWO WEEKS FROM NOW. I'LL EMAIL YOU THE DETAILS.
MMM . . . OKAY.
HEY, DREW, WANNA SEE MY NEW VIDEO GA-
NO, GRAHAM.
CLUBS

OMELET

CHAPTER
5

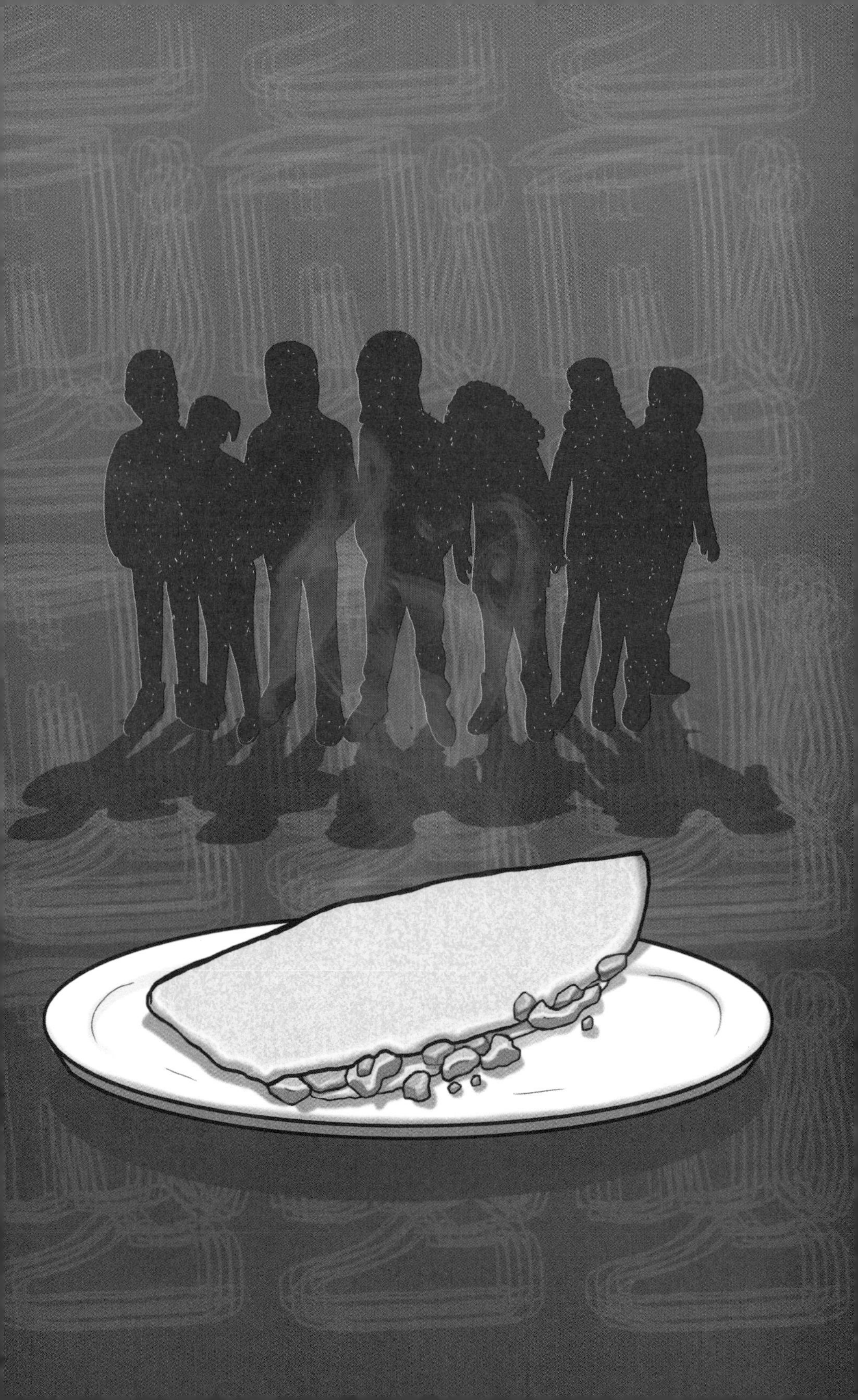

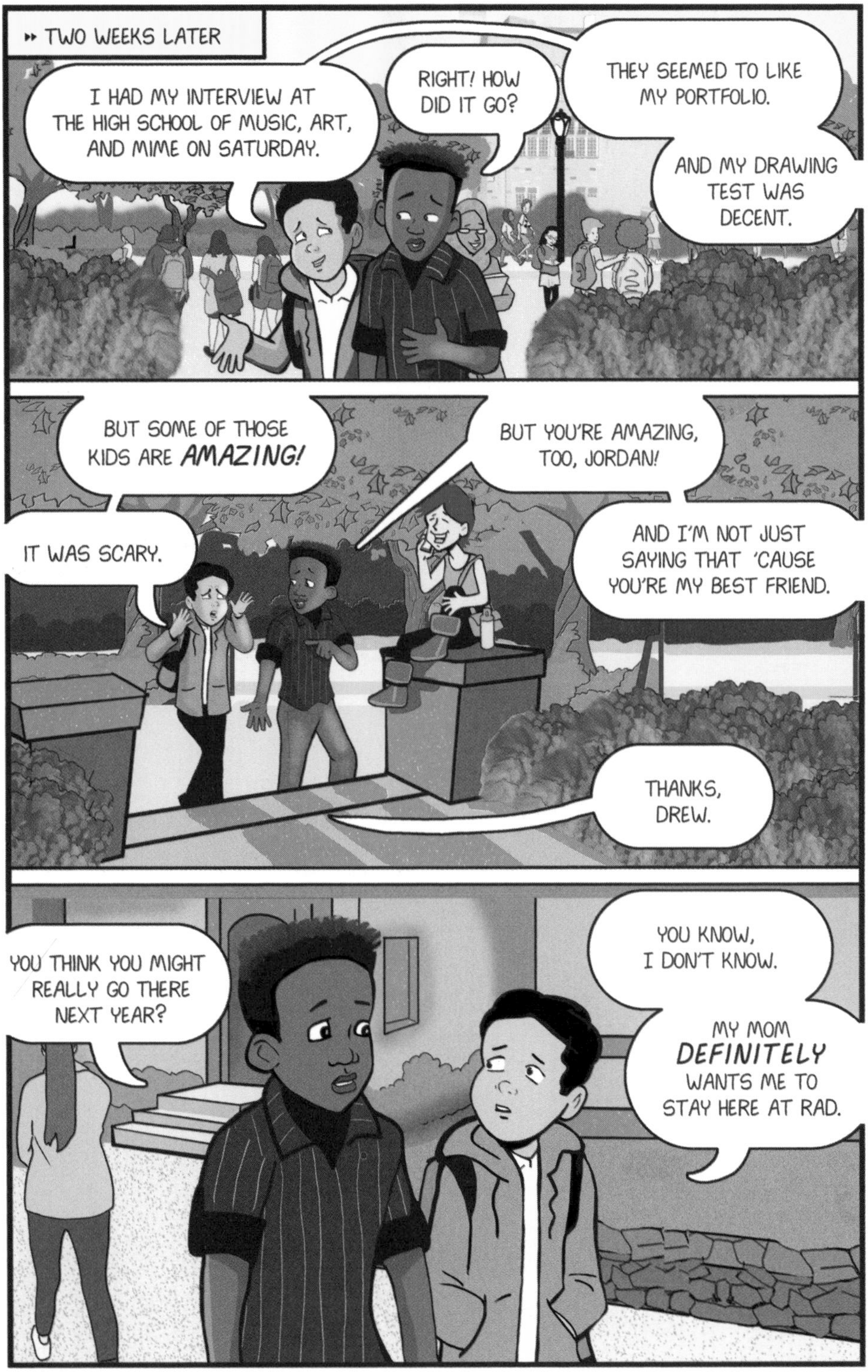
TWO WEEKS LATER
I HAD MY INTERVIEW AT THE HIGH SCHOOL OF MUSIC, ART, AND MIME ON SATURDAY.
RIGHT! HOW DID IT GO?
THEY SEEMED TO LIKE MY PORTFOLIO.
AND MY DRAWING TEST WAS DECENT.
BUT SOME OF THOSE KIDS ARE AMAZING!
IT WAS SCARY.
BUT YOU'RE AMAZING, TOO, JORDAN!
AND I'M NOT JUST SAYING THAT 'CAUSE YOU'RE MY BEST FRIEND.
THANKS, DREW.
YOU THINK YOU MIGHT REALLY GO THERE NEXT YEAR?
YOU KNOW, I DON'T KNOW.
MY MOM DEFINITELY WANTS ME TO STAY HERE AT RAD.

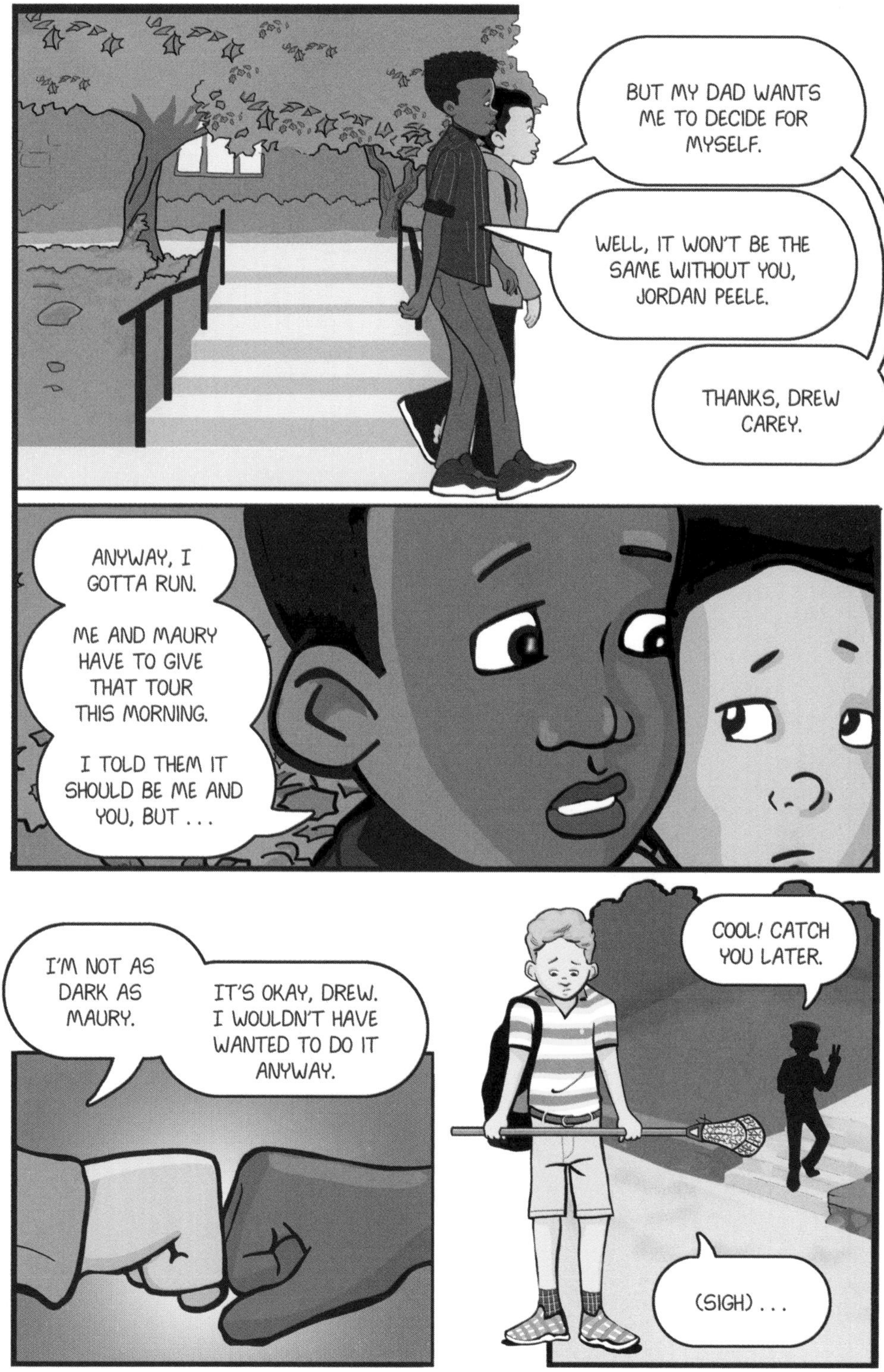
BUT MY DAD WANTS ME TO DECIDE FOR MYSELF.
WELL, IT WON'T BE THE SAME WITHOUT YOU, JORDAN PEELE.
THANKS, DREW CAREY.
ANYWAY, I GOTTA RUN.
ME AND MAURY HAVE TO GIVE THAT TOUR THIS MORNING.
I TOLD THEM IT SHOULD BE ME AND YOU, BUT . . .
I'M NOT AS DARK AS MAURY.
IT'S OKAY, DREW. I WOULDN'T HAVE WANTED TO DO IT ANYWAY.
COOL! CATCH YOU LATER.
(SIGH) . . .

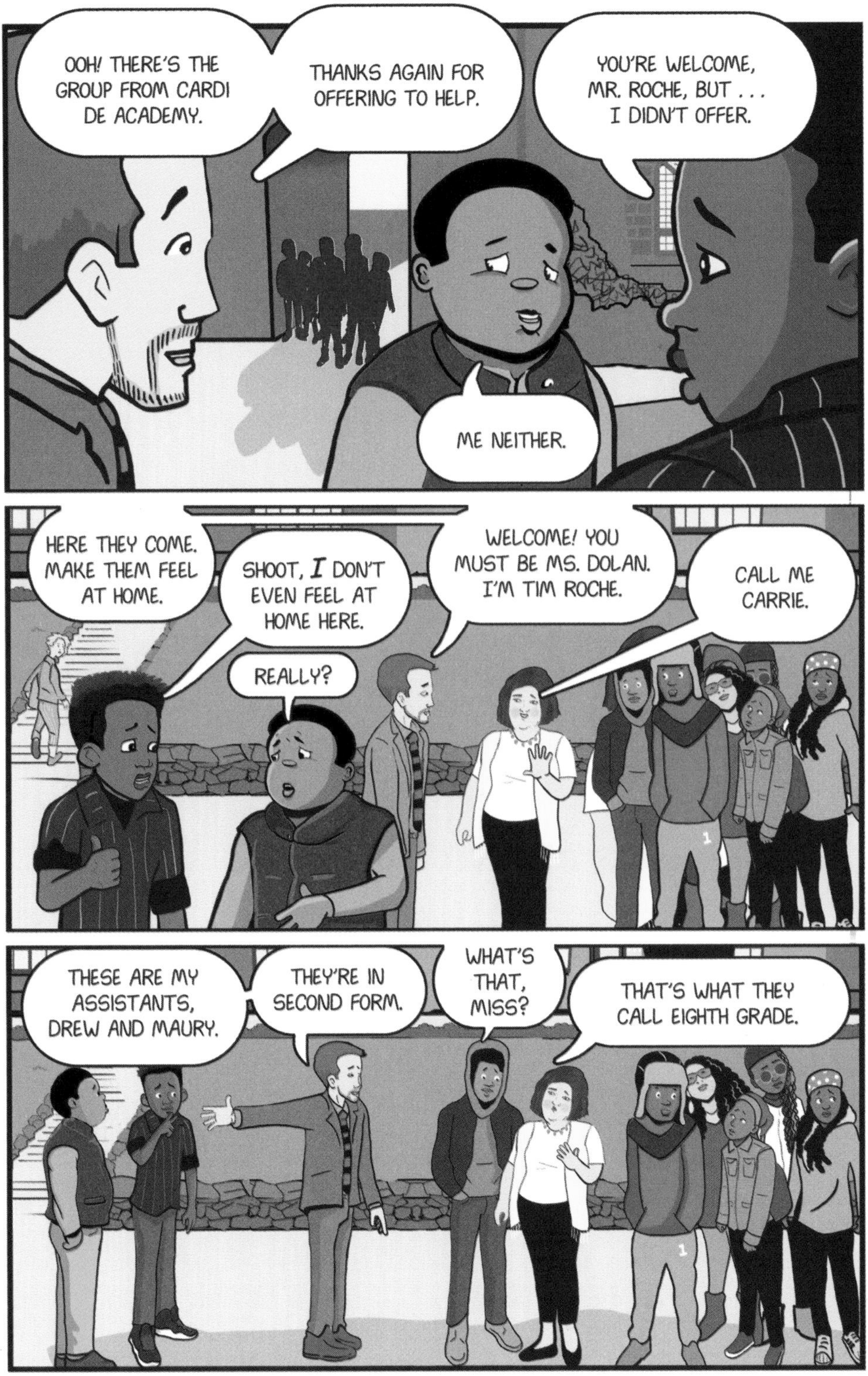
OOH! THERE'S THE GROUP FROM CARDI DE ACADEMY.
THANKS AGAIN FOR OFFERING TO HELP.
YOU'RE WELCOME, MR. ROCHE, BUT . . . I DIDN'T OFFER.
ME NEITHER.
HERE THEY COME. MAKE THEM FEEL AT HOME.
SHOOT, *I* DON'T EVEN FEEL AT HOME HERE.
REALLY?
WELCOME! YOU MUST BE MS. DOLAN. I'M TIM ROCHE.
CALL ME CARRIE.
THESE ARE MY ASSISTANTS, DREW AND MAURY.
THEY'RE IN SECOND FORM.
WHAT'S THAT, MISS?
THAT'S WHAT THEY CALL EIGHTH GRADE.

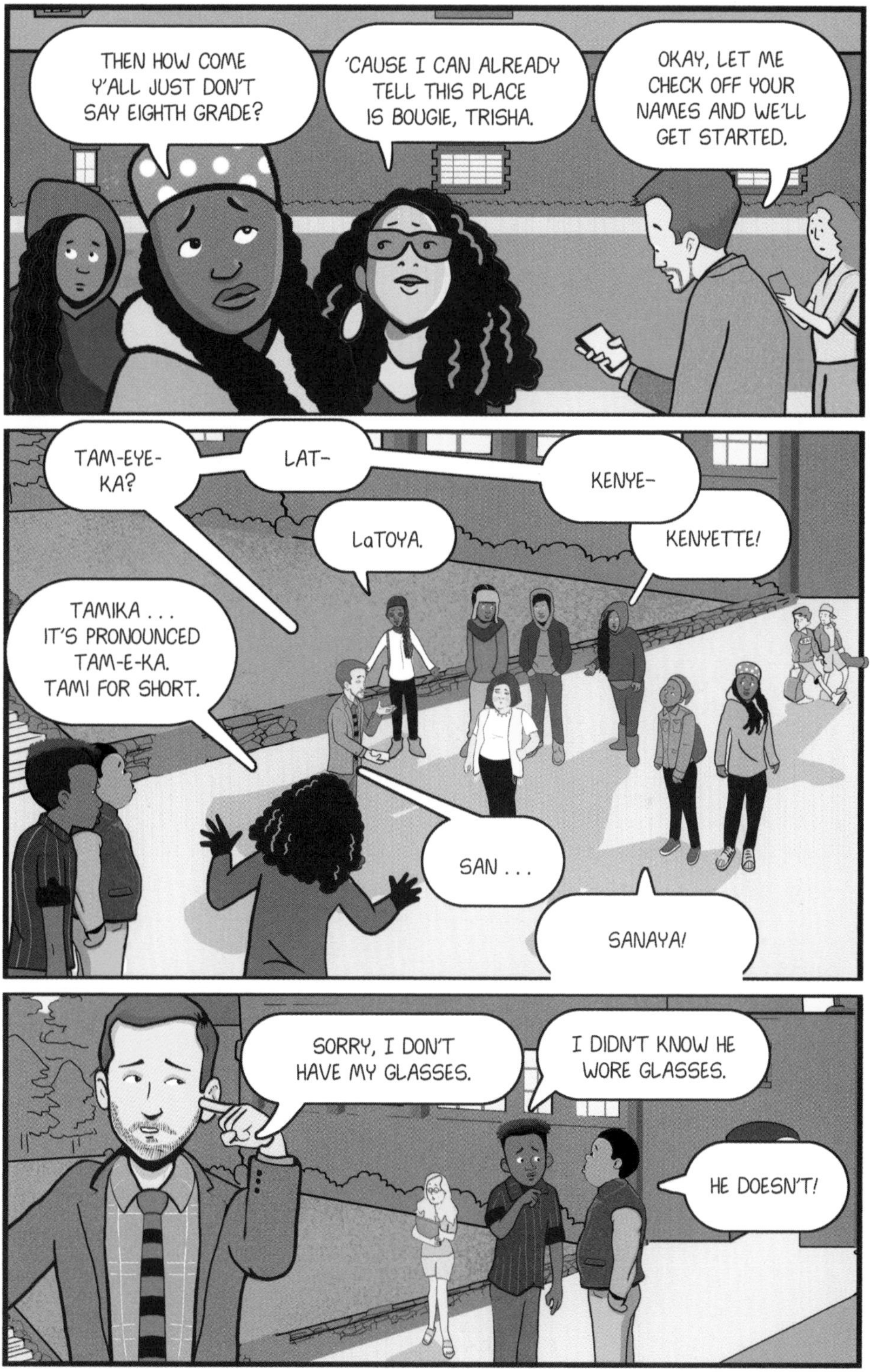
THEN HOW COME Y'ALL JUST DON'T SAY EIGHTH GRADE?
'CAUSE I CAN ALREADY TELL THIS PLACE IS BOUGIE, TRISHA.
OKAY, LET ME CHECK OFF YOUR NAMES AND WE'LL GET STARTED.
TAM-EYE-KA?
LAT-
KENYE-
LaTOYA.
KENYETTE!
TAMIKA . . . IT'S PRONOUNCED TAM-E-KA. TAMI FOR SHORT.
SAN . . .
SANAYA!
SORRY, I DON'T HAVE MY GLASSES.
I DIDN'T KNOW HE WORE GLASSES.
HE DOESN'T!

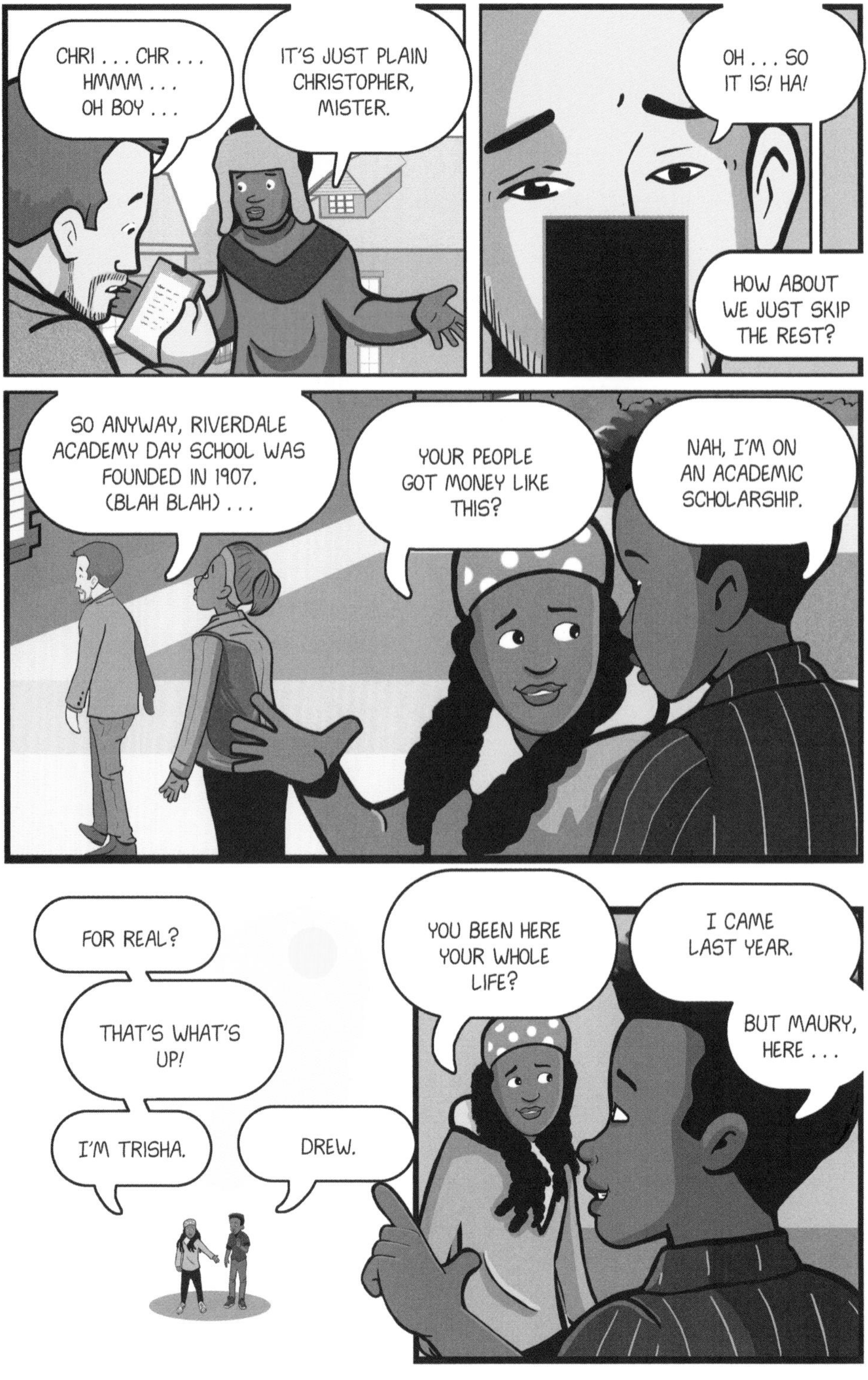
CHRI . . . CHR . . . HMMM . . . OH BOY . . .
IT'S JUST PLAIN CHRISTOPHER, MISTER.
OH . . . SO IT IS! HA!
HOW ABOUT WE JUST SKIP THE REST?
SO ANYWAY, RIVERDALE ACADEMY DAY SCHOOL WAS FOUNDED IN 1907. (BLAH BLAH) . . .
YOUR PEOPLE GOT MONEY LIKE THIS?
NAH, I'M ON AN ACADEMIC SCHOLARSHIP.
FOR REAL?
THAT'S WHAT'S UP!
I'M TRISHA.
DREW.
YOU BEEN HERE YOUR WHOLE LIFE?
I CAME LAST YEAR.
BUT MAURY, HERE . . .

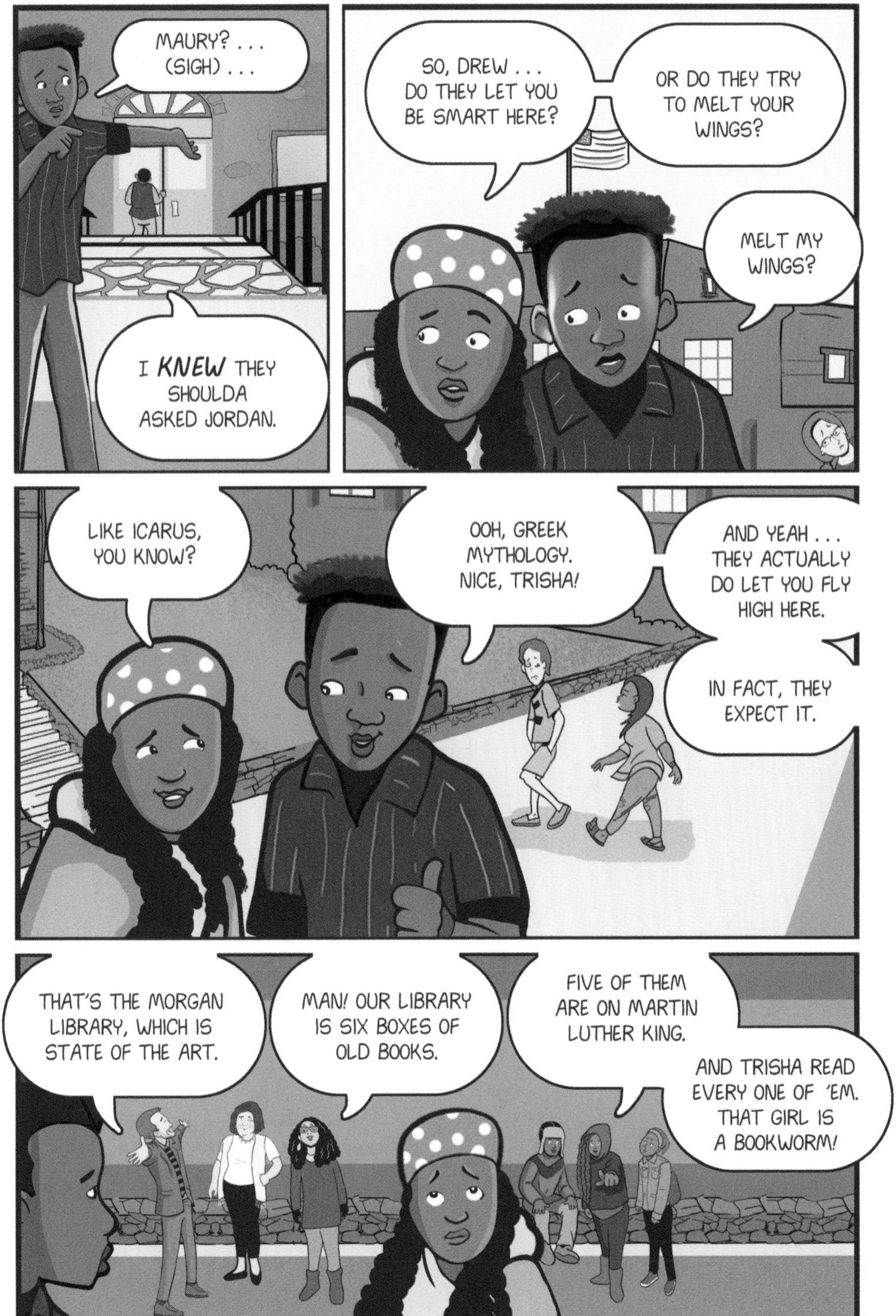
MAURY? . . . (SIGH) . . .
I KNEW THEY SHOULDA ASKED JORDAN.
SO, DREW . . . DO THEY LET YOU BE SMART HERE?
OR DO THEY TRY TO MELT YOUR WINGS?
MELT MY WINGS?
LIKE ICARUS, YOU KNOW?
OOH, GREEK MYTHOLOGY. NICE, TRISHA!
AND YEAH . . . THEY ACTUALLY DO LET YOU FLY HIGH HERE.
IN FACT, THEY EXPECT IT.
THAT'S THE MORGAN LIBRARY, WHICH IS STATE OF THE ART.
MAN! OUR LIBRARY IS SIX BOXES OF OLD BOOKS.
FIVE OF THEM ARE ON MARTIN LUTHER KING.
AND TRISHA READ EVERY ONE OF 'EM. THAT GIRL IS A BOOKWORM!

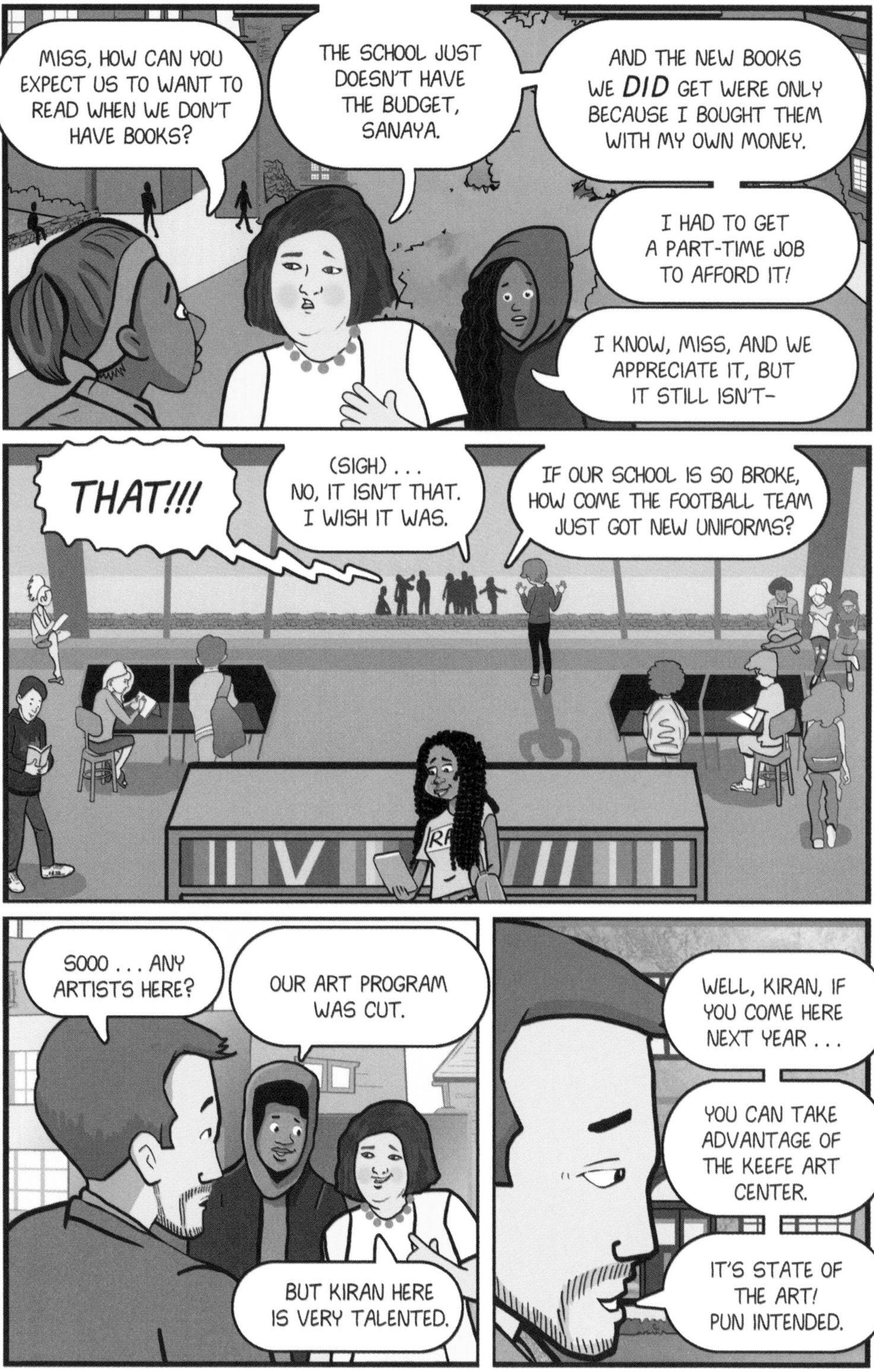
MISS, HOW CAN YOU EXPECT US TO WANT TO READ WHEN WE DON'T HAVE BOOKS?
THE SCHOOL JUST DOESN'T HAVE THE BUDGET, SANAYA.
AND THE NEW BOOKS WE *DID* GET WERE ONLY BECAUSE I BOUGHT THEM WITH MY OWN MONEY.
I HAD TO GET A PART-TIME JOB TO AFFORD IT!
I KNOW, MISS, AND WE APPRECIATE IT, BUT IT STILL ISN'T-
THAT!!!
(SIGH) . . . NO, IT ISN'T THAT. I WISH IT WAS.
IF OUR SCHOOL IS SO BROKE, HOW COME THE FOOTBALL TEAM JUST GOT NEW UNIFORMS?
SOOO . . . ANY ARTISTS HERE?
OUR ART PROGRAM WAS CUT.
BUT KIRAN HERE IS VERY TALENTED.
WELL, KIRAN, IF YOU COME HERE NEXT YEAR . . .
YOU CAN TAKE ADVANTAGE OF THE KEEFE ART CENTER.
IT'S STATE OF THE ART! PUN INTENDED.

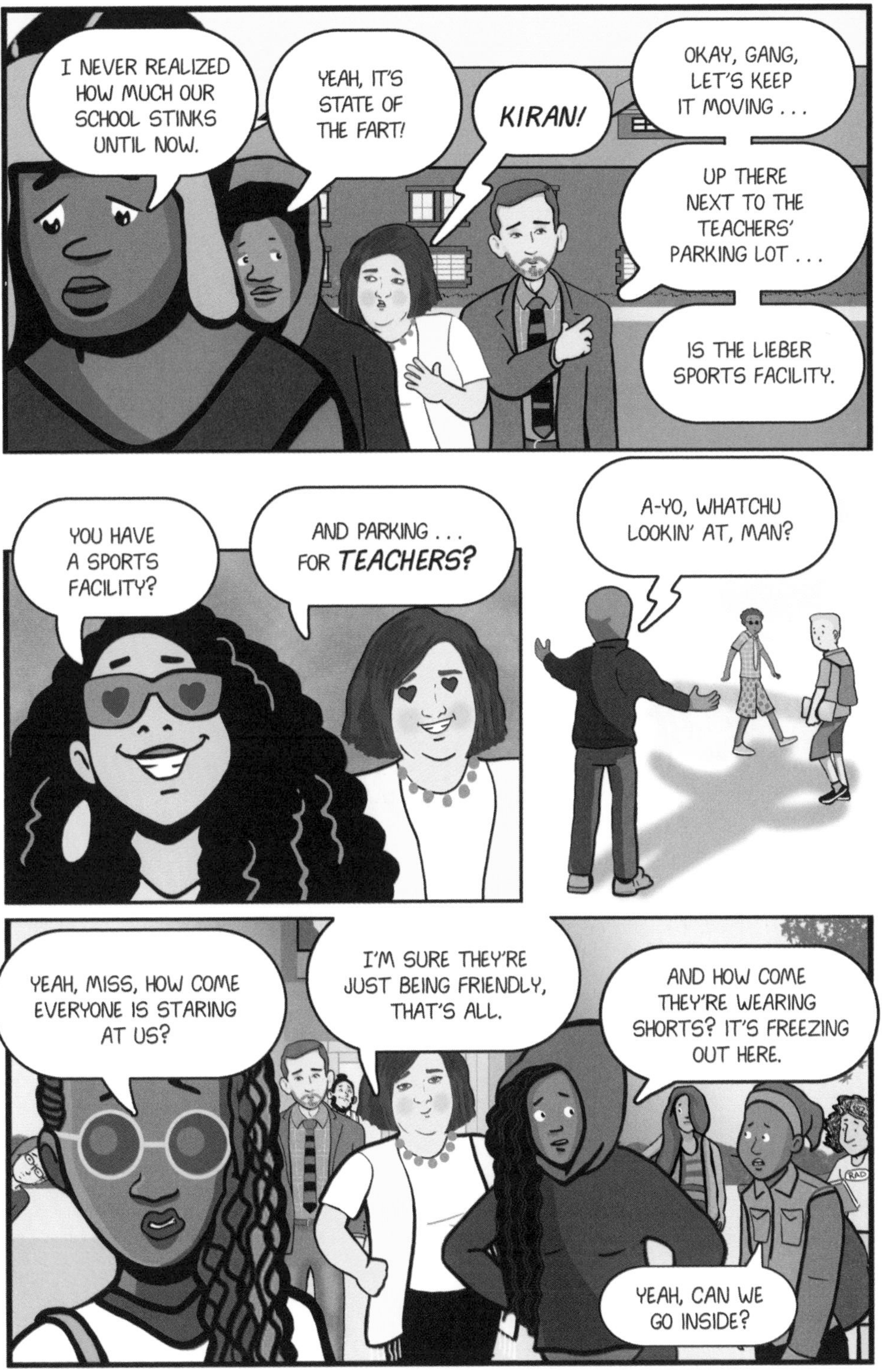
I NEVER REALIZED HOW MUCH OUR SCHOOL STINKS UNTIL NOW.
YEAH, IT'S STATE OF THE FART!
KIRAN!
OKAY, GANG, LET'S KEEP IT MOVING . . .
UP THERE NEXT TO THE TEACHERS' PARKING LOT . . .
IS THE LIEBER SPORTS FACILITY.
YOU HAVE A SPORTS FACILITY?
AND PARKING . . . FOR TEACHERS?
A-YO, WHATCHU LOOKIN' AT, MAN?
YEAH, MISS, HOW COME EVERYONE IS STARING AT US?
I'M SURE THEY'RE JUST BEING FRIENDLY, THAT'S ALL.
AND HOW COME THEY'RE WEARING SHORTS? IT'S FREEZING OUT HERE.
YEAH, CAN WE GO INSIDE?

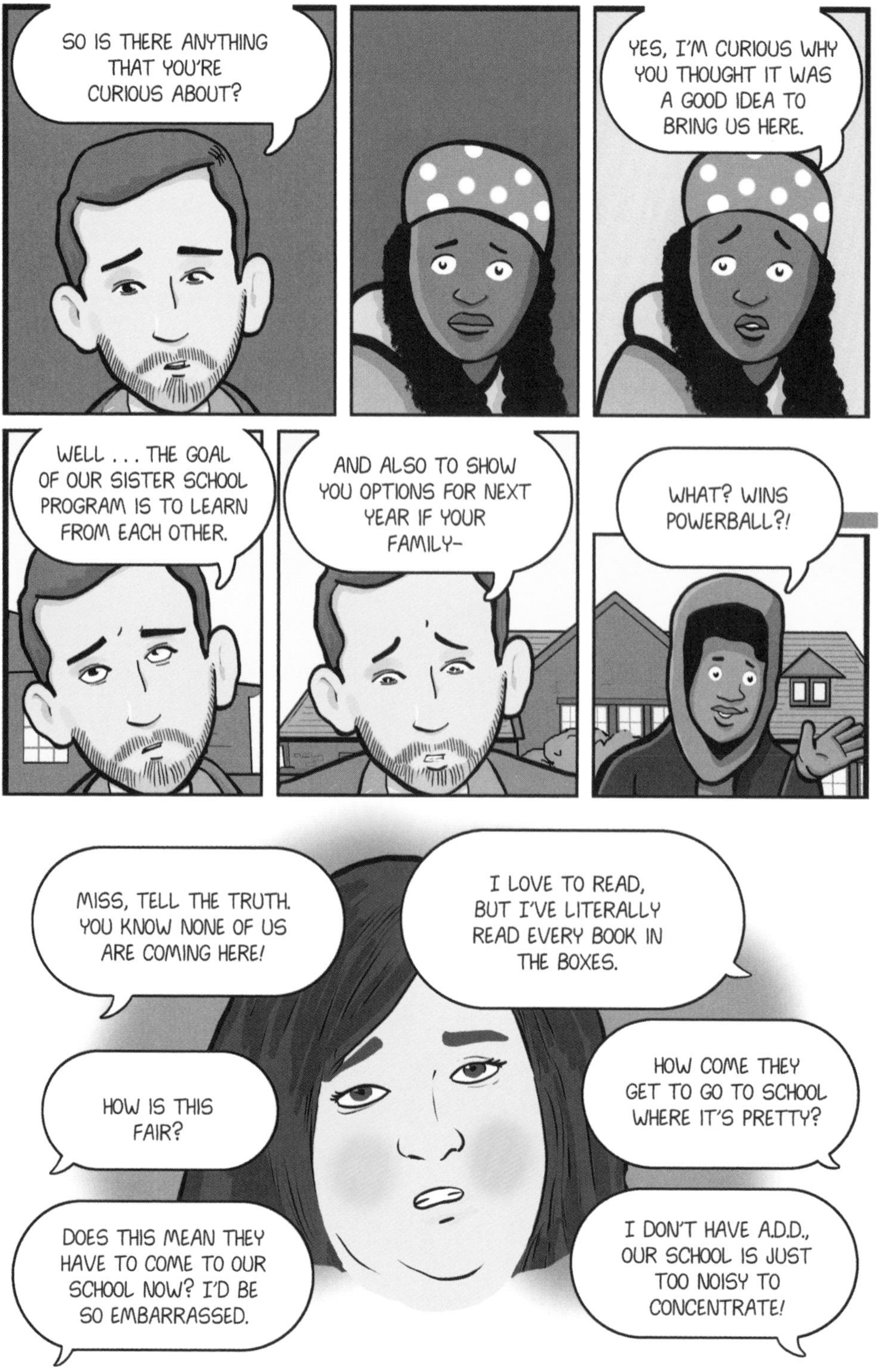
SO IS THERE ANYTHING THAT YOU'RE CURIOUS ABOUT?
YES, I'M CURIOUS WHY YOU THOUGHT IT WAS A GOOD IDEA TO BRING US HERE.
WELL . . . THE GOAL OF OUR SISTER SCHOOL PROGRAM IS TO LEARN FROM EACH OTHER.
AND ALSO TO SHOW YOU OPTIONS FOR NEXT YEAR IF YOUR FAMILY–
WHAT? WINS POWERBALL?!
MISS, TELL THE TRUTH. YOU KNOW NONE OF US ARE COMING HERE!
I LOVE TO READ, BUT I'VE LITERALLY READ EVERY BOOK IN THE BOXES.
HOW IS THIS FAIR?
HOW COME THEY GET TO GO TO SCHOOL WHERE IT'S PRETTY?
DOES THIS MEAN THEY HAVE TO COME TO OUR SCHOOL NOW? I'D BE SO EMBARRASSED.
I DON'T HAVE A.D.D., OUR SCHOOL IS JUST TOO NOISY TO CONCENTRATE!

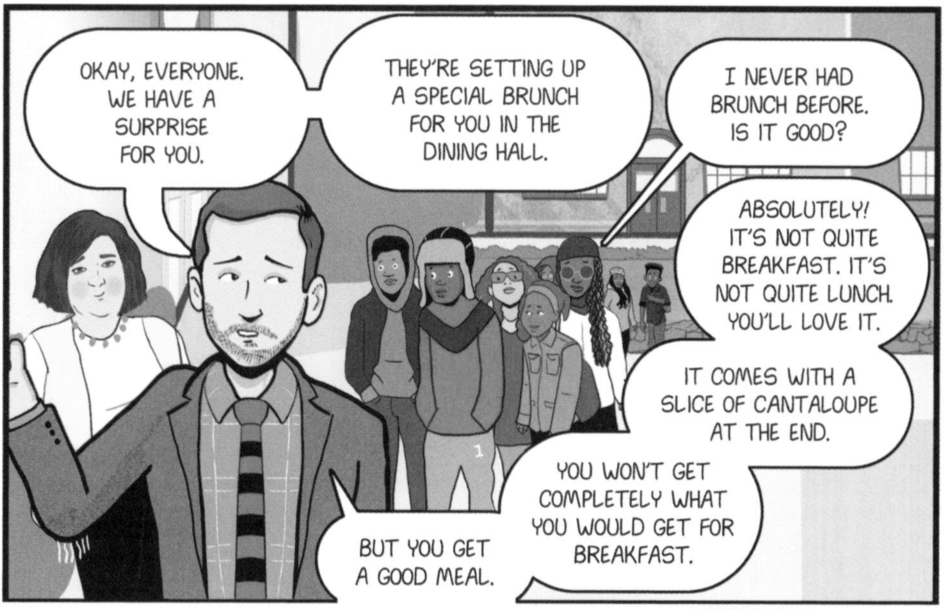
OKAY, EVERYONE. WE HAVE A SURPRISE FOR YOU.
THEY'RE SETTING UP A SPECIAL BRUNCH FOR YOU IN THE DINING HALL.
I NEVER HAD BRUNCH BEFORE. IS IT GOOD?
ABSOLUTELY! IT'S NOT QUITE BREAKFAST. IT'S NOT QUITE LUNCH. YOU'LL LOVE IT.
IT COMES WITH A SLICE OF CANTALOUPE AT THE END.
YOU WON'T GET COMPLETELY WHAT YOU WOULD GET FOR BREAKFAST.
BUT YOU GET A GOOD MEAL.

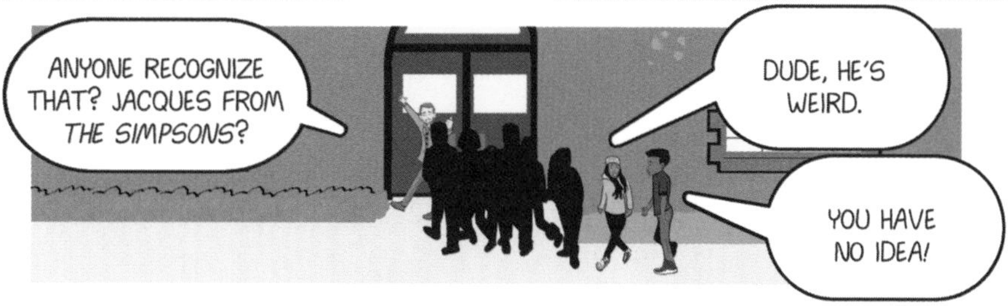
ANYONE RECOGNIZE THAT? JACQUES FROM *THE SIMPSONS*?
DUDE, HE'S WEIRD.
YOU HAVE NO IDEA!

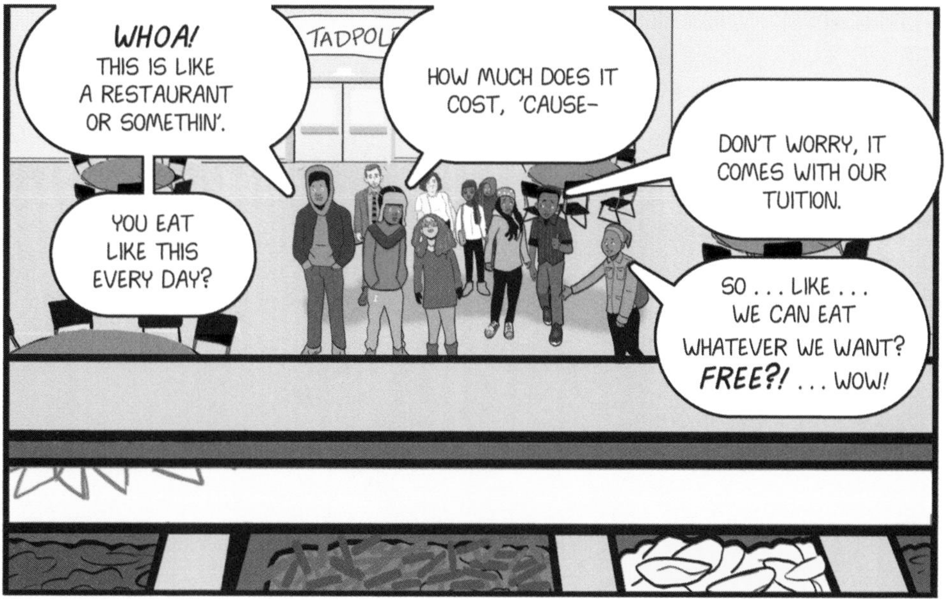
WHOA! THIS IS LIKE A RESTAURANT OR SOMETHIN'.
TADPOL
YOU EAT LIKE THIS EVERY DAY?
HOW MUCH DOES IT COST, 'CAUSE–
DON'T WORRY, IT COMES WITH OUR TUITION.
SO . . . LIKE . . . WE CAN EAT WHATEVER WE WANT? ***FREE?!*** . . . WOW!

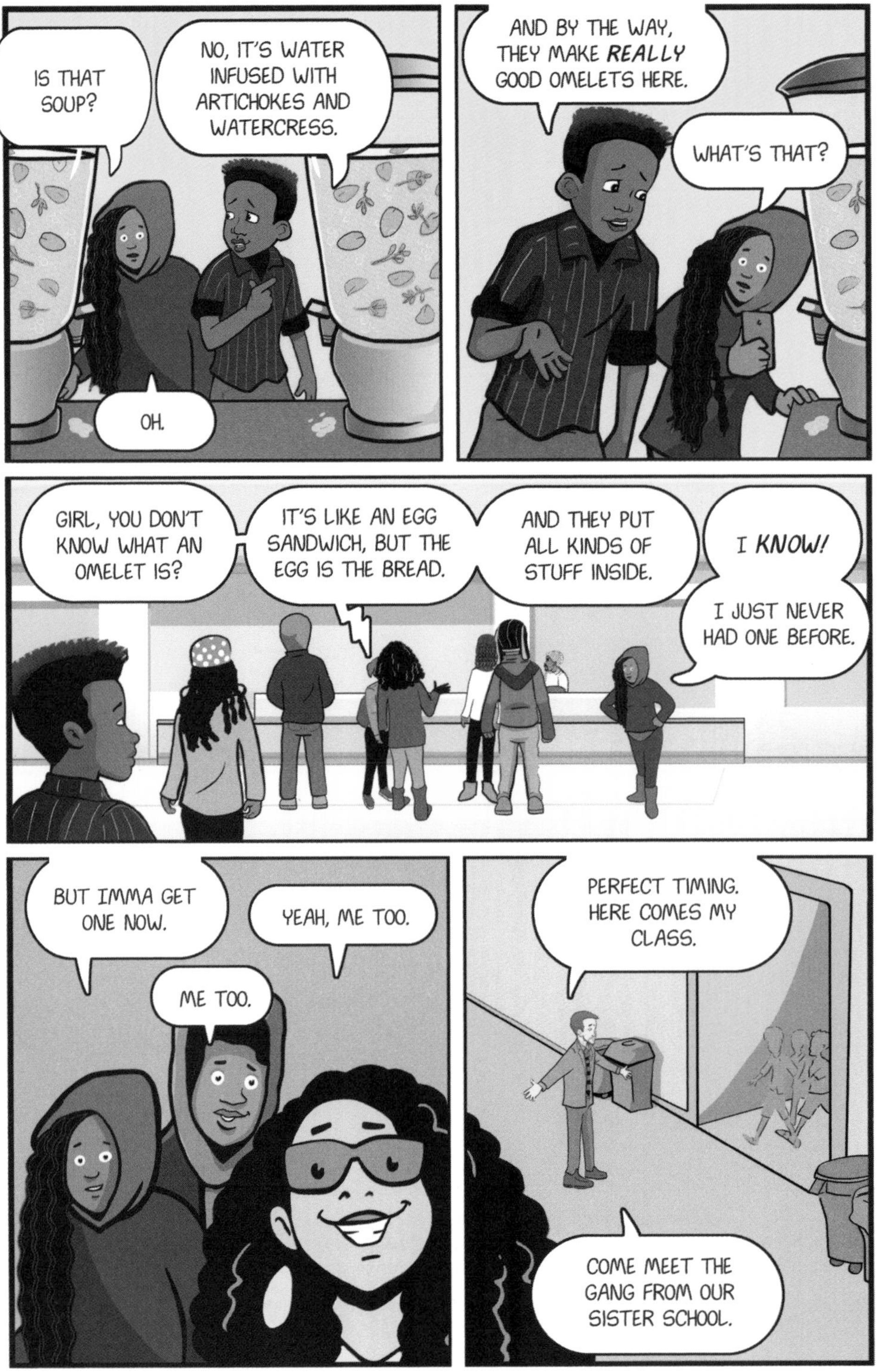
IS THAT SOUP?
NO, IT'S WATER INFUSED WITH ARTICHOKES AND WATERCRESS.
OH.
AND BY THE WAY, THEY MAKE **REALLY** GOOD OMELETS HERE.
WHAT'S THAT?
GIRL, YOU DON'T KNOW WHAT AN OMELET IS?
IT'S LIKE AN EGG SANDWICH, BUT THE EGG IS THE BREAD.
AND THEY PUT ALL KINDS OF STUFF INSIDE.
I **KNOW!**
I JUST NEVER HAD ONE BEFORE.
BUT IMMA GET ONE NOW.
YEAH, ME TOO.
ME TOO.
PERFECT TIMING. HERE COMES MY CLASS.
COME MEET THE GANG FROM OUR SISTER SCHOOL.

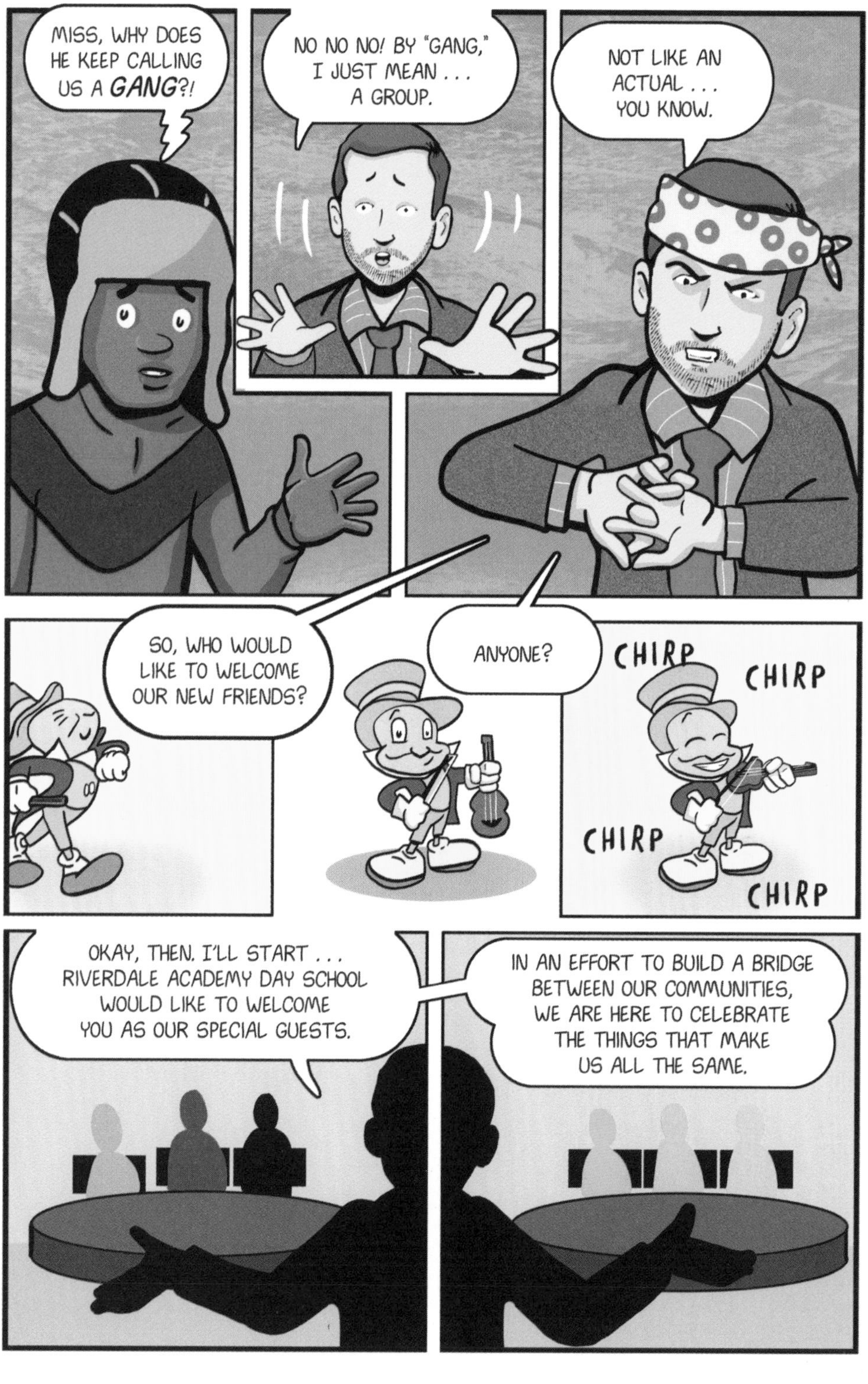
MISS, WHY DOES HE KEEP CALLING US A ***GANG***?!
NO NO NO! BY "GANG," I JUST MEAN . . . A GROUP.
NOT LIKE AN ACTUAL . . . YOU KNOW.
SO, WHO WOULD LIKE TO WELCOME OUR NEW FRIENDS?
ANYONE?
CHIRP
CHIRP
CHIRP
CHIRP
OKAY, THEN. I'LL START . . . RIVERDALE ACADEMY DAY SCHOOL WOULD LIKE TO WELCOME YOU AS OUR SPECIAL GUESTS.
IN AN EFFORT TO BUILD A BRIDGE BETWEEN OUR COMMUNITIES, WE ARE HERE TO CELEBRATE THE THINGS THAT MAKE US ALL THE SAME.

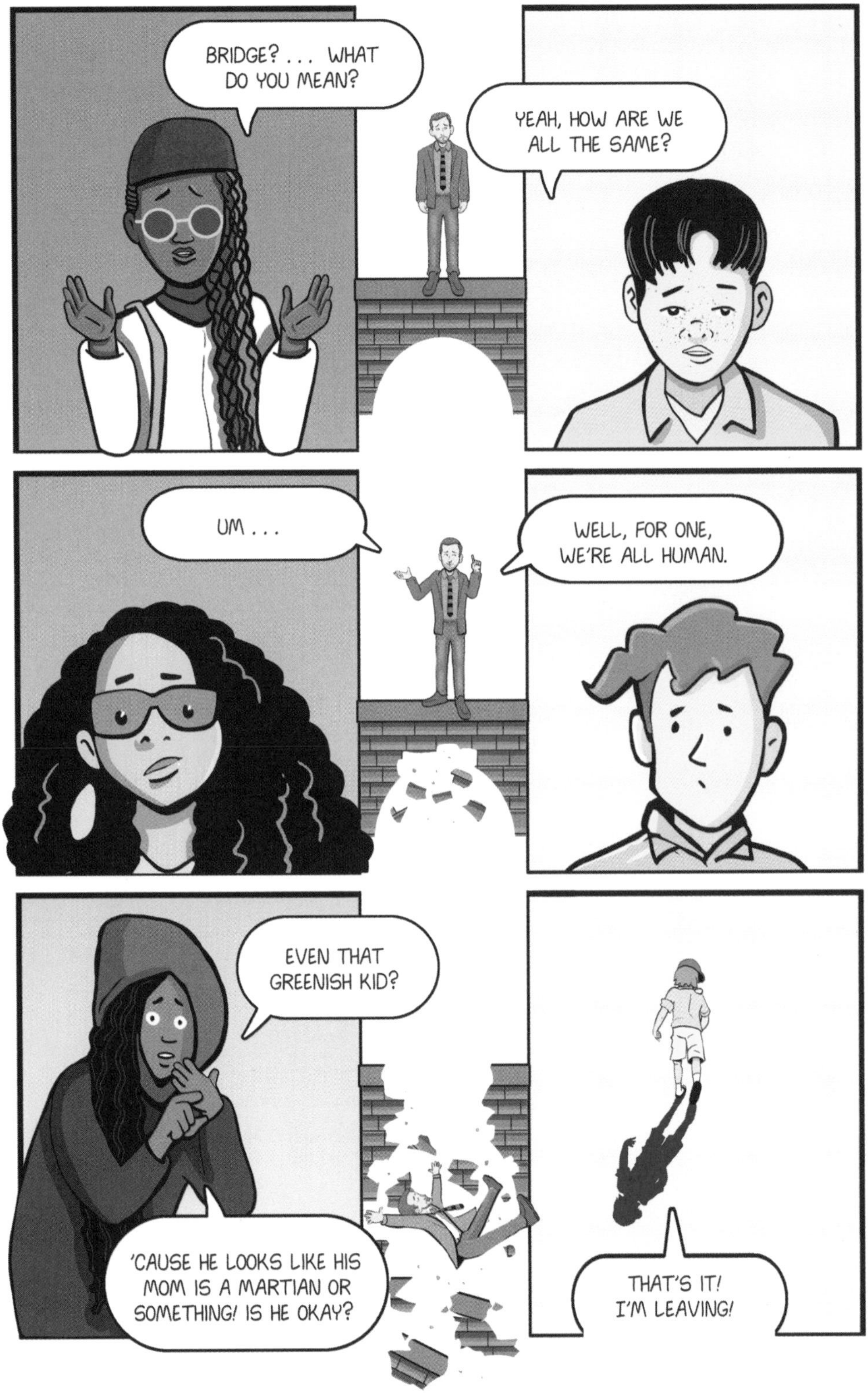
BRIDGE? . . . WHAT DO YOU MEAN?
YEAH, HOW ARE WE ALL THE SAME?
UM . . .
WELL, FOR ONE, WE'RE ALL HUMAN.
EVEN THAT GREENISH KID?
'CAUSE HE LOOKS LIKE HIS MOM IS A MARTIAN OR SOMETHING! IS HE OKAY?
THAT'S IT! I'M LEAVING!

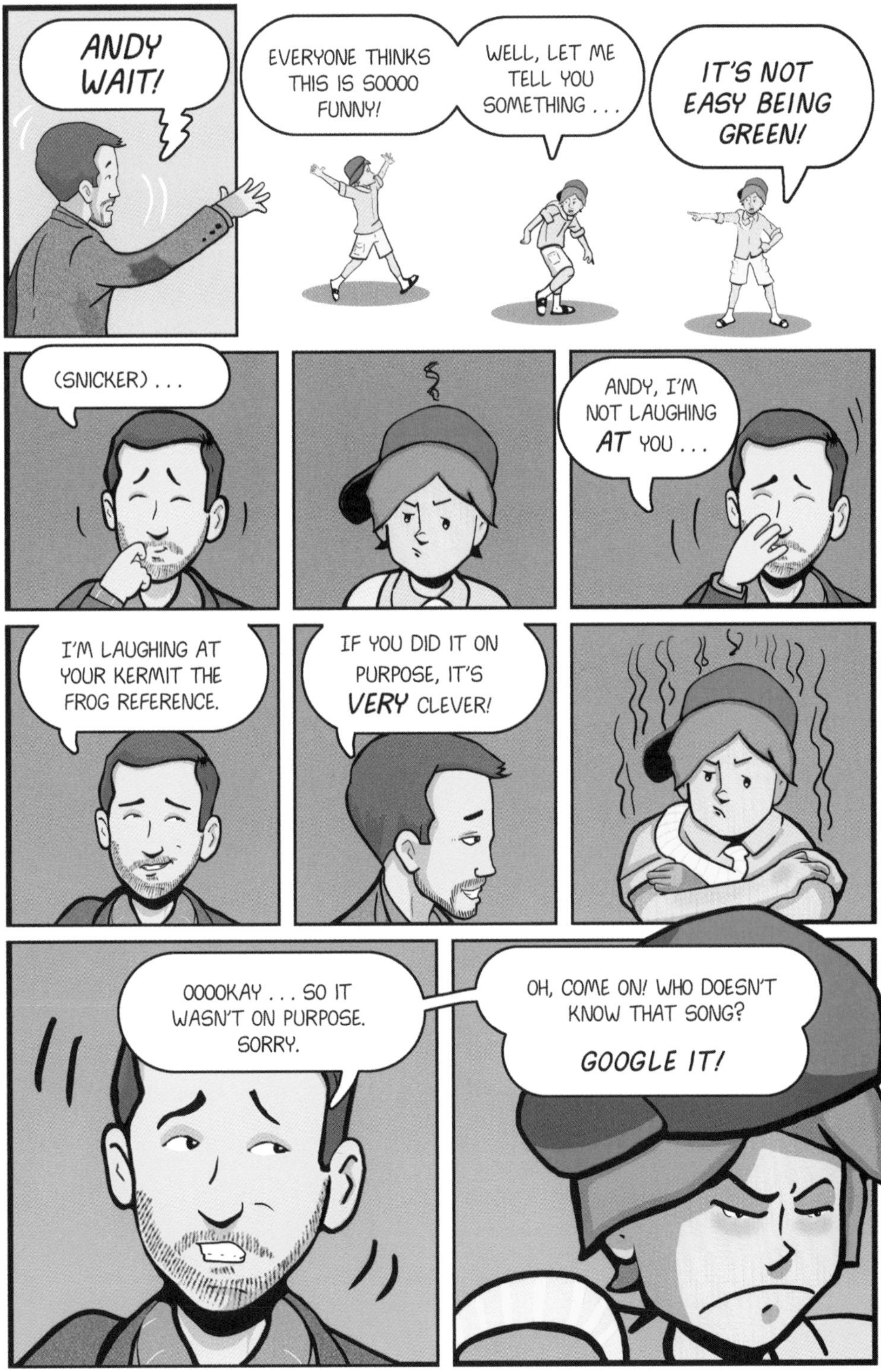
ANDY WAIT!
EVERYONE THINKS THIS IS SOOOO FUNNY!
WELL, LET ME TELL YOU SOMETHING . . .
IT'S NOT EASY BEING GREEN!
(SNICKER) . . .
ANDY, I'M NOT LAUGHING AT YOU . . .
I'M LAUGHING AT YOUR KERMIT THE FROG REFERENCE.
IF YOU DID IT ON PURPOSE, IT'S VERY CLEVER!
OOOOKAY . . . SO IT WASN'T ON PURPOSE. SORRY.
OH, COME ON! WHO DOESN'T KNOW THAT SONG?
GOOGLE IT!

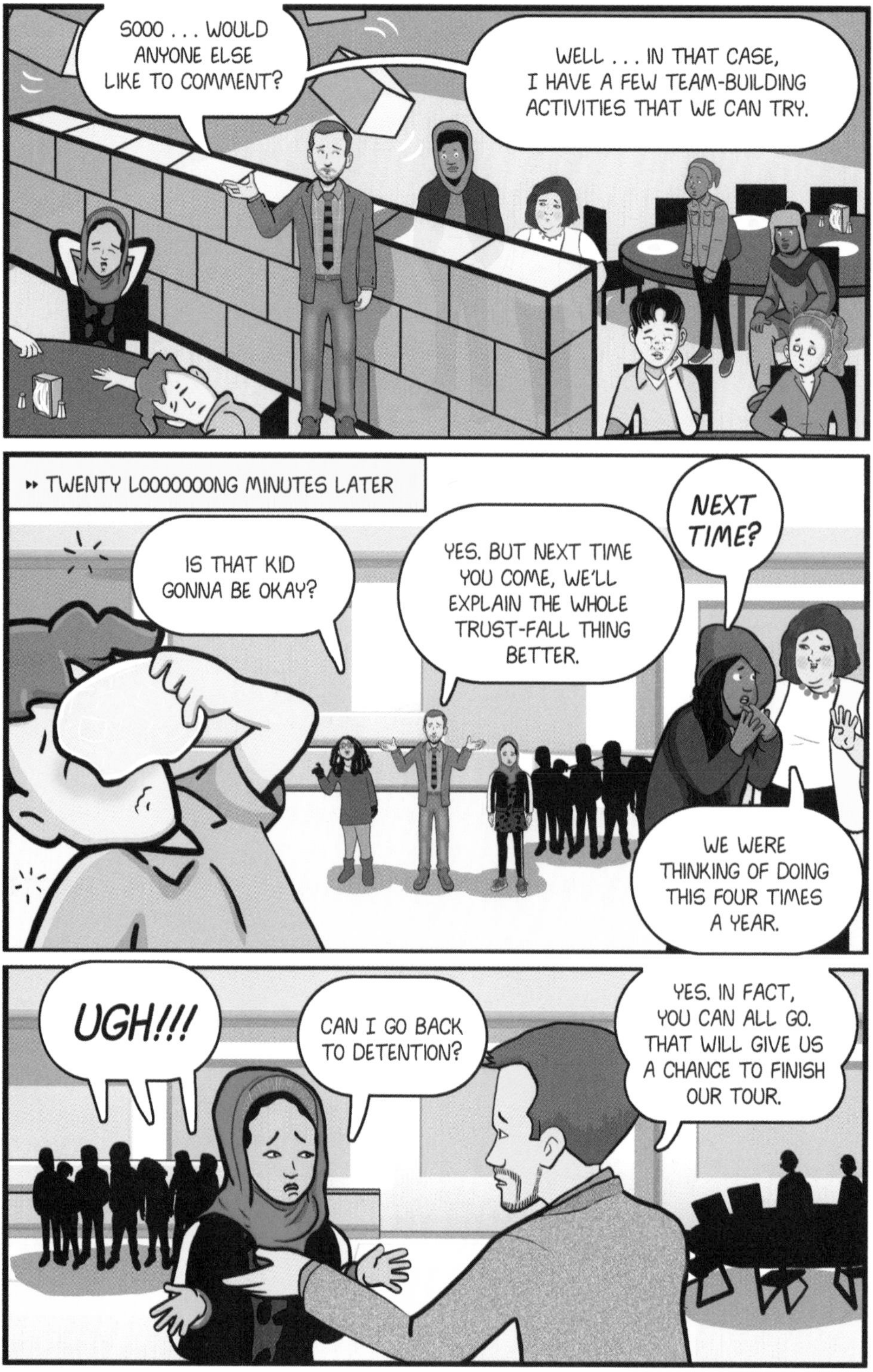
SOOO . . . WOULD ANYONE ELSE LIKE TO COMMENT?
WELL . . . IN THAT CASE, I HAVE A FEW TEAM-BUILDING ACTIVITIES THAT WE CAN TRY.
TWENTY LOOOOOOONG MINUTES LATER
IS THAT KID GONNA BE OKAY?
YES. BUT NEXT TIME YOU COME, WE'LL EXPLAIN THE WHOLE TRUST-FALL THING BETTER.
NEXT TIME?
WE WERE THINKING OF DOING THIS FOUR TIMES A YEAR.
UGH!!!
CAN I GO BACK TO DETENTION?
YES. IN FACT, YOU CAN ALL GO. THAT WILL GIVE US A CHANCE TO FINISH OUR TOUR.

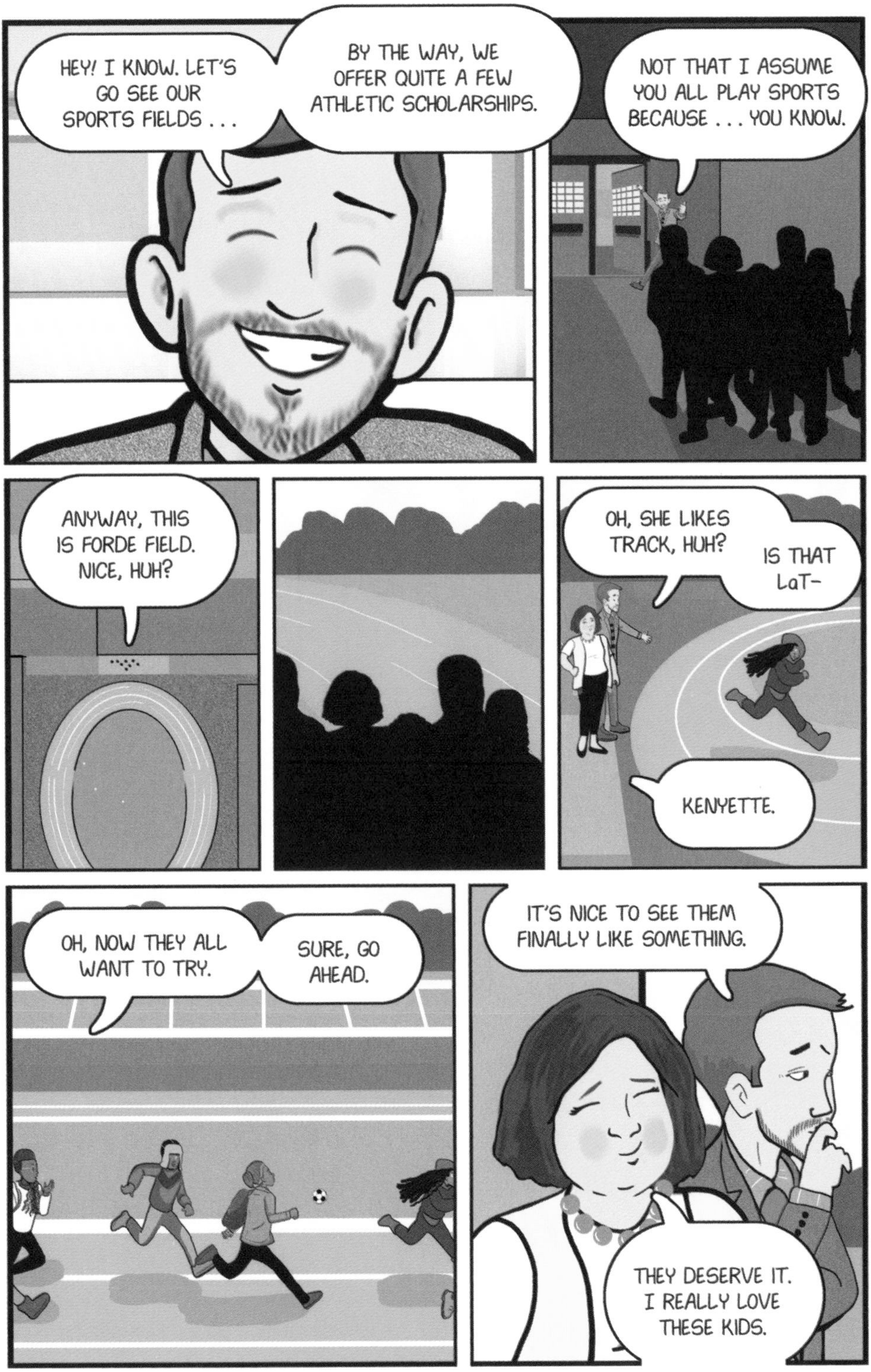
HEY! I KNOW. LET'S GO SEE OUR SPORTS FIELDS . . .
BY THE WAY, WE OFFER QUITE A FEW ATHLETIC SCHOLARSHIPS.
NOT THAT I ASSUME YOU ALL PLAY SPORTS BECAUSE . . . YOU KNOW.
ANYWAY, THIS IS FORDE FIELD. NICE, HUH?
OH, SHE LIKES TRACK, HUH?
IS THAT LaT-
KENYETTE.
OH, NOW THEY ALL WANT TO TRY.
SURE, GO AHEAD.
IT'S NICE TO SEE THEM FINALLY LIKE SOMETHING.
THEY DESERVE IT. I REALLY LOVE THESE KIDS.

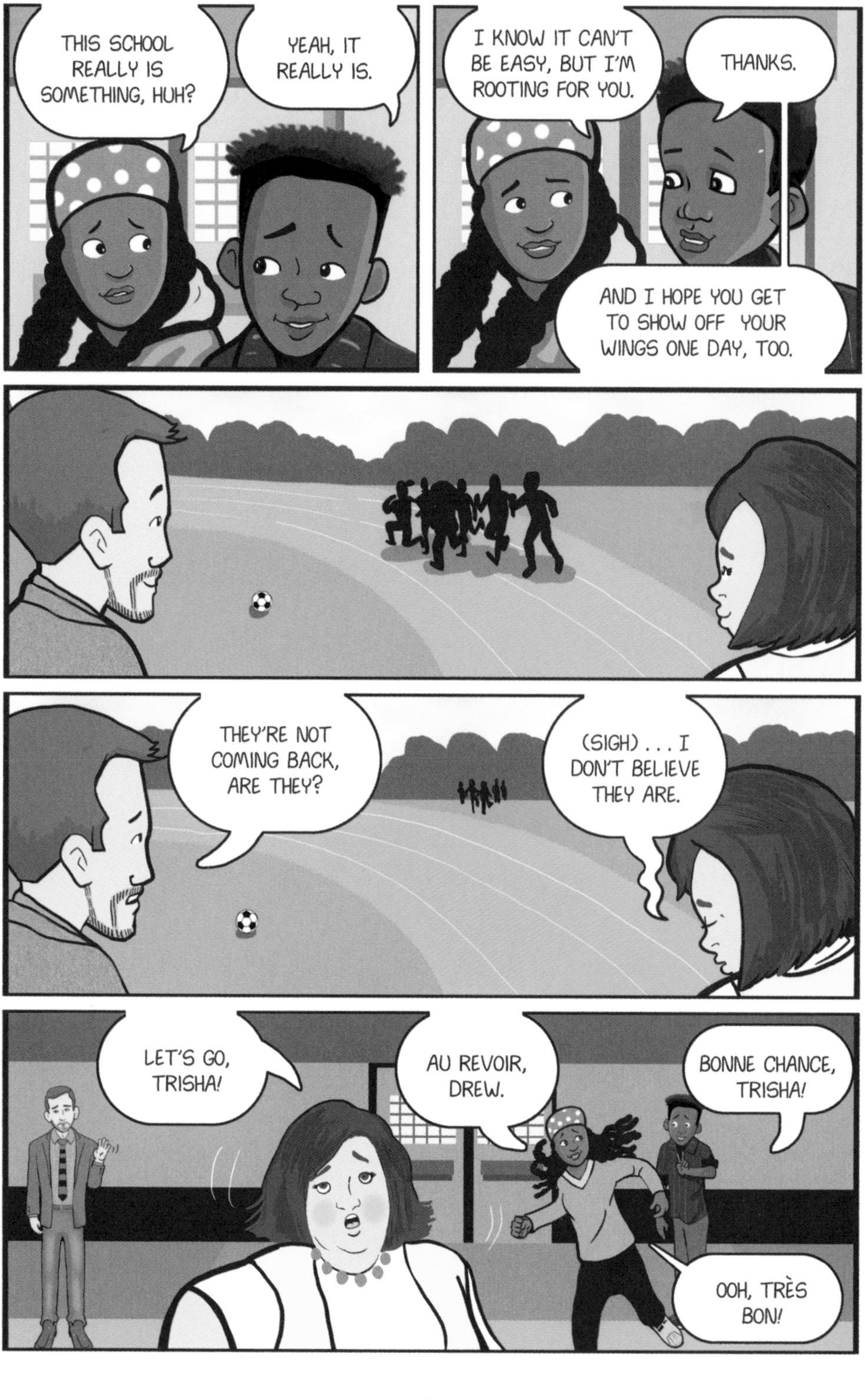
THIS SCHOOL REALLY IS SOMETHING, HUH?
YEAH, IT REALLY IS.
I KNOW IT CAN'T BE EASY, BUT I'M ROOTING FOR YOU.
THANKS.
AND I HOPE YOU GET TO SHOW OFF YOUR WINGS ONE DAY, TOO.
THEY'RE NOT COMING BACK, ARE THEY?
(SIGH) . . . I DON'T BELIEVE THEY ARE.
LET'S GO, TRISHA!
AU REVOIR, DREW.
BONNE CHANCE, TRISHA!
OOH, TRÈS BON!

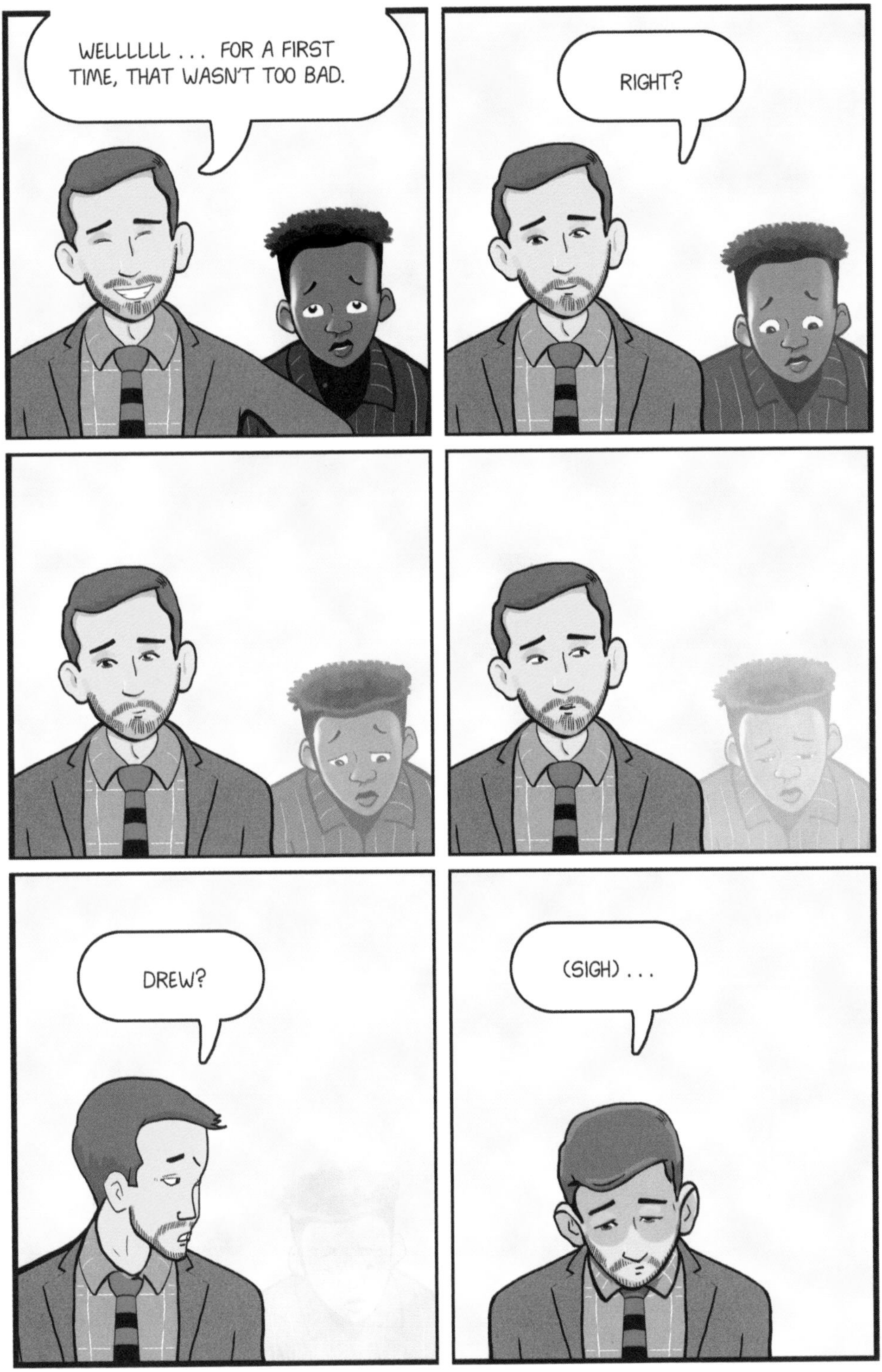
WELLLLLLL . . . FOR A FIRST TIME, THAT WASN'T TOO BAD.
RIGHT?
DREW?
(SIGH) . . .

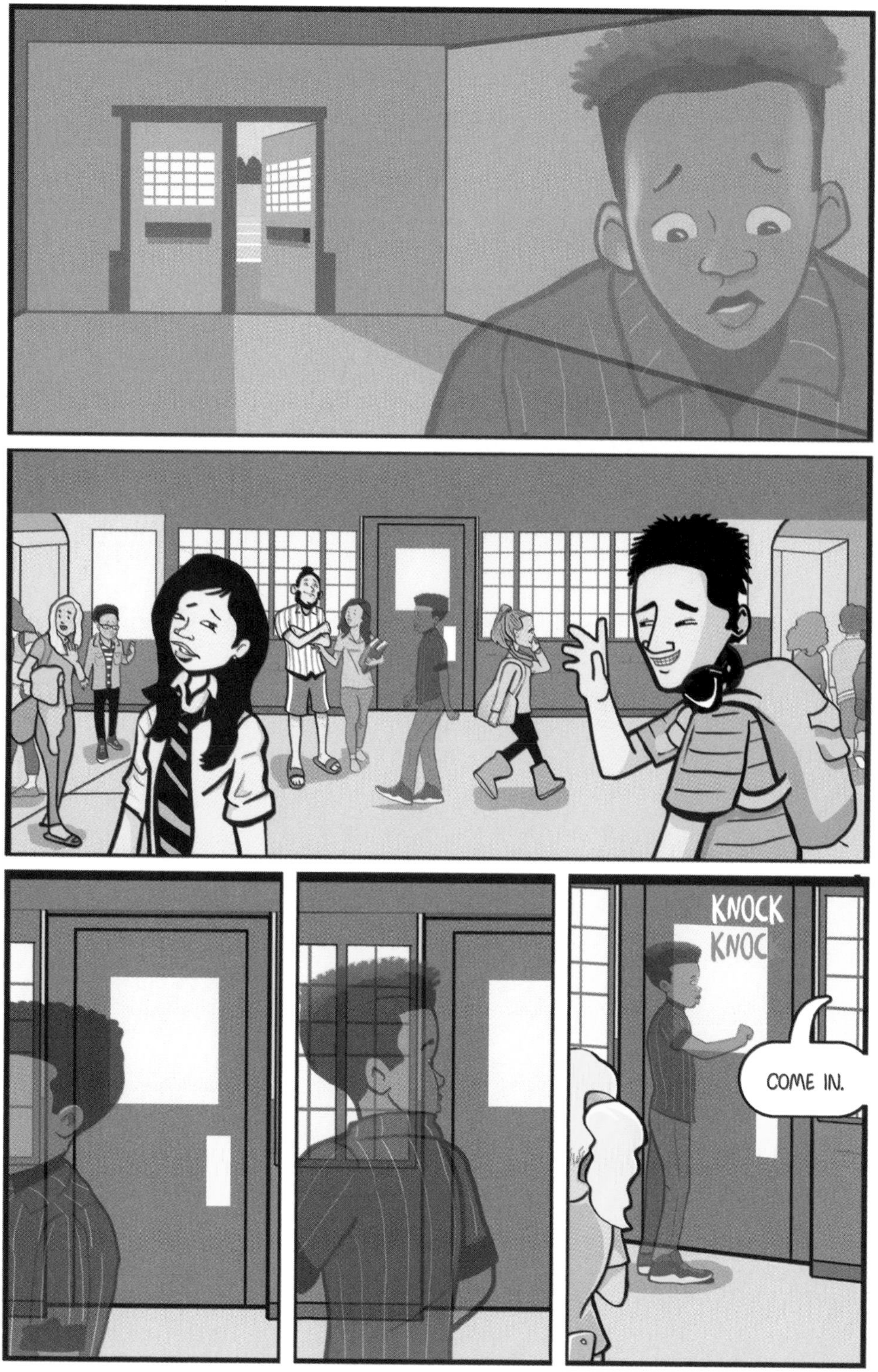
KNOCK
KNOCK
COME IN.

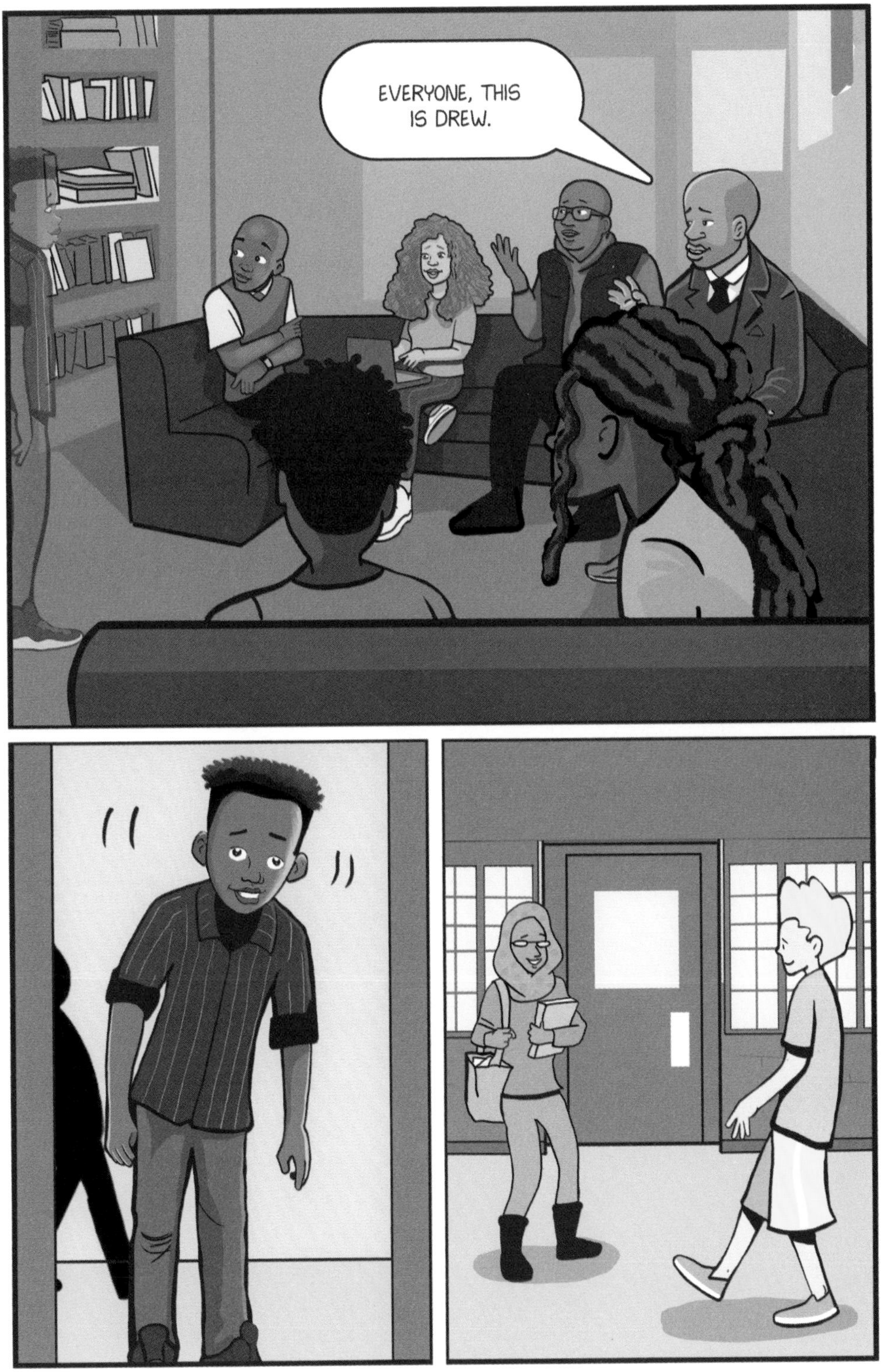
EVERYONE, THIS
IS DREW.

INVISIBLE
m.e.

CHAPTER
6

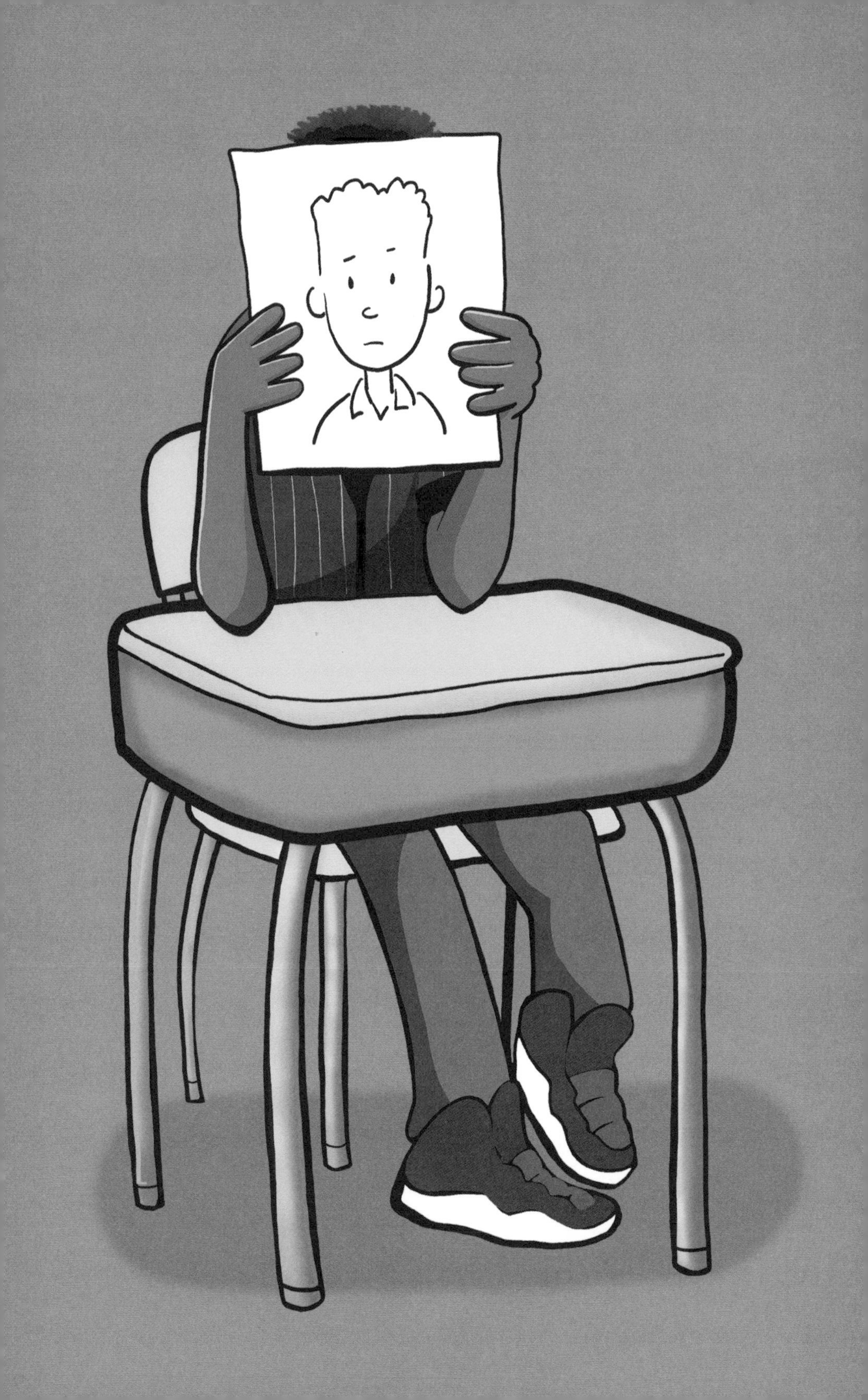

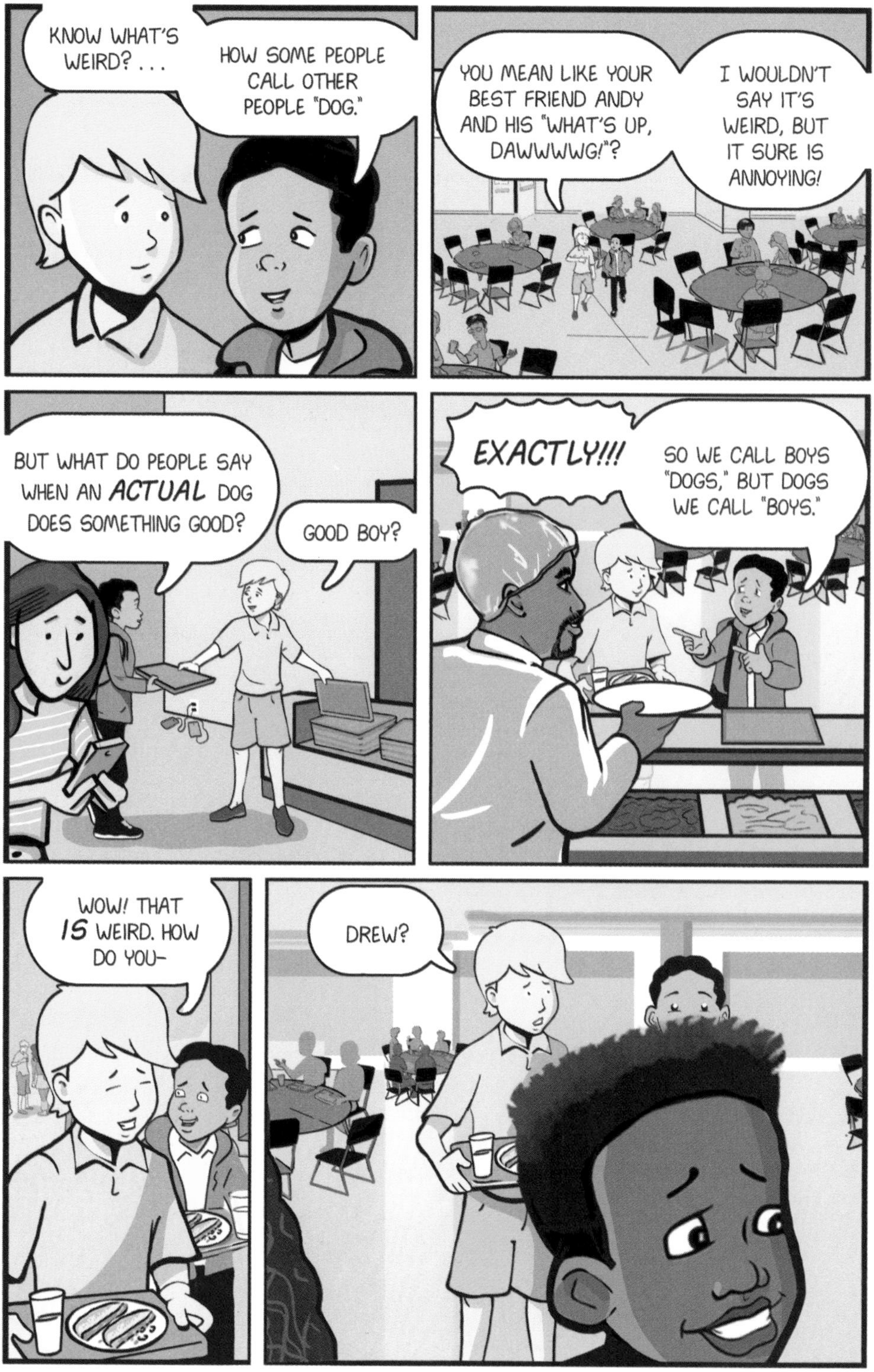
KNOW WHAT'S WEIRD? . . .
HOW SOME PEOPLE CALL OTHER PEOPLE "DOG."
YOU MEAN LIKE YOUR BEST FRIEND ANDY AND HIS "WHAT'S UP, DAWWWWG!"?
I WOULDN'T SAY IT'S WEIRD, BUT IT SURE IS ANNOYING!
BUT WHAT DO PEOPLE SAY WHEN AN ACTUAL DOG DOES SOMETHING GOOD?
GOOD BOY?
EXACTLY!!!
SO WE CALL BOYS "DOGS," BUT DOGS WE CALL "BOYS."
WOW! THAT IS WEIRD. HOW DO YOU-
DREW?

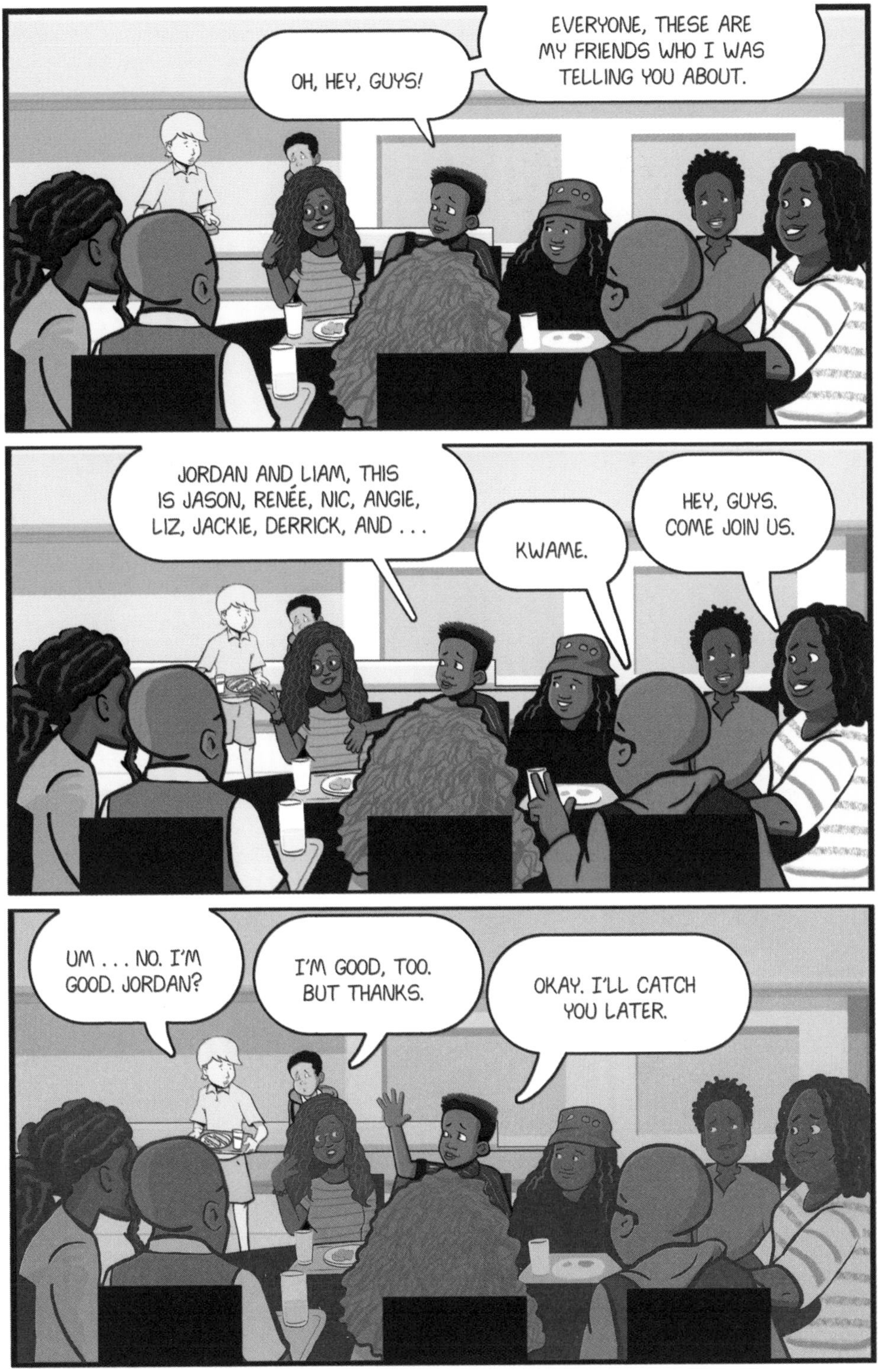
OH, HEY, GUYS!
EVERYONE, THESE ARE MY FRIENDS WHO I WAS TELLING YOU ABOUT.
JORDAN AND LIAM, THIS IS JASON, RENÉE, NIC, ANGIE, LIZ, JACKIE, DERRICK, AND . . .
KWAME.
HEY, GUYS. COME JOIN US.
UM . . . NO. I'M GOOD. JORDAN?
I'M GOOD, TOO. BUT THANKS.
OKAY. I'LL CATCH YOU LATER.

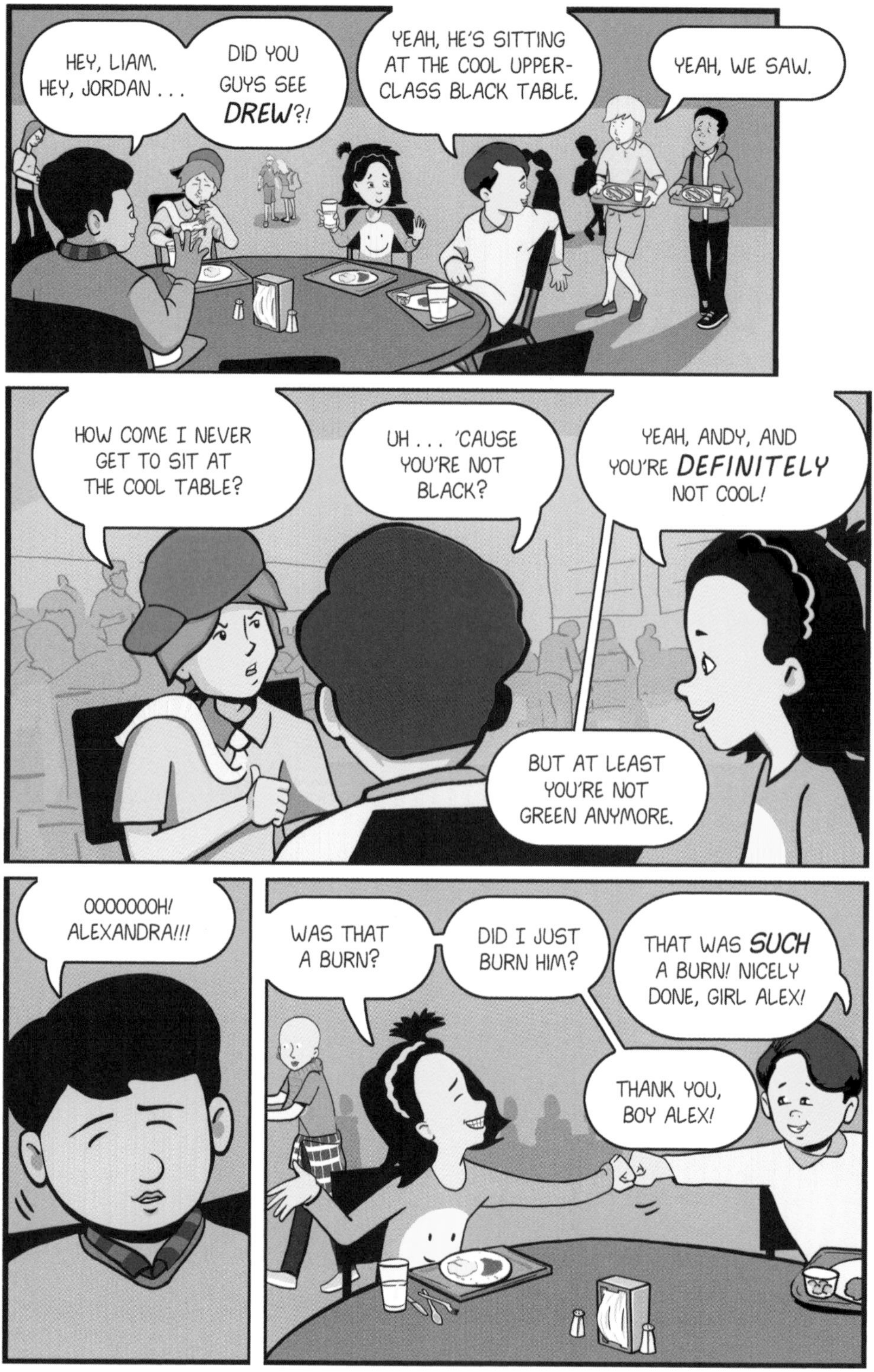
HEY, LIAM. HEY, JORDAN . . .
DID YOU GUYS SEE DREW?!
YEAH, HE'S SITTING AT THE COOL UPPER-CLASS BLACK TABLE.
YEAH, WE SAW.
HOW COME I NEVER GET TO SIT AT THE COOL TABLE?
UH . . . 'CAUSE YOU'RE NOT BLACK?
YEAH, ANDY, AND YOU'RE DEFINITELY NOT COOL!
BUT AT LEAST YOU'RE NOT GREEN ANYMORE.
OOOOOOOH! ALEXANDRA!!!
WAS THAT A BURN?
DID I JUST BURN HIM?
THAT WAS SUCH A BURN! NICELY DONE, GIRL ALEX!
THANK YOU, BOY ALEX!

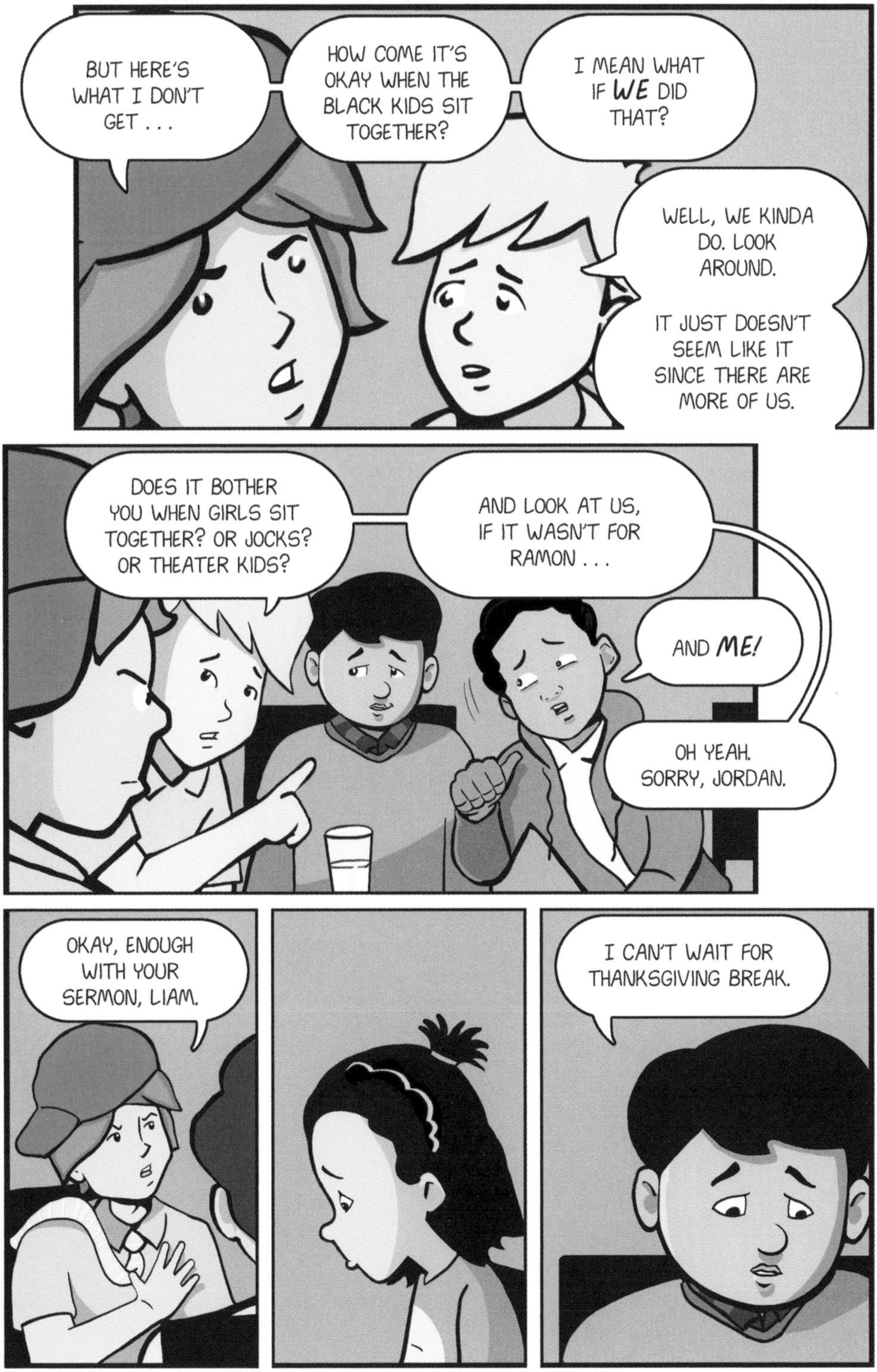
BUT HERE'S WHAT I DON'T GET . . .
HOW COME IT'S OKAY WHEN THE BLACK KIDS SIT TOGETHER?
I MEAN WHAT IF WE DID THAT?
WELL, WE KINDA DO. LOOK AROUND.
IT JUST DOESN'T SEEM LIKE IT SINCE THERE ARE MORE OF US.
DOES IT BOTHER YOU WHEN GIRLS SIT TOGETHER? OR JOCKS? OR THEATER KIDS?
AND LOOK AT US, IF IT WASN'T FOR RAMON . . .
AND ME!
OH YEAH. SORRY, JORDAN.
OKAY, ENOUGH WITH YOUR SERMON, LIAM.
I CAN'T WAIT FOR THANKSGIVING BREAK.

104

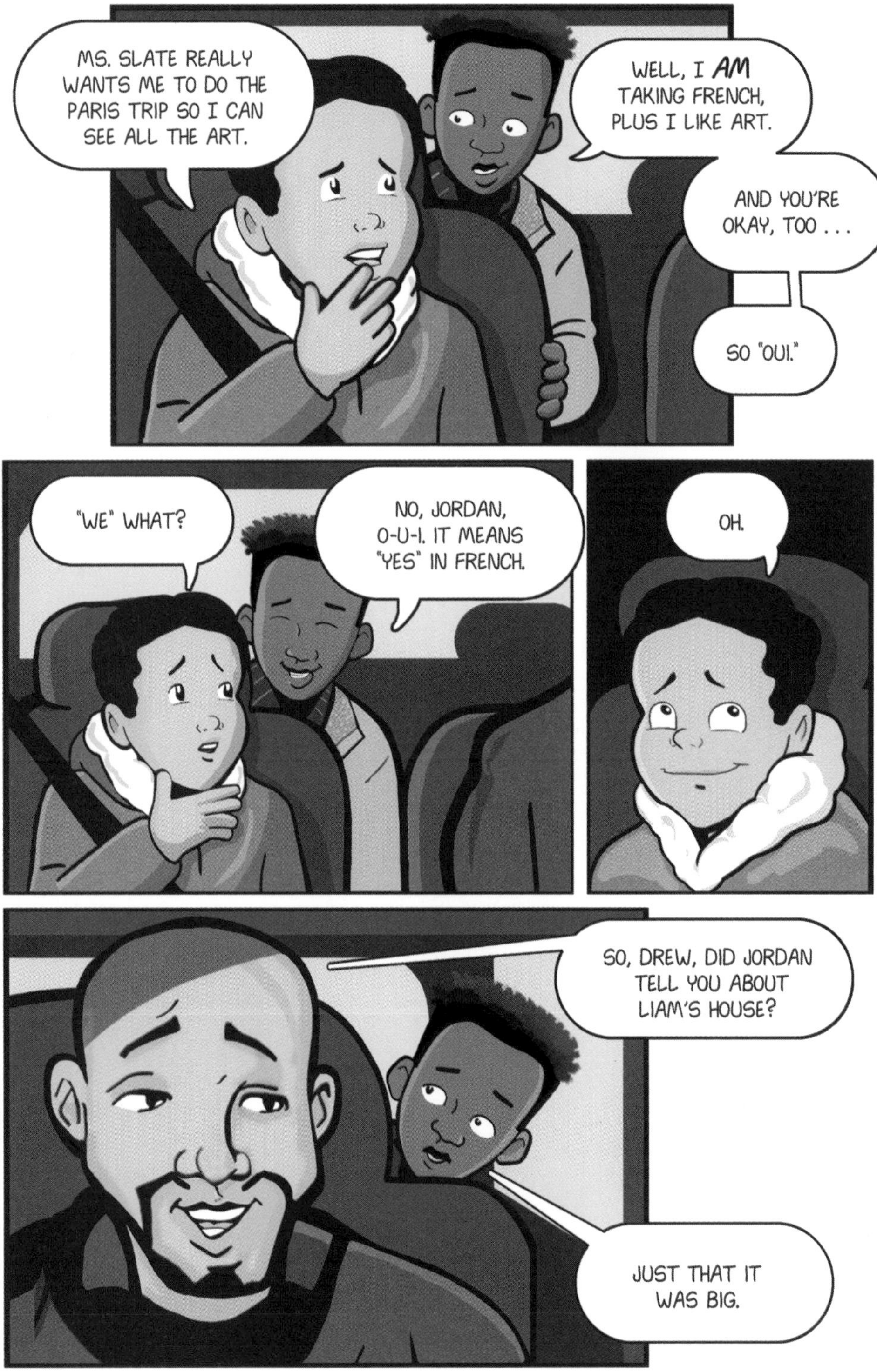
MS. SLATE REALLY WANTS ME TO DO THE PARIS TRIP SO I CAN SEE ALL THE ART.
WELL, I *AM* TAKING FRENCH, PLUS I LIKE ART.
AND YOU'RE OKAY, TOO . . .
SO "OUI."
"WE" WHAT?
NO, JORDAN, O-U-I. IT MEANS "YES" IN FRENCH.
OH.
SO, DREW, DID JORDAN TELL YOU ABOUT LIAM'S HOUSE?
JUST THAT IT WAS BIG.

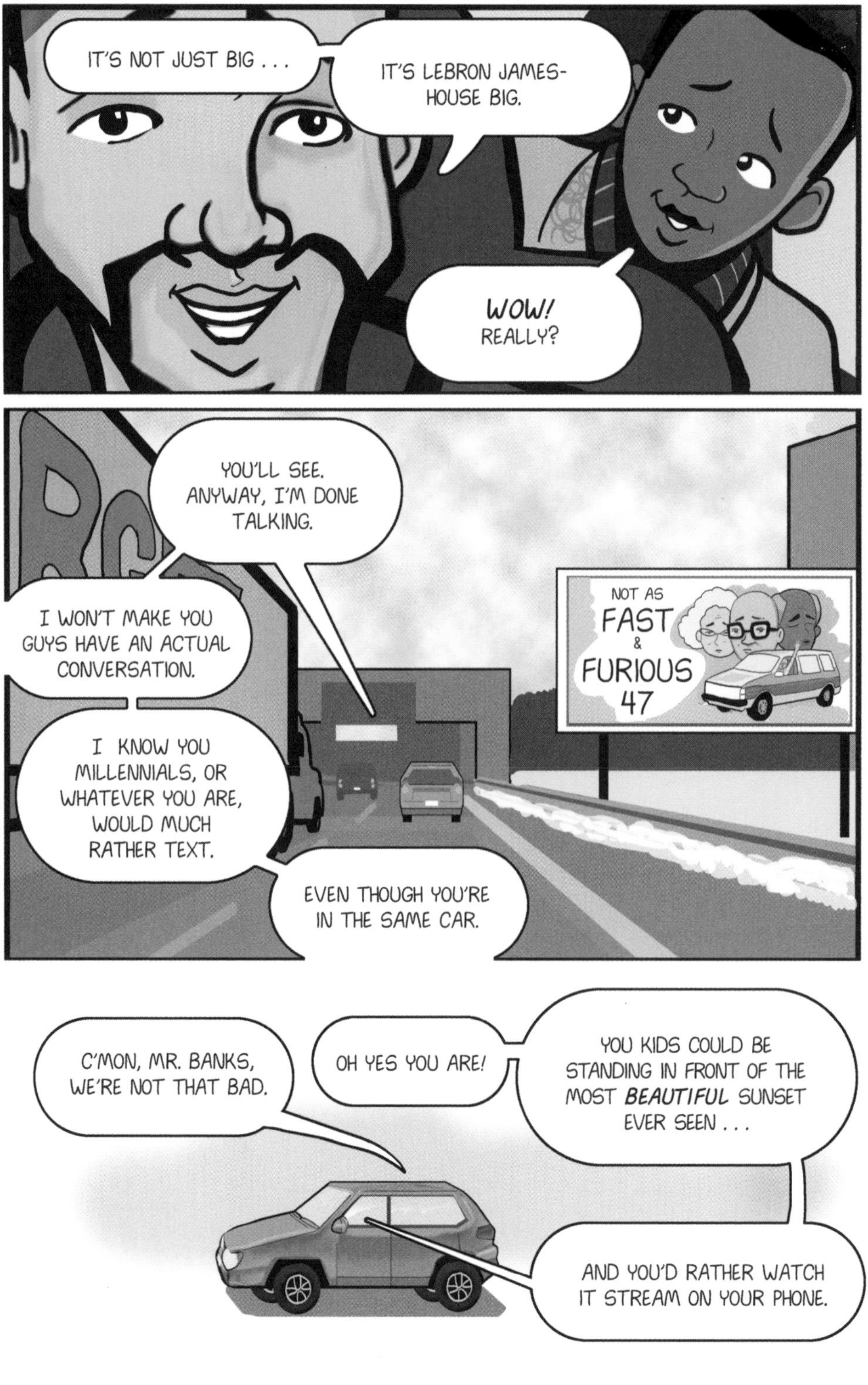
IT'S NOT JUST BIG . . .
IT'S LEBRON JAMES-HOUSE BIG.
WOW! REALLY?
YOU'LL SEE. ANYWAY, I'M DONE TALKING.
I WON'T MAKE YOU GUYS HAVE AN ACTUAL CONVERSATION.
I KNOW YOU MILLENNIALS, OR WHATEVER YOU ARE, WOULD MUCH RATHER TEXT.
EVEN THOUGH YOU'RE IN THE SAME CAR.
NOT AS FAST & FURIOUS 47
C'MON, MR. BANKS, WE'RE NOT THAT BAD.
OH YES YOU ARE!
YOU KIDS COULD BE STANDING IN FRONT OF THE MOST BEAUTIFUL SUNSET EVER SEEN . . .
AND YOU'D RATHER WATCH IT STREAM ON YOUR PHONE.

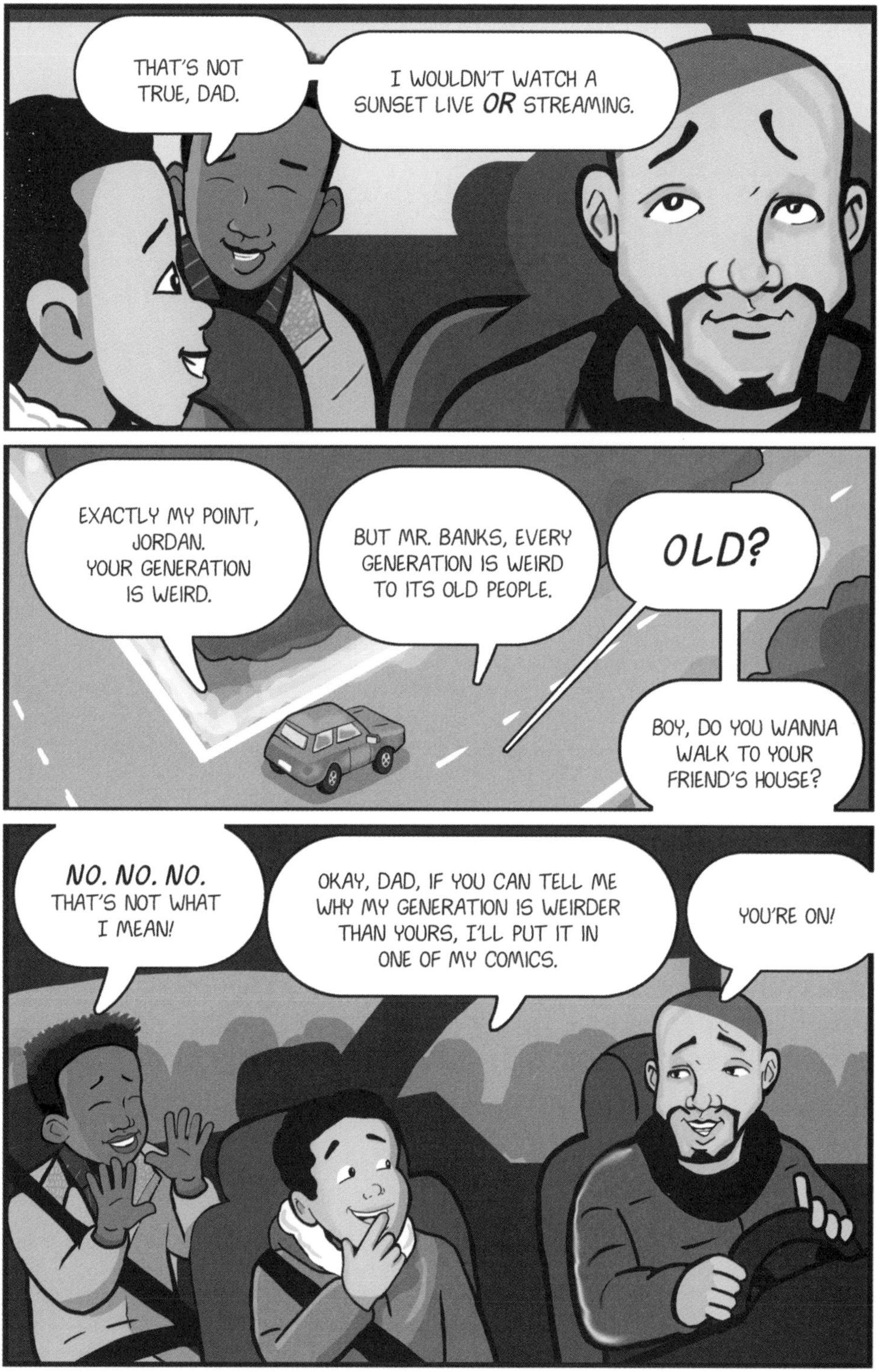
THAT'S NOT TRUE, DAD.
I WOULDN'T WATCH A SUNSET LIVE *OR* STREAMING.
EXACTLY MY POINT, JORDAN. YOUR GENERATION IS WEIRD.
BUT MR. BANKS, EVERY GENERATION IS WEIRD TO ITS OLD PEOPLE.
OLD?
BOY, DO YOU WANNA WALK TO YOUR FRIEND'S HOUSE?
NO. NO. NO. THAT'S NOT WHAT I MEAN!
OKAY, DAD, IF YOU CAN TELL ME WHY MY GENERATION IS WEIRDER THAN YOURS, I'LL PUT IT IN ONE OF MY COMICS.
YOU'RE ON!

I Lost the Bet

written by Chuck Banks   art by Jordan Banks

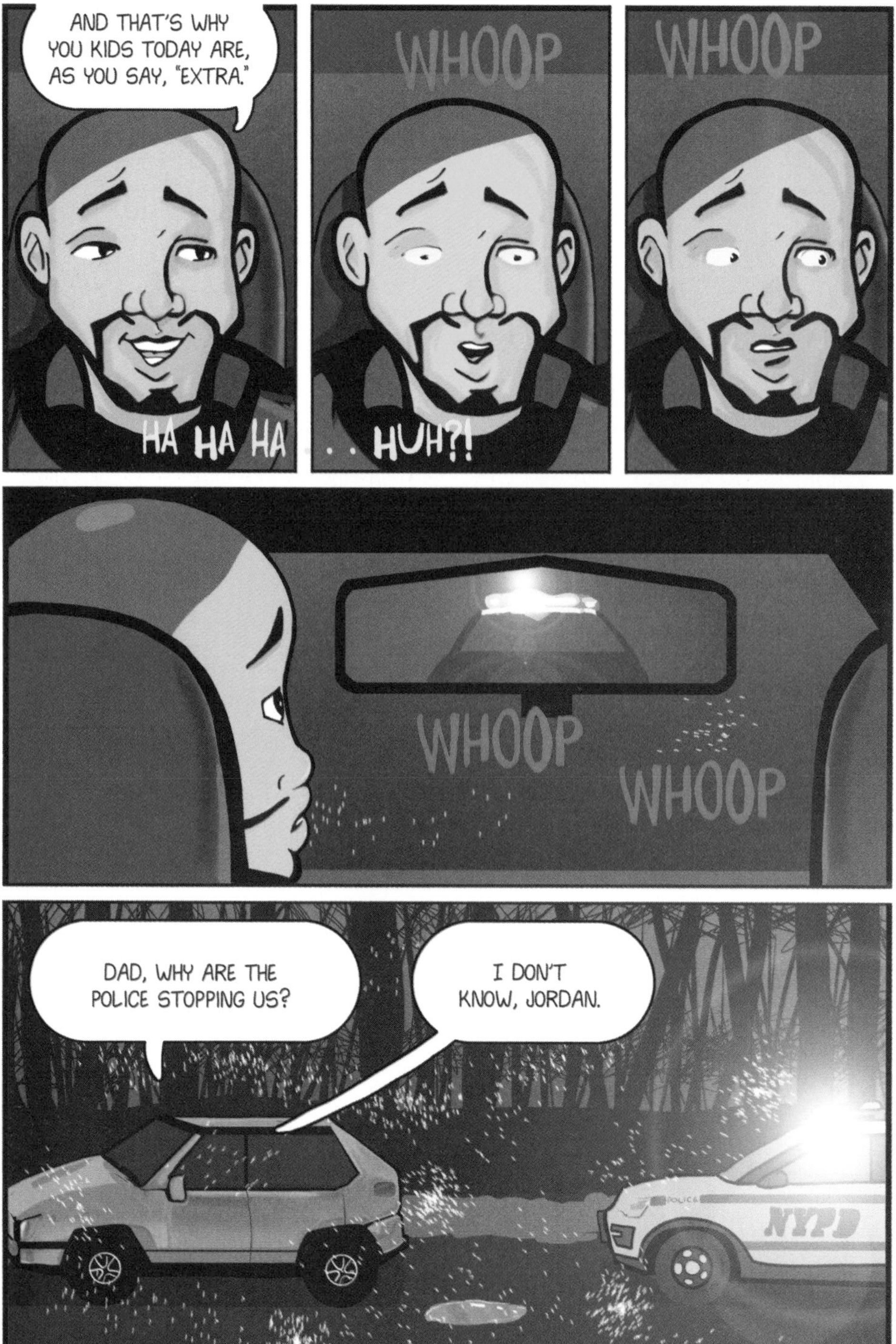
AND THAT'S WHY YOU KIDS TODAY ARE, AS YOU SAY, "EXTRA."
HA HA HA . . .
WHOOP
HUH?!
WHOOP
WHOOP
WHOOP
DAD, WHY ARE THE POLICE STOPPING US?
I DON'T KNOW, JORDAN.
NYPD
POLICE

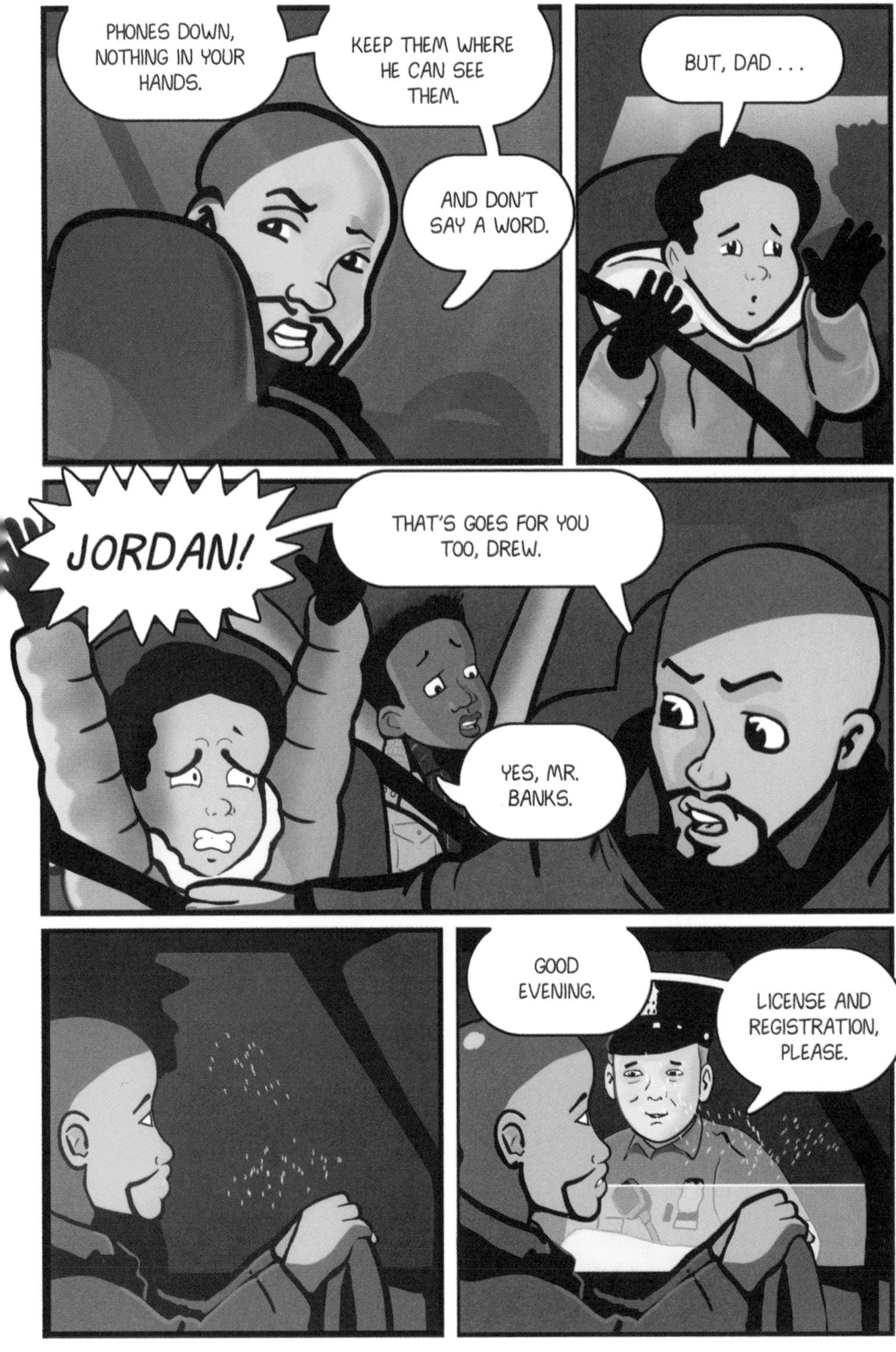
PHONES DOWN, NOTHING IN YOUR HANDS.
KEEP THEM WHERE HE CAN SEE THEM.
AND DON'T SAY A WORD.
BUT, DAD . . .
JORDAN!
THAT'S GOES FOR YOU TOO, DREW.
YES, MR. BANKS.
GOOD EVENING.
LICENSE AND REGISTRATION, PLEASE.

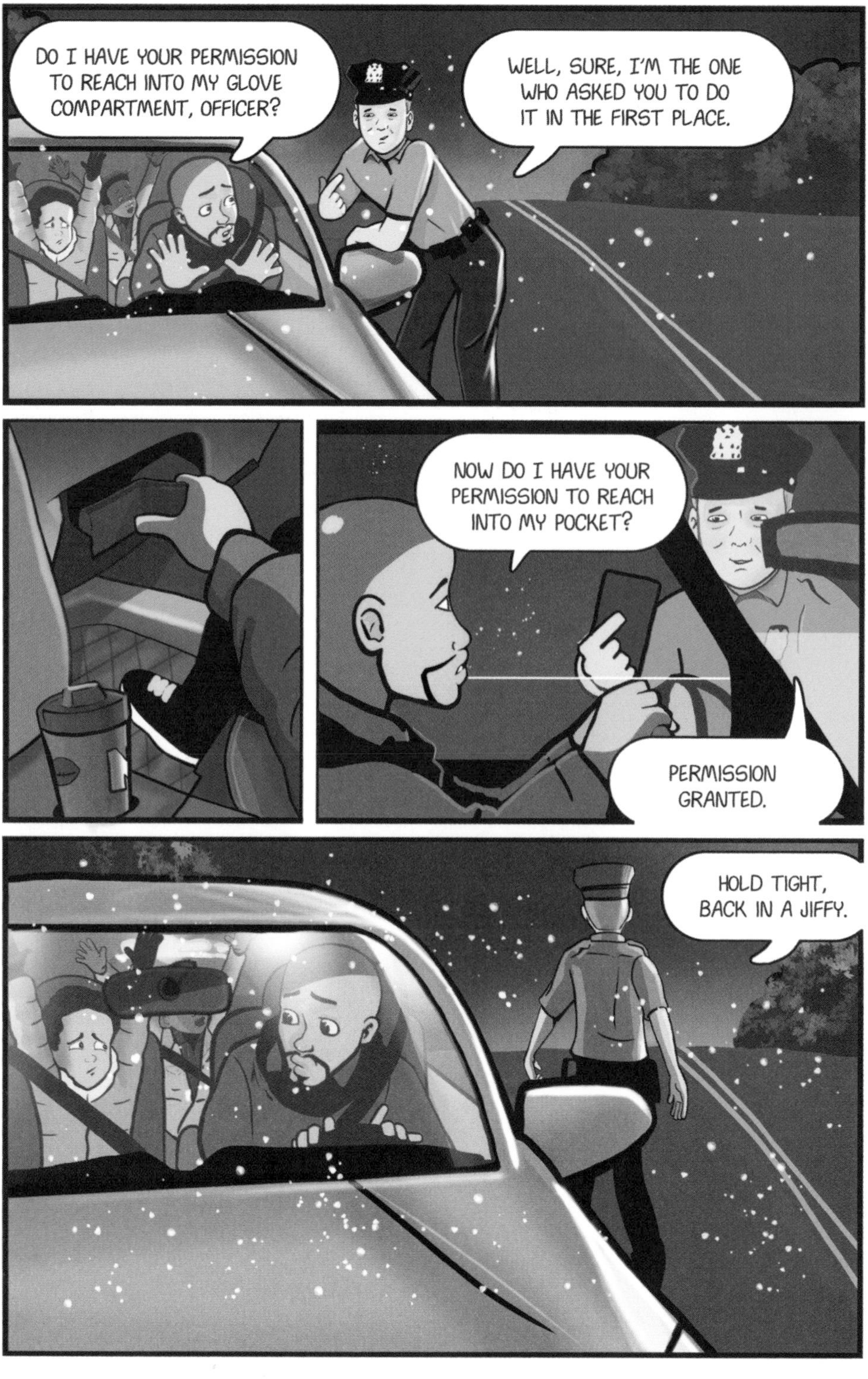
DO I HAVE YOUR PERMISSION TO REACH INTO MY GLOVE COMPARTMENT, OFFICER?
WELL, SURE, I'M THE ONE WHO ASKED YOU TO DO IT IN THE FIRST PLACE.
NOW DO I HAVE YOUR PERMISSION TO REACH INTO MY POCKET?
PERMISSION GRANTED.
HOLD TIGHT, BACK IN A JIFFY.

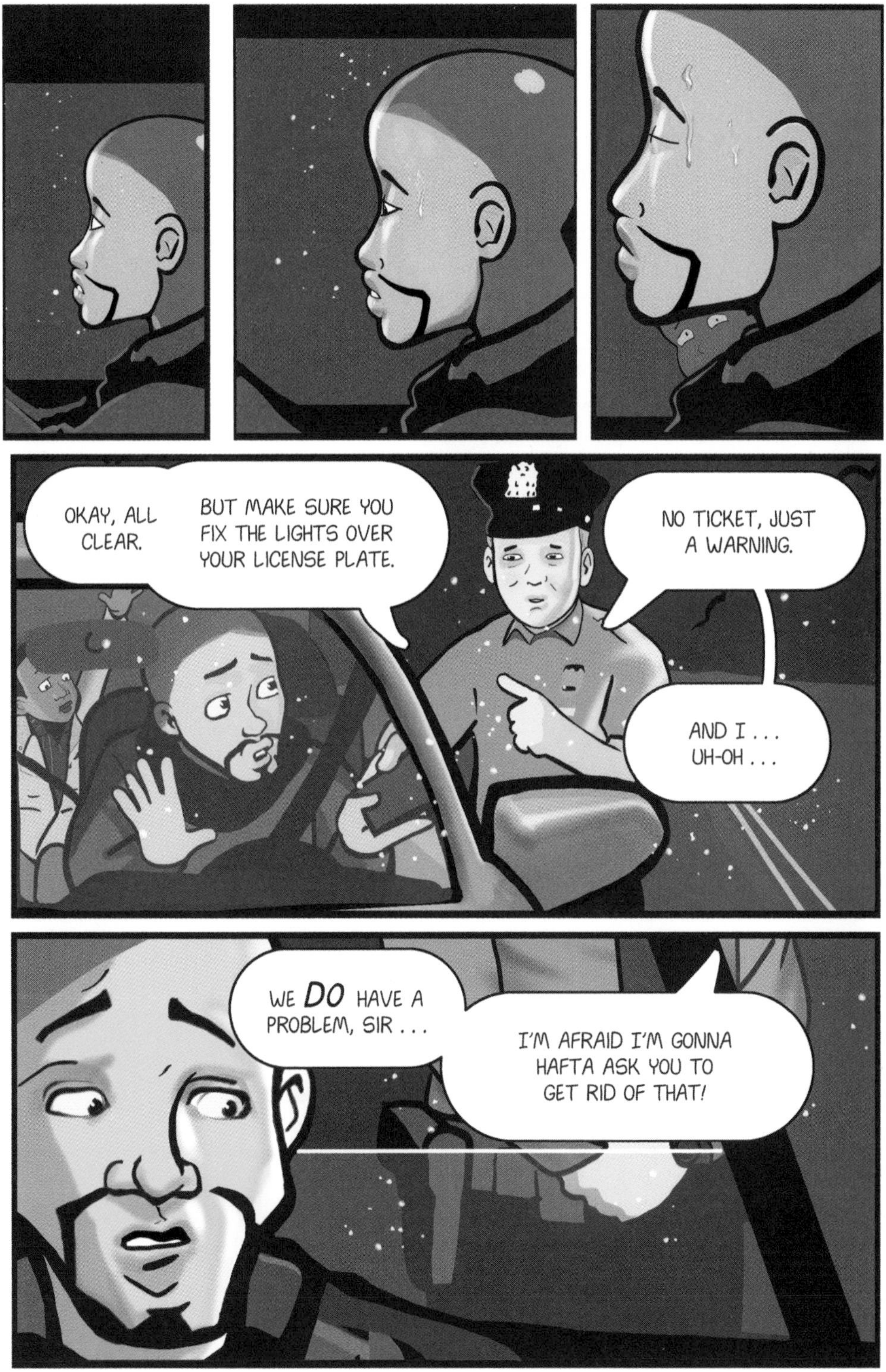

OKAY, ALL CLEAR.
BUT MAKE SURE YOU FIX THE LIGHTS OVER YOUR LICENSE PLATE.
NO TICKET, JUST A WARNING.
AND I . . . UH-OH . . .
WE DO HAVE A PROBLEM, SIR . . .
I'M AFRAID I'M GONNA HAFTA ASK YOU TO GET RID OF THAT!

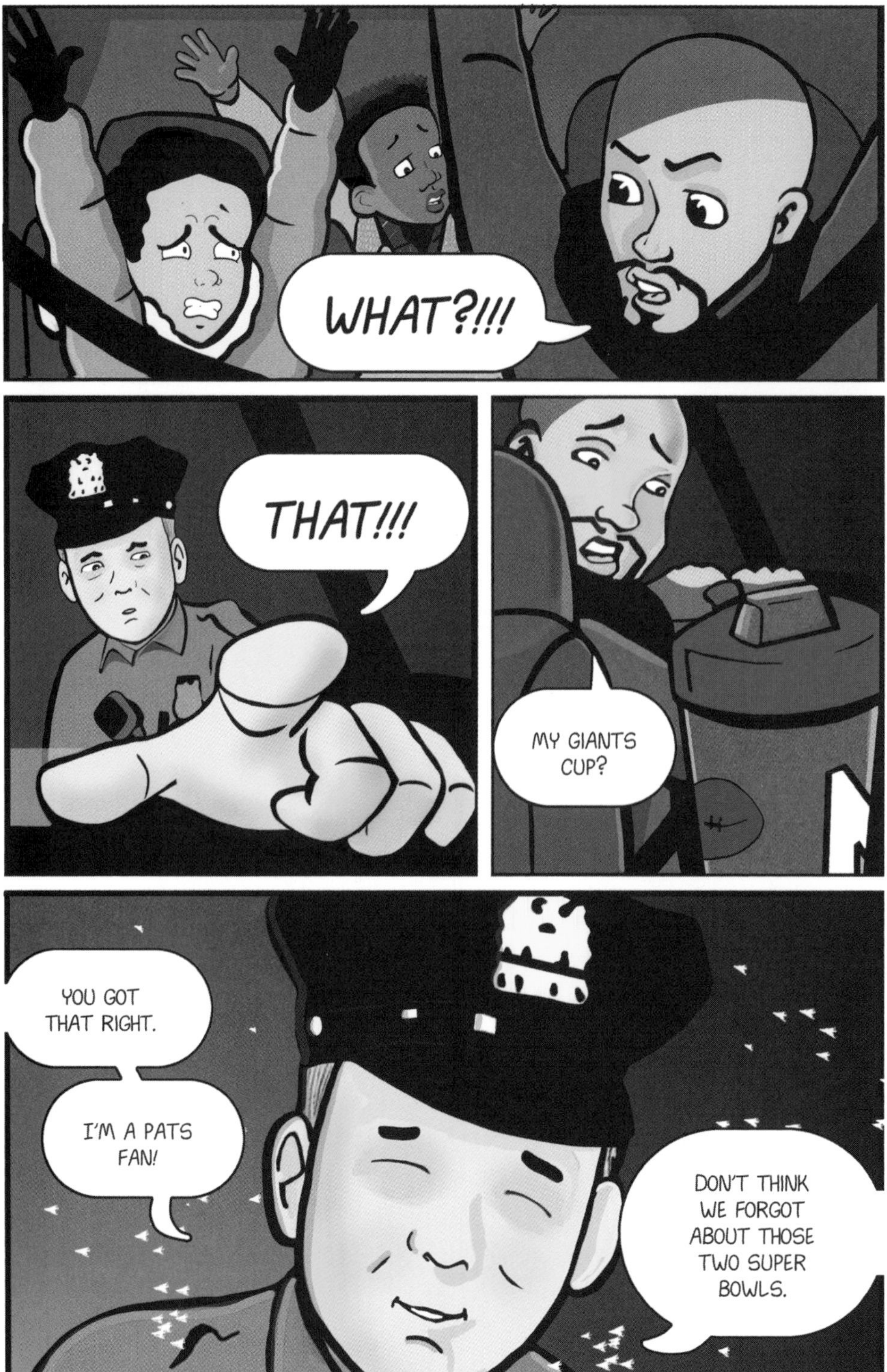
WHAT?!!!
THAT!!!
MY GIANTS CUP?
YOU GOT THAT RIGHT.
I'M A PATS FAN!
DON'T THINK WE FORGOT ABOUT THOSE TWO SUPER BOWLS.

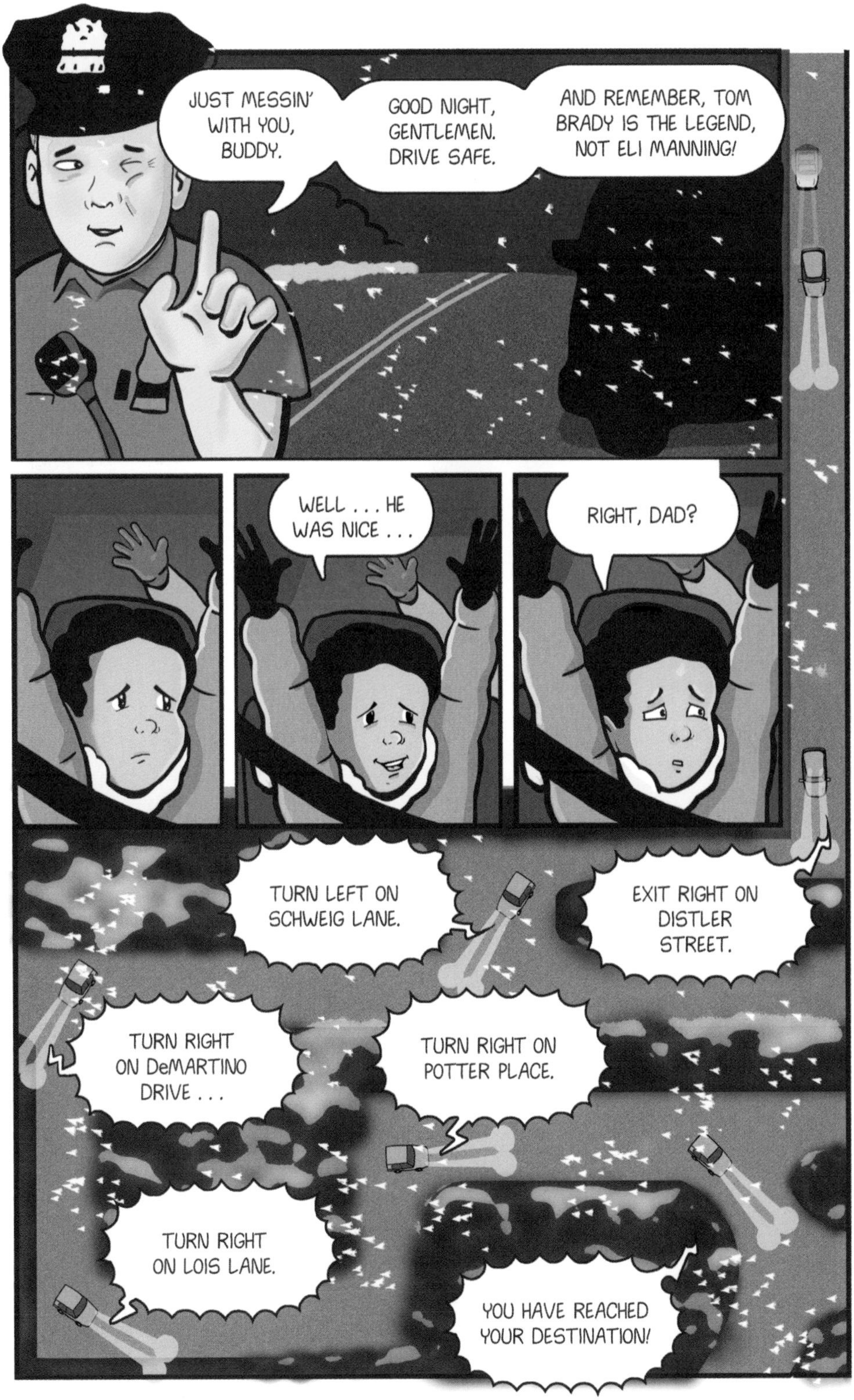
JUST MESSIN' WITH YOU, BUDDY.
GOOD NIGHT, GENTLEMEN. DRIVE SAFE.
AND REMEMBER, TOM BRADY IS THE LEGEND, NOT ELI MANNING!
WELL . . . HE WAS NICE . . .
RIGHT, DAD?
TURN LEFT ON SCHWEIG LANE.
EXIT RIGHT ON DISTLER STREET.
TURN RIGHT ON DeMARTINO DRIVE . . .
TURN RIGHT ON POTTER PLACE.
TURN RIGHT ON LOIS LANE.
YOU HAVE REACHED YOUR DESTINATION!

116

117

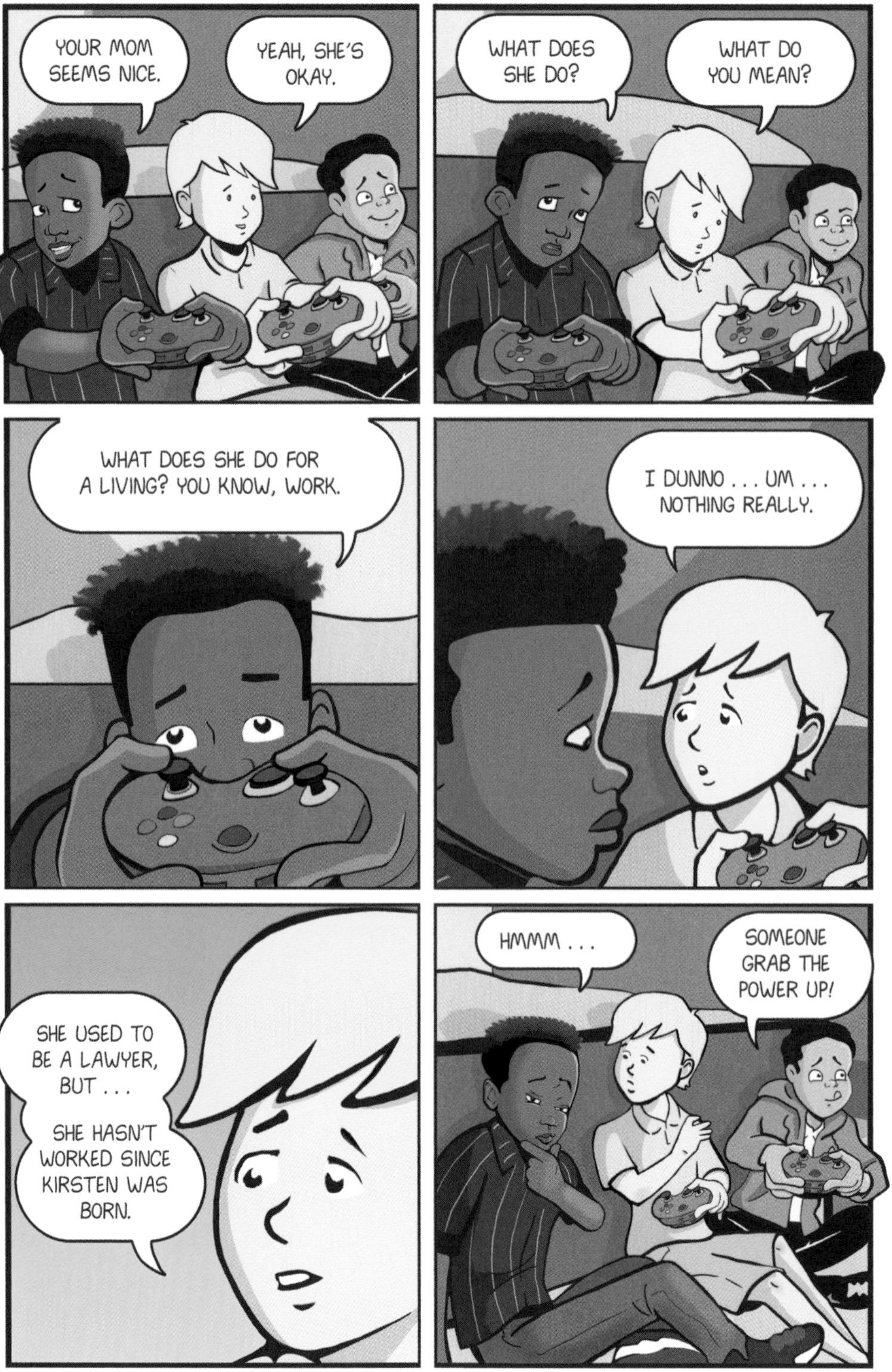
YOUR MOM SEEMS NICE.
YEAH, SHE'S OKAY.
WHAT DOES SHE DO?
WHAT DO YOU MEAN?
WHAT DOES SHE DO FOR A LIVING? YOU KNOW, WORK.
I DUNNO . . . UM . . . NOTHING REALLY.
SHE USED TO BE A LAWYER, BUT . . .
SHE HASN'T WORKED SINCE KIRSTEN WAS BORN.
HMMM . . .
SOMEONE GRAB THE POWER UP!

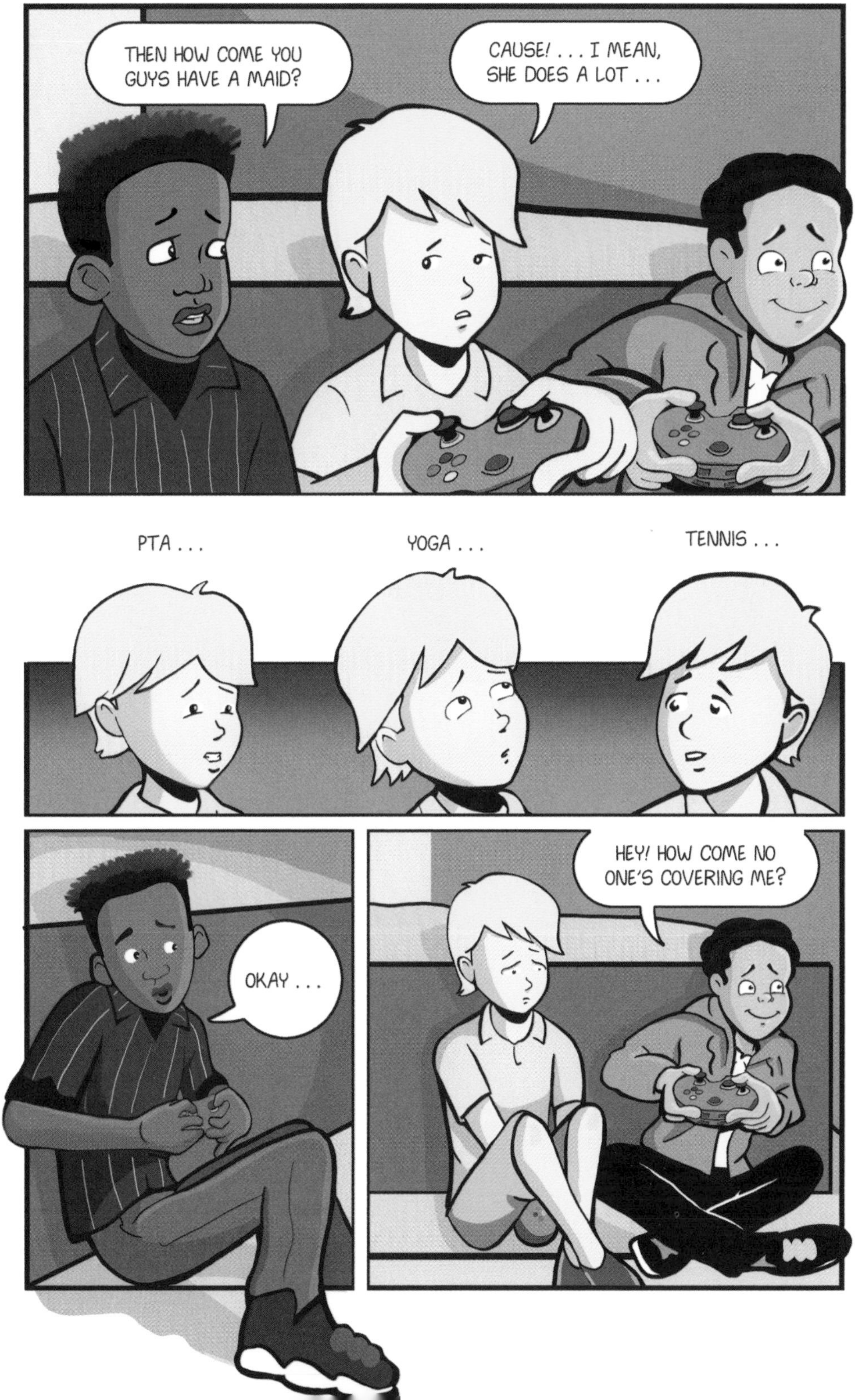
THEN HOW COME YOU GUYS HAVE A MAID?
CAUSE! . . . I MEAN, SHE DOES A LOT . . .
PTA . . .
YOGA . . .
TENNIS . . .
OKAY . . .
HEY! HOW COME NO ONE'S COVERING ME?

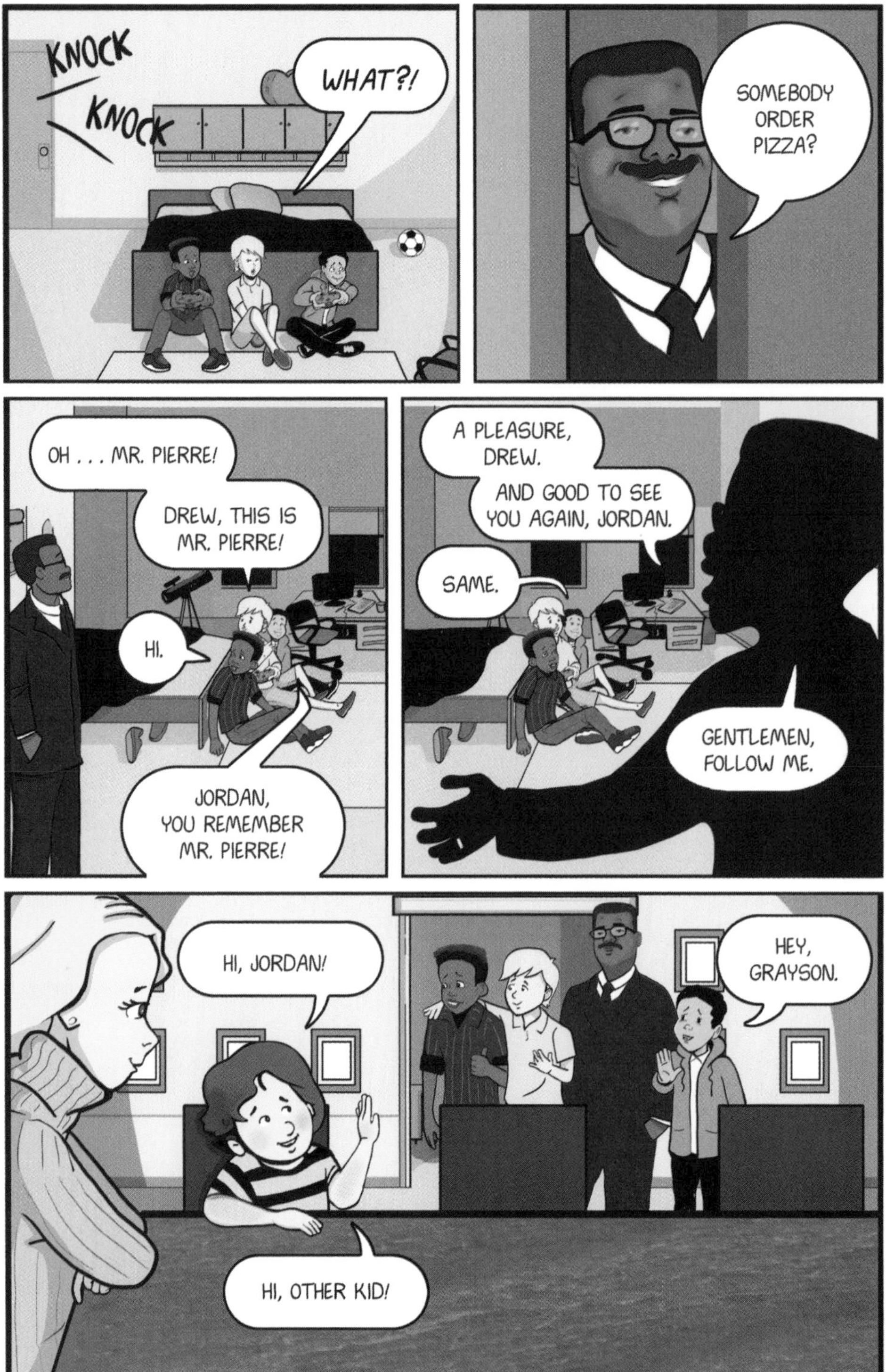
KNOCK
KNOCK
WHAT?!
SOMEBODY ORDER PIZZA?
OH . . . MR. PIERRE!
DREW, THIS IS MR. PIERRE!
HI.
JORDAN, YOU REMEMBER MR. PIERRE!
A PLEASURE, DREW.
AND GOOD TO SEE YOU AGAIN, JORDAN.
SAME.
GENTLEMEN, FOLLOW ME.
HI, JORDAN!
HEY, GRAYSON.
HI, OTHER KID!

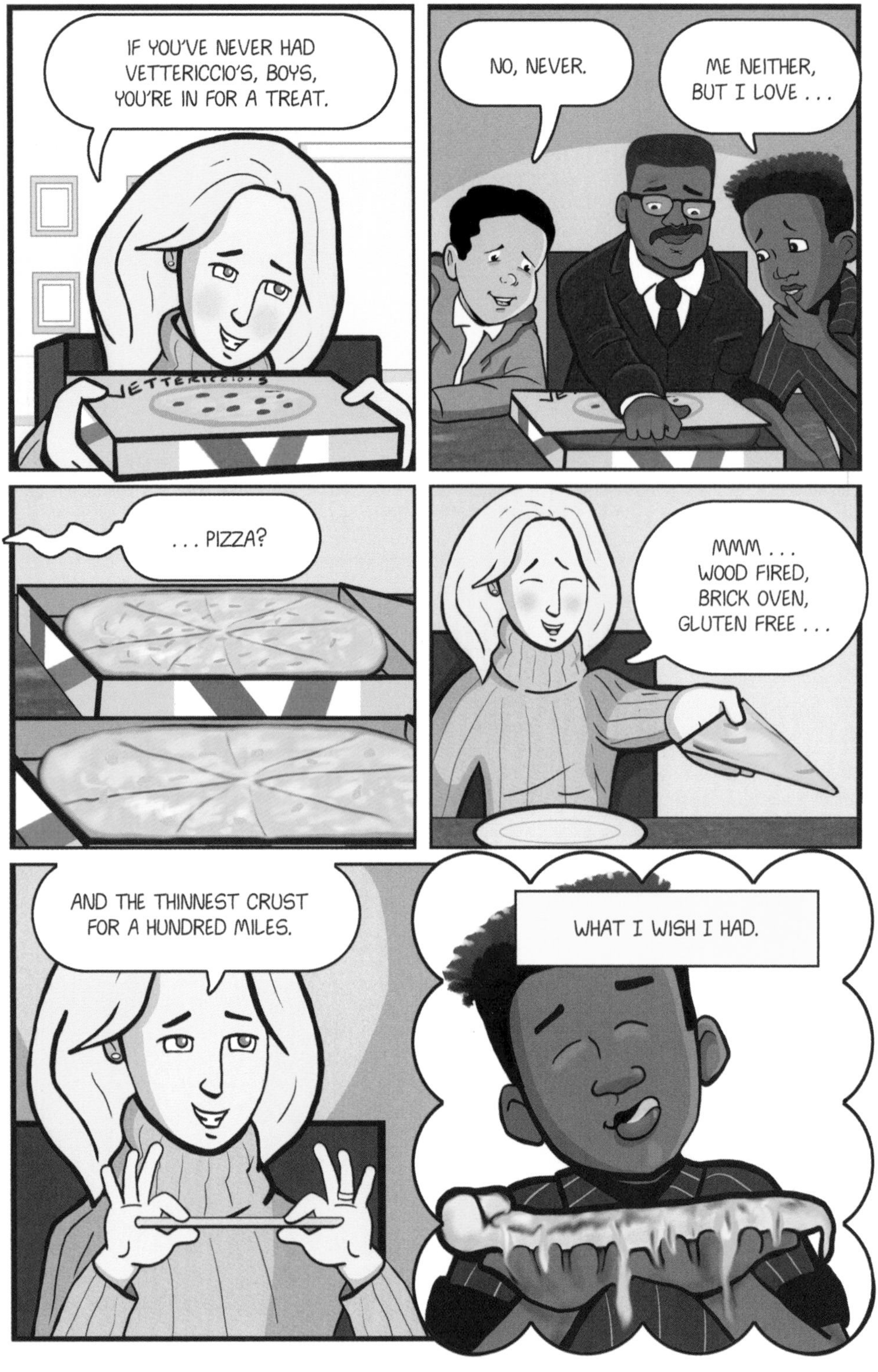
IF YOU'VE NEVER HAD VETTERICCIO'S, BOYS, YOU'RE IN FOR A TREAT.
VETTERICCIO'S
NO, NEVER.
ME NEITHER, BUT I LOVE . . .
. . . PIZZA?
MMM . . . WOOD FIRED, BRICK OVEN, GLUTEN FREE . . .
AND THE THINNEST CRUST FOR A HUNDRED MILES.
WHAT I WISH I HAD.

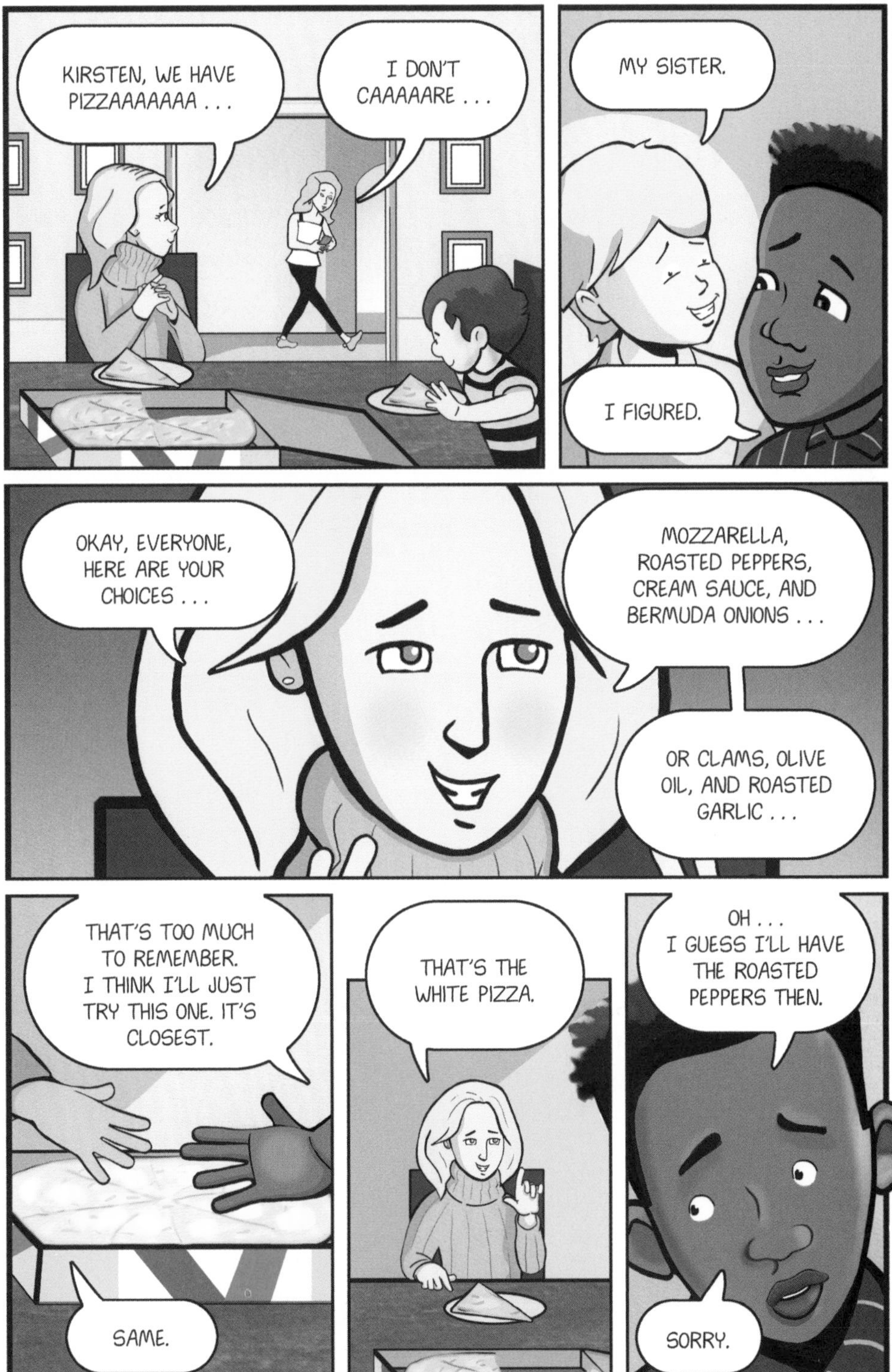
KIRSTEN, WE HAVE PIZZAAAAAAA . . .
I DON'T CAAAAARE . . .
MY SISTER.
I FIGURED.
OKAY, EVERYONE, HERE ARE YOUR CHOICES . . .
MOZZARELLA, ROASTED PEPPERS, CREAM SAUCE, AND BERMUDA ONIONS . . .
OR CLAMS, OLIVE OIL, AND ROASTED GARLIC . . .
THAT'S TOO MUCH TO REMEMBER. I THINK I'LL JUST TRY THIS ONE. IT'S CLOSEST.
SAME.
THAT'S THE WHITE PIZZA.
OH . . . I GUESS I'LL HAVE THE ROASTED PEPPERS THEN.
SORRY.

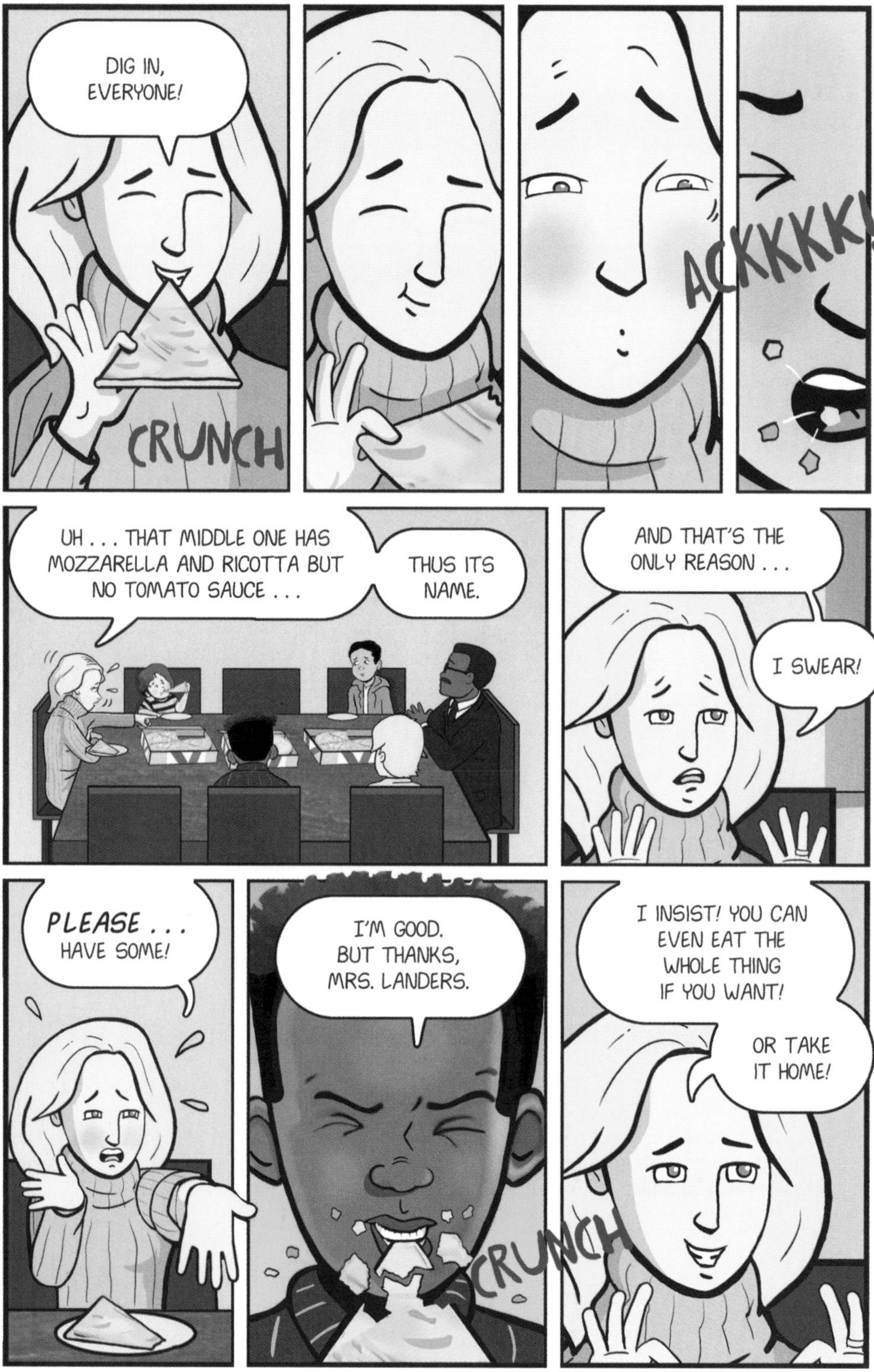
DIG IN, EVERYONE!
CRUNCH
ACKKKK!
UH . . . THAT MIDDLE ONE HAS MOZZARELLA AND RICOTTA BUT NO TOMATO SAUCE . . .
THUS ITS NAME.
AND THAT'S THE ONLY REASON . . .
I SWEAR!
PLEASE . . . HAVE SOME!
I'M GOOD. BUT THANKS, MRS. LANDERS.
CRUNCH
I INSIST! YOU CAN EVEN EAT THE WHOLE THING IF YOU WANT!
OR TAKE IT HOME!

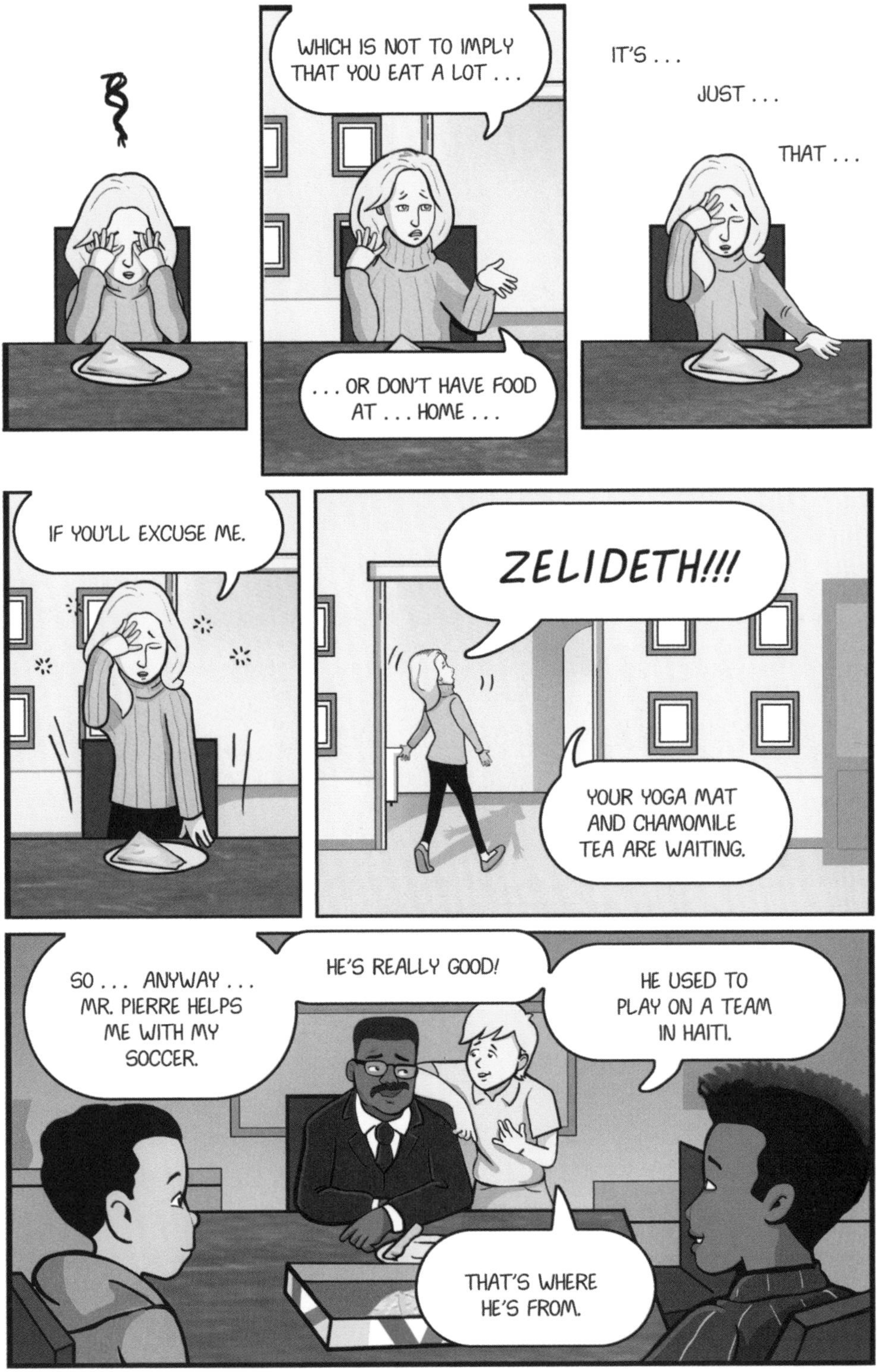
WHICH IS NOT TO IMPLY THAT YOU EAT A LOT . . .
. . . OR DON'T HAVE FOOD AT . . . HOME . . .
IT'S . . .
JUST . . .
THAT . . .
IF YOU'LL EXCUSE ME.
ZELIDETH!!!
YOUR YOGA MAT AND CHAMOMILE TEA ARE WAITING.
SO . . . ANYWAY . . . MR. PIERRE HELPS ME WITH MY SOCCER.
HE'S REALLY GOOD!
HE USED TO PLAY ON A TEAM IN HAITI.
THAT'S WHERE HE'S FROM.

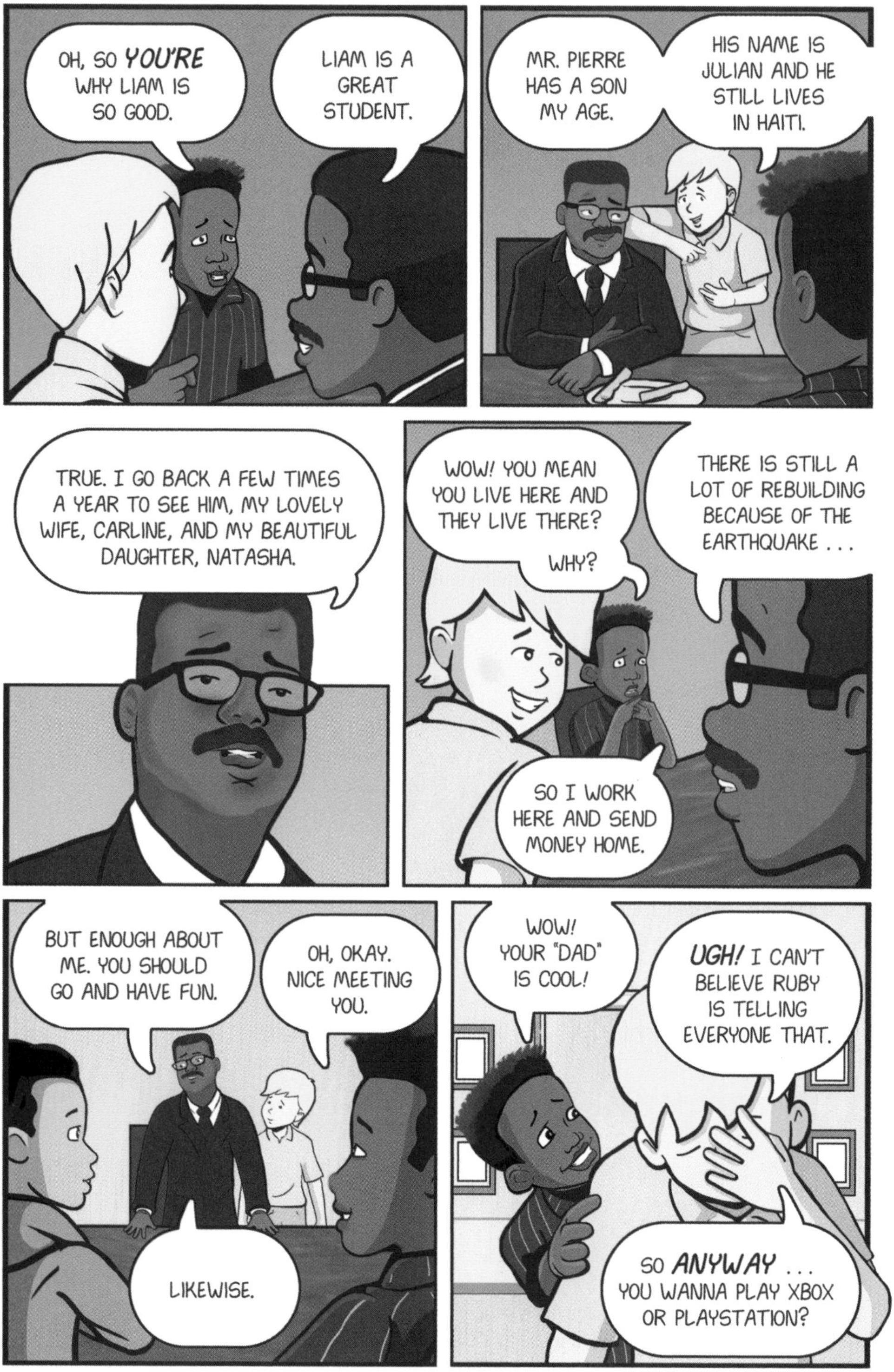
OH, SO ***YOU'RE*** WHY LIAM IS SO GOOD.
LIAM IS A GREAT STUDENT.
MR. PIERRE HAS A SON MY AGE.
HIS NAME IS JULIAN AND HE STILL LIVES IN HAITI.
TRUE. I GO BACK A FEW TIMES A YEAR TO SEE HIM, MY LOVELY WIFE, CARLINE, AND MY BEAUTIFUL DAUGHTER, NATASHA.
WOW! YOU MEAN YOU LIVE HERE AND THEY LIVE THERE?
WHY?
THERE IS STILL A LOT OF REBUILDING BECAUSE OF THE EARTHQUAKE . . .
SO I WORK HERE AND SEND MONEY HOME.
BUT ENOUGH ABOUT ME. YOU SHOULD GO AND HAVE FUN.
OH, OKAY. NICE MEETING YOU.
LIKEWISE.
WOW! YOUR "DAD" IS COOL!
UGH! I CAN'T BELIEVE RUBY IS TELLING EVERYONE THAT.
SO ***ANYWAY*** . . . YOU WANNA PLAY XBOX OR PLAYSTATION?

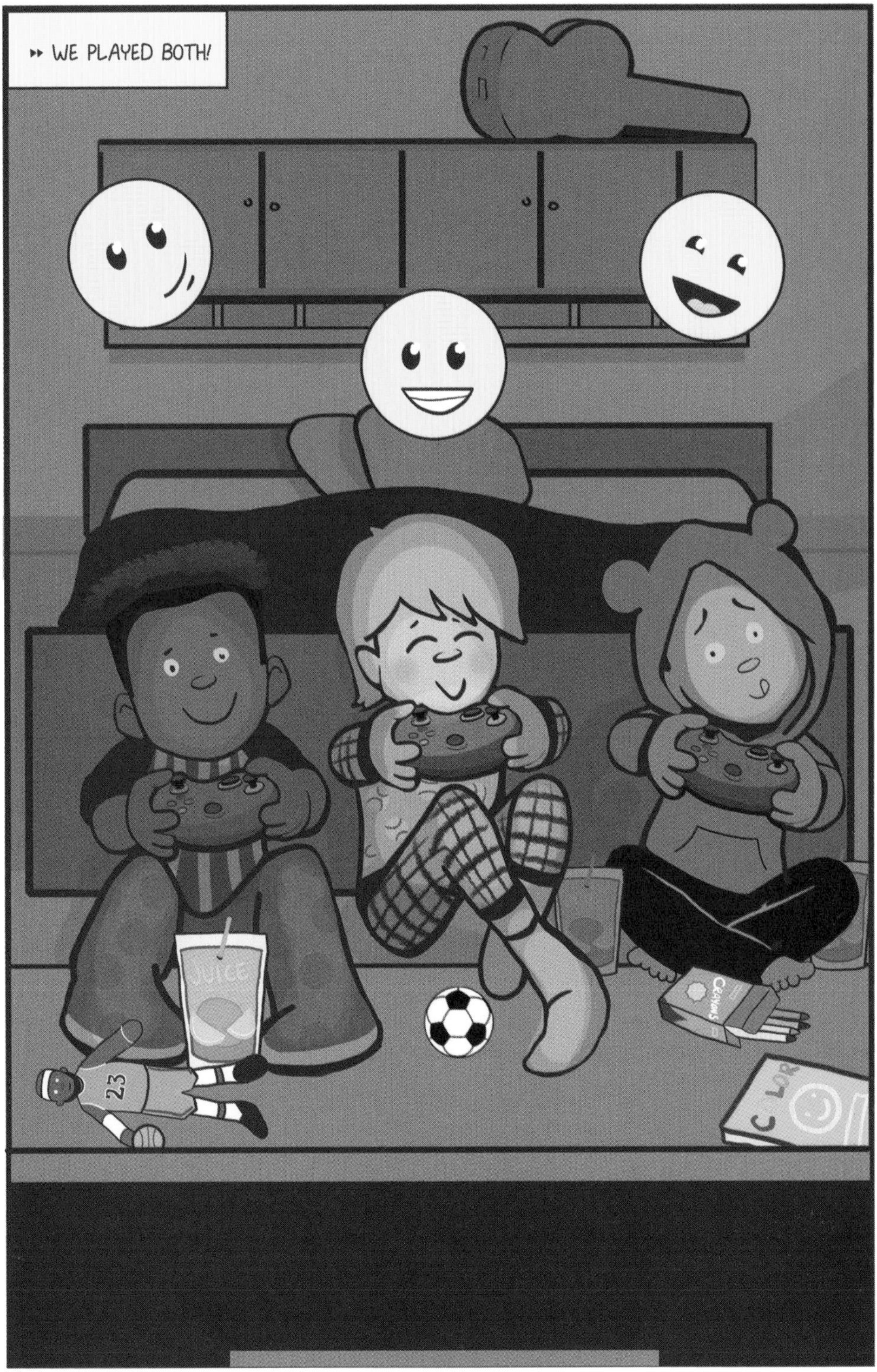
▸▸ WE PLAYED BOTH!
JUICE
23
CRAYONS
COLOR

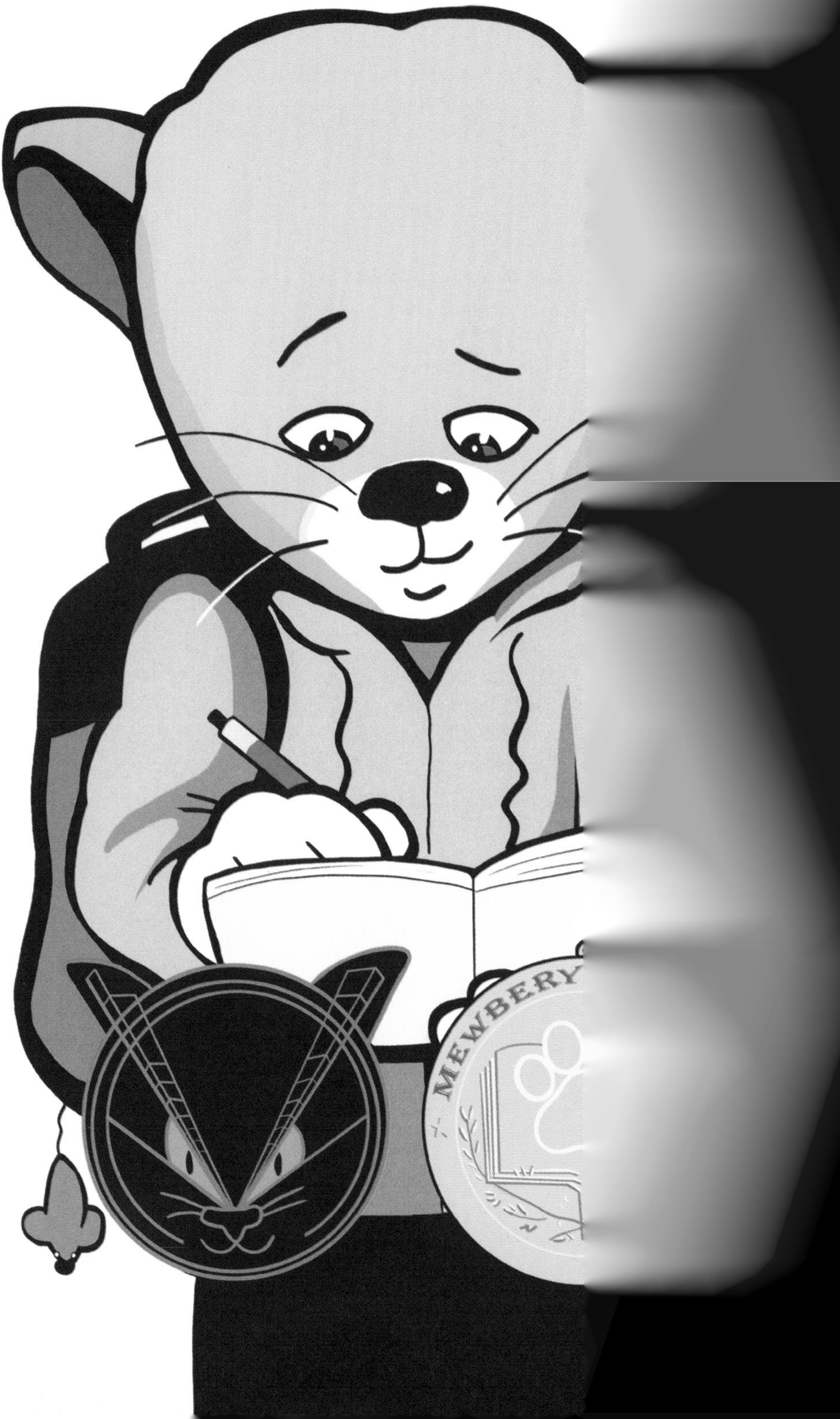
MEWBERY

Obedience school
is hard enough
without being the . . .

MEW KID

CHAPTER 7

Mew York Times bestselling pawthor

FURRY CRAFT

"Furry, sharp claws, and totally real.
Jordan Manx is the cat
everyone will be talking about."
-Jeff Kitty
Author of *Diary of a Wimpy Cat*

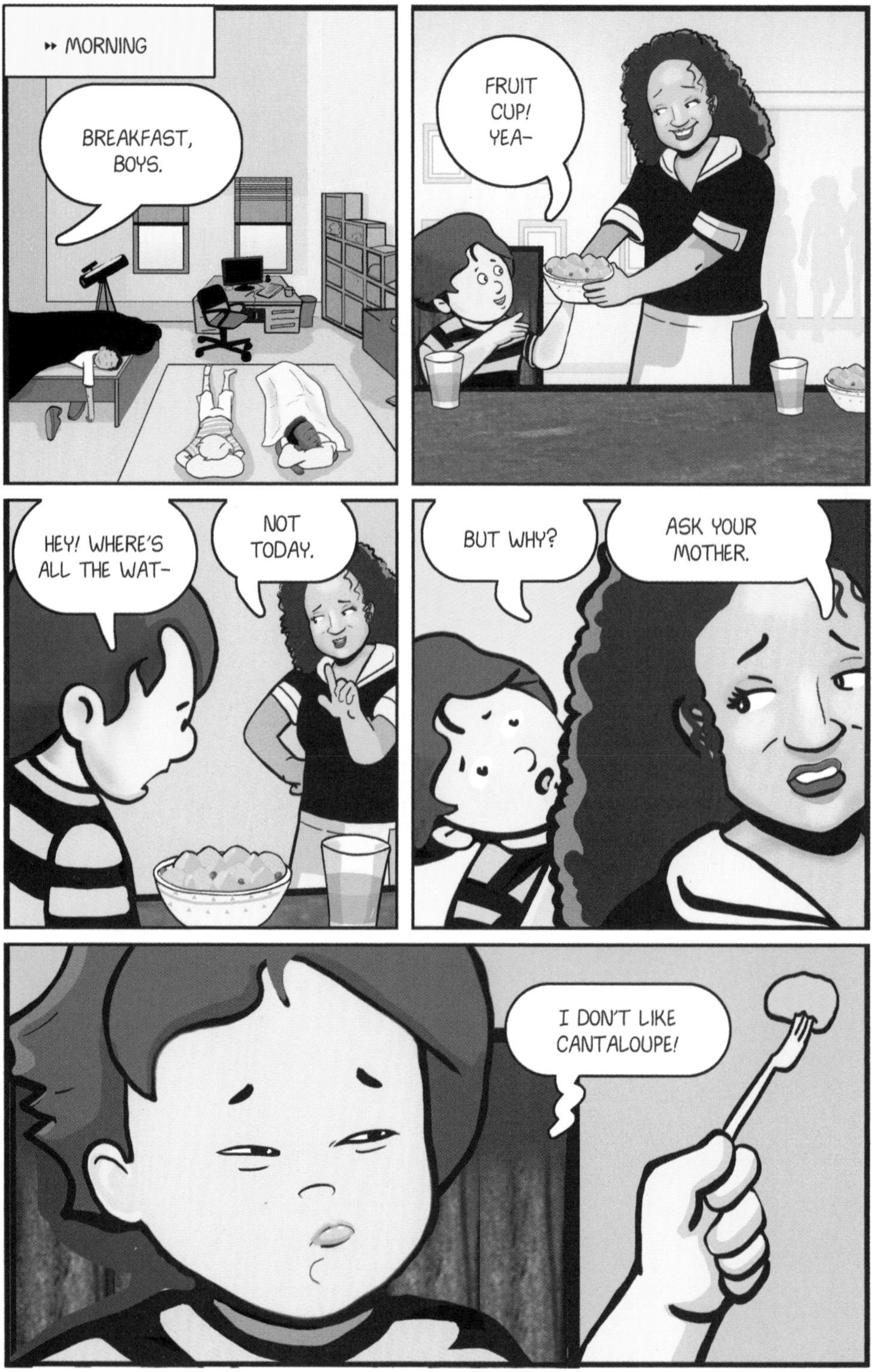
MORNING
BREAKFAST, BOYS.
FRUIT CUP! YEA-
HEY! WHERE'S ALL THE WAT-
NOT TODAY.
BUT WHY?
ASK YOUR MOTHER.
I DON'T LIKE CANTALOUPE!

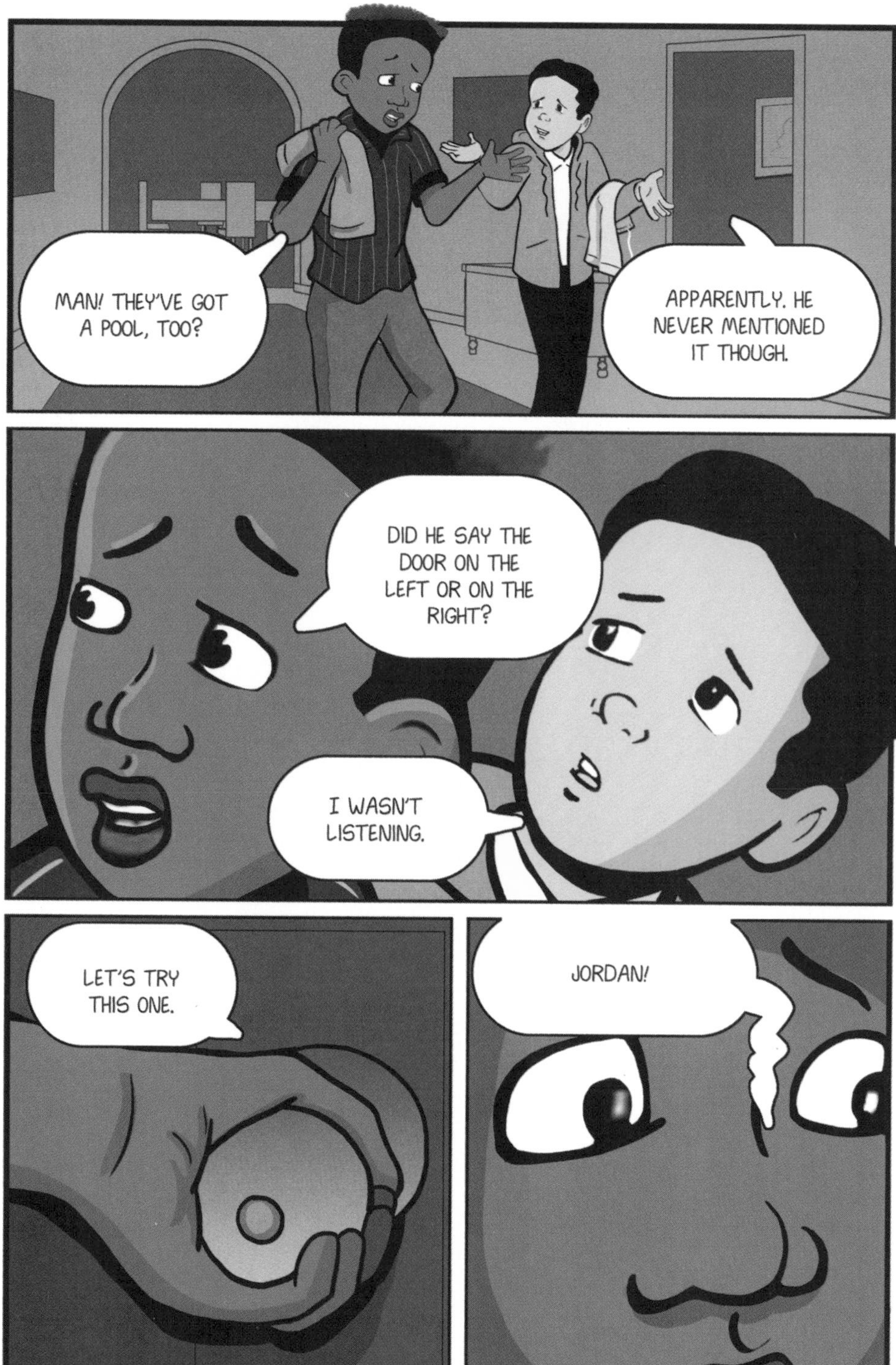
MAN! THEY'VE GOT A POOL, TOO?
APPARENTLY. HE NEVER MENTIONED IT THOUGH.
DID HE SAY THE DOOR ON THE LEFT OR ON THE RIGHT?
I WASN'T LISTENING.
LET'S TRY THIS ONE.
JORDAN!

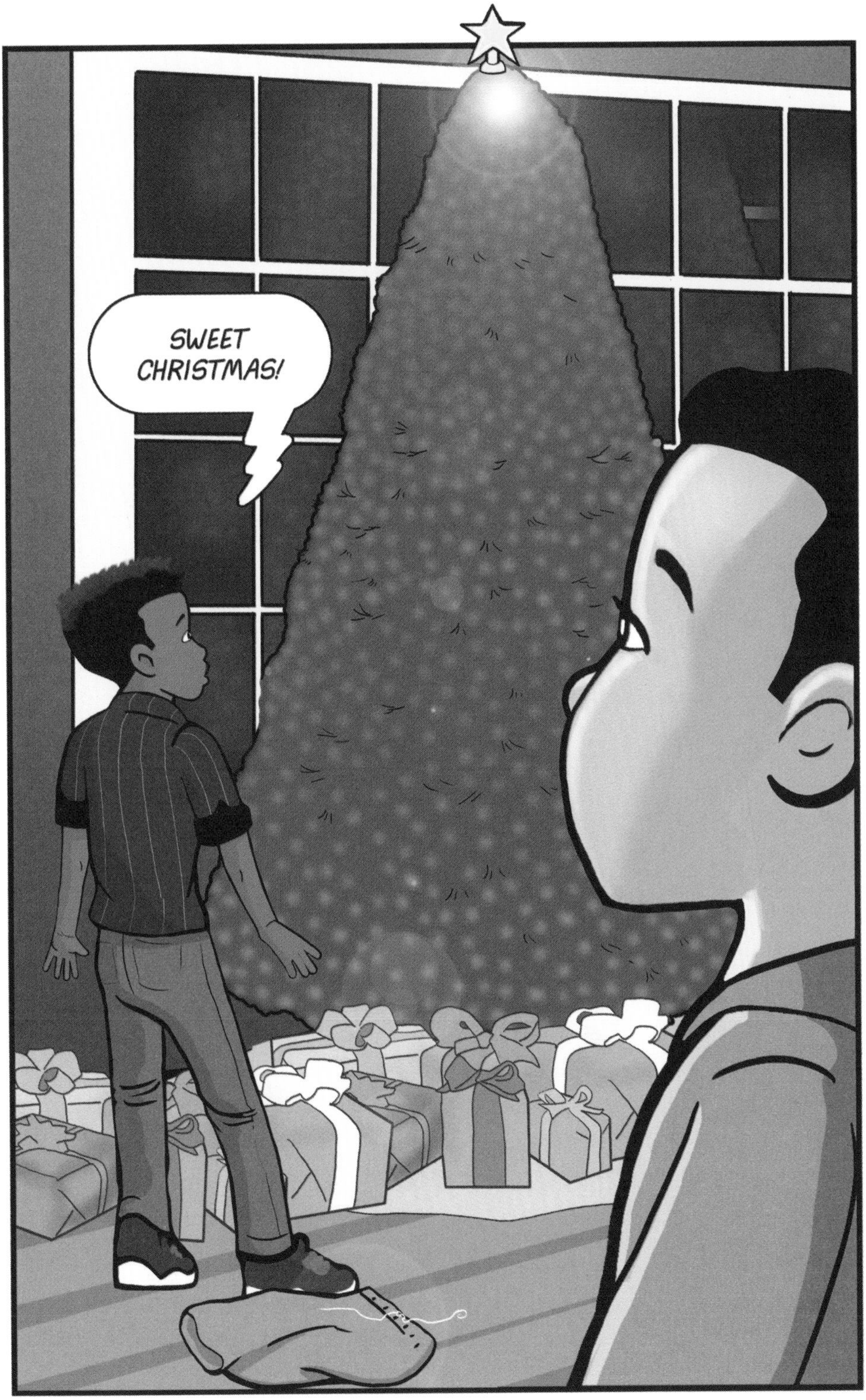
SWEET CHRISTMAS!

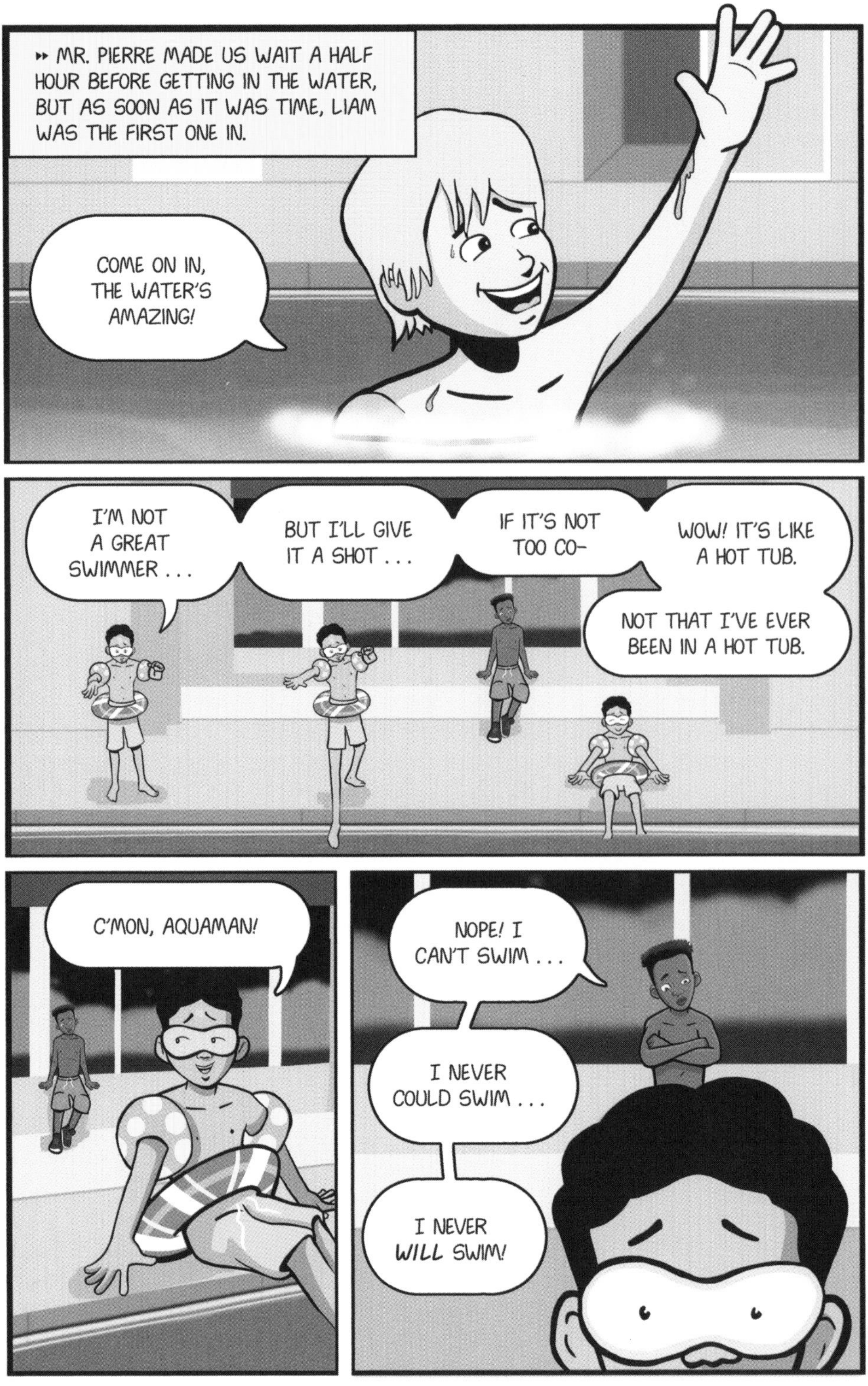
MR. PIERRE MADE US WAIT A HALF HOUR BEFORE GETTING IN THE WATER, BUT AS SOON AS IT WAS TIME, LIAM WAS THE FIRST ONE IN.
COME ON IN, THE WATER'S AMAZING!
I'M NOT A GREAT SWIMMER . . .
BUT I'LL GIVE IT A SHOT . . .
IF IT'S NOT TOO CO–
WOW! IT'S LIKE A HOT TUB.
NOT THAT I'VE EVER BEEN IN A HOT TUB.
C'MON, AQUAMAN!
NOPE! I CAN'T SWIM . . .
I NEVER COULD SWIM . . .
I NEVER *WILL* SWIM!

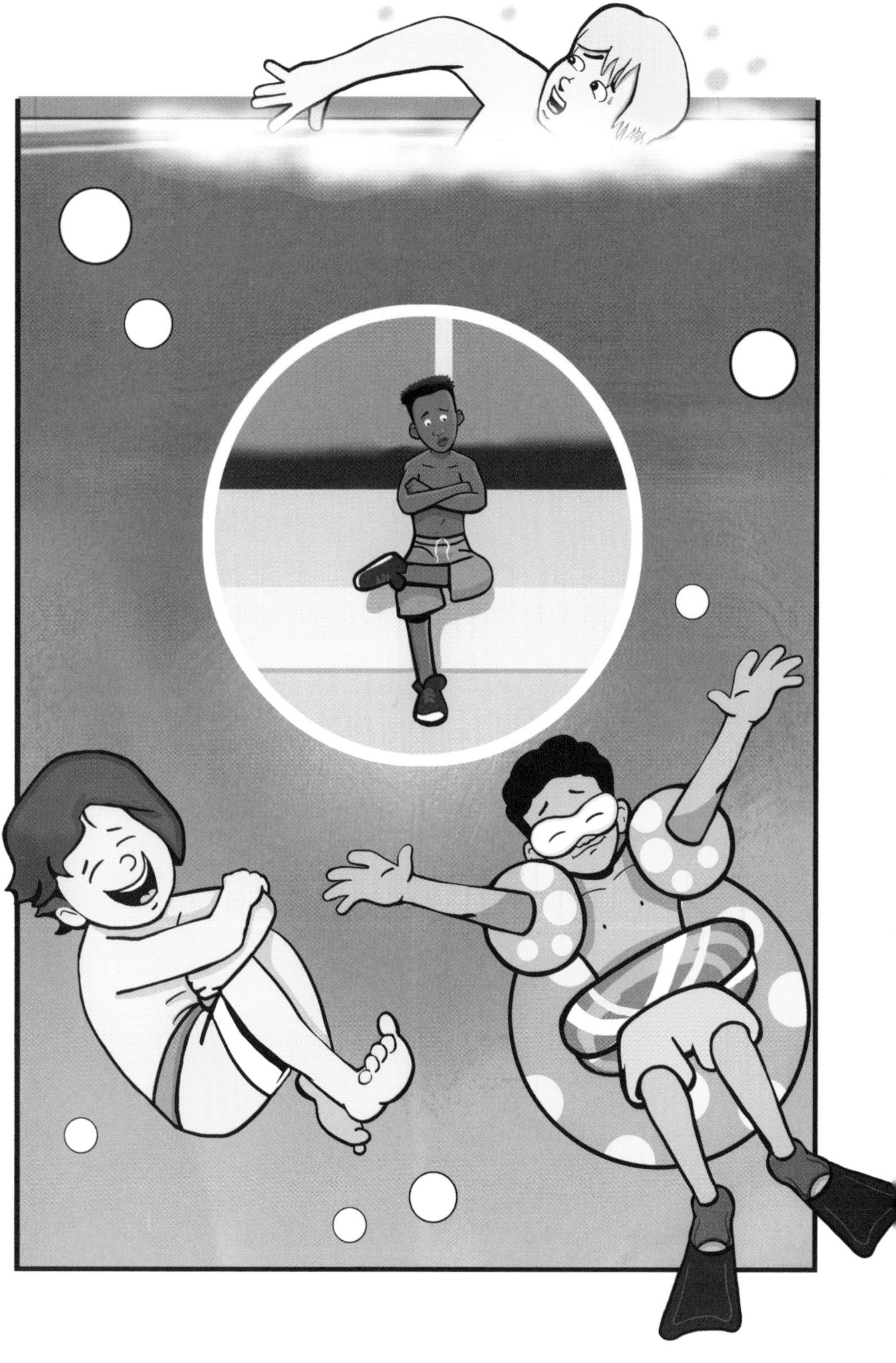

138

146

147

148

149

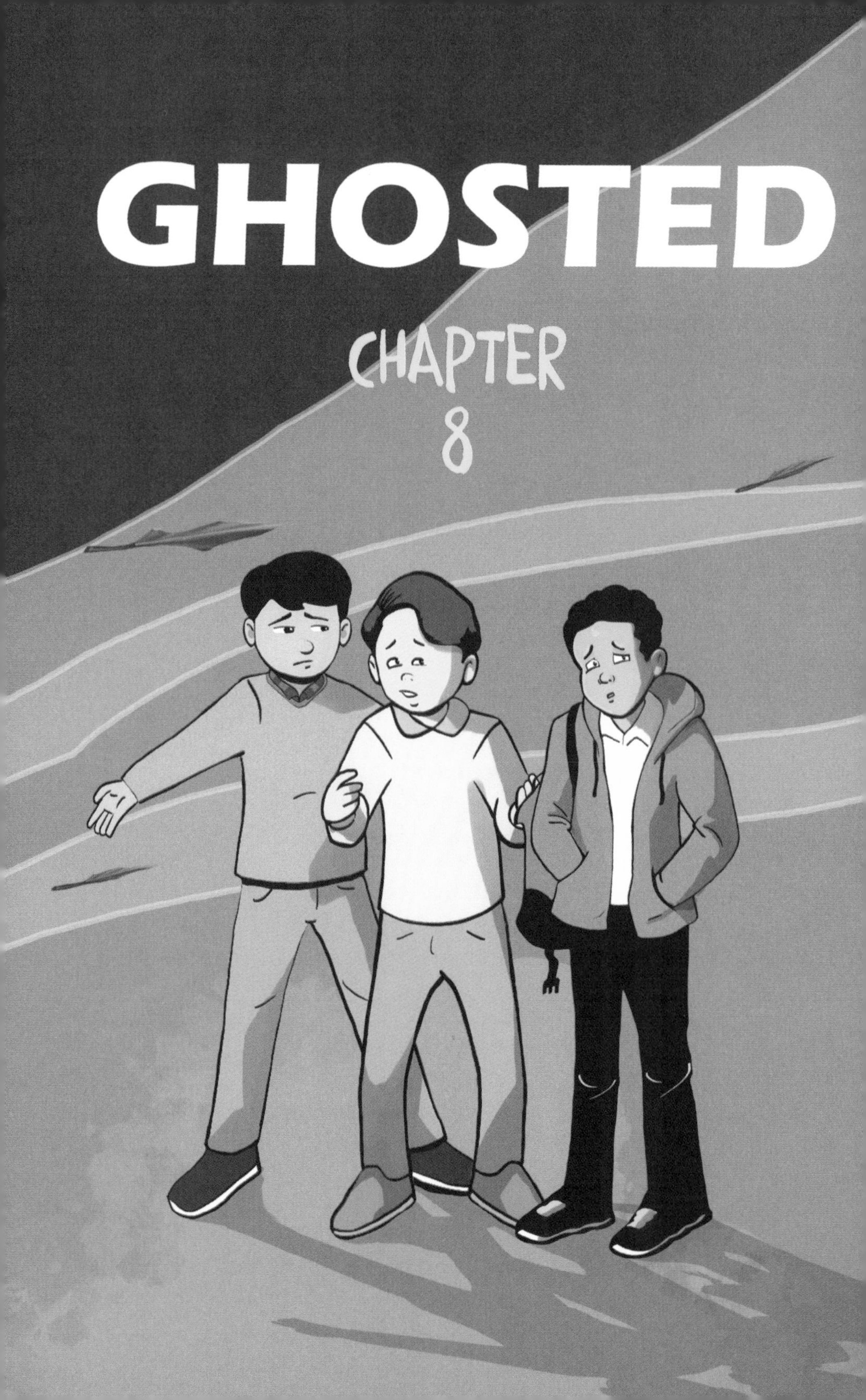
GHOSTED
CHAPTER
8

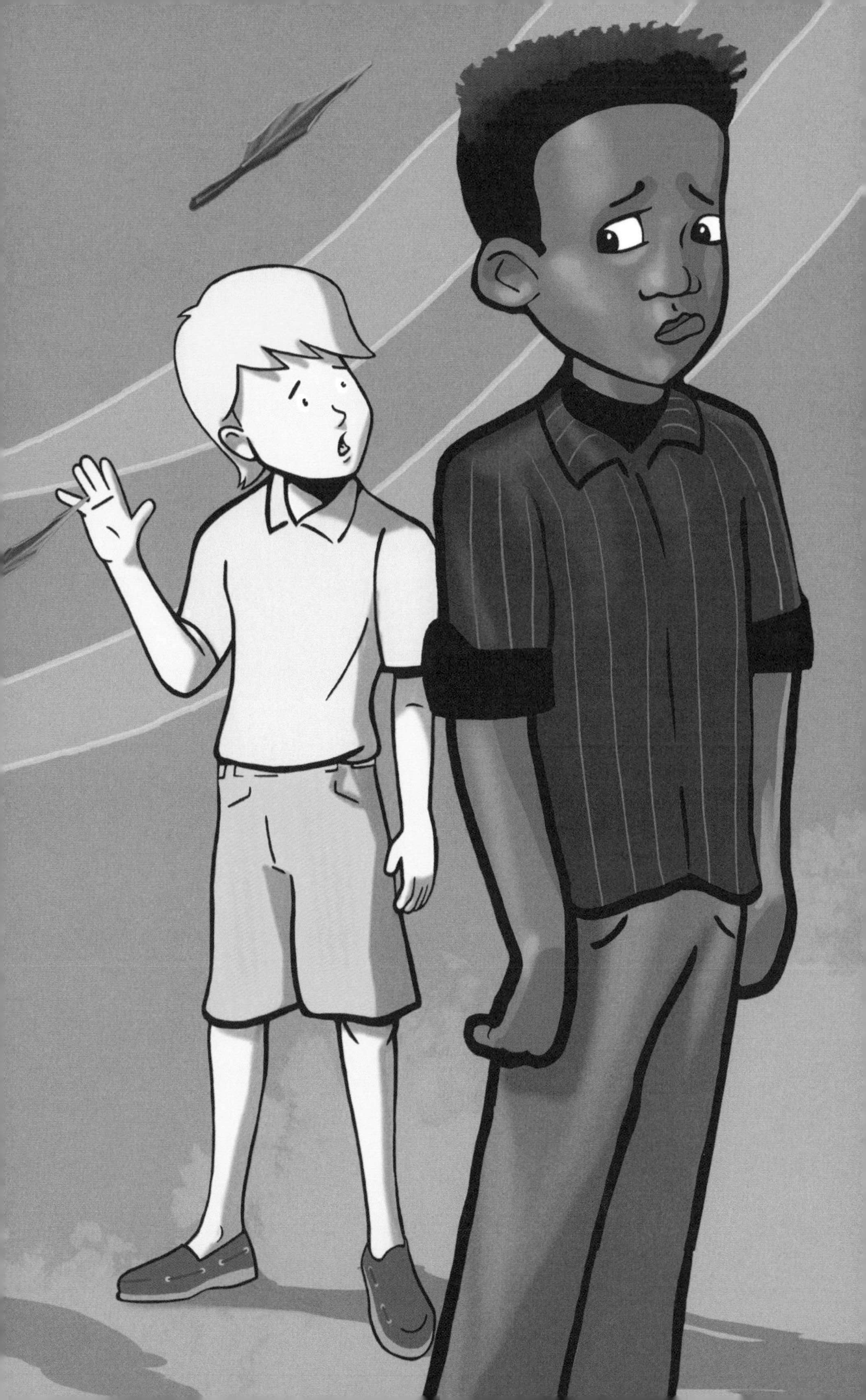

153

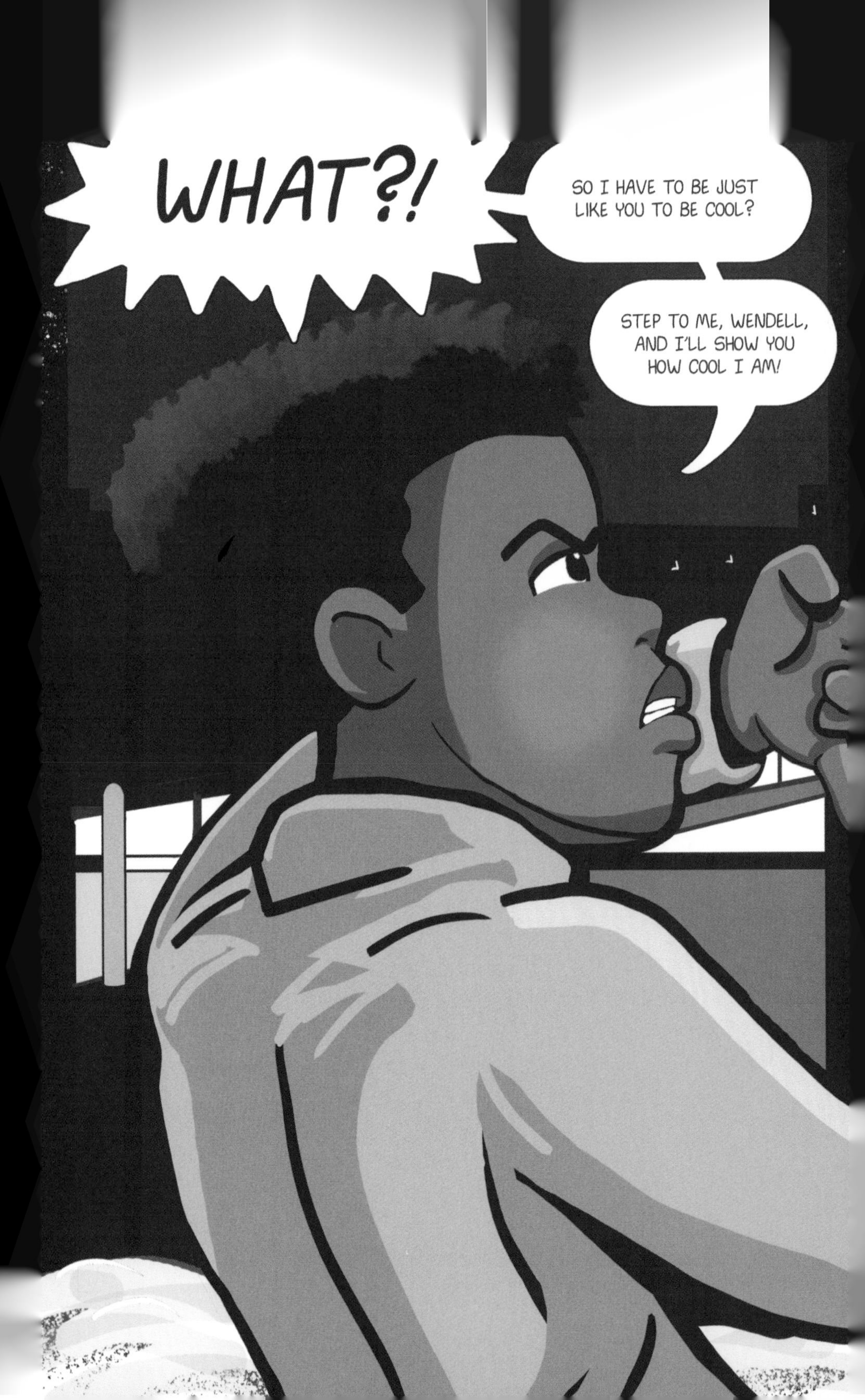
WHAT?!
SO I HAVE TO BE JUST LIKE YOU TO BE COOL?
STEP TO ME, WENDELL, AND I'LL SHOW YOU HOW COOL I AM!

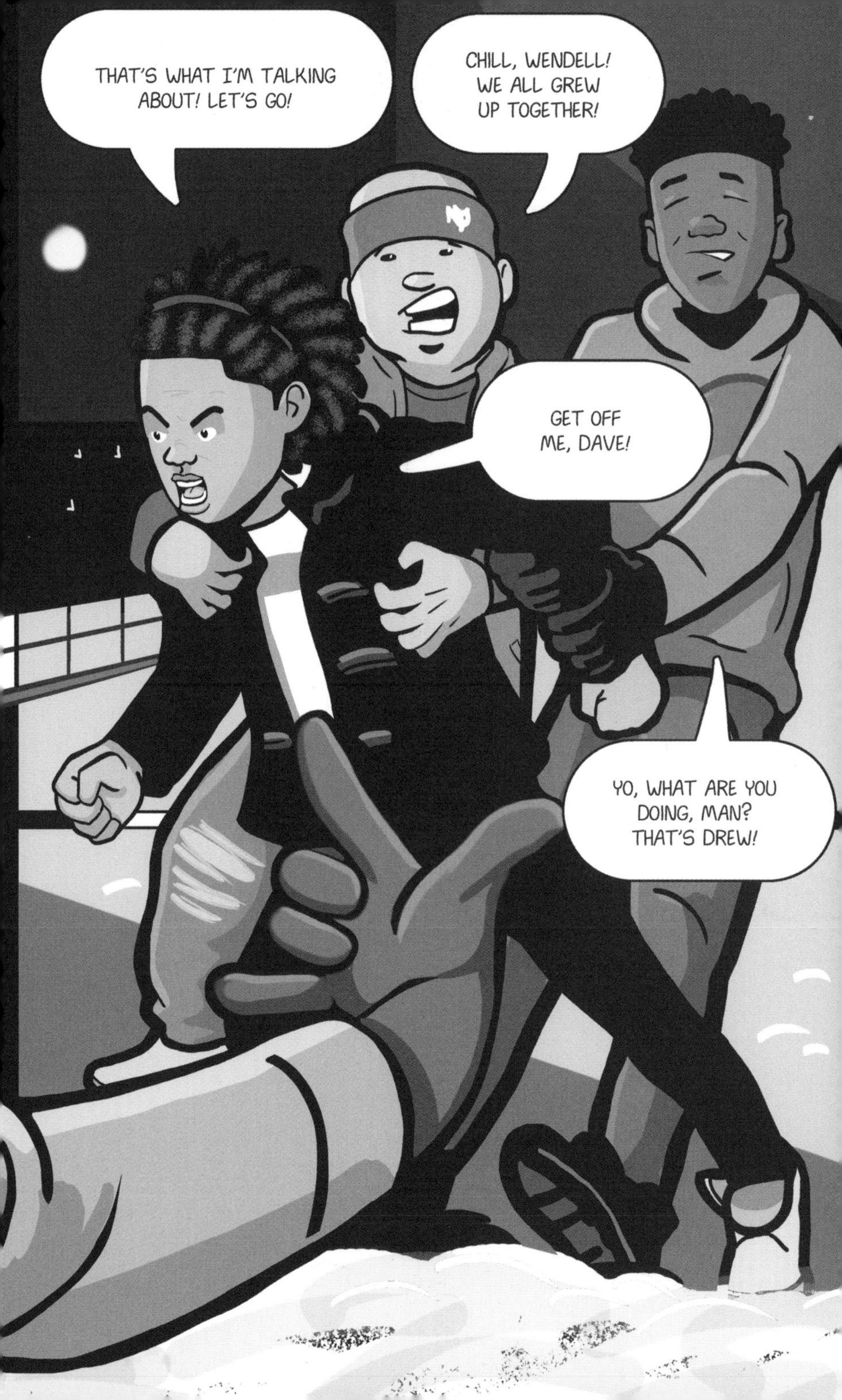
THAT'S WHAT I'M TALKING ABOUT! LET'S GO!
CHILL, WENDELL! WE ALL GREW UP TOGETHER!
GET OFF ME, DAVE!
YO, WHAT ARE YOU DOING, MAN? THAT'S DREW!

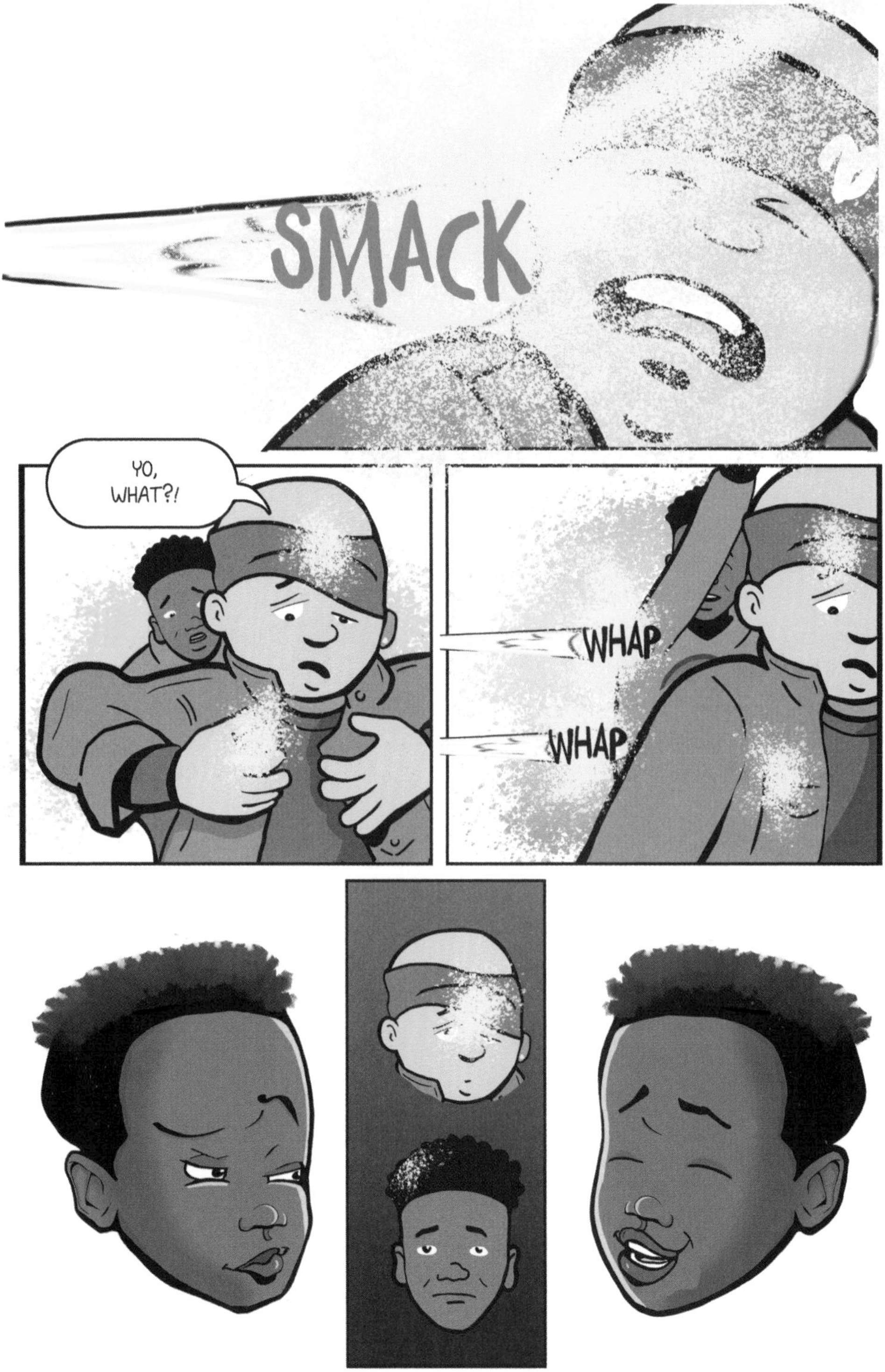
SMACK
YO, WHAT?!
WHAP
WHAP

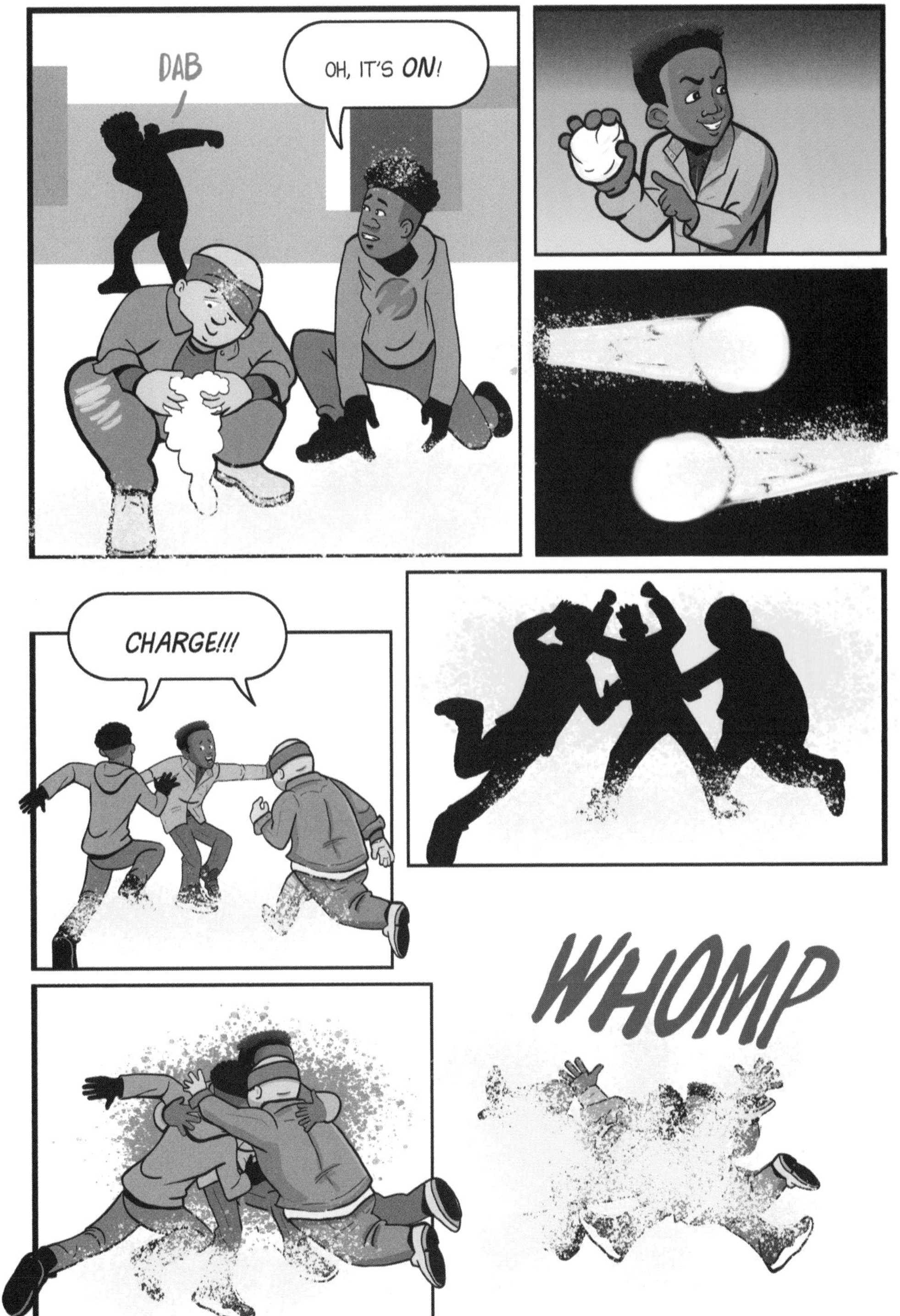
DAB
OH, IT'S ON!
CHARGE!!!
WHOMP

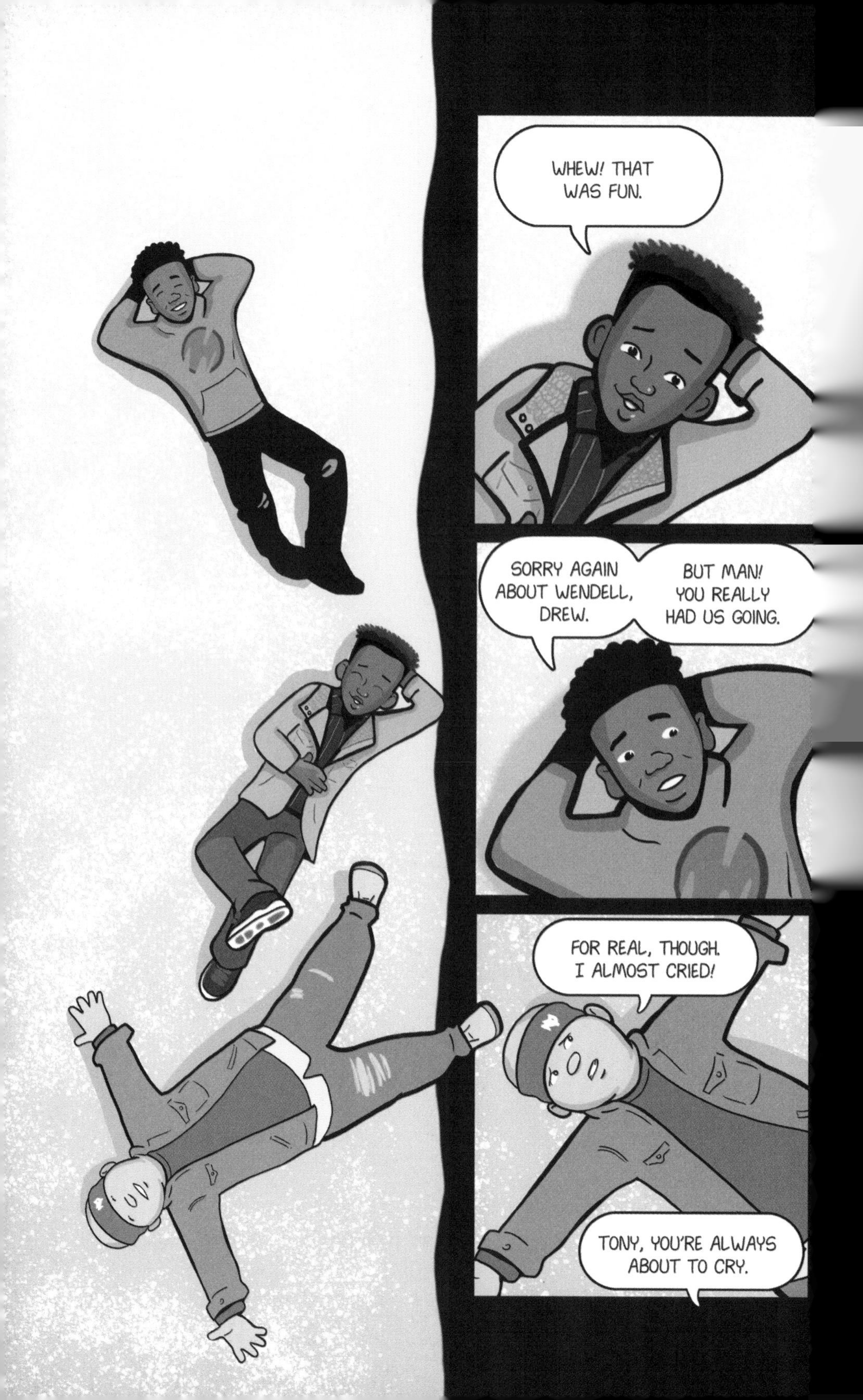
WHEW! THAT WAS FUN.
SORRY AGAIN ABOUT WENDELL, DREW.
BUT MAN! YOU REALLY HAD US GOING.
FOR REAL, THOUGH. I ALMOST CRIED!
TONY, YOU'RE ALWAYS ABOUT TO CRY.

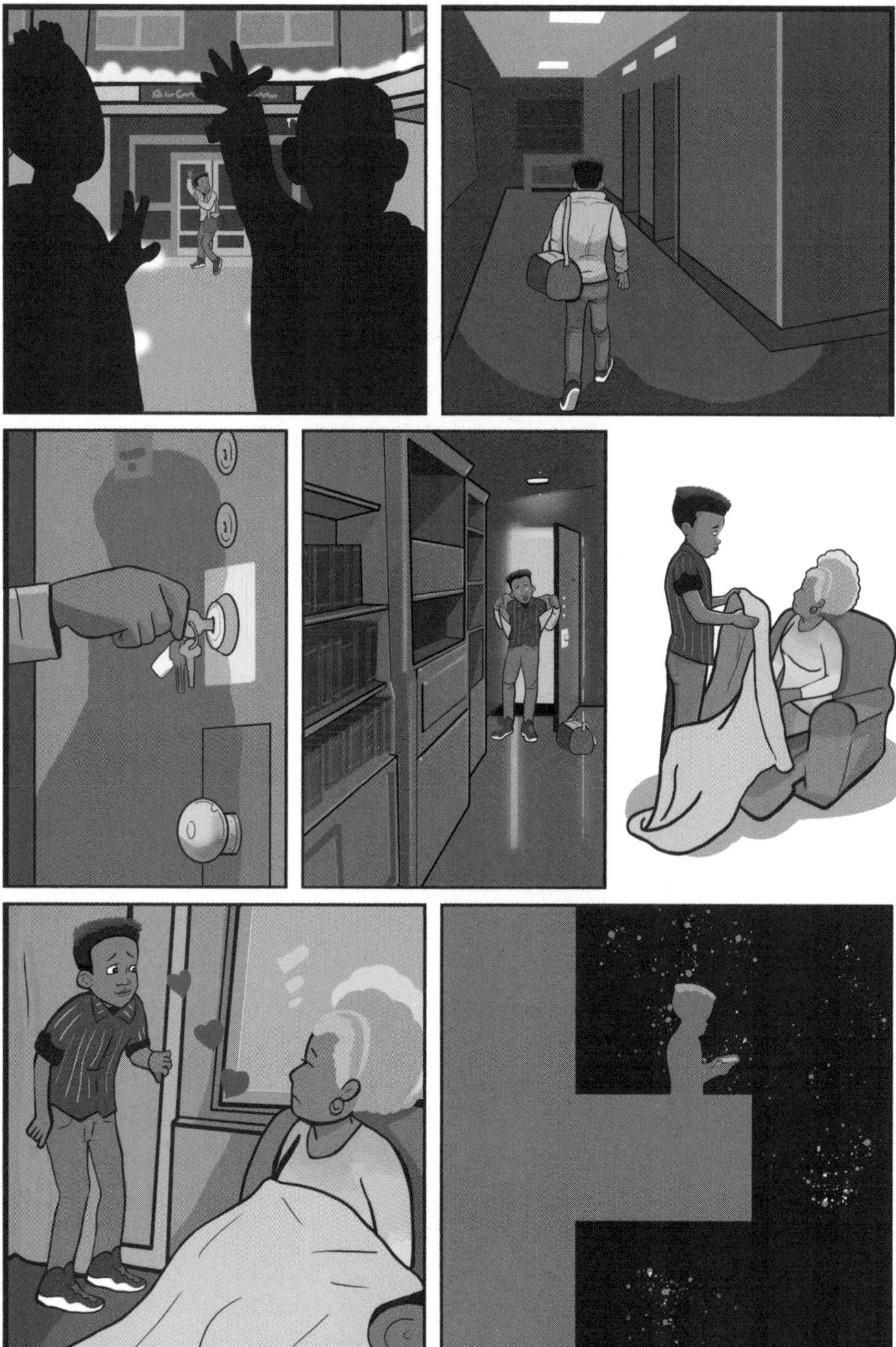

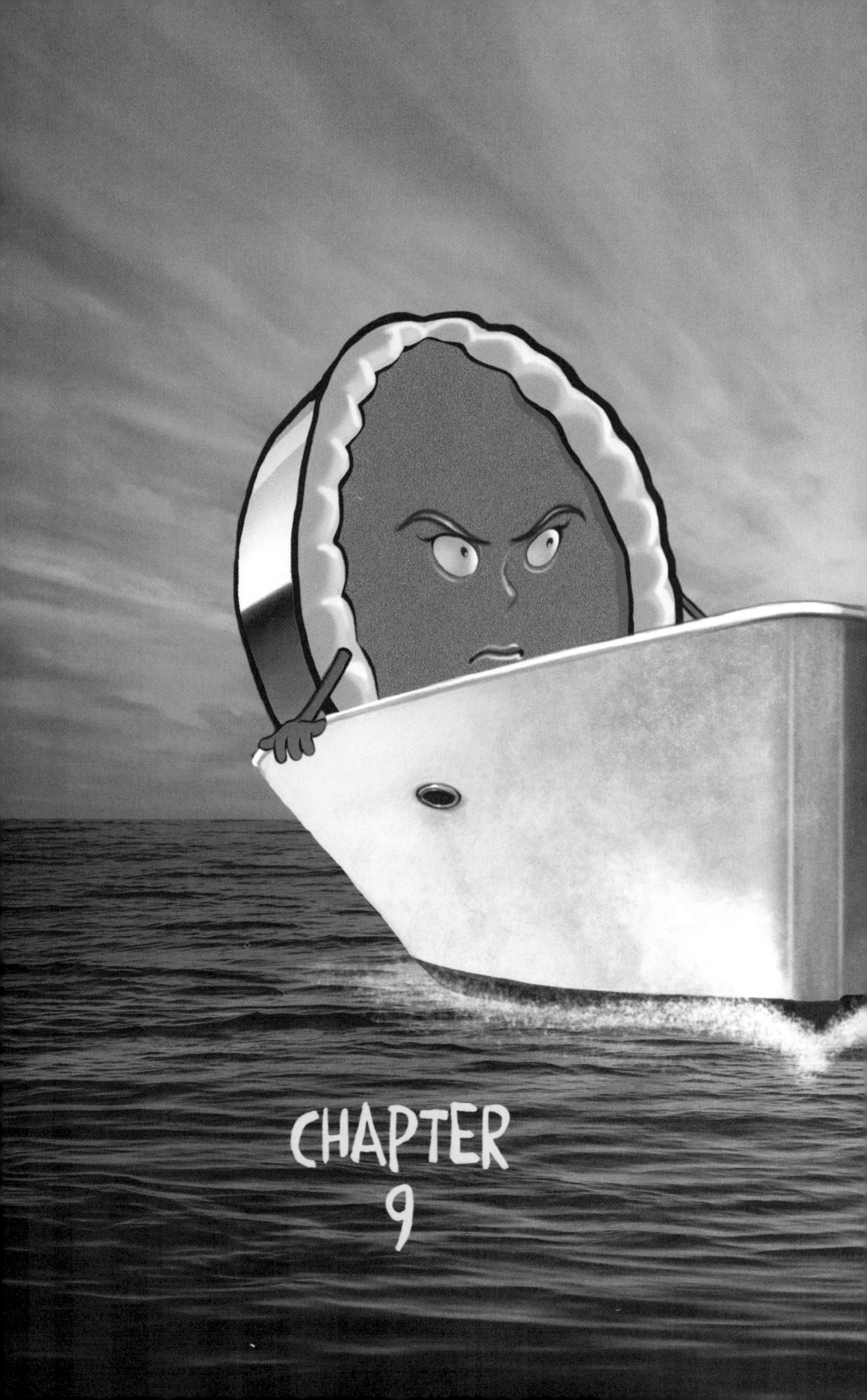
CHAPTER
9

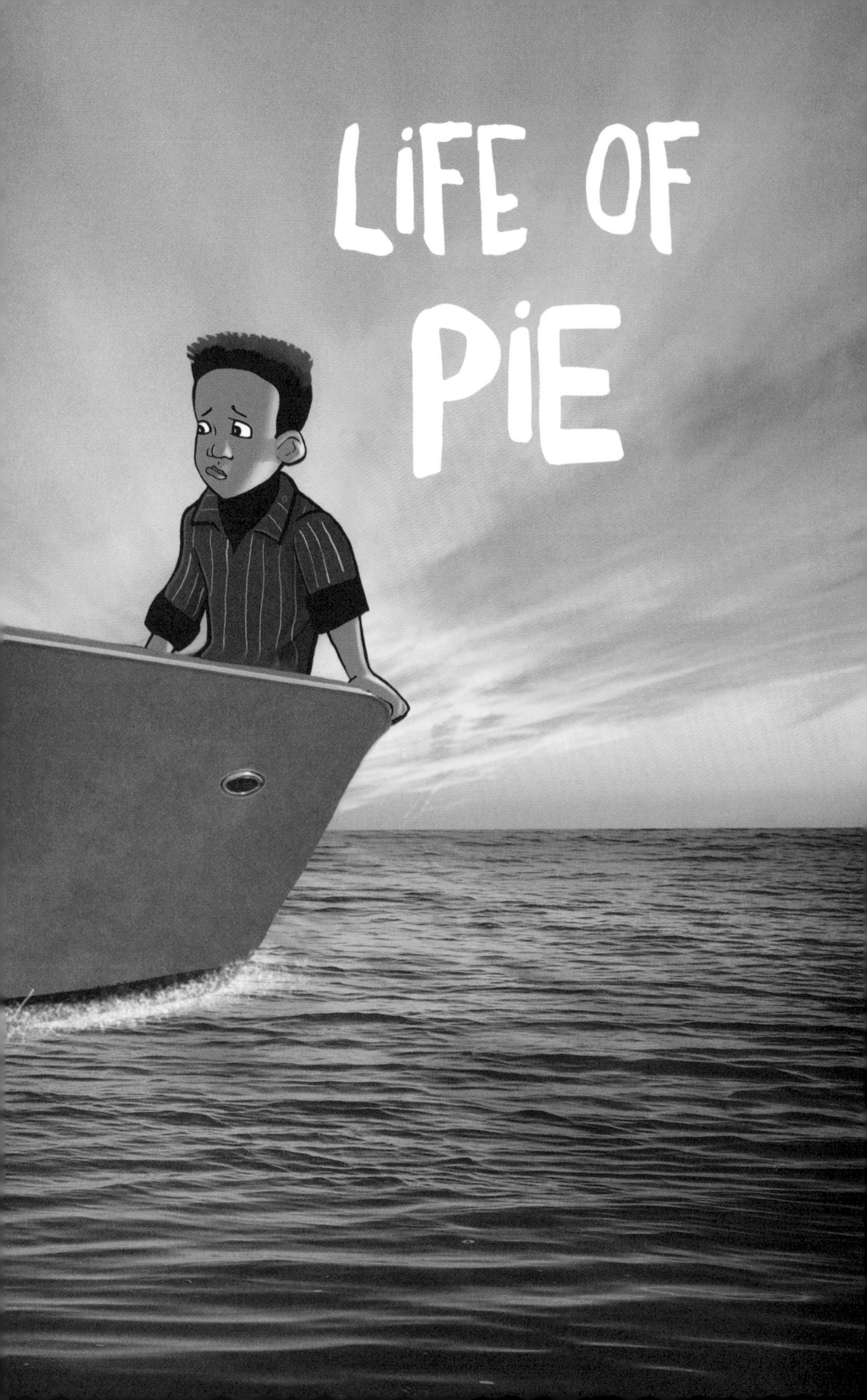
LIFE OF
PIE

167

168

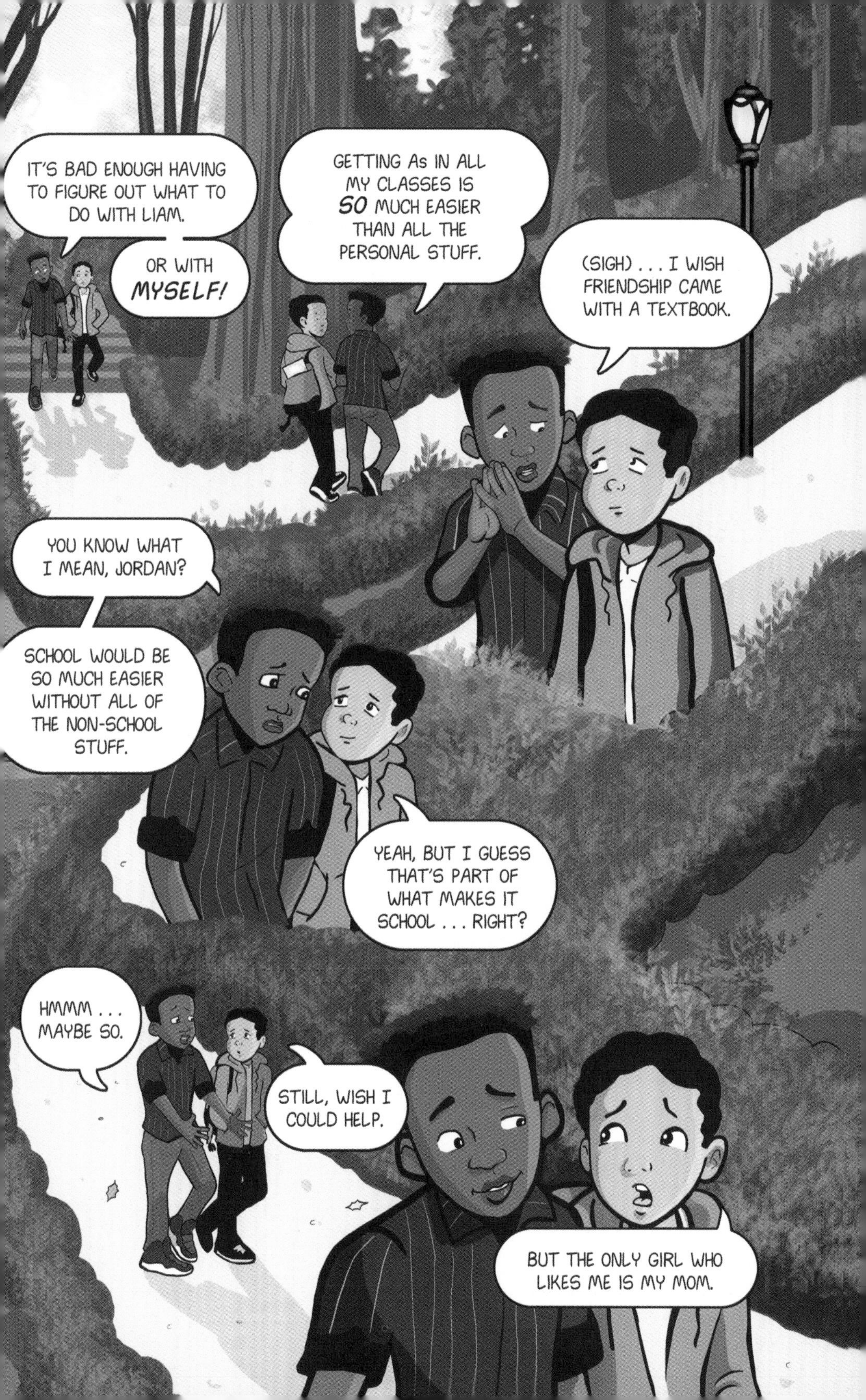
IT'S BAD ENOUGH HAVING TO FIGURE OUT WHAT TO DO WITH LIAM.
OR WITH *MYSELF!*
GETTING As IN ALL MY CLASSES IS *SO* MUCH EASIER THAN ALL THE PERSONAL STUFF.
(SIGH) . . . I WISH FRIENDSHIP CAME WITH A TEXTBOOK.
YOU KNOW WHAT I MEAN, JORDAN?
SCHOOL WOULD BE SO MUCH EASIER WITHOUT ALL OF THE NON-SCHOOL STUFF.
YEAH, BUT I GUESS THAT'S PART OF WHAT MAKES IT SCHOOL . . . RIGHT?
HMMM . . . MAYBE SO.
STILL, WISH I COULD HELP.
BUT THE ONLY GIRL WHO LIKES ME IS MY MOM.

171

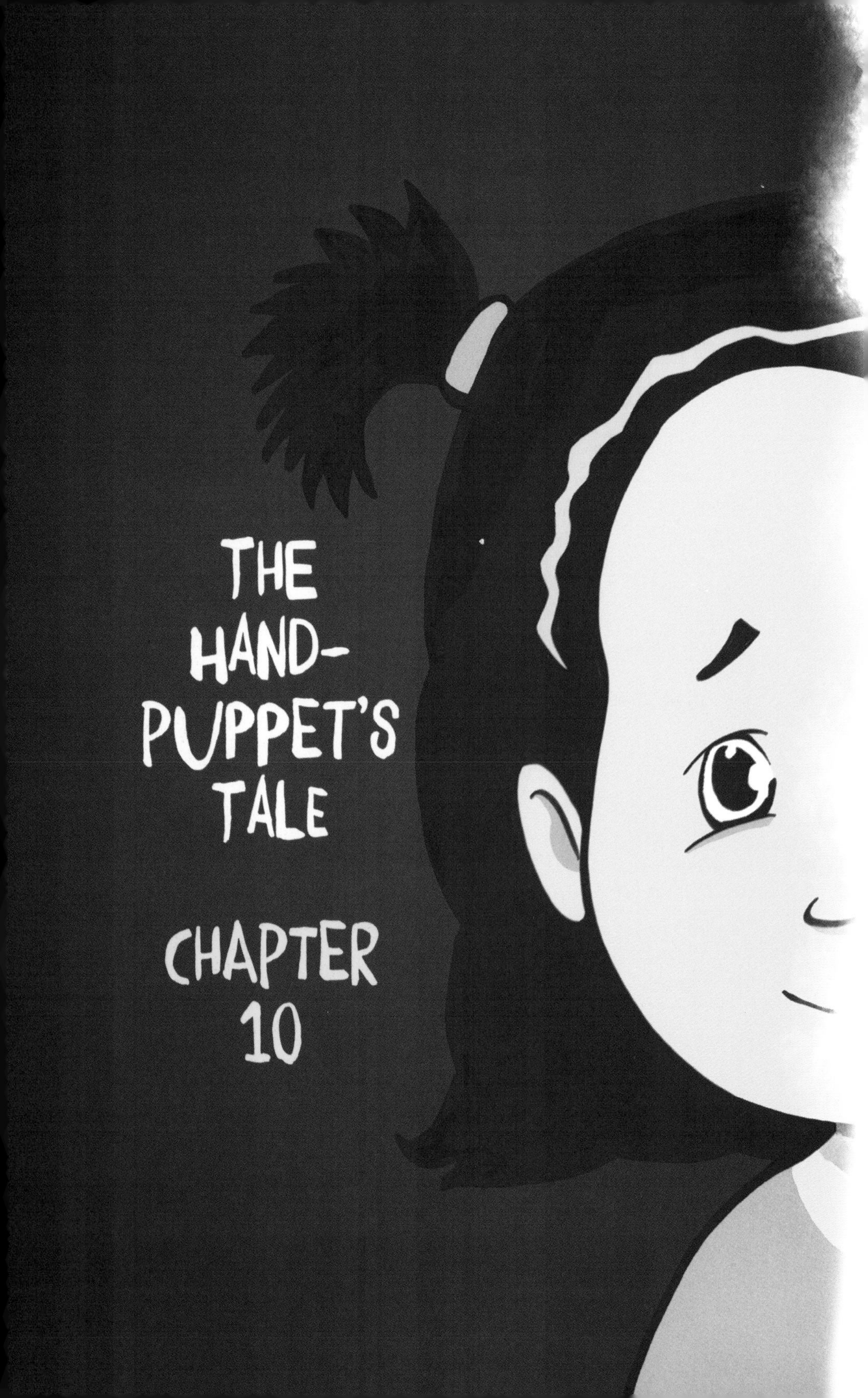
THE HAND-PUPPET'S TALE
CHAPTER 10

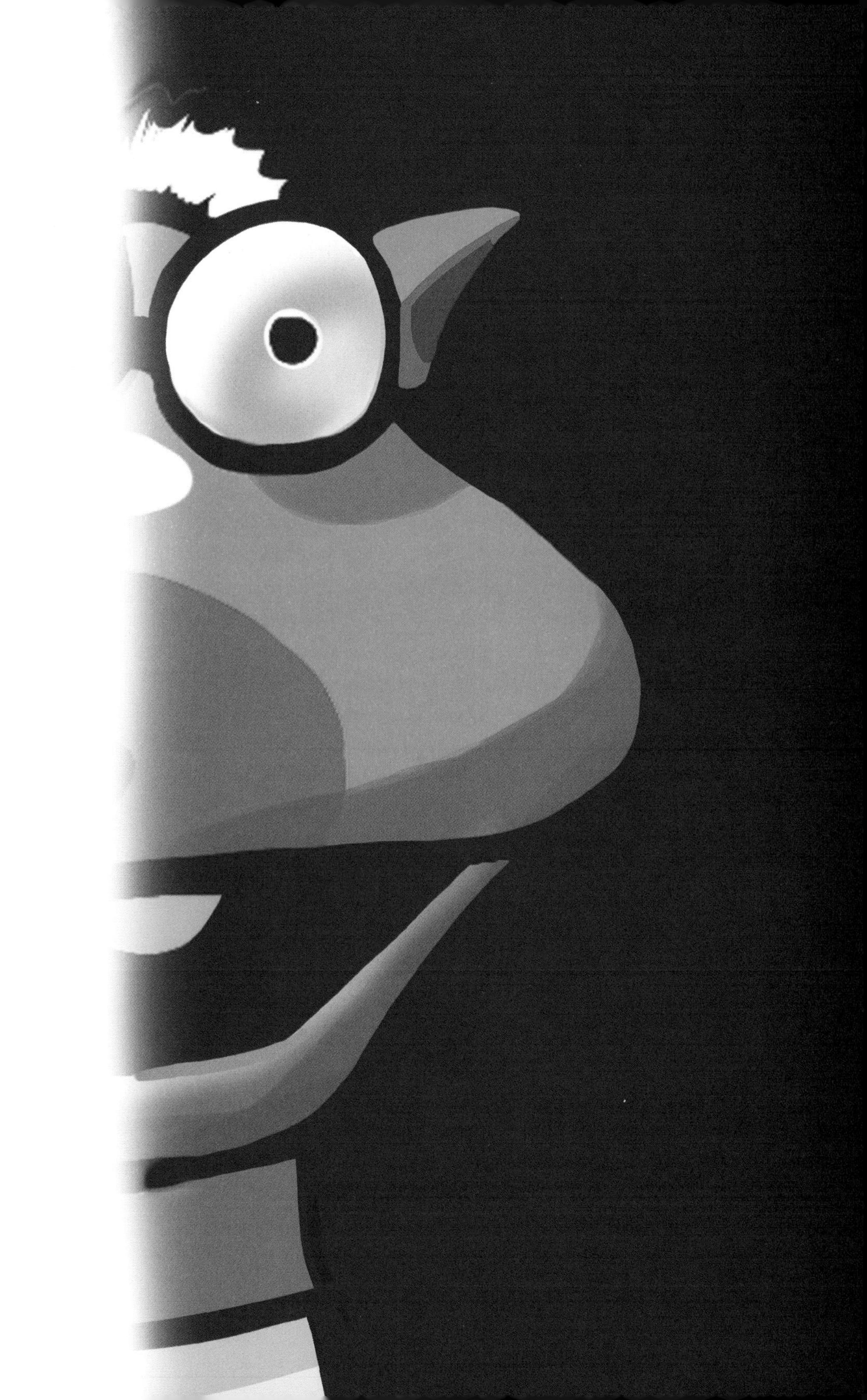

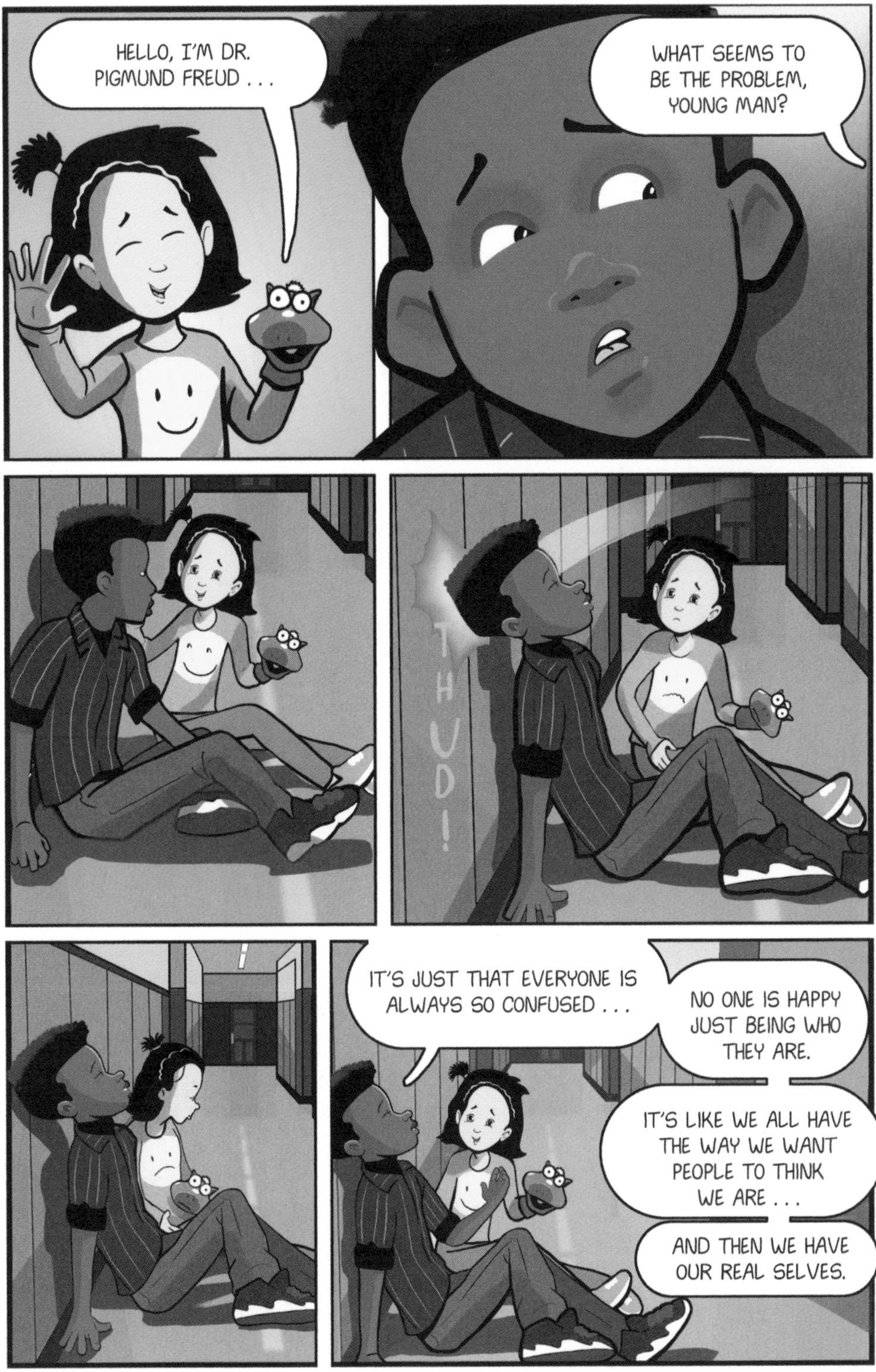
HELLO, I'M DR. PIGMUND FREUD . . .
WHAT SEEMS TO BE THE PROBLEM, YOUNG MAN?
THUD!
IT'S JUST THAT EVERYONE IS ALWAYS SO CONFUSED . . .
NO ONE IS HAPPY JUST BEING WHO THEY ARE.
IT'S LIKE WE ALL HAVE THE WAY WE WANT PEOPLE TO THINK WE ARE . . .
AND THEN WE HAVE OUR REAL SELVES.

IF YOU'RE BIG, THEN THE WORLD WANTS YOU TO BE SMALL . . .

BUT IF YOU'RE SMALL, YOU WANNA BE BIG!

IF YOU'RE SHY, THEY WANT YOU TO BE OUTGOING . . .

BUT IF YOU ALREADY ARE, THEN YOU NEED TO BE HUMBLE.

I DON'T *LIKE* YOU, BUT I WANNA BE JUST *LIKE* YOU!

THEN AGAIN, MAYBE IT'S BECAUSE YOU LOOK LIKE ME THAT I DON'T LIKE YOU AT ALL!

OR THEY SPEND SO MUCH TIME TALKING ABOUT OTHERS THAT NO ONE ACTUALLY KNOWS *THEM!*

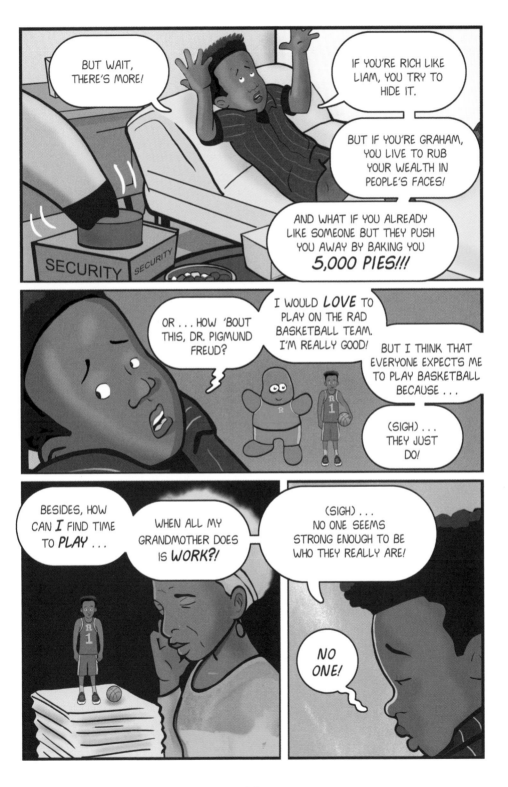

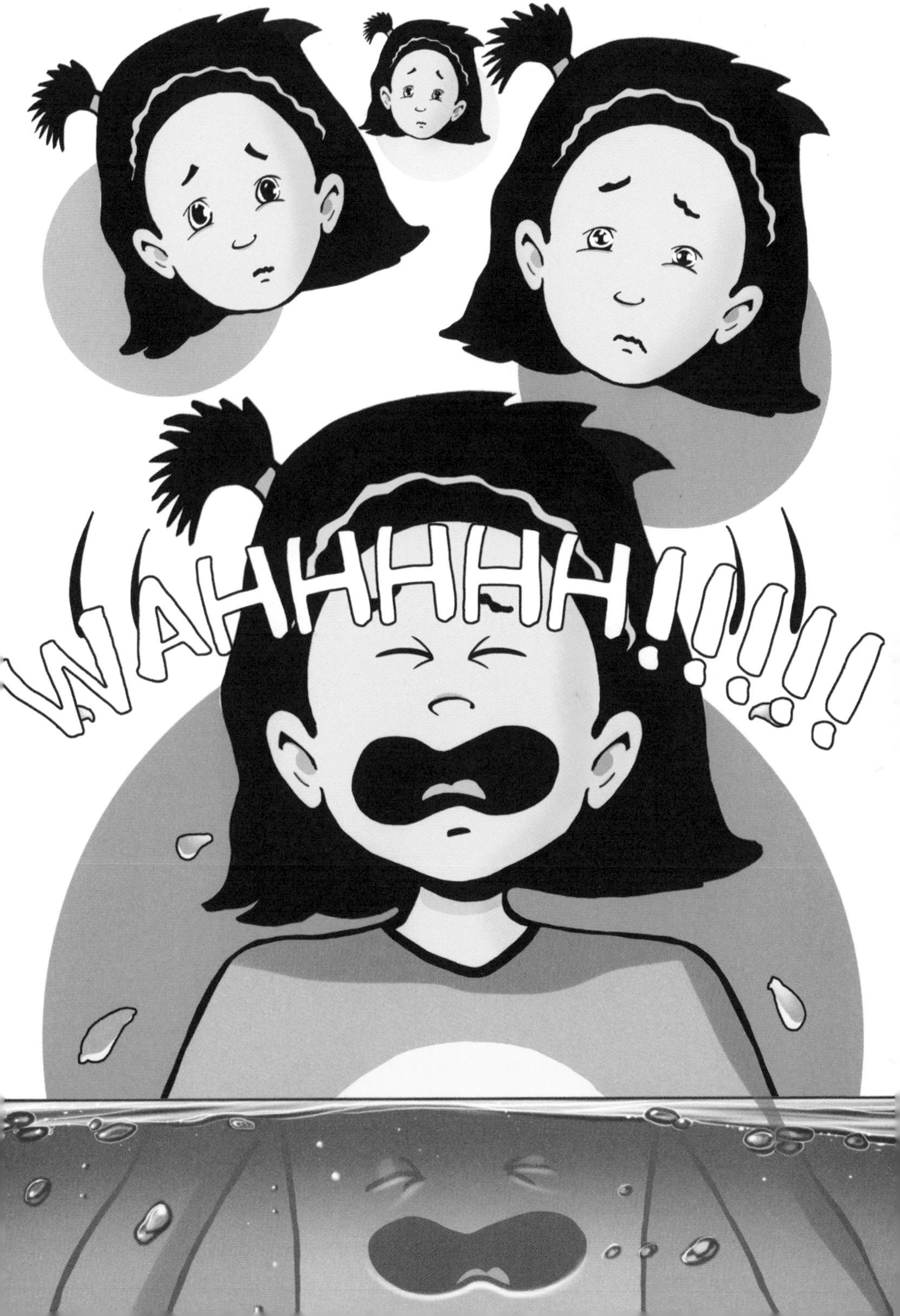
WAHHHHH!!!!!!

185

188

189

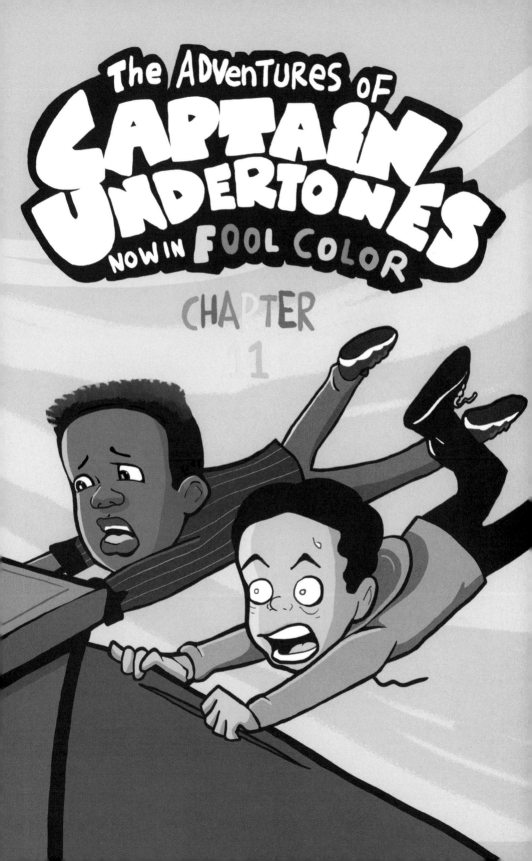

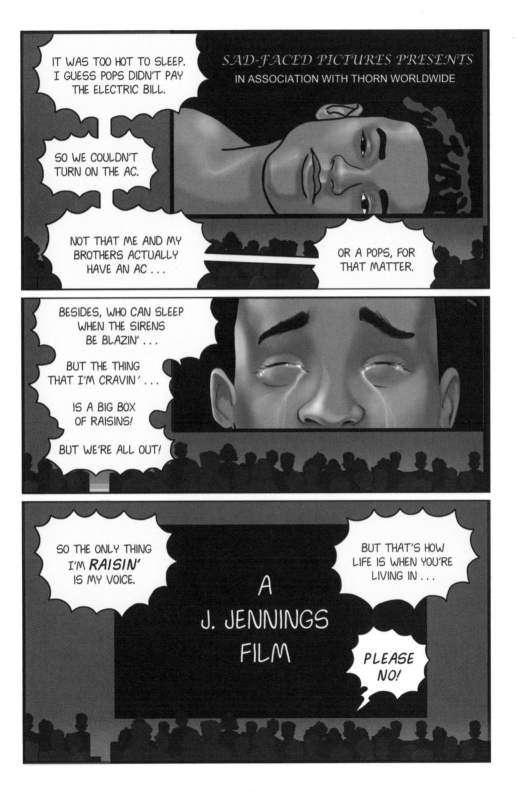

197

▶▶▶▶▶ FIVE THOUSAND HOURS (AND A SURPRISE VISIT FROM THE AUTHOR OF THE BOOK) LATER

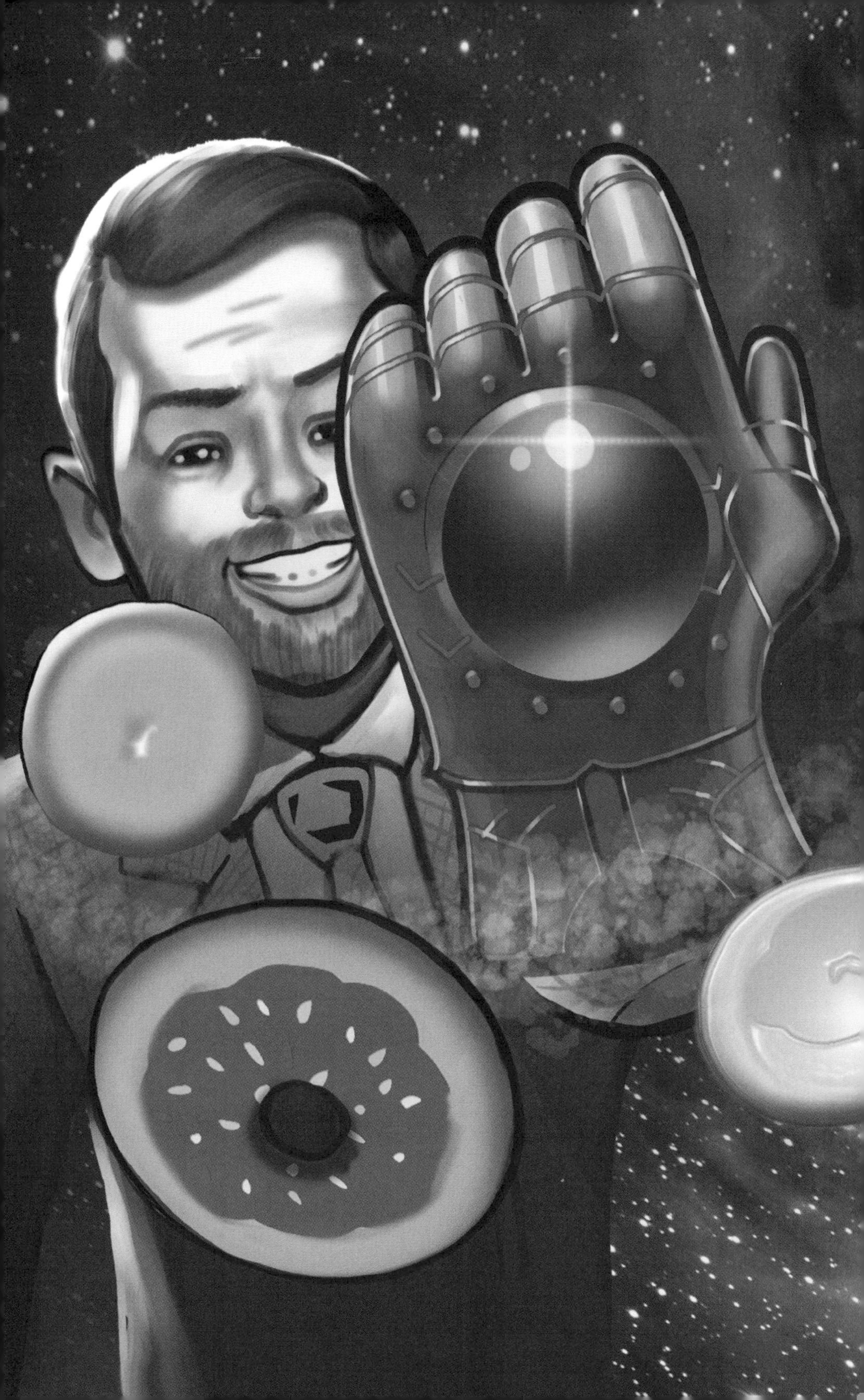

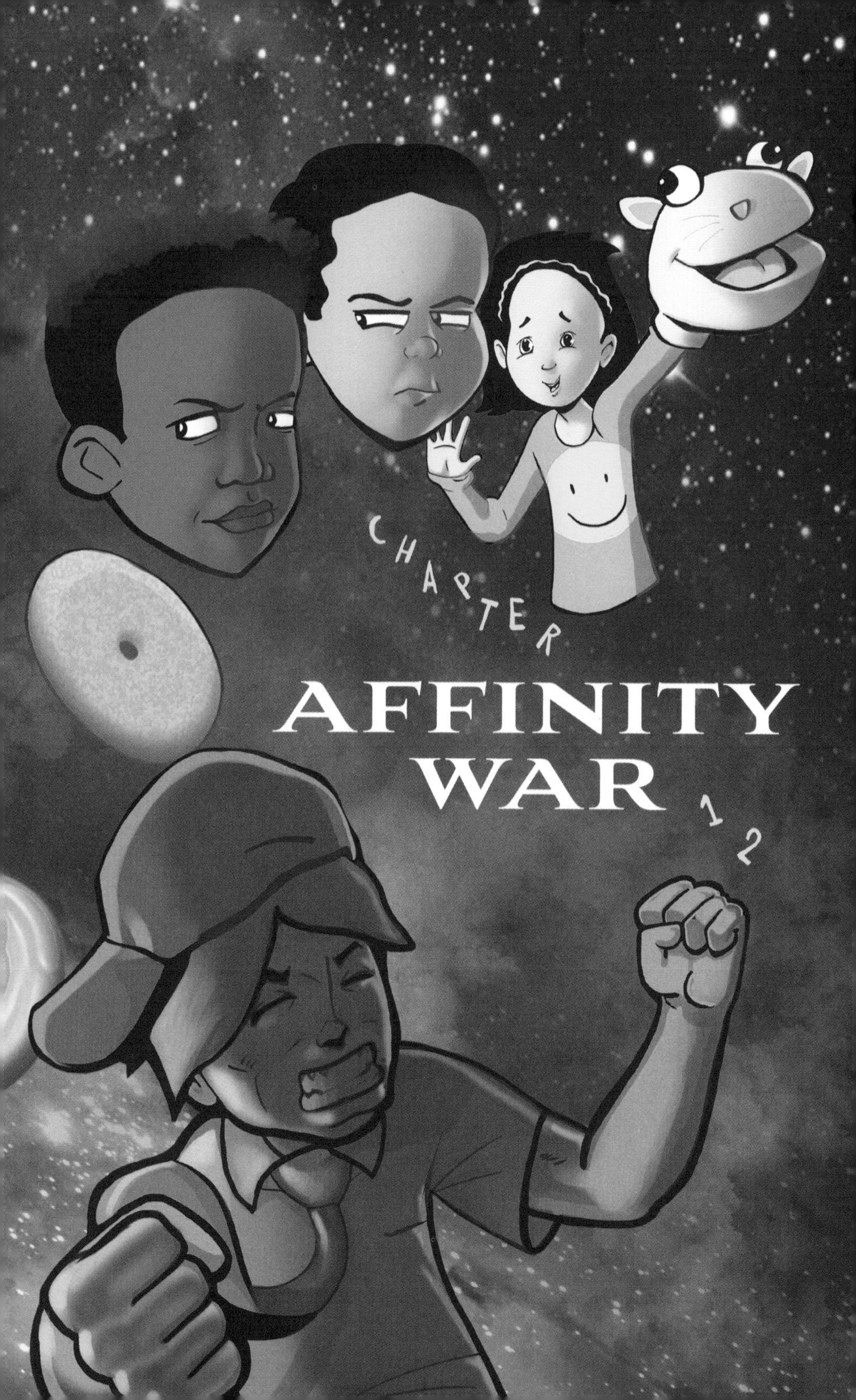
CHAPTER
AFFINITY WAR
12

212

NAY, KIDDO

CHAPTER
13

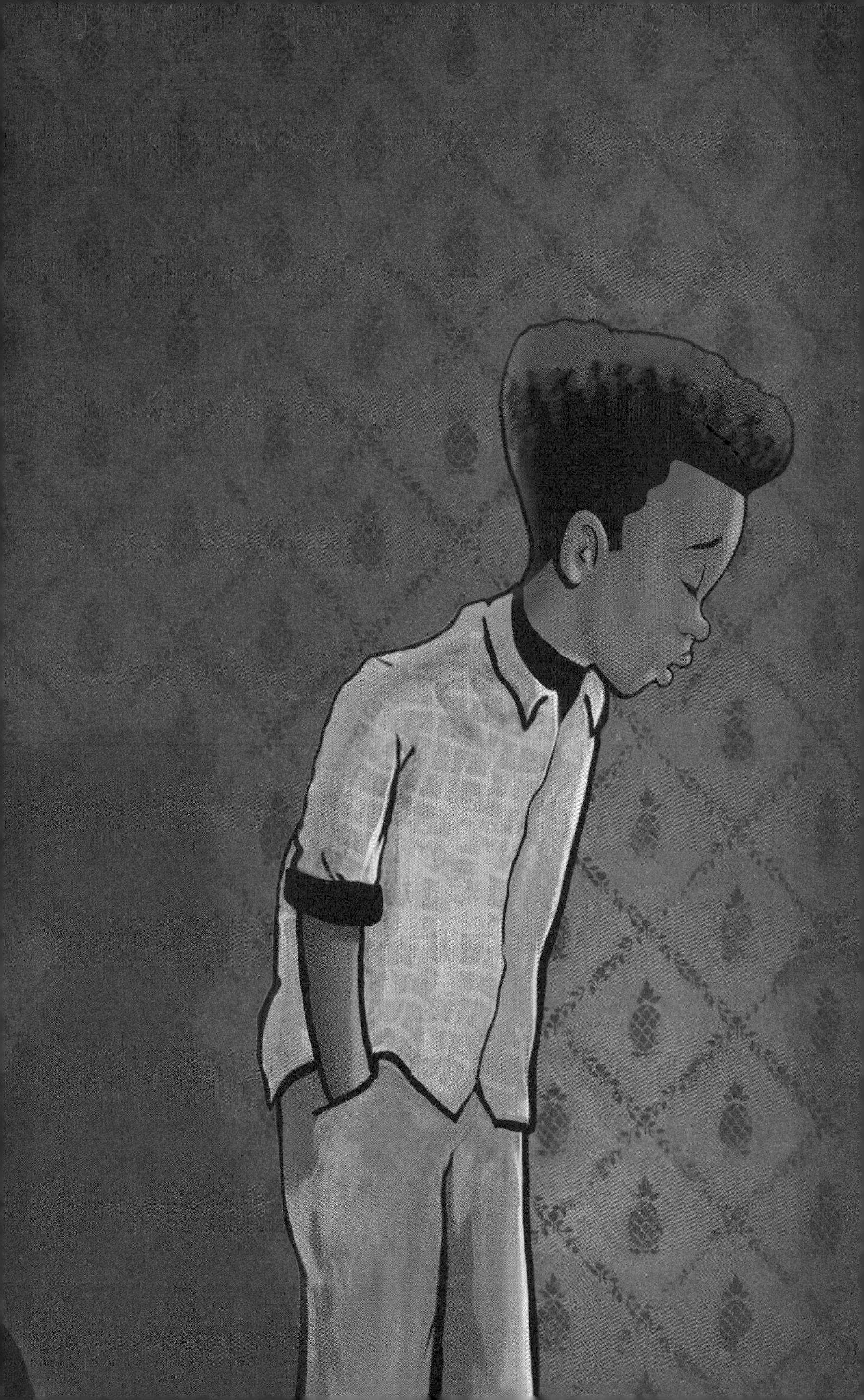

227

231

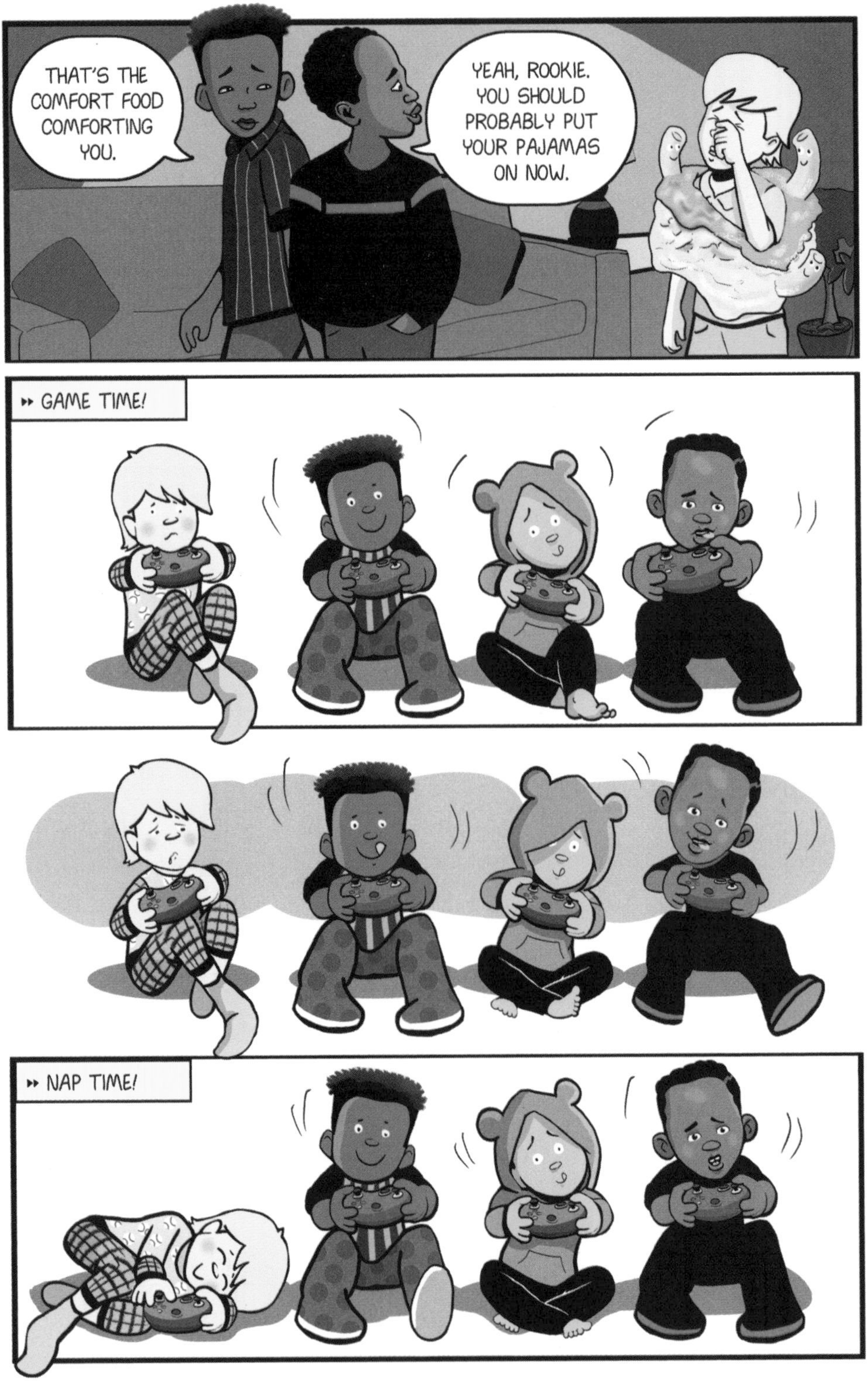
THAT'S THE COMFORT FOOD COMFORTING YOU.
YEAH, ROOKIE. YOU SHOULD PROBABLY PUT YOUR PAJAMAS ON NOW.
GAME TIME!
NAP TIME!

241

245

246

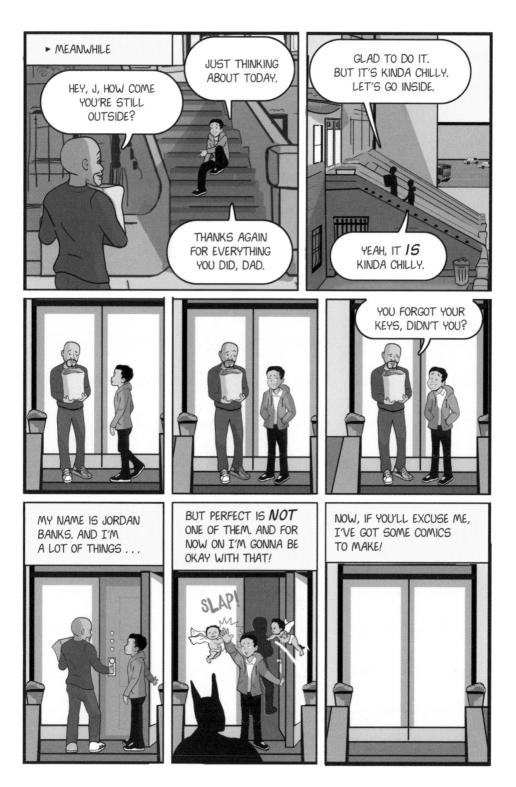

Thank you to the amazing M'shindo Kuumba
for taking my colors to an entirely different level!

To my family, Aren, Jay, and Autier.
My sons have always been, and continue to be, my inspiration.

Thank you to Suzanne Murphy; Rosemary Brosnan; Patty Rosati;
my editor, Andrew Eliopulos; my publicist, Jacquelynn Burke;
my designer, Cat San Juan; my art director, Erin Fitzsimmons;
and the rest of my amazing team at HarperAlley/Quill Tree Books
for believing in me enough to give me the opportunity
to tell my story my way.

A huge thank you to my agent, Judy Hansen,
who has stood with me from the very beginning
to help bring *New Kid* and *Class Act* to life.

Thank you to all of the authors and artists who gave me
their blessing to use their work in my chapter headings:
Jeff Kinney (*Diary of a Wimpy Kid*); Barry Deutsch (*Hereville:
How Mirka Got Her Sword*); Ryan Andrews (*This Was Our Pact*);
Shannon Hale & LeUyen Pham (*Real Friends*); Kazu Kibuishi (*Amulet*);
Terri Libenson (*Invisible Emmie*); Raina Telgemeier (*Ghosts*);
Dav Pilkey (*Captain Underpants*); and Jarrett J. Krosoczka (*Hey, Kiddo*).

Thank you to my fellow authors who gave me permission to use them
as Easter eggs throughout *Class Act*: Kwame Alexander, Jason Reynolds,
Jacqueline Woodson, Elizabeth Acevedo, Renée Watson, Derrick Barnes,
Nic Stone, Angie Thomas, Tami Charles, and Eric Velasquez.

Thank you to my art assistant, John-Raymond De Bard.

Thank you to Carol Fitzgerald, Andrea Colvin, and most of all
to my fans: The kids. The teachers. The librarians. The parents.
The book groups. The reviewers. The bloggers. The publications.
And the award committees who showed *New Kid* so much love.